CHILDREN of the FLEET

By Orson Scott Card
From Tom Doherty Associates

ENDER UNIVERSE

Ender Series

Ender's Game
Ender in Exile
Speaker for the Dead
Xenocide
Children of the Mind

Ender's Shadow Series

Ender's Shadow
Shadow of the Hegemon
Shadow Puppets
Shadow of the Giant
Shadows in Flight

Children of the Fleet

The First Formic War
(with Aaron Johnston)

Earth Unaware
Earth Afire
Earth Awakens

The Second Formic War
(with Aaron Johnston)

The Swarm

Ender Novellas

A War of Gifts
First Meetings

THE MITHERMAGES

The Lost Gate
The Gate Thief
Gatefather

THE TALES OF ALVIN MAKER

Seventh Son
Red Prophet
Prentice Alvin

Alvin Journeyman
Heartfire
The Crystal City

HOMECOMING

The Memory of Earth
The Call of Earth
The Ships of Earth
Earthfall
Earthborn

WOMEN OF GENESIS

Sarah
Rebekah
Rachel & Leah

THE COLLECTED SHORT FICTION
OF ORSON SCOTT CARD

*Maps in a Mirror: The Short Fiction
of Orson Scott Card*
Keeper of Dreams

STAND-ALONE FICTION

Invasive Procedures
(with Aaron Johnston)
Empire
Hidden Empire
The Folk of the Fringe
Hart's Hope
*Pastwatch: The Redemption of
Christopher Columbus*
Saints
Songmaster
Treason
The Worthing Saga
Wyrms
Zanna's Gift

CHILDREN OF THE FLEET

FLEET SCHOOL

Orson Scott Card

TOR

A TOM DOHERTY ASSOCIATES BOOK

NEW YORK

CHILDREN OF THE FLEET

Copyright © 2017 by Orson Scott Card

A Tor Book
Published by Tom Doherty Associates
175 Fifth Avenue
New York, NY 10010

www.tor-forge.com

Tor® is a registered trademark of Macmillan Publishing Group, LLC.

The Library of Congress Cataloging-in-Publication Data is available upon request.

ISBN 978-0-7653-7704-3 (hardcover)
ISBN 978-1-250-16950-1 (international, sold outside the U.S.,
subject to rights availability)
ISBN 978-1-250-16214-4 (signed edition)
ISBN 978-1-4668-5340-9 (ebook)

Our books may be purchased in bulk for promotional, educational, or business use. Please contact your local bookseller or the Macmillan Corporate and Premium Sales Department at 1-800-221-7945, extension 5442, or by email at MacmillanSpecialMarkets@macmillan.com.

First Edition: October 2017

Printed in the United States of America

0 9 8 7 6 5 4 3 2 1

To Scott Allen
All these years,
You've been with me
Every step along the way

CHILDREN of the FLEET

1

Student Name: Dabeet Ochoa

Assignment: Fable in Your Own Words

The nun Geppetto came from a family of woodworkers and was among the best of them before her religious vocation took her to a place where she never expected to have a knife and block of wood in her hands again. But the boss nun wanted to present a pageant at Christmas time, and when Sister Geppetto tentatively suggested that a puppet show might allow the nuns to perform without personally wearing costumes on a stage, the boss nun assigned her to carve all the puppets.

Sister Geppetto had a year before the next Christmas, but she had to allow time for even the clumsiest nuns to learn to operate the puppets, so she spent every waking moment in woodcarving. The boss nun relieved her from all other duties and admired her rapid progress.

All the puppets were carved, put together, painted, and strung to the control units by August, and while other nuns worked on the script, the voices, and learning to operate the puppets, Sister Geppetto carved the last of the puppets—the one that would be used the very least in the pageant, and yet the one that was most important. The Baby Jesus.

All the Baby Jesus had to do was get lowered in and lie in the manger. Three strings would be enough to ensure that he didn't get skewampus as he was lowered. But this seemed irreverent to Sister Geppetto, to treat the God of Heaven as if he were a mere prop in someone else's story, instead of what he was: The Story Itself.

So she made articulated arms and legs, and designed a different control unit so that the limbs could all waggle like an infant's, without raising the baby from the manger.

The boss nun praised it as quite clever and immediately placed this wiggly baby puppet in the show. Then she thanked Sister Geppetto, and officially reassigned her to working in the garden through the harvest season, so that the nuns working on the pageant could be free to master their parts.

However, Sister Geppetto was not satisfied. It was wrong to make the Baby Jesus into a prop with wiggly limbs; she might have done the same with a puppet octopus or beetle.

No, Baby Jesus had to be able to grow up into a toddler. The limbs that waggled in the manger needed to be able to rotate into place for crawling and then walking. This required so much ingenuity that through all her gardening work, Sister Geppetto thought of nothing but ways to create joints that could do such different tasks, and then at night tried out each idea to see how well it worked.

In mid-November, when she had solved all the mechanical problems and was assembling the working baby-to-toddler version of Baby Jesus, the thought came to her: I chose to be a nun, which means to have no children; and yet I have this child, and he will grow from infant into boychild as if he were alive. I have incarnated a being in the image of God.

This thought turned into a prayer: O Holy Mother, Our Lady of Hope and Love, grant this image of Thy Good Son the gift of speech, even if only I can hear his voice. I wish to know from his own lips if this offering is acceptable to Him. Forgive me if I sin in saying this prayer, and forgive me for making this puppet secretly when I was commanded to be done with woodcarving and work in the garden instead.

At once she heard the voice of the Baby Jesus, though the lips of the puppet did not move. "Attach my strings, O mother of mine," said the baby. "How can I dance my joy if you do not raise me up?"

Dabeet Ochoa was halfway through fifth grade, which was just right for a ten-year-old, when he decided it was time to stop living in his mother's dream world. It's not that she cocooned him—he had friends to talk to, in person and on the nets. He got along well with all his teachers. He rarely made errors on examinations. He was well-informed about events in the wider world.

But now that the third and final Formic War was over, and the world was getting back to something like normal, Dabeet realized that all his mother's lies were going to be put to the test, and he didn't want his life to come crashing down along with her delusions.

The problem was that with the end of the war, the families of the International Fleet were being reunited. Many of those who had served in the IF were coming back down to Earth or Luna, where their spouses and children awaited them. Many others were staying with the Fleet, and their families were being ferried up into space, to join them in space stations, warships, cargo ships, asteroid stations, and the moons of various farflung planets.

Somewhere among those soldiers and officers was Dabeet Ochoa's father—presumably a man of Indian ancestry, though Mother had never been quite clear on why Dabeet had an Indian first name. Dabeet had not dared to ask whether his father would return to Earth or bring them up into space. Why did he hesitate? He finally admitted to himself that he was like an American child who was almost completely certain about Santa Claus, but dared not ask for fear the answer would lead to the end of the annual largesse of Christmas.

Is my father, the brave officer of the Fleet, a myth my mother made up, to console me for being fatherless? Or was he invented to impress the neighbors, so they wouldn't think of Mother as a common tramp who fell for some idiotic lies and got pregnant?

Dabeet suspected it was the latter, because she had never regaled him with stories of his father until she was insinuating herself into their Hispanic neighborhood in Elkhart, Indiana. Dabeet first learned about his father from remarks like, "He's with the Fleet, of course." The way she said it, everyone knew she meant the International Fleet—spaceships, not wet-bottom ocean ships. Her "of course" meant that they could not possibly imagine she would have had a child with someone who was not a valued participant in the war to save the human race.

Best of all, no one could question the absence of a father who might be deep in the reaches of the Kuiper Belt, years of travel away from Earth. But a year ago, someone's pointed remark about the war being over triggered a revelation that took Dabeet—and no one else—by surprise. "Yes, the war is over," said Mother, "but the Fleet has its own laws, and no court on Earth—not even the courts of the Hegemony—has any jurisdiction over him."

"Why would the courts be involved?" Dabeet was glad that a nosy neighbor woman asked the question, so he didn't have to trigger a spate of crying by asking her himself.

"Because if an officer of the Fleet has a spouse up *there,* then that's the only marriage that IF law will recognize."

Gasps. Moans of how unfair it was. "And you are not that spouse! Nuestra señora, tan atroz! Maria Rafaella, you poor thing. And your baby, legally fatherless! Better that your man had died in the war and left you a widow than this scandalous treatment!"

At this point, Mother burst into tears. "I was so young, and he was so glorious, an officer already, he gave his *word,* but now he denies that he would have carnal knowledge of a fifteen-year-old, because that's how old I was, how old I *had* to be, when dear little Dabeet formed within my body. My family disowned me, so the whole fortune of the Ochoas of Barrio Campina in Ciudad Bolivar is beyond my reach forever."

It was Dabeet's firm and immediate conviction that if there were any Ochoas in Ciudad Bolivar in Venezuela, either they had no fortune or they were no relation to Mother. For all he knew, her name was Moreno and she came from Saltillo, Mexico. When she spoke Spanish, it was without a trace of any South American accent Dabeet had ever heard, and her face and body revealed far too much Aztec or Carib or Guajiro ancestry for her to claim to have much of the blood of Spain. And the great wealthy families of Latin America guarded their bloodlines too carefully to produce a daughter who looked as Amerindian as Mother.

Her claim to be Venezuelan probably sprang from a wish to associate herself with the great Venezuelan war hero Victor Delgado—though "El Victor" never lived in Venezuela, having been spaceborn in a free mining family in the Kuiper Belt.

This much was undeniable: Mother had given him half his DNA, and that meant she was half responsible for the wits he was born with. And those wits had earned him the test scores Mother always bragged about. "It wasn't I who brought little Dabeet to America, it was Dabeet who brought me! Test scores! Achievements! At the age of *five* he was so brilliant that the US Immigration and Naturalization Department brought us in under the Genius Exception instead of one of the South American quotas."

This always made Hispanics ooh and aah, though by now Dabeet knew perfectly well that they were all thinking, "Little bastard," or, "So you're saying my kids are stupid?"

And since Dabeet *was* a little bastard, and Mother *was* saying their children were stupid, Dabeet thought that it was not unfair of them to feel that way. Though, to their credit, few of them said it aloud, or even allowed it to show on their faces until they were away from Mother.

Instead they nodded politely, listening with varying degrees of patience as the serious brag began. "If the war hadn't ended when it did, my Dabeet would have been one of those children taken up to Battle School. For all we know, he might have been The One instead of Ender Wiggin."

Everyone, especially Dabeet, knew this idea was ridiculous, so they smiled indulgently at a mother's pride and went on to talk about something else, like the way all the children in Battle School were coming back to their home countries on Earth, and such terrible things went on in Battle School that it was good that it had been shut down, and it's better for the children of Earth to be educated on Earth.

"But Dabeet is *not* a child of Earth," said Mother, every time. "Dabeet is a child of the Fleet. As much as anyone else, he is a child of the Fleet and my son *will* receive his benefits, no matter how much the Great Seducer of Underage Venezuelan Girls tries to avoid confirming his rights."

Now, at age ten, Dabeet had realized a fact so obvious that only courtesy could have kept any of the neighbors from stating the obvious: Regardless of whether Maria Rafaella had any legal standing as the spouse of some IF officer, DNA did not lie. If Dabeet's DNA had been tested against his purported father's DNA, then the Fleet's lawyers would immediately have stepped in to enforce Dabeet's rights as a child of the Fleet.

They had not, which might mean any of several things. Perhaps Mother had not known the officer's name, in which case the IF would not know to whom they should compare Dabeet's DNA. Or perhaps Dabeet's father had died in some explosion so spectacular that not even a fragment of his body had remained.

Or perhaps Mother had slept with a Fleet officer, but he was not the only man, and when she had Dabeet's DNA tested, she learned that the most motile sperm had no connection with the Fleet.

Or, most likely, Mother had never made any formal claim and had never offered Dabeet's DNA for testing. Their silence was understandable because they did not know that he existed.

And now that Battle School had been refitted as Fleet School, accepting only children who were part of an off-Earth family, why would she refrain from the obvious step of submitting his DNA so he would qualify?

Because it was all a lie. Perhaps Mother knew perfectly well who Dabeet's father was, and what Latin American hamlet or city he was hiding in. She kept claiming he was with the Fleet because now she was stuck with the lie.

Sooner or later, though, the lies and concealment would catch up with her—and Dabeet would pay the price. There were kids at school who already muttered "muchopadre"—many-fathers.

Why should Dabeet be trapped in Mother's fantasy world when it all came crashing down?

Maybe trapping him was the point. His intelligence could not be denied, and if he were to be certified as a child of the Fleet, he would surely be taken to Fleet School.

Where no parents were allowed.

Maybe every word that Mother said was true, maybe his DNA had been tested and he was certified, and Mother simply would not apply to install him in Fleet School, and would actively fight any attempt to take him away from her control.

Getting out from under Mother's control was Dabeet's main reason for wanting to go into space.

It was time to get answers and make decisions of his own.

So Dabeet found the file containing his genome in the Elkhart School District's database, copied it, and then began attaching it to all kinds of applications.

Using the school computers along with information he pried from Mother's smartphone, Dabeet applied, in his mother's name, for Fleet-child status for her only child—himself. He found a site intended for offworlders that administered the admissions test for Fleet School, took the test, and submitted the results along with his mother's application for him to be admitted.

He also submitted his test results to a dozen different boarding schools on Earth and Luna, always pretending to be his mother, always giving the best information he could find about her finances to make sure he qualified for need-based scholarships. He needed a full ride, not just tuition.

Then, having done all that was within his power and much that officially was not, Dabeet went about his days with confidence that he was only a sojourner in this place. Soon he would be plucked out of Elkhart,

Indiana, and sent to a school on Luna, or in Russia, Brazil, Italy, Kikuyu, New Zealand, or Japan.

He did not allow himself to wonder what he would do if none of these places offered him a full scholarship, or if his forgery was discovered and Mother were able to intervene to block him. All that was in his power was to give himself more opportunities and choices. It was up to Mother to decide, once he was admitted somewhere, to either let him go or launch an all-out, lifelong war between the two of them.

For he would never forgive her if she did not let him go.

No one could have guessed that he harbored such thoughts. He was always polite and instantly obedient to his mother. He never allowed himself to show embarrassment or doubt when she discoursed about his father and his heritage.

Having examined his appearance impartially in mirrors and in photographs, he decided that his father might very well be from India or Southeast Asia, and so he studied videos of Malays, Tamils, and Bengalis so he could master the cultural markers of males of low status in such lands: a beaming, toothy smile upon meeting, downcast eyes when speaking, hand half-concealing his mouth when disagreeing with an adult.

"I don't like the way you hide yourself from people who are stupid compared to you," said Mother once. And another time, "When did you learn to bow your head like that? These people are not lords in some medieval time." And more than once, "When you cover your mouth like that, no one can hear you, and yet your words are the most important ones they'll hear all day."

And, most telling, her constant mantra: "You are superior in mind and heart to everyone you meet. Hold yourself with pride, instead of apologizing with your bows and mumbles."

She noticed what he was doing, but had no understanding of why. If some cruel fate decided to keep him in Elkhart, he was determined that none of the Anglos or Asians that controlled American education and business would have any cause to fear his keen intelligence. "He is not here to take my place and rule over me," they would assure themselves. Thus they would admit him into positions from which he could take their places and rule over them.

Meanwhile, he fulfilled all his assignments and took all his tests, performing as a model student at the Charles G. Conn School for the Gifted. In fact, he overperformed.

If the test had six essay questions—at Conn, true-false and multiple-choice tests were forbidden—then Dabeet answered all six with well-reasoned and well-supported essays. Then he would pose two more questions that were much better than the ones the teacher had come up with, and answer those as well.

When the assignment was to retell one of Aesop's fables in his own words, he wrote a perfectly competent retelling of "The Tortoise and the Hare," followed by a refutation of the principle that "slow and steady wins the race," using counterexamples from history. And finally he wrote his own fable based loosely on the Italian tale of Geppetto and his wooden puppet.

If his teachers felt themselves overwhelmed by the sheer volume of work that he turned in, they made no complaint. They did not even comment positively. They simply accepted what he gave them, and then graded everything, including comments on the extra material, showing that they read and appreciated it. But, guided by rules designed to minimize competitiveness and bullying, the teachers never singled him out for praise in a way that might lead other students to resent or envy him.

This did not matter to Dabeet. He did not need their words to tell him that his program of making himself hopelessly overqualified for Conn was working. Every teacher—even ones he had never met—greeted him by name in the halls. Visiting dignitaries who spoke to no students individually were nevertheless brought to his classroom, where Dabeet could always see that they had been told which seat was his, for they counted across and down until their eyes rested on him. Whereupon he did his best look-down-modestly, then locked his eyes attentively on the teacher until the visitor went away.

Even when the rumor flew through the school that the great Hyrum Graff was visiting, the man who had been put on trial for his supposed crimes in the way he educated Ender Wiggin in Battle School, Dabeet meant to change his routine not a whit.

Sure enough, the stout man rumored to be Graff himself was brought into the classroom, ostensibly because it was a "typical example" of a Conn classroom; but instead of counting across and down the rows, Graff's eyes went immediately to Dabeet.

It was too late to pretend that he had not seen that he was seen. So Dabeet flashed the Graffish man his best Indo-Malay smile, and only then ducked his head modestly and then focused again on the teacher.

Even as he did these things, Dabeet thought: This is a not a man who needs to see me as unthreatening. This is a man who needs to see me as the most dangerous creature in the state of Indiana. I should have met his gaze, smiled, and then frozen the smile and stared at him unblinking, the smile unwavering, until he left.

I did as I did, he told himself. Let Graff—if it *was* Graff—make of it whatever he wants.

2

Student Name: Dabeet Ochoa

Assignment: Fable in Your Own Words

Teacher Response: An interesting response to the Italian story of Pinocchio (Pine-eyes), with the Baby Jesus as the puppet. However, the fable seems incomplete to me. Was that the ending you intended? Or is there more to the story? Ending the story where you do, it sounds as if the purpose of this secret puppet was entirely fulfilled by its achievement of speech. Doesn't it matter what *else* the Baby-Jesus puppet might have to say? Is the puppet capable of independent thought? Does it think like a baby, or like a wooden puppet, or like a god-made-flesh?

Student Response: Here is the rest of the story:

The nun Geppetto attached strings and made the fully articulated Baby Jesus crawl and then walk and then run and then dance. The Baby Jesus laughed with joy at each new movement, even as Geppetto exhausted herself with learning the intricate hand movements that allowed the Baby Jesus to carry out his lifelike activities.

Because this Baby Jesus was not part of the play, and no one was quite aware of what Geppetto had been carving, there were no scheduled rehearsals and he was never on a stage. So the Baby Jesus did not seem to understand the reason for limitations. "Why did you not come to me when the sun was shining?" asked the Baby Jesus. "Why do you not take me out into the courtyard? Why can't I go down to the village?"

"I had to work in the garden while the sun shone."

"It's winter and nothing is growing."

"The turnips and carrots are in the ground, and I must prepare the soil for next year's seeds. Also, the geese are gleaning the field so we and the poor who eat at our table can get all the food value from the fallen grain when we roast the geese at Christmas."

"Then take me into the garden with you," said Baby Jesus.

"How can I do my work while my hands are making you walk and run and dance? Or how can I make you move while my hands are busy with my work?"

"Take me down into the village, then. I hear laughter from the children there, even over the walls of this nunnery."

"I am not one of the sisters who is allowed to go into the village."

"Then send me with one of the sisters who *is* allowed."

"They must not know that you exist, because I did not have permission to make you."

"But now that I exist, why should I be forbidden to play among the other children?" asked the Baby Jesus.

"The children would watch you in a show," said Geppetto, "but they can't play with you. They'd tangle your strings and pull on your limbs and break or bend your hinges so you didn't work right anymore. Children can be rough and brutal, and you wouldn't like how they treated you."

"I love the sound of their laughter," said Baby Jesus, "and I need to be one of them."

"That is not in my power."

"Then as long as I belong to you, and you keep me secret solely in order to protect yourself, I am not free."

To Geppetto this was a terrible accusation because she knew that it was true. She had made this puppet to satisfy her own vanity, but she had pretended that she made it to honor God. She begged for it to have the power of speech, but for her own sake, not for the sake of the puppet. Did I create this in order to keep it as my prisoner? As my slave?

What should I do with this pretended Baby Jesus? she prayed to God.

But the only answer she heard in her heart was, How can you call it a pretended Baby Jesus, when it speaks to you like a real child?

"Cut my strings," said Baby Jesus whenever she took him from his hiding place. "Set me free among the children."

"Without your strings you cannot move at all," said Geppetto.

"Without my strings I cannot move *under your control*," said Baby Jesus. "It is your control that you don't want to lose. My freedom means nothing to you."

"There is no freedom if you can't act on your own decisions," said Geppetto.

"There's no freedom when you hold my strings," said Baby Jesus.

Then came the day when the Boss Nun found the hiding place of the Baby Jesus. Naturally the Baby Jesus said nothing to the Boss Nun, or if he did, she could not hear. When Geppetto came in from the garden, the Boss Nun showed her the puppet and said, "I do not remember this puppet in the Christmas play."

Then Sister Geppetto confessed all, and, weeping, begged the Boss Nun to tell her how she could earn forgiveness.

"The workmanship of this puppet is the best of all your carving," said the Boss Nun. "All the other puppets were used in a play to delight the people, excite their wonder at the story of Christ, and thus glorify God. What was the purpose of this puppet?"

"To satisfy my own vanity, and to be the child that I will never have."

"So this puppet represents worldly pride and your last doubts about your vocation as a nun?" asked the Boss Nun.

"I fear that it is so."

"Then let us set you free from that fear," said the Boss Nun. "Yet I cannot bear the thought of burning something so beautifully made."

"Oh, I beg you not to burn it, for that would be like burning my own child. Don't you know that I have heard this baby's voice inside my head? He begs me to set him free and let him play with the children."

"Then that is what you must do," said the Boss Nun.

That very night, the Boss Nun led Sister Geppetto to the town square. At this hour, no one was there. Geppetto used her carving knife to cut all the strings, one by one. Then she laid the Baby Jesus beside the well at the center of the square.

"Oh, thank you," said Baby Jesus.

"This will not end well for you," said Sister Geppetto.

The Boss Nun had not heard him. "Did he speak to you?"

"He thanked me for his freedom."

"Then the words you told him are the words God could say to all humankind, were it not for the sacrifice of his Only Begotten."

Geppetto kissed the forehead of the inert Baby Jesus and wept as the Boss Nun took her back inside the convent.

The next night, the Boss Nun took her back to the square. They walked all around the square but did not see the Baby Jesus puppet, until finally they stopped at the town's well in the middle and Geppetto heard the Baby Jesus calling out to her.

"Oh I am broken!" he cried. "Tie a string to me and raise me out of here!"

"He's at the bottom of the well," said Sister Geppetto. "And he's broken."

"You hear his voice?" asked the Boss Nun. "You believe this?"

"He never lied to me," said Geppetto.

The Boss Nun looked as if she had much to say, but at last all she did was turn the crank and raise up the bucket full of water. The puppet was not in the bucket.

"Please let me try again," said Geppetto. "We only need to get the bucket under him. He's wooden, so he must be floating."

So patient and understanding was the Boss Nun that she stayed with Sister Geppetto until she raised up the Baby Jesus on the third try. All the puppet's metal joints were bent, though none had fully come apart; one wooden arm was broken, but the cloth of the shirt plus a few splinters held it in place.

"And still he speaks to you?" asked the Boss Nun doubtfully, as she examined the puppet to assess the damage.

"He weeps in pain," said Sister Geppetto, "and he also says that freedom is a strange gift, because without strings he had no power even to protect himself."

"Nor have any of us," said the Boss Nun. "Have you also learned this lesson?"

"I have learned that when I do not obey the rule of my order, I have no power to do good, but only power to do harm, even when I meant it to be good."

"Then this puppet of Baby Jesus has done its work and completed its mission in your life. I will pray for the Spirit of God to cease quickening this puppet so you no longer hear its voice. But I will let you keep this wooden body as a reminder of all you learned."

All I learned, thought Sister Geppetto, and all I loved, for this Baby Jesus was the god of my idolatry and all that I will ever love so completely in my life.

Seventy-five years later, having served long years as the Boss Nun herself,

Sister Geppetto died as a feeble old woman and, according to instructions that she left, a certain old broken puppet was laid beside her body in the coffin when it was lowered into the ground. Only then did anyone remember that yes, it was Sister Geppetto who carved the puppets that were used in the Christmas pageant every year. But as for this puppet, which had never been a part of the show, no one knew what it had been made for, or why it was broken, or why she had kept it without ever repairing it.

Five women from neighboring apartments rushed to the Ochoa apartment to tell them that a car from the International Fleet had stopped in front of the building. "The man asked if you lived here!" they reported, and soon variants also were said: "The man asked about Dabeet." "The man is here to take Dabeet to Fleet School."

Dabeet knew that it was barely possible that the man had spoken Mother's name, and that all the rest was people leaping to conclusions and telling Mother what they knew she wanted to hear.

By the time Hyrum Graff, Minister of Colonization, came to their door, he was out of breath, and there was nowhere in the apartment for him to sit, because neighbors were occupying every surface and leaning against all the open wall space.

Graff stood leaning on the doorframe, a younger man in a much crisper uniform standing near him. "Four flights is a long way up for a fat old man," said Graff.

Dabeet said nothing.

Mother said nothing.

"I need to talk to Dabeet Ochoa alone," said Graff.

After a few moments, everybody got up and filed out of the apartment. When no one was left but Dabeet and Mother, Graff shook his head. "*Dabeet* Ochoa. Alone."

"He may not be interviewed outside the presence of his parents."

"You know the law," said Graff. "Insist on it, and I'll leave right now. If you want me to stay, then *you* leave." He looked at his watch.

Mother got up and left the apartment, slamming the door behind her.

Graff sat down on the tallest chair, the one with sturdy arms. He sighed as he lowered himself into it. "I have to sit in a chair I have some hope of getting up out of without assistance," he said.

Dabeet simply looked at him. He had not expected Graff to come.

"Do you know why I'm here?" asked Graff.

"I do not, sir," said Dabeet.

"But you have a guess?"

"If you were still head of Battle School, I would imagine you had come to tell me that I was accepted, or to give me some kind of final test to see if I were qualified."

"But I am now Minister of Colonization," said Graff.

"That means that you're really the boss of the International Fleet," said Dabeet.

"Oh, no, that's far from the truth. The International Fleet is ready to fight an interstellar war at any time, and I play no part in war readiness and training."

"Neither does Battle School," said Dabeet.

"We are no longer drafting the brightest potential commanders from among Earth's children, because there is no present enemy and the nations have withdrawn our authority to take such actions," said Graff.

"The IF still takes volunteers," said Dabeet.

"As adults, age seventeen and above. All volunteers are then screened for command potential. You still have . . . six years left?"

"Battle School has been repurposed as Fleet School," said Dabeet.

"It's a very different school now," said Graff. "We aren't really training soldiers there anymore."

"Commanders, though."

"Commanders of exploratory, recon, outpost, and colonizing missions. A very different set of tasks than we require of war leaders."

"But a nearly identical set of qualifications," said Dabeet. He did not say what they both knew: that command of an exploration, reconnaissance, outpost, or colonization mission required exactly the skill set of a military commander—and more.

"Less centered on killing," said Graff.

"You only recruit among the children of the Fleet," said Dabeet.

"And here you are, a boy without a birth certificate, but making claims based on . . . what?"

"My mother's word," said Dabeet.

"Do you believe your mother?"

"I neither believe nor disbelieve," said Dabeet. "I have submitted my DNA to be tested against the IF rolls. Either I'm the son of an IF soldier or I'm not. You know the answer, and I don't."

"Your mother does, or thinks she does," said Graff.

"What I know is that the Minister of Colonization has come to visit a poor eleven-year-old Venezuelan immigrant to the United States in his mother's humble apartment, presumably in response to either my mother's petitions, if she ever really made them, or my own repeated submission of my test results and my DNA through every channel I could find."

"Most of those channels having nothing to do with admissions to the IF or Fleet School or . . . anything."

"My test scores are very, very good," said Dabeet. "I thought they might make their own channels."

"They did," said Graff. "Which is why every single one of your submissions has been brought to my attention, regardless of the channel you submitted it through."

"A year of silence," said Dabeet. "And now . . . you."

"If you couldn't bear a year of silence," said Graff, "what possible use could we make of you? Every voyage our ministry undertakes is at least thirty years long."

Dabeet rolled his eyes. "I know about relativity. Nobody will experience all thirty years."

Graff smiled. "But everybody they leave behind will be at least sixty years' worth of old or dead by the time they get back. If they ever do."

It was fine to discuss abstractions, but Dabeet saw that Graff was steering around the questions that mattered right now. "What about my mother's petitions?"

"What you're really asking is whether your mother actually made those petitions. What you're asking is if she ever really meant for you to go into space."

"I'm asking about whether you received any petitions from my mother."

Graff nodded. "I know what you're asking and what you're not asking, what you don't know and what you do know."

"But you're not answering."

"You're an eleven-year-old boy."

"Nearly twelve. I'm vastly more mature than I was a year ago." Dabeet hoped that the irony would make Graff smile.

It didn't. "Why should I provide you with information that your mother hasn't given you?"

Dabeet did not believe there *was* any such information. "Because you're a man of integrity who respects the wisdom of children," said Dabeet.

"And you would know this because . . ."

"I read the trial transcripts," said Dabeet.

"Ah, yes, my court-martial for causing the deaths of two children and abusing countless others."

"There was a war. We won. As a direct result of your training methods."

"I heard the verdict," said Graff. "I believe the court-martial ended with my receiving a medal, a commendation, a reprimand, a suspended sentence, and an honorable discharge from the International Fleet."

"And an immediate appointment by the Hegemon, the Polemarch, and the Strategos as Minister of Colonization, with an enormous budget and the authority to construct exploratory, reconnaissance, outpost, and colonization ships," said Dabeet. "'With Battle School placed under the Ministry of Colonization to serve as a preparatory school for children of the Fleet who showed promise as future commanders of such ships and expeditions.'"

"Word for word," said Graff. "Demonstrating that your ability to memorize and retain is remarkable."

"I don't care who my father is, Minister. I don't care if he's still in the Fleet, denying he ever slept with a native girl, or if he harvested bananas on a plantation and was stung by a dozen tarantulas and died an agonizing death."

"You just want to get into Fleet School."

"There's no law *against* a child of Earth being admitted to Fleet School."

"There's also no budget to pay for lifting some worthless piece of human cargo to a place where he cannot possibly benefit any nation on Earth."

"Give me a scholarship," said Dabeet. "You can't have an oversupply of children as qualified as I am."

"Though there are quite a few as vain as you are," said Graff.

"Vanity is self-regard for trivial things—appearance, manner. Humility is recognition of the truth about oneself. The truth about me is that however I was conceived, I have abilities far beyond the capacity of the Charles G. Conn School for the Gifted in Elkhart, Indiana."

"There are four national schools for gifted students in the United States," said Graff, "and there are sixteen Hegemony schools, two of them in North America."

"Those were the also-ran schools, for students not taken for Battle School."

"Many brilliant students were passed over for Battle School because they weren't quite right for our very narrow purposes."

"You didn't know what was quite right for your very narrow purposes," said Dabeet. "You still don't know. You don't know why Ender

Wiggin succeeded and others never came close to his abilities. Which test scores promised the results you got from him? Which students that you weeded out might have done even better, except that you measured them against criteria that had never been proven to have anything to do with military command success?"

"My point exactly," said Graff. "These Earthside schools are excellent, with superb faculty and, in most cases, a commitment to creativity that allows students to explore and become whatever they want to be."

"I want to be an explorer and a colonizer," said Dabeet. "Which Earthside school has a career path leading there?"

"Wait till you're seventeen and enlist."

"I can finish a Ph.D. program in that time," said Dabeet. "But it will all be wasted if I do it here on Earth."

"Well, you make a strong case," said Graff.

"But you're unpersuaded."

"We have rules for a reason," said Graff.

"So you can hide behind them as you deny my application for reasons having nothing to do with those rules."

Finally, Graff smiled. "For a boy who has never worked in government, you understand something about how it works."

"Nobody understands how it works," said Dabeet.

"No, Dabeet. *I* understand how it works. I play the instruments of government as if they were kazoos and ukeleles. They make a horrible din but at least when I play them, the music reaches an end."

"The ugly noise of ambition," said Dabeet.

"If I wanted to make sure I got an early retirement because somebody else had maneuvered me out of my position," said Graff, "I would invite you to come and be an intern in my office."

Dabeet felt a thrill of victory. Graff saw him as a potential threat. "I don't want that job."

"Yes you do," said Graff. "You want any job that gets you out into space and leaves your mother behind."

Dabeet had no answer. He knew that this would be one of the benefits of entering Fleet School, because it was the one school he could enter where Mother could *not* maneuver her way into following him. But Graff was saying that this was Dabeet's main goal. To get away from his mother. Was it?

Maybe.

"Nobody ever wants just one thing," said Dabeet.

"I read your little retelling of the Pinocchio story. There are so many versions, but you're the first person ever to make Geppetto into a nun."

"I think nuns are interesting," said Dabeet.

"No you don't," said Graff.

Dabeet did not make a sarcastic reply about how Graff seemed to think he knew everything about somebody he had only just met. If Graff didn't know how to read people, he wouldn't have the vast power that he held.

"Then what do I think about nuns?" asked Dabeet.

"I have no idea, because Sister Geppetto in your story isn't really a nun. She isn't even the Holy Mother. She's *your* mother."

"My mother didn't carve me out of wood."

"Yes she did," said Graff. "And now she won't let go of the strings."

Dabeet had almost forgotten the story, once he wrote it. It had been nothing but a stupid, meaningless assignment, and he treated it like kleenex—he blew a snotty little story into it and then tossed it into the wastebasket of his teacher's mind.

"I don't remember the story that well," said Dabeet.

"You remember everything," said Graff.

"I remember everything I care about," said Dabeet.

"You care intensely about everything," said Graff, "and so you remember everything."

"Aren't those useful traits?"

"Your Baby Jesus puppet demanded that his strings be cut, even though it made him powerless and destroyed him."

"Puppets can't do anything without strings."

"They can't do anything *with* strings, either. They only have things done to them."

"Instead of trying to read an absurd amount of psychological twaddle into a throwaway story," said Dabeet, "why don't you just tell me what you think you learned from it?"

"That you would rather die at the hands of the village children than continue to live under your mother's control."

Dabeet sat and thought about this, trying to see whether it was true or not. Finally he said, "I can't unwrap myself and see the truth. What you say might be true. Maybe I unconsciously revealed some deep inner hunger in a story that meant nothing."

"It was *because* it meant nothing and you never expected anyone who mattered to read it that you were free to say unconsciously truthful things," said Graff.

"War criminal, bully, dictator, and psychoanalyst," said Dabeet.

"You've only dipped a toe into the ocean of my résumé," said Graff. "Tell me why you are *not* so deeply troubled that you'd be nothing but a disruptive influence in Fleet School."

"Without my mother," said Dabeet, "I wouldn't have—"

"Without your mother you wouldn't have a pot to piss in—or any basis for your arrogant disregard for the feelings of other people."

"Are you saying I'm not *nice*?" asked Dabeet. "There's now a *niceness* test for getting into Battle School?"

"There always was," said Graff. "But I'm sure you can be charming if you decide to be. No, what you seem utterly to lack is the ability to imagine the feelings of other people and adapt your program in order to fulfil their needs along with your own."

"My 'program' has nothing to do with anybody but me."

"If you made it into Fleet School, there would be someone else who did not get that place."

"He should have done better on the tests."

"Here's a test for you: Why not apply your adequate intelligence to figuring out what qualities would make a good leader of an expedition, or a colony, or a scouting or reconnaissance mission? Then see which of those qualities you lack, making it meaningless to bring you into Fleet School."

"You could have sent me an email saying all this."

"But then I couldn't have seen the stubbornness in your face as you rejected every idea I offered you without even a moment's consideration that you might have something to learn from me."

"I consider everything."

"You consider everything impossible unless you want it, and then it already belongs to you, in which case anyone who stands in your way is a thief."

Dabeet inwardly reeled back at this blow. To him, stubbornness had always meant his mother, her refusal to adapt to reality or to realize how ridiculous or offensive she seemed to others. Graff was saying that these were Dabeet's flaws as well.

The thought of his mother's many faults brought Dabeet back to the only important thing he had to learn from Graff. "You had my DNA tested," he said. "Have the decency to tell me if my mother is right about my parentage."

Graff chuckled with what seemed to be real amusement. "You want the truth of your parentage."

"Am I a child of the Fleet?"

"Your mother was not so promiscuous as that. At most, you would be a child of one member of the Fleet."

It took a moment for Dabeet to remember the old epithet "child of the Regiment," which was a cruel term for someone whose mother had slept with every soldier when a regiment was stationed in her town. "So you amuse yourself at my expense," said Dabeet, "and yet you can't tell me a simple truth that you possess and I have a right to know."

"A right to know," said Graff, "eventually, when the time is right."

"Now is the right time," said Dabeet.

Graff cocked his head slightly, and his smile faded to grimness. "If you were not such a preternaturally brilliant child, I would never give you an accurate answer until you came of age. But now I see that receiving the answer you ask for is as much of a test as any other test I could devise. So we'll see what you make of it."

Dabeet knew that Graff was hinting that the answer would be something unpleasant. But he had imagined so many possible fathers that . . .

"Your father is most definitely an officer of the International Fleet. He knows about you, and if you possessed the qualifications for Fleet School, you would be admitted as a legitimate child of the Fleet."

Dabeet knew that *this* could not be the information that would stagger him, that would be a test of his qualifications. "You could have told this to me or my mother at any time."

"That's not the information that your mother withheld from you," said Graff. "She's been saying it all along. But your DNA also told us that you have no closer relationship to Maria Rafaella Ochoa than to any other woman with some degree of Amerindian ancestry."

It took Dabeet a moment to register what Graff had said. "She isn't my mother?"

"Nor your aunt, nor your cousin, nor your cousin's cousin's cousin. She barely qualifies as your neighbor. Neither she nor you comes from Venezuela. She is a native-born citizen of the United States, and she learned Spanish as a second language when she was about your age, and *her* mother was a career diplomat stationed in Ecuador."

"But . . ."

"Dabeet Ochoa, at a loss for words?" asked Graff.

"Why would she . . ."

"Why would she devote her life to you like a mother? Why would she claim to be what she was not? Why would she lie to you? Or—and this is the most interesting question—why would a genius like you never question how his extraordinary intelligence could possibly have sprung from an above-average but not-extraordinary intelligence like hers?"

"Because she . . ."

"Because you lived in a world entirely of her shaping, and you showed not the slightest ability to question the basic parameters of the stories she told you."

"I doubted all her stories!"

"You doubted the ones that sounded false," said Graff. "That your father was a Fleet officer, that your mother's family was wealthy—and they are, by the way. But you never doubted the ones that were most outrageous—that she is a Venezuelan yet has no trace of that accent, and that she is the mother of a son like you."

"Did she kidnap me?" asked Dabeet.

"Now you're flailing about, trying to turn this into some romantic or tragic farce," said Graff. "Your real mother was unable to raise you. You were placed into the foster care system in the place where your mother abandoned you—though she saw to it that anonymous donations were made to provide for your upkeep and education. And you were lucky enough to come quickly under the care of an extraordinarily devoted and loving foster mother, who recognized your extraordinary abilities and knew that you would never reach your real potential in that place. So she brought you to the United States—legally, I might add, because she *could* prove that she was an American citizen, and, by claiming parentage, won *you* the rights and privileges of citizenship."

"What can I . . . what am I supposed to *do* with this information?" asked Dabeet.

"Nothing at all," said Graff. "You would gain nothing by denying her parentage, and lose much, including residency in the United States. She would also suffer, because she kidnapped you from your native country."

"Ecuador?"

"I think I've told you enough to show you that knowledge you have no use for is rarely worth having. The secret, by the way, is not to avoid learning useless knowledge. It's to make use of whatever knowledge you have."

"Thank you for the astonishingly wise counsel," said Dabeet.

"Sarcastic little bastard to the bone," said Graff. He pressed down on the arms of the chair and lurched to his feet, groaning. "Oh, for the pleasures of low gravity."

"So that's it? You're leaving me with nothing?"

"I left you with true information, and a serious test. Now let's see how you use the information and try to pass the test."

"How can I contact you when I'm ready?" asked Dabeet.

Graff was already out the door. "If you're ever ready for anything that pertains to me, I'll let you know." By then he was halfway to the stairs. He moved much faster than his bulk should have allowed.

All the neighbors were outside, watching both Graff and Dabeet. Many were clustered around Mother, muttering questions or judgments. With such an audience, Dabeet dared not call out after Graff. Nor did he want to demean himself by running after him in order to ask one more question.

Besides, he had no idea what that question would be.

The car moved off. Mother headed back inside.

Do I still call her Mother? Of course I do. She sacrificed everything to bring me here, and even if she surrounded me with lies, the lies were all meant to elevate me and advance me and help me achieve my potential. What child has had a more dedicated parent than this one? She may be ridiculous, but she has earned the title Mother far more than the woman who bore me, who was, like my father, little more than a gene donor.

"I don't think it went very well, Mother," said Dabeet quietly when she ushered him back into the apartment.

"Tell me everything."

So Dabeet spoke to his mother for an hour, and almost nothing that he said was any truer than the stories his mother had told him all his life, and so when he had satisfied her curiosity, he felt empty and wicked and angry and deeply, deeply sad.

I am never going to Fleet School, because Graff doesn't like me, and whatever attributes he doesn't like, they aren't likely to change.

Besides, Dabeet realized, I don't have the same urgency to get away from Mother. She's my one protector in a hostile world where minds like mine are a commodity to be captured or killed or exploited by governments—haven't we seen what happened to the Battle School students when they came home to Earth? I would have to be a fool to get out from under her protection.

And under that was a feeling so deep and so irrational that Dabeet was ashamed that it formed part of his reason for no longer seeking to leave her behind: She did not deserve to lose contact with the child for whom she had sacrificed her former life.

Only gradually did he realize that somewhere, apparently still living, were his birth parents. They must be brilliant to have been Dabeet's genetic sources. How can they possibly be as obscure as Mother? Somewhere, in some country, his birth mother now lived the life she had abandoned him in order to pursue. Did she rule a nation? Run a great corporation? Had she produced works of art or literature? Was she a performer? Was she famous in some way? She must have Amerindian blood—Graff had said so. As for Dabeet's father, he was in the Fleet, he knew about Dabeet's existence . . . was there some way to figure out, perhaps from his picture, who he might be?

Stop it! Dabeet ordered himself silently. If they wanted to help you they'd already be helping. There's only one person who will help you, and that's Mother, and it's time you treated her with the respect she has earned from you.

3

—That was too provocative, going to see him.

—How could I make any intelligent decision about him without meeting him?

—You could have called him in. You didn't have to show your face.

—It's on the front of my head. And bringing him in would be even *more* provocative.

—You know what's going on right now. You know it's only beginning. And now you've put a target on him.

—I don't see how. He's never had even the slightest military training. He's useless to them.

—Whoever "them" is, are they going to think that matters? Ender Wiggin aced all the tests. Dabeet Ochoa aced all the tests. This is a matter of record and yes, of *course* they'll find a way to access those records.

—I wish I had foreseen all these potential consequences.

—You foresee everything.

—I'm not God, you know. *If* he sees everything, either, which I'm not sure he does.

—You want them to take him.

—A child? You think I want them to—

—I think you want to see what *he'll* do.

—He's eleven. Which of the other kids was able to *do* anything?

—You placed a tracker on him?

—"Them" would find anything like that.

—You just can't stand to let anybody in on your plans, even when it's their legal responsibility to know what you're doing to a child.

—It's sweet that you imagine that I *have* plans. That's why I shouldn't have admirers working with me.

—I don't admire you. I distrust you intensely.

—Yet you're *sure* I have a plan.

—You always have plans, sixty-four layers deep, and reaching forward generations.

—I have aspirations. Let's watch Dabeet carefully and see who *does* have plans for him.

The day after the Minister of Colonization visited him, Dabeet went to school as he normally did, but he could hardly concentrate on anything. Not that he *needed* to concentrate in order to answer in-class questions or deal with teachers. But he kept spinning through the tests that the minister had assigned to him.

The first test had been explicit: Figure out the qualities of a good colony leader and then see which of those qualities Dabeet lacked. Answers that immediately came to mind were: I don't make friends with other children. I'm arrogant and they resent me. But the adults admire and respect me. Will I be leading a team of children or of adults, if I'm a Fleet School graduate? Adults, of course. But perhaps when I'm an adult, other adults will resent me and fear me the way other children do now. I need to think more about that.

Then there was the hypothetical test—that maybe receiving the answer Dabeet was asking for would be as much of a test as any other. And which answer *was* the one he was looking for? He had wanted to know if his father was with the International Fleet, and now Dabeet knew that he was. Why would knowing that be a test?

Or did Graff think that telling him his mother was *not* his mother was the answer he had been looking for? Absurd. It was probably a lie anyway. Children were often smarter than their parents. At least smart children were.

Unless even smart children are too ignorant and naive to understand just how smart their mothers really are.

That's what the man wants. To set me thinking in circles and see if I can make rational decisions anyway.

The third test might not have been a test at all. But the man phrased it as a challenge. That made it a test. "The secret is not to avoid learning useless knowledge. It's to make use of whatever knowledge you have."

Which knowledge did he mean? About Mother? About his putative father? About his rumored birth mother? About the fact that he was not considered qualified for Fleet School?

That was such nonsense. A man like that does *not* come to the home of an unqualified applicant to reject him in person. He comes to an eminently qualified student in order to test him further by pretending to reject him.

Now, *there* was some of the "knowledge" Dabeet had—that he wasn't being taken up to Fleet School. But was it true? Was *any* of his "knowledge" true? And if it was not true, was it knowledge?

The word "epistemology" flashed into his mind. He's making me question which of my sources of information is reliable, and the answer is: None of them. Everyone has their own purposes in what they choose to say or not say, and then they have the purposes they don't even *know* that they have, which means that I can't actually "know" anything, if that's supposed to mean possessing certainty about the truth-value of any portion of the information I "know."

Mother had been lying to him? Well, what child didn't get lied to regularly? The question really is, Which things that she said were lies, and which were things that she believed to be true, which were actually false, and which were things she believed, which also happened to be true? A mother-centered epistemology wasn't going to get him far. But at least she had his best interests at heart. Though of course she couldn't possibly know what was best for him. Neither could the Minister of Colonization. Neither could Dabeet himself.

Make use of whatever knowledge you have. All knowledge was tentative, untrustworthy. You had to act on what you believed, but constantly test it to see if it was not believable after all, and then adapt your plan. . . .

Thus his mind spun around and around. Uselessly, because right now he had no power to act on any of the information he had. What was he going to do, stow away on a supply shuttle and turn up in Fleet School as a volunteer student? "Please, sir, may I audit your classes here?" "No, lad, as a pirate, you're going to walk the plank!"

At lunch, Dabeet ate alone, though he could have sat with any of several groups. He was *not* hated by the other students, and he liked many of them and regarded several as friends. Being very intelligent put off some of the other kids, but his penchant for covertly ridiculing the teachers or their lessons made him something of a hero to some students, and a source of entertainment to others. But he was not so close to anyone that, when he chose to be alone, anyone presumed to intrude on his lunchtime isolation.

Dabeet was lost in thought—in daydreams, to tell the truth, about what Fleet School might be like, and how boring it probably was now that the war was over—when an adult hand gripped his shoulder, not so tightly as to cause pain, but firmly enough that Dabeet understood the pointlessness of resistance.

Other children were looking at whoever had hold of him. If Dabeet had been more observant, he would have realized this and couldn't have been taken by surprise. I'm not observant enough. That's a test and I just failed it.

"Could you come with me, Master Ochoa?"

Ah. It was the principal himself. In the lunchroom. In order to bring Dabeet out in person. Dabeet could hear people whispering his name as the principal guided him past their tables. Dabeet was not sure he liked this kind of celebrity.

In the corridor, where no one else could hear, Dabeet asked, "Can you tell me, sir, why I'm not being allowed to finish my lunch?"

"You were just moving food around on your tray, Dabeet," said the principal. "I have instructions to deliver you into the custody of your father."

My father. The idea ran through him with a thrill. And then, immediately, he disbelieved it. "My father doesn't know I exist."

"He seems to think that he does," said the principal. "Do you imagine we didn't do the DNA exam required before delivering a child into the custody of a parent not already known to us by retinal scan? This man provided you with your Y chromosome."

They reached the school offices and Dabeet tried to hang back. After all these years, after spending many of them quite sure that his father was a myth entirely invented by Mother, Dabeet did not want to meet him now, not under these circumstances. Because, with the principal's testimony, he might believe that it was true.

They passed through the outer office, where none of the staff even looked up, and then past the principal's private secretary and into the inner sanctum, the holy of holies, the place where students went to have authority work its magic on them.

There was no one there.

"But he was here only a few . . ."

The principal didn't finish his sentence, because he slumped to the floor.

Dabeet barely had time to register this, and then he took one breath too many and he, too, felt himself slipping downward, the room spinning, and then . . . darkness.

—

Dabeet awoke on a large airplane, attached to a seat by an ordinary seat belt. This was the only restraint on him, and yet he felt like a prisoner. Of course, all passengers in an airplane in flight were prisoners, because they couldn't leave the cage in which they were confined. And all children surrounded by adults were prisoners, because they were not free to make even the slightest decisions for themselves.

Dabeet tested this idea by unfastening his seat belt.

Immediately, a uniformed man stood in front of him. "Please fasten your seat belt, Dabeet," he said.

Dabeet realized—as he should have realized immediately, he knew—that this was not a normal commercial airliner. He had seen movies. He knew that he should have been in a row of five or six or seven or nine seats, all facing forward. But his seat had its back against the wall of the fuselage, and there was a wide space between him and the seat on the opposite wall, facing his. It was unoccupied.

"I need to micturate," said Dabeet.

The uniformed man didn't bat an eye at the deliberately rare word; nor did he look contemptuous at Dabeet's attempt at intellectual bullying. "No, you do not," said the man. "The gas that was used to render you unconscious also causes your body to retain water, and hardly anything has been taken up by your kidneys in the hours since you were taken."

The man was actually being rather candid, which was a good thing. How far would it extend? "While I'm sitting here wishing I could take a piss and forbidden to do so," said Dabeet, "can you give me some information about who kidnapped me, where I'm being taken, what the purpose of this expedition is, what happened to the principal of my school, and whether my father really was the person who came to my school to get me?"

"Quite a list," said the uniformed man.

"And yet you can see that these are all reasonable things for me to ask about," said Dabeet.

"Reasonable, and yet premature," said the man.

"You're a colonel," said Dabeet, "and your uniform is gaudy enough that I assume you're from a Latin American country. Your accent suggests that you are not Brazilian, so I assume you speak Spanish. You look European, so I also assume you're from an Andean country where Amerindians like me are an oppressed, low-status minority that has little chance of advancing to high rank. The chance of Chile or Ecuador mounting a kidnapping in the United States is nil, and the Bolivian economy couldn't supply a plane this luxurious to be used on a clandestine mission. This smacks of the perks of high-ranking officials."

"It *used* to be a presidential plane," said the officer, "but it's been repurposed."

"So the president now has a better plane. That suggests a prosperous economy, and yet a nation eager to thumb its nose at the United States. Venezuela or Peru."

"All Latin American nations are happy to thumb their noses at the norteamericanos," said the officer. "I'm a general but you couldn't have known that because this is not the uniform of my own country and it does not display my true rank. Nor is this airplane the one-time property of the top political leader of *my* country."

"I think I'm going to wet my pants now."

"Whatever pleases you," said the general. "You will still have to sit in it until we land, and you will not be allowed to change clothing until bedtime tonight. You're free to decide how childish you want to appear and how smelly you wish to be when you arrive at your new home."

"I liked my old home, and wherever you're taking me, I will never regard it as my home."

"It's the nation of your birth," said the general. "The United States was not. And whether this fits the overly sentimental American meaning of the word 'home,' it will definitely be tu casa. Your dwelling place for the foreseeable future."

"Does my mother know what's happened to me?"

"She knows that you left school with your father," said the general.

"Did I?"

"I'm not that person, if that's what you're asking."

"Nobody involved with this operation is my father," said Dabeet, "because he's with the International Fleet, and the IF does not carry out any kind of operation on the surface of Earth."

"At least not while wearing the uniform of the IF," said the general. "Really, Dabeet, you keep leaping to conclusions and relying on public information which might be, for all you know, disinformation. Be as bright as your reputation says you are. Try to think at least a few words ahead of your mouth."

Dabeet said nothing more.

The general reached down and rebuckled Dabeet's seat belt.

Dabeet unbuckled it.

The general bent over as if to whisper in Dabeet's ear, but instead jabbed Dabeet sharply in the upper stomach, just below the ribs. Dabeet doubled over, unable to breathe.

"Are we in agreement now? About your continuing to wear a fully fastened seat belt?" asked the general softly.

Dabeet, unable to catch enough breath to answer, nodded.

"Smart enough to learn from experience," said the general. "But not smart enough to recognize the power structure in a new environment without direct and painful experience. You're already such a disappointment." The general walked away.

There were other people seated or walking back and forth in this cabin of the airplane, but nobody spoke to him or looked at him. Dabeet's mouth was very dry. His skin felt dry. They couldn't want him to dehydrate. But he didn't feel inclined to ask for anything at the moment.

He tried to do as the general had suggested, and think through his situation and extrapolate more information from the crumbs the general had let fall. But the gas they had given him left him groggy and he had a headache. He wasn't thinking at his best.

Or maybe everything had been faked from the start. Maybe he had been *told* he was smart, and had been given wildly inflated scores on all his tests. Maybe the easy tests he took were *not* the same ones Ender Wiggin had been given. Maybe the Charles G. Conn School for the Gifted was nothing of the kind, and the visit of the Minister of Colonization had not been because Dabeet was anything special, but because the Minister wished to provoke exactly this kidnapping. Because Dabeet really was a rather stupid boy, with a reputation for genius, if Dabeet happened to be killed or left in the custody of some monstrous foreign power, it would be no loss to anyone except, perhaps, Mother.

But this was obviously not true. The tests had been genuine. The questions had been hard. Dabeet had answered them all correctly. The other children at Conn Gifted were, in fact, quite clever in their way. Dabeet was a genuine target for genuine kidnappers.

And now he realized what was going on. Graff *had* set him up. The news media had carried several recent stories of Battle School alumni and students who were either kidnapped or assassinated upon their return to Earth. Some said this was why Ender Wiggin himself remained in space, because he was too much at risk. Newly released from the constraints of the Formic Wars, nations were maneuvering for advantage and preparing for wars; Battle School–trained children might be the secret weapons that could be used to save one nation—or destroy another.

The country that has taken me doesn't think it has enough clever Battle Schoolers, and so they want me. Or they want to deprive some other country of my services.

But I have no training in war. I didn't think I'd need any. Yes, I've read about Ender Wiggin and I've read about other generals, but not with any serious intent. Fleet School has different purposes now. So whoever has taken me, they're going to be disappointed with my performance.

Disappointing them won't lead to any good outcome for me.

So I'll pretend to know whatever they need, and then I'll learn it in order to perform superbly. *If* I decide I want to help them. If not, I'll figure out how to *seem* to be helping while actually sabotaging them.

At about that point in his thinking the grogginess and inaction overcame him, and he slept again.

——

When he awoke he was sitting in a different chair. Still strapped in, but now he looked over the top of a rather large desk to see a man in a civilian suit, sipping at a tiny coffee cup while another voice droned on in a language that only sometimes sounded like Spanish. Dabeet looked for the source of the other voice, and finally concluded, from the periodic breaks and cracks in the voice, that he was listening to a speakerphone that carried a signal via satellite.

Dabeet understood colloquial Spanglish, the language of the immigrant community in Indiana, and he had learned some formal Spanish. But this sounded as if a Frenchman had inserted his DNA into the conversation.

Nasals. Otherwise Spanish-like. Português. Brazilian, then? Why in the world would Brazil, one of the major powers, need a definitely not-Brazilian boy untrained in war?

No, the other people on the plane had spoken Spanish flawlessly and smoothly. It was quite possible that for some reason Brazil had funded a poorer Latin-American country in this kidnapping. Perhaps Brazil wanted to help one of its dependent countries prevail in some minor local squabble without getting directly involved itself.

Finally the man behind the desk spoke—and in Spanish, but slowly, as if to allow the man on the other end of the conversation to understand him more easily. Dabeet learned little from the conversation: "The visitor is awake and listening. I will find out what I can."

So Dabeet would be interrogated. About what, he did not know, since he possessed no state secrets, and, between his mother's lies and Graff's, he did not know if he knew the things he did know.

"Your visitor," began the man behind the desk.

Dabeet knew at once that the man wished to ask about Graff. So Dabeet would pretend not to understand him. "No, sir," said Dabeet—in English. "I am not your visitor, nor am I your guest. I am your captive, and I'm a child as well."

"The boy pretends to be an idiot," said the man, in Spanish.

After a second: "No," said the Brazilian on the speakerphone, this time in English. "He pretends to believe *you* are an idiot."

"You are all idiots," said Dabeet in low Spanish, guessing that the Brazilian would not understand him, especially because he added a few colorful fighting words to the statement.

As Dabeet had hoped, the man behind the desk was forced to interpret his words, though he paraphrased considerably. All the while, he placidly looked Dabeet in the eye, like a cow chewing its cud.

After a couple of seconds of satellite lag, the voice over the telephone, again in English, said, "We are curious to know why a genius is so stupid as to insult those who hold his life in their power."

"You are playing into the hands of the Minister of Colonization," said Dabeet. "You noticed me because he came and spoke to me. But what did he say? That there was no more Battle School. Now they train the children of the Fleet to explore and colonize, and I am badly suited to such a mission. So even though I *am* a child of the Fleet, I will not be taken off Earth to study. *This* is the prize you have captured."

"He's convinced me," said the man at the desk. "He's worthless to us."

"I'm a child of the Fleet," said Dabeet. "Do you imagine that the Ministry of Colonization has not been watching everything you do? I'm quite sure this airplane is being watched from space. I'm sure the IF knows who is aboard this plane, where it took off, and where you think it will land. Even if they have no use for me, do you think that the IF will overlook any harm you might do to a child of the Fleet?"

"The IF has no authority on the surface of the Earth or the Moon," said the man at the desk.

"Authority is one thing," said Dabeet. "The ability to kill you at will, from space, is something else." At that moment, another thought occurred to him. "You wanted me because you represent a nation so feeble that no Battle School students or graduates returned to you when the school was disbanded. You must have enemies that you fear, and you hoped that a Battle School commander would make a difference in the war that you know is coming."

The man at the desk smiled sarcastically. "You know nothing about us."

Dabeet decided not to mention that he knew the man on the phone was Brazilian. That alone might guarantee that Dabeet would be killed, once he proved to be useless. "I know something about the International Fleet," said Dabeet. "They aren't staying out of all the little wars that are poised to start in the next while because they have no authority. If they wanted to enforce the hegemonic peace, they'd do it. Why don't they? Because they *want* Earth to be filled with warfare."

Two seconds of silence.

"What do they gain from that?" asked the man on the telephone.

"Refugees. People who have lost everything, who have fled their homes, and need a place to go. The IF will offer them that place—on colony ships headed for the empty Formic worlds, and then to the new planets they expect to discover and colonize."

The man at the desk smiled. "Do you seriously expect us to believe that—"

But the man on the phone interrupted. "I can see that this will be the outcome, if not the purpose, of their policy."

"Lots of little wars, or a handful of big ones," said Dabeet. "That's why they let all the Battle School children go home—no, *made* them go home, even though there were some who would rather have stayed with the Fleet. So that the wars would not be quick, decided by military hardware and raw numbers. Instead, clever commanders will face each other, and the armies and navies will maneuver all over the map, creating more and more refugees with every move they make."

"So you think that we are the puppets of the IF," said the Brazilian on the phone.

"Of course you are. Kidnapping me was just one more instance of falling into the IF's trap."

Desk Man was not buying it. "You give MinCol far too much credit—he has no authority within the Fleet, he's merely a vestigial part of the Hegemony."

"So it is meant to seem," said Dabeet, thinking more deeply into this story as he talked. "But the vast treasury of the Fleet has not been returned to the nations that paid it as taxes and assessments, has it? That money is being used to build ships. Not warships, but colony ships. Exploration and colonization are the primary activities of the IF. How important is the Minister of Colonization to such a fleet?"

"So he comes all the way to Earth so that he can tempt us to kidnap *you*," said Desk Man scornfully.

"You saw my test scores, or why else would you have taken the Minister's bait?"

"You think that MinCol really means to take you after all?" asked the Brazilian.

"I think that MinCol is still testing me," said Dabeet, adopting the military title for Graff. "If I can't talk you out of keeping me or killing me, then I'm not the boy he wants."

"But the decision isn't yours," said Desk Man. "No matter how you plead."

"This doesn't depend on my being persuasive. This depends on your recognizing the truth when someone tells it to you—even if it's an eleven-year-old boy."

"What truth is that?" asked the Brazilian.

"The IF doesn't care who wins these wars on Earth. The IF doesn't care if your nations are swallowed up or destroyed. But you do."

"Yes," said Desk Man, "we do."

"You have me in hopes that I'll help you *win* your war. But in the process, you're being funded by a much larger nation—and whether you win or lose, how much independence do you think you'll have?" Dabeet decided to roll the dice on telling them what he had figured out. "I know, I know, Brazil has no imperial ambitions. But suppose your little nation chooses a government that no longer wants to be so cooperative with Brazilian foreign policy? Brazil has to act in its own interest. Right now, Brazil's interest coincides with your own. Whatever happens militarily, however, you will be a tool of Brazilian foreign policy, and you will produce refugees to fill the IF's colony ships. Which aspects of this were part of your plan for your nation's future?"

Neither Desk Man nor the Brazilian spoke. For at least half a minute, which felt like forever.

"I have the plan you need," said Dabeet.

"Your plan," said Desk Man, "is to sow distrust between our patron and ourselves."

"His plan," said the Brazilian, "is to point out to us that no matter what we do, the IF will get what it wants, and nobody else will."

"*You* will," said Dabeet. "There are nine nations capable of launching rockets at escape velocity, without having to use the shuttle system that is still controlled by the IF. These rockets are intended to launch scientific and communications satellites. But what if one of them could send a payload out to L-5, where the Fleet School hovers?"

"Are you that desperate to get to Fleet School?" asked Desk Man.

"I'll already be at Fleet School," said Dabeet. "You will not only let me live, you'll return me to Indiana, and, because I passed this test, the Minister of Colonization will take me up to Fleet School. I'll be there, ready to cooperate with your venture."

"And what, exactly, is this venture supposed to be?" asked the Brazilian.

"Think about what Fleet School represents. The best of the children of the Fleet are there. An attack on the station doesn't have to 'succeed,' it only has to take place. No nation will claim credit for it. The only message the mission will give to the IF is this: If you continue to abandon Earth to endless warfare, then you will not remain untouched by war."

"This hypothetical expedition is expected to fail," said Desk Man.

"The mission will succeed no matter what happens, because the IF can't absorb such a blow. It will have to come to Earth and exert authority, and once it has taken that step, it will have no choice but to restore the Hegemony and guarantee the peace as it did during the Formic Wars."

"But what will this expedition do—besides die with disinformational notes in their pockets?"

"A sensible plan would be to take over the entire station without harming any of the children. A message is sent to the IF. Then the invaders seize one of the Fleet School shuttles and take it back to Earth, with a few dozen children aboard, along with the surviving members of the expedition."

"So the IF won't shoot it down," said Desk Man.

"The IF doesn't have to worry about publicity," said the Brazilian.

"So they can shoot it down and write off those children as casualties of war. They could claim that *we* exploded the shuttle."

"They *could* do that," said Dabeet, "except that they *do* have to worry about publicity. Nobody is more suspicious of official statements from the high command than soldiers and junior officers are—they know from experience that most of what the high command says is bullshit. So if the IF high command wishes to retain their lofty offices, and to have the loyalty and obedience of the soldiers and officers under them, they will proceed with great caution. They would far rather see your expedition get back to Earth, if it means the children survive, than to punish it, if that would harm the children."

"You've never been in the IF," said Desk Man, "so you have no idea what they—"

"You know he's right," said the Brazilian. "You know that your own military functions exactly that way."

Again, silence. Desk Man might disagree with the Brazilian, but it would do him no good to argue with him, or even show Dabeet that he was frustrated. If he was. Desk Man was good at keeping his face blank. Or else Dabeet wasn't skilled enough in reading facial expressions to be able to read him.

"It's quite possible," said the Brazilian eventually, "that the child is right about the IF setting a trap for us. I don't think they're interested in catching and punishing us, as long as we return the boy—in this, his situation exactly parallels what he says of the Fleet School hostages we would take, if we were insane enough to pursue his plan."

"So all of this was for nothing," said Desk Man.

"Not at all," said the Brazilian. "We have made the acquaintance of a remarkable child, and we can only hope that he's as big a source of irritation and inconvenience for MinCol as he has been for us."

"Setting him free is a mistake," said Desk Man. "If we intend to *use* his plan, and he ends up in Fleet School, he can warn them of what's coming."

Dabeet chuckled. "Why would I do that?" he asked.

"Why wouldn't you?" asked Desk Man.

Dabeet unbuckled his seat belt, stood up, and leaned on the desk, so his face wasn't far from Desk Man's. "I don't like the Minister of Colonization. I really don't like his having rejected me for Fleet School unless I passed this dangerous test. If I fail, I'm either a captive or I die—so if I live, tell me what it is that I owe to MinCol? Loyalty? He had no loyalty to me."

"This feeling will pass," said Desk Man.

"The IF is manipulating Earth," said Dabeet, "at great cost to all nations, including yours. When your people start dying in the wars that are coming, how quickly will your rage at the IF 'pass'?"

Desk Man remained silent until the Brazilian spoke. "Here's what we'll do, my young friend. *If* you get taken up to Fleet School, then you will find a way to open an entry point on the outside of the station. Choose a spot that will face Earth while the door is open."

"And you'll be watching?" asked Dabeet.

"Let's say you do it twice. Open it for a period of time, close it for the *same* period of time, then open it again. That will tell us that you are capable of helping us, on a schedule, and that we still have your loyalty."

"A traitor can open a door," said Desk Man.

"Once we know that there's a door that might open," said the Brazilian, "we'll decide whether to risk the lives of a team of soldiers in order to pursue your insane plan. *If* we can figure out a way to approach the station undetected, and *if* we think the plan will have the outcome you predict, and *if* the situation on Earth becomes as dire as you claim to believe it will, *then* we'll consider your plan. If we decide to proceed, we'll find a way to let you know the day and time of arrival, and you will be there to open the door."

Dabeet nodded and sat back down. "If Victor and Imala could find a way to approach the Formic scout ship in the First Formic War, then surely you, with much greater knowledge of the technologies and practices of the IF than they had of the Formic ship, will find a way."

"Pois é. You're just like MinCol, full of little tests for other people to pass, if they can. Now the airplane that you are on will turn around immediately, because there's still plenty of fuel to make it back to the airport you left from."

"They'll be watching that airport," said Desk Man.

"Of course they will," said the Brazilian. "You're counting on that, because as soon as you realized that someone had smuggled an unconscious child on board the plane, you turned around to return him. You had nothing to do with his being kidnapped, and you are horrified and embarrassed that your airplane was used for such an evil purpose."

"Where was he supposedly hidden?" asked Desk Man.

"Be resourceful," said the Brazilian. "If you can't figure out a plan, get the boy to come up with one. He'll go along with all this, at least until you refuel and take off again. Won't you, Dabeet Ochoa?"

"I will," said Dabeet. "It's in the interest of every party to this conversation to demonstrate good faith and loyalty—to each other, not the IF or the local authorities in Indiana."

"It has been no pleasure at all doing business with you," said the Brazilian. "And, just so you know, I'm not a Brazilian."

What was he, then, Portuguese? Angolan? Neither country had the means to do what he was doing. But . . . of course he was Brazilian. He was simply warning Dabeet that whatever else he said or did, he'd better not implicate Brazil in this. Dabeet would decide, when the time came, whether to comply with this request. "No one ever thought you were, sir," said Dabeet.

It took Dabeet about five minutes to find a space on the plane that he could fit into, concealed. Since this was a diplomatic aircraft, there were plenty of stowage areas for smuggling weapons, bombs, drugs, or whatever else needed the protection of a diplomatic pouch while it was delivered. Dabeet picked one that was inside a bench seat in the less-comfortable part of the plane where, presumably, persons of lesser status were transported. It was flattering to realize that he had been given fairly good treatment, compared to how it might have been.

Dabeet spent fifteen minutes of the return flight inside that bench, so that if there was a forensic examination, traces of his presence would be found. Then he came back out, enjoyed the meal he was served, and talked enough with the crew that despite their strict reticence, he learned that the nation of origin for Desk Man and his officers was Ecuador.

But of course this information was probably not a slip at all, but the cover story they had been told to let him "discover" for himself. Other comments, much more oblique, led him to suspect a country with mountains much lower than the Andes, and lots of coastline not far from those mountains. He suspected either Panama or a Caribbean island—and from the facial features and skin color of Desk Man and his officers, Dabeet concluded that they were *not* from a Caribbean island. Panama then, or maybe Costa Rica. But of course he might be wrong and they could be from Argentina for all he knew. Or it might be the plane's crew—and perhaps the plane itself—that originated in Panama, while Desk Man was, in fact, from Ecuador. Or Mexico. Possibly Venezuela, because Mother might not have been lying about that.

Thus did Dabeet pass the time on the way home, refusing to anticipate what would happen to him once he was turned over to the American authorities. He would be interrogated, of course, so he would have to act like a confused child who could remember almost nothing because of the effects of the drug he'd been given. But he would have to be true to his own character, because he was known, and if he didn't exude the same level of confidence—no, be honest now, *arrogance*—that he normally displayed, someone might suspect he was deliberately hiding something.

What, exactly, was MinCol testing here? Was it enough that he got the plane turned around and saved his own life? Or was he expected to have figured out more than he had? Was the real test going to be how honest and forthright he was when the IF sent someone to debrief him?

If Dabeet couldn't even be sure of his captors' country of origin, how could he hope to outguess the manipulations of a man like Minister of Colonization Hyrum Graff?

4

—I can see that it might appear to you that this was some kind of test, and it was, in a general sense. And while I recognize that my coming to see you might have called undue attention to you, it was certainly not my plan to expose you to any kind of danger.

—I suppose, then, that I passed the test "in a general sense."

—I wonder how you managed it, since they went to a lot of trouble to abduct you, only to return you without receiving anything in return.

—Perhaps you should regard the decipherment of that conundrum as *your* test. In a general sense.

—I can think of several solutions to the puzzle that do not redound to your credit.

—How odd. I can't think of any. But perhaps we can trade information.

—I've already told you everything I know about your parentage. Except your father's actual identity, which you have no need to know.

—No, it's a new question. A small one. I don't believe for a moment that my father, whoever he is, was involved with my kidnapping. Yet the principal said that the man who came to claim me passed the DNA test, affirming that he was my father.

—Oh, Dabeet, do you really need me to answer that?

—My assumption now is that the DNA test that the principal mentioned consisted of a sum of money being passed to him from a foreign agent.

—The principal is being detained until we can determine whether that is true. He might have been under duress. He claims, of course, that he was taken completely by surprise by the gas attack on the two of you. But he has no plausible reason for having brought you to his office in the middle of lunch hour.

—"Until *we* can determine"?

—Because you are a child of the Fleet, the IF is participating in the investigation.

—So my status as a child of the Fleet has been openly declared at my school?

—To the local police, but I'm sure they've already mentioned it at Conn. Thus you are vindicated to the faculty and students who thought you and your mother were falsely claiming Fleet status.

—I'm ashamed that it matters to me, but it does.

—You're ashamed that you were ashamed? Soon you'll be ashamed of being ashamed of being ashamed. This will have no happy ending.

—I assume that my captors were allowed to leave.

—The airplane is, technically speaking, a diplomatic pouch. The local authorities had no authority to inspect it or, for that matter, detain it.

—But the IF does what it likes.

—At our first indication of interest, Fleet inspectors were invited to enter. They were shown a compartment under a seat that contained, not only your DNA from sweat and skin, but also the residue of various drugs, explosives, and other munitions. Also three species of animals that it is illegal to traffic in. But I assume you weren't actually confined there?

—No, they had me in a very comfortable seat. Only when they had decided to return me did we need to find a place to make it appear that I had been hidden on board, and then I needed to be confined there long enough to leave those traces that you found.

—How did you persuade them to return you instead of making you disappear over the Atlantic?

—I assumed that we were over the Caribbean.

—You thought they were taking you to a Latin American country.

—I told them that the IF would be tracking them with your enormous satellite surveillance system, and that you had the power to take them out of the air at any time.

—They know that we wouldn't do that.

—I convinced them that I'm so important that you might. And people who would do anything for power can't believe that the IF, with more power than anybody, might really refrain from using it.

—Interesting insight.

—Obvious, and therefore not an insight, just an observation.

—What did you promise them?

—Everything I could think of. I have no idea which was the promise that tipped the balance.

—They'll hold you to it.

—The best way to avoid any such outcome is for me to leave planet Earth.

—The Moon?

—I had Fleet School in mind, sir.

—But you haven't passed *my* tests, Dabeet.

—I matter to you, Minister Graff, or you would not have invested so much time in me. If you're uncertain whether I have the qualifications you require, why not take me to Fleet School and make the attempt to inculcate me with them? Do I need to be curious? Do I need to be capable both of following and of leading in groups? Do you need to know whether I'll be obedient? Or whether I'll disobey orders when that's the course that will have the best outcome for my team or my mission? Take me to Fleet School and let's both find out whether I have judgment to match my native intelligence.

—A decent stab at my first test, I must admit.

—The Formic Wars are over, sir. Not so much is at stake. If I'm a bust, what have you lost, really? With my test scores and my parentage, no one will fret that I didn't deserve a chance at Fleet School. If your curriculum is worthwhile, trust me to make the most of it.

—You make a strong argument, but it isn't the only argument.

—On board the airplane, the civilian in charge was on satphone with a Portuguese-speaking man who was clearly the ultimate source of authority for the mission to kidnap me.

—Brazilian, then, you think?

—He made sure to insist that he was not.

—And a civilian was in charge.

—He had the private office and the big desk and the comfortable chair. The general in colonel's uniform was relegated to making sure I kept my seat belt on.

—And why did you tell me this now, instead of before?

—I waited until I thought you might need a demonstration of my loyalty before deciding to take me off planet.

—So you thought you were coming close to persuading me.

—I also know you're not the kind of leader who changes his plan just to prove that a subordinate is wrong.

—You know? Or you hope?

—How could you be where you are, if you acted out of petty vanity?

—Someday I'll ask you to tell me where, exactly, you think I am.

—You're in charge of whatever you care to be in charge of, sir. You care most about colonization, so that's the position from which you lead the International Fleet and seek to control events on Earth.

—Events can't be controlled, Dabeet. They can only be influenced.

—Just like people.

—You've passed all my tests now, Dabeet. Welcome to Fleet School.

What do you do when all your plans work out? When all your dreams come true?

In his heart, Dabeet was already gone. From the moment Graff told him he was accepted into Fleet School, Dabeet detached from his friends. None had been close—or so it seemed to Dabeet, since he never felt toward his friends the kind of relentless dependency that others seemed to feel. He noticed when he wasn't included in some event—a party, a movie, a new game—but he didn't mind much, because he had other things to do. And now that he was preparing to go to Fleet School, he declined such invitations as he received. There was no point in investing any more time and effort with people he would never see again.

His friends, if they noticed his increased distance, said nothing about it. It was the teachers who were most demanding. Dabeet had not understood until now how much his teachers valued him. They were so eager to congratulate him—not just once, but over and over. And without Dabeet telling a soul about it, news of his acceptance into Fleet School flew through Charlie Conn. But only the teachers seemed to think it mattered much.

There was only one real surprise for Dabeet—how painful it was to think of leaving Mother. For more than a year, he had bent all his efforts to get away from her, preferably with many miles of empty space between them. Now that he was really leaving, he began to realize how completely she had given over her life to him, and how dependent he was on her. Perhaps one of the reasons he hadn't minded that he didn't have close friends was that his mother cared about everything he did, praised what was praiseworthy, commiserated with his miseries, and constantly told others how gifted he was. That which had been most annoying about her—the constant brag, the promises and lies—

was now the mainstay of his life, and he could not imagine living without seeing her every day.

And yet when she immediately started trying to think of ways to come with him, he resisted her almost instinctively. Yes, he would miss her, and going to this new school would be frightening because of her absence. But he also knew that it would be disastrous if, through some fluke, she were allowed to come along.

"They must need some kind of nursing staff for the children," said Mother. "It wouldn't take me long to take a refresher course."

"Nursing staff?" asked Dabeet.

"I was a school nurse, once upon a time," said Mother.

It was the first Dabeet had ever heard of it. "Then why aren't you working in medicine?"

"Because I chose not to," said Mother. "I chose to work at the same kind of job as the other women in the neighborhood."

"They hate their jobs."

"And so do I," said Mother. "Why do they do their jobs even though they hate them?"

"To put food on the table for their families."

Mother shrugged as if that answer would do for her, as well.

"Mother, with a nursing job you could put far more food on the table!"

"Have you ever been hungry? Did you aspire to be fat?"

"Why would you work at a job beneath your ability when—"

"And they probably need cleaning staff in Fleet School, too. Anything. I could be useful."

"It's a boarding school, Mother," said Dabeet. "Do you want to infantilize me by being the only mother who followed her child to school?"

"Nobody even has to know I'm your mother."

"Then what would be the point?" asked Dabeet. "Stay here and . . . get a real job, one you *like*."

"I have the job I like, Dabeet."

"But that job is disappearing. This household is being downsized, from two persons to one. You're the one. Now it's time for you to take care of yourself."

Mother's eyes filled with tears so suddenly that Dabeet thought for a moment that tears had squirted out away from her face instead of merely spilling over her lids and down her cheeks. "What self do you think I have left?" she asked softly.

Dabeet's first response was the one that Mother had intended: He threw his arms around her and began to weep as well.

But his mind could not stop working, and he thought: She took me when I was too young to ask. She freely offered the gift of caring for me, and I'm grateful. But I'm not in bondage to her. In the sense that I never consciously incurred a debt, being a child, I owe her nothing, not in a way where she has a right to compel me to repay. "Am I not what you raised me to be?" whispered Dabeet. "Am I not doing what you always said you wanted me to do?"

"I wanted your father to recognize you," Mother answered in a voice made almost unintelligible by weeping. "I wanted you to have your heritage. But I never thought I'd lose you."

"Every mother loses every child," said Dabeet.

"Not when they're ten!"

"Some much younger than eleven," said Dabeet. "You let the child go when it's for the child's own good." Almost he added, The way my birth mother gave me to you. But it was better to let her believe that he still believed her version of his birth and infancy.

"Dabeet, I always said that I meant for you to go to Fleet School, but I never . . ."

"You never actually applied," said Dabeet. "You never even submitted my DNA for analysis."

She wept even more bitterly.

"Why else do you think I went ahead and submitted the application myself?" he asked.

"I should have known you'd take matters into your own hands," she said. "You've always been such a responsible boy."

Buying groceries and bringing back the correct change was about all the experience she had with his "responsibility." That and doing his own homework without nagging. "You let me ride my bicycle to the store, carrying money."

"It was safe enough. None of the mothers would let their boys rob you or steal your bike. *That's* why I didn't work at a better job. I wanted the other women to know me and trust me."

And that's one of the lessons Graff wants me to learn, Dabeet realized. Mother could have had more money, more prestige—but it was more important, more useful for her to be able to trust in the neighbor women so they would watch over her child. Mother knew it already. She *is* a wise woman. Who's to say I couldn't have acquired whatever wits I have from her?

"Mother, all your plans have worked out well, and now I'm going to

Fleet School. The war's over, so they don't censor mail now—I looked it up. We're going to be free to email each other."

That only made her cry a little harder as she waved him away. But he didn't leave the room.

"Do you think I don't know how much you sacrificed for me, Mother? How much I owe you?" Of course she *didn't* know that he knew how much she had done for a child who was, after all, no kin of hers.

Then again, it was also possible that Graff was lying to him.

But if he asked her for the truth, she would only affirm the same lies she had always told him—if they were lies. He would know no more than now, and she would be even sadder in the bargain. Or angry—it might make her angry. What was the point of that?

"Oh," she said. "Oh. I almost forgot." Her tears stopped. She seemed eager, for a moment. She stood up and got a box from beside the sink. She unplugged from it a cord that was attached to the wall. "It's a little old-fashioned, I know, but this was delivered for you today."

It was a phone. Not an expensive one, but he saw that several games were pre-installed, along with various programs that looked promising. It was the kind of phone that could access anything and function as a real computer, if you attached the right things to it.

"Why would they give me this?" asked Dabeet. "There's no phone service between Fleet School and Earth."

"Are you sure?" asked Mother.

"*You* didn't order this for me, did you?" Dabeet asked.

"Ay, que pudiera," she said. "But if I had that kind of money, would I buy you a phone you couldn't use in space?"

Only then did Dabeet realize that this phone was not from Fleet School, either. They would almost certainly have the most capable holographic desks for their students, not a flat-screen phone. This came from the people who had kidnapped him. This was certainly part of the plot that he had proposed—to open an entry point to an invading force.

I have to take it, even if I never use it.

Then he realized that the phone was also a message. We know who and where your mother is. Don't think you can betray us with impunity just because you're up in space. As long as your mother is on Earth, we can hurt you.

Maybe she *could* be brought into space. . . .

"What are you thinking? Do you like it?"

"It's a strange thing for them to give me," said Dabeet. "Maybe it's a mistake." Then he grinned. "If it is, I can't think of a single reason to correct it."

Dabeet did not use the phone at all—he kept it switched off and never connected it to his mother's laptop. He did keep it charged, because why not?

But he was aware of it whenever he was at home, clinging to its lifeline plugged into the wall. Wireless charging was out of the question, because Mother believed it wasn't safe to have loose electricity ricocheting off the walls. And they didn't make wireless chargers these days that didn't automatically connect the device with any computer or net connection in the house.

Dabeet continued going to school every day, but he only went to the few classes that interested him, and otherwise stayed in the library, reading or, when he had an idea worth working on, writing. He found that unexpressed ideas remained inchoate, with only a few broad strokes clearly in mind. But the moment he started to write them down, all sorts of complications and implications emerged, requiring further tweaking or exploration before the thoughts could be considered worthy of full-fledged idea status.

Only a week ago, there would have been complaints about Dabeet's nonattendance. Long ago the administrators and teachers had realized that the argument "You're going to fall behind" simply did not apply to Dabeet, who seemed perpetually to fall *ahead*.

So the argument of choice became "You're setting a bad example for students who do need to attend class in order to keep up," and Dabeet had learned enough about social niceties to leave unspoken the obvious point that it wasn't his problem if they didn't do what was required to excel.

"They're in a school for the gifted," Dabeet would reply. "If they haven't the sense to do the work they need to do, they don't belong here. The sooner they flunk back into regular schools, the better."

He had once heard an adult behind a closed door say, quite clearly, a single word: "Merciless." Dabeet had had no idea whether the word applied to him. He wasn't so vain as to think himself the subject of every conversation among the faculty. But he took the word personally, all the same.

Why should I show mercy to those who choose not to make the most of their abilities and opportunities? Let them show mercy to themselves first. So he had carried the word "merciless" inside his head as if it were a tattoo he was rather proud of wearing.

Only after Graff issued his challenges did Dabeet realize that perhaps mercy was an attribute of a good leader. Suppose I'm on an expedition and one of my team has a moment of mental weakness, making a dangerous mistake. Suppose it costs the life of another team member. It would be simple justice to kill the offender—that way he could never endanger anyone else by his careless errors.

On the other hand, it was quite likely that all the team members were chosen because of the contribution they would make to mutual survival and the success of the mission. How would it benefit those goals to add a second corpse to the first? Or even to inflict some kind of punishment on the offender? He would, as a leader, have to take that person's weakness into account. But he would still need to show enough mercy to allow the weakling to continue doing whatever had made him valuable enough to be on the expedition in the first place.

Graff never asked him about that or any other hypothetical, because Graff didn't ask him anything, really, after he had informed him he was being tested. Besides, Graff didn't know how the word "merciless" was graven in Dabeet's heart. I would be merciful, Graff, if mercy would work for the good of the team and the mission. And if harsh justice would be the best course, then I know how to be merciless as well.

When it came to lazy students who might follow Dabeet's example of class-cutting, Dabeet's feeling was, If, like me, you cut class in order to study and think and write at a much higher level than anything in the curriculum, then you should do it. I'm the hardest-working student in this school, which is why I don't always have time for class.

Besides, I'm going into space soon. Or at least *sometime*. So why should I get involved in any of my classes, if I'm only going to be torn away at short notice? Well begun is a waste of time, if you can't also finish.

It was a nice spring day, with the lawn thick and dry on the practice field, when Dabeet took his notebook out to sit by the fence and jot ideas as they came to mind. A dirt maintenance road ran along the outside of the fence.

A motorcycle came sputtering along, moving barely fast enough to keep from tipping over. It stopped directly opposite Dabeet.

Dabeet deliberately did not look up.

The engine turned off. "Please climb the fence and come with me," said a man. It was the general from the airplane.

"If this is another kidnapping," said Dabeet, "you're going about it all wrong."

"It's a private conversation," said the general. "But no conversation on the grounds of this school can possibly be private."

"People will see me go with you. Cameras will see me climb over the fence."

"People see what they see. Our business is that they not hear what they shouldn't hear."

Dabeet reached over the fence and handed his notebook to the general. "Treat the book with respect," Dabeet said. "I may be saving the human race on one of those pages."

"You're not," said the general, "unless you added something preternaturally brilliant since we last scanned it at three A.M. today."

"How intrusive you are," said Dabeet. "And stealthy."

"We prefer 'sneaky,'" said the general. "Don't think we aren't intrigued by the things you write. You just haven't saved the world yet."

While they talked, Dabeet made it over the fence—which was meant to be more of a boundary marker than a serious barrier. Soon he was behind the general on the motorcycle, and away they rode, slowly on the dirt road, then at the posted speed limit on paved roads.

It was at the top of a grassy, windswept hill that the general brought the motorcycle to a stop and switched it off.

"You got the phone," the general said at once.

"I did."

"It never occurred to you that we might want to call you?"

"It occurred to me," said Dabeet. "Did it occur to you that I didn't want to be called?"

"It became clear within a few days. That's when we started our nocturnal visits. You kept it completely off, but also completely charged."

"I might have had a use for it," said Dabeet.

"You really *didn't* try to use it, not even once, or you'd know that no matter what number you dial, your calls are directed to a single phone number."

"Yours?" asked Dabeet.

"Whoever's on duty at the time. Even sneaky people need to sleep."

"What's the real purpose of the phone?" asked Dabeet.

"It contains information."

"You know they'll inspect my phone at Fleet School, if they even let me keep it."

"The information is hidden."

Dabeet thought about this for a moment. "You can't hide information on any computer. Anything that smacks of concealment, and they'll be suspicious. If not alarmed."

"It's hidden in plain sight."

"As what, a game?"

"Games are hard to use as a disguise for data. To be believable, the game has to be good enough that they would believe someone of your intelligence would play it."

"So . . . in a graphics file."

"In a painting, very expressionistic. It's one of your favorites."

"I don't have a favorite painting. I don't have any paintings."

"You have three paintings, all of which you treasure. In these roughed-in parts of each painting, there are several that seem smeary or pixelated. These actually contain code. If you run the exercise-charting program, using the painting as data input, it will show you a three-dimensional map of Fleet School, at least as it was during its Battle School days about eight years ago."

"What's to stop the school authorities from doing that?"

"It shows you an error message, and you have ten seconds, without any visible feedback or instructions, to type in the password."

"And what is the password?"

"Whatever you type, the first time you run it. I suggest you do that here on Earth, as soon as possible. Run the exercise program on all three paintings, and you'll have as much information as we have that might help you. And the address to which you should send instructions about what portal you'll open for our little invasion force. We'll watch for it to open, close, reopen, and close again. Then we'll tell you the date and time you need to open it for our force."

"No," said Dabeet. "I'll tell *you*. You won't know what times I'll be free, what times the spot I chose will be accessible. I'll let you know when the window will open and stay open."

"I don't believe this will work," said the general. "But other people think that poking the bear is a dandy idea, because after all, what harm can an angry bear do?"

"I'm a kid," said Dabeet. "What could go wrong, following the plans of some immigrant kid?"

"My point exactly, but who listens? Each time you pull up one of the pictures to access the information, when you quit your session, all traces of the decoded data will be erased. Just so you know that your phone will always be secure."

"Secure as long as their searches are perfunctory. If they ever think they have something to worry about and become thorough, nothing will be secure," said Dabeet.

"It's good that you know that," said the general. "Emails can be sent to and from Fleet School. Watch for us. Check your filtering software— our messages will always go straight into your spam folder. They'll never come from the same address twice, so *never* answer. Only write to the address concealed in one of the picture files."

"Which they'll detect, if they want to."

"It never leads to the same place twice. And if you receive no message from us for more than thirty days, send a message to your mother complaining of the weather in Fleet School. We'll know that means we must write to you through her as well."

"So you'll be reading my mother's mail?"

"We will," said the general. "Are you going to complain that her constitutional rights are being violated?"

Dabeet said nothing. If they thought he would be more loyal to them because they would be in such close control of his mother, they were mistaken. He owed them nothing. Nor did he owe their stupid plan even token compliance.

The general could not be reading his thoughts. Yet he said, "This is *your* plan, so don't be skittish. There are risks, and you volunteered to take them."

"My plan is to try to involve the IF in Earthside wars, to put a stop to them. If there's nothing to put a stop to—"

"The first fighting has already begun on many battlefields. And Russia has made a play at kidnapping many of the top Battle School students. Whether that benefits them is unknowable, but it certainly harms those nations from which the Battle Schoolers were taken."

So the plan *was* regarded as necessary to preserve the independence of small countries. "Just make sure that when you come, you don't hurt anybody," said Dabeet. "Not one serious injury. Not one death."

"That's our goal."

"You don't think it will happen that way," said Dabeet.

"Live bullets will fly," said the general. "No plan survives in the face of the enemy."

Unspoken, of course, was this: The moment Dabeet secretly let the invaders into Fleet School, he would have no more control over their actions than would any other child. It did not matter if the Trojan horse had second thoughts once the concealed Danaean soldiers had left its belly.

"I consider myself warned," said Dabeet. "Take me home, please. School's over for the day by now."

5

—You are going to a great deal of trouble for one boy, whose worth is unproven and whose loyalty is nil.

—We have a responsibility to all the children left over from our wartime programs.

—His native intelligence was gift enough. You know that he'll thrive without any intervention from us.

—Even if that were true, which is by no means secure, he has legal rights. He *is* a child of the Fleet. He *does* want to study at Fleet School. How, then, do *we* have the right to refuse him?

—Do you think I'm naive enough to think you would lose sleep over depriving someone of their "right" if granting it would atrapalliate some program you value?

—Why should some nation on Earth have the use of him, when he may prove valuable as an explorer or expedition commander or colony governor?

—Since we don't know how your experiment with Ender Wiggin as a colony governor is going to turn out, I hope you're not thinking of trying this with other children.

—I'm in no hurry. We can wait to see who he becomes in training. I am quite sure that within a few more years, we'll have a good idea of what this boy will or won't be worth to us.

—And if he's dangerous?

—A combat position is possible. Then his dangerousness will be directed against the enemy.

—We're not at war. The Formics are destroyed.

—It's difficult to imagine that there'll be no combat in his lifetime.

—You're not going to train him for war, anyway.

—If he needs to learn war, he'll learn it.

—Why did you continue this bizarre program, once we had Ender and Bean?

—We had no way of knowing how long the war would last, or how thoroughly Ender and his jeesh might lead us to victory. Many scenarios were possible in which the war lasted long enough for Dabeet to be part of the next generation of child warlords.

—It's always such a bother, disposing of war surplus goods.

—I'm taking that as a joke, my friend. Because Dabeet is definitely a *person* not a "good." A person, I might add, whose good side it may someday be very important for you to be on.

—With any luck, I'll be dead by then.

—It's all about *how* you die, my friend.

—If he's that dangerous, then kill him now.

—The bear and the bee are only dangerous if you provoke them.

—Warning taken.

They finally gave him a date for his departure in the lunar shuttle, and from lunar orbit, he'd board an outbound supply craft that would be making a stop at Fleet School. During the Formic Wars, there had been direct shuttles to Battle School, each one full of new students. But now that the school was no longer recruiting on Earth, it was cheaper to funnel all Earth–to–Fleet School transport through ordinary IF channels. Civilian clothes, in a civilian shuttle to lunar orbit, and only then boarding an IF supply ship to finish the trip.

Dabeet read as much as he could about spaceflight, especially near-Earth shuttles. The only thing that frightened him about it was weightlessness. So many people got very sick the first few times they went through it. Some never lost that uncontrolled nausea. Wouldn't it be ironic if they had to send him back because he couldn't function in zero-gee?

Life in Fleet School was mostly in a near-Earth-gravity environment, but the battleroom—which still, according to what he could learn, played a large role in the curriculum—was in null-gee, and if Dabeet couldn't stop puking, his future with the IF would be in considerable doubt.

None of the other students will have problems like that, because they grew up in space, or at least they've been off Earth long enough to get over the nausea.

And that led him to realize: They'll all think of themselves as True Children of the Fleet, and I'll be a child of Earth, a complete outsider. If I'm puking in the battleroom, what choice will they have but to shun me? One dose of vomiting, and I'll have lost my value to Fleet School. If they send me home right away, then Mother and I really will have to go into hiding, because I won't be there to open the door for a tiny invading army. Which won't happen because they ban all private electronics so I won't have their stupid phone.

Dabeet got his mother to take him to a doctor to inquire about medicine for space sickness. The doctor merely looked at him as if he were insane. "Are you planning a space voyage soon?"

"Not a 'voyage,' but yes, a trip. To L-5."

"There's nothing there but the old Battle School, and they don't allow tourists," said the doctor.

"If there's a preventive for motion sickness, I'd appreciate a good dose. I don't suppose there's anything like an inoculation."

"Motion sickness isn't caused by an infectious agent, Dabeet."

"Perhaps something with laser or ultrasound involving the semicircular canals in the ears?"

"You don't want to mess with those delicate organs."

"I don't want to puke my guts out, either, especially when I'm in the null-gee battleroom."

The doctor, who hadn't made any kind of study of Battle School, had no idea what Dabeet was talking about. "If there's some kind of problem that arises in space, I'm sure the IF doctors already have appropriate treatments for it."

Including the option of sending pukers home.

"But here's my advice. Relax about it. Don't fill your body with stress. Trust that you probably won't get sick—most people don't, or it passes within a couple of minutes. And if you do, they'll have a way to treat it."

"Very comforting," said Dabeet.

Yet all his worry was in vain, because when the shuttle took off and, more importantly, when he was in the cargo ship flying from Luna to Fleet School, he felt not even the slightest twinge of nausea.

Shouldn't I have felt *something*? he asked himself. But when he asked one of the cargo ship's crew if it was natural to feel nothing out of the ordinary, the man laughed. "It's natural to turn green and live on soda crackers or dry toast for a week, that's what's natural."

"That didn't happen to me at all, and this is my first voyage."

"You must be heroically lucky. Like all the idiots in the stories, who get the help of some fairy because they pulled a thorn out of the fairy's ass, or something like that."

Dabeet assured him that there was no fairy—or fata, or djinn, or leprechaun.

The man smiled at that. "Well, nausea or not, work at getting your space legs. It takes several years to stop lurching around like a drunk. Though children may learn faster. Good luck."

In the shuttle from Earth to the Moon, there had been a strict requirement that everybody stay belted in. In the cargo ship, there was room for him to move around and practice flying. He wouldn't arrive in Fleet School without being competent enough at zero-gee to avoid the scorn of the other kids.

It was only as the cargo ship approached its docking station alongside Fleet School that it occurred to Dabeet that there was no reason for him to have a natural immunity to space sickness. It was one of the crewmen on the vessel, who kept asking him if he was in any kind of distress. "Are you sure this is your first space voyage?"

"I think I would have noticed," said Dabeet.

The man laughed. "I guess so. But everybody feels nauseated the first time they go into freefall. The human body just isn't designed to feel OK like that. The kids raised out in the belts, in the Miner families— they get over it when they're infants. They learn to float and grab before they can walk. But you've lived your whole life on Earth."

"As long as I can remember," said Dabeet. "I have a very good memory."

"You remember being a baby?" asked the man.

Dabeet smiled, and the man clapped him on the shoulder and floated away. But the question bothered him. What *was* his earliest memory? Was it possible that he had once lived in space? Perhaps Mother didn't even know about it. But if he had been in space as an infant, would he still be acclimated to freefall?

If Graff was telling the truth—a huge *if*—then there wasn't time for him to have lived in space. So was there another reason he might be immune to the nausea of freefall?

Being Amerindian might be part of it. Didn't they use some norte-americano tribe to build skyscrapers? Navahos? Or was that just the code-talking in World War II? No, it was Iroquois, mostly Mohawk, who worked on skyscrapers, because those were the Native Americans who lived near Manhattan during the early days of skyscraper-building. And it wasn't that they weren't afraid of falling, it's that they learned from an early age not to show fear.

Besides, this wasn't about fear of falling. This was about being in freefall, which is something which, on Earth, you don't live through, because it means you already fell from a high place. You fall from a skyscraper frame, you don't have time on the way down to the ground to even notice whether, in addition to terror, you're also feeling sick to your stomach.

Dabeet had never heard of Amerindians having some kind of immunity to motion sickness or freefall nausea—and he *would* remember, if he had ever read it. He also had never heard that *everyone* was susceptible to it. In fact, he knew that in the old days of ocean-going ships, some people never got over seasickness completely, even on the largest, most stable ships, while others quickly adapted.

But that was the point. They adapted. They felt the nausea, and then they got over it. Did anybody *not* feel the nausea?

Me. I don't feel it. Yet my balancing organs function properly—I don't fall over or bump into things. So I'm sensing all the balance issues that other people feel. I'm simply not bothered by them.

Why am I fretting about this so much? Why is this capturing my thought?

Because there's something important about this. Some question that is *answered* by my immunity to freefall nausea.

Dabeet closed his eyes and let his thoughts drift. His immediate thought was that closing his eyes should have made the discomfort of freefall worse—it was well known that the best self-treatment for sea-sickness was to focus on the distant horizon, not the pitching deck or the nearby waves. And dancers were able to remain vertical through long spins by focusing on a single point and finding it again the moment they could whip their heads around on the next spin. Yet closing his eyes had no effect on him.

He allowed a piece of music to enter his mind. He had long ago learned to enter a meditative state by rejecting his own conscious control of his thoughts. He had noticed that when he became aware of music playing in the back of his mind, it was a fully-scored orchestra or mariachi band or pop ensemble, all the instruments playing with all the rhythms and harmonies. But as soon as he tried to take conscious control of the music, or even follow it closely, thinking about it, all that fullness faded and what was left was the single melody line of his attention.

So he had trained himself to let his mind go, without consciously controlling his thoughts, and resist the temptation to examine those thoughts closely. He needed to let the music come up from his unconscious and continue to move forward in its fullness, its intricate interconnectedness, and be aware of it without paying attention to it.

As the cargo vessel docked with Fleet School, that was the meditative trance that Dabeet put himself into. And what emerged from it was this:

The IF did not know that Ender Wiggin and his jeesh would be so spectacularly successful in their invasion of the Formic worlds. Every enemy fleet destroyed, then the home world itself blown to bits and every hive queen with it. For all the IF high command knew, at least one Formic world might have survived, and therefore a new invasion of Earth was likely. Also, it was possible that a Formic fleet had embarked forty years before and would enter the solar system ten years after the human invasion of the Formic worlds was over.

This still might happen. There might yet be a Fourth Formic War.

So why, then, did they dismantle Battle School and replace it with a school whose purpose was colonization and exploration?

It was a good strategy, in the long term, because the human race could never again afford to be caught clinging to only one planet, whose destruction would mean the end of our species. Graff was probably quite sincere in that policy, that in the long run the protection of the human race depended on dispersal rather than fortification.

And maybe they had information Dabeet could not know, that affirmed there would be no Formic invasion fleet popping up at near lightspeed at the fringes of the solar system. In that case the closing of Battle School made sense. So did the International Fleet's unhooking itself from the Hegemony, so they were no longer dependent on or obedient to any Earthbound institution.

But all those decisions were reached after Ender Wiggin's victory. Until that moment, the IF had to be planning for a much longer war, for a struggle at least as epic as the one between Rome and Carthage, a back-and-forth, ever-escalating struggle to the death with a resourceful and implacable enemy.

They would need commanders even smarter than Ender Wiggin and his brilliant jeesh. That meant that Graff and the IF high command would have already set in motion plans to get those commanders.

What part did I play in those plans?

The docking was complete. The cargo vessel was entirely inside a docking bay—they were designed for each other, and for every other ordinary null-gee cargo bay throughout the solar system. The artificial gravity had kicked in; there was an audible sigh of relief from those suffering from nausea. Now it was time to unfasten seat belts and set foot again on a floor that knew it was a floor, and not a wall or ceiling.

Stepping out through the door onto a gangway, Dabeet held tightly to the railing on his right so that he could free his eyes to take in the surrounding area. The cargo vessel was a snug enough fit, and now conveyor belts were taking cargo from the ship into the bowels of the Fleet School space station. Dabeet wanted to follow the cargo and see how it was dispersed and stowed, but a cough from behind him reminded him that he was supposed to be moving forward down the gangway.

Waiting at the foot of the ramp was a tall blond lieutenant—Dabeet had memorized all the insignias of the IF—who introduced himself as Odd Oddson. "And yes," the lieutenant continued, "my parents were singularly uncreative, and I know that it makes an amusing pun in English."

"I hope you'll explain it to me sometime, sir," said Dabeet.

Odd looked at him a bit askance, but then grinned. "A dry sense of humor is unusual among the children, Mr. Ochoa. But not unwelcome, or at least not to me. In the old days, you would have arrived with a squad of greenies, and I would have led you to your new barracks. These are less formal times, and nobody comes from Earth, so we have no ordinary ritual for receiving you."

"I'm glad you were kind enough to meet me, sir," said Dabeet.

"I was assigned, so the kindness all came from Commandant Urska Kaluza."

Dabeet instantly made the associations. "A Slovene name," he said. "Urska is short for Ursula—does she really use her nickname?"

"She is addressed as Commandant and Sir," said Oddson. "By you, at least. Colonel Kaluza by those of high enough rank to address her by name rather than office."

"I wouldn't dream of informality, sir," said Dabeet. "At least not without invitation."

"It will never come, I promise you," said Oddson. "And now you'll get a chance to practice all your courtesies, because she wanted to meet you upon arrival. Follow me."

Dabeet hadn't been in such a complex three-dimensional structure in his life. Planetside buildings tended toward rectangles, and floors were level. Here, the main corridors ran around the wheel of the space station, with the outer surface of the wheel forming the floor. Dabeet was sure this must be a holdover from the earliest days of space colonization, when a kind of pseudo-gravity was achieved by spinning the whole station, so that centrifugal force would make a kind of "down" for the inhabitants.

But artificial gravity had been around since the days of Ukko Jukes, and now a complex set of computations kept real gravity very nearly balanced throughout the station, except in the battleroom cubes at the center. That central placement would have made them effectively weightless when they were first built; now they were sealed off from all gravity so that the battlerooms had no heavy or light spots, and objects flew straight from one side to the other. Again, Dabeet's pre-voyage study made it unnecessary for him to ask questions.

Nor was Dabeet feeling chatty. Instead of commenting on what he saw during the trip from deck to deck, from spoke to spoke of the wheel, he filed everything away, along with excellent estimates of the distances involved, as he began to construct his internal map of Fleet School. Already he knew just how far it was when the upward curve of the long corridors made the feet of someone moving away from him disappear. As he grew taller, that distance would change.

Commander Urska Kaluza did not rise from her chair when Lieutenant Oddson introduced him and then immediately left. "I thought we'd seen the last Earthside student."

Not knowing whether she was pleased or displeased to have her expectation broken, Dabeet said nothing.

"You tried hard enough to get here—yes, we saw all your applications and petitions and pathetic pleas and test scores. Now I'd like to know what you expect from this school. If you have in mind a panacea for all your problems, you're going to be disappointed."

"Disappointments are unavailable to those without expectations," said Dabeet.

"What a strutting little prig you are," she commented, seemingly without rancor or distaste. "It will be interesting to see if you make any friends at all."

Dabeet restrained himself from saying, My strutting priggishness may be nearly as great a handicap to friend-making as your complete disregard for the feelings of others. Instead, he stood in silence, regarding her without a trace of an expression that might be construed as a response to her rudeness.

I'm like a machine that self-programs to get through social situations.

In this case, a complete lack of expression was the most challenging response he could give Urska Kaluza, because she could not possibly detect anything in his face for which she could punish or even criticize him, and yet it would be infuriating that her rudeness had no effect whatsoever. "Deadface," Dabeet called this expression, and it was his favorite to use with adults who were impressed with their own authority.

He thought of several things to say. "Where are you going to place me, to maximize my opportunity to make no friends?" or "Since you're my only friend now, I hope I can visit here often," or "What did you say? I'm sorry, I was praying." He could use such verbal jabs with teachers at Conn, because they were used to him and sometimes they would even laugh. But with Kaluza, it would be taken as insubordination at a level that might get him sent back to Earth. So she got deadface, and nothing else, until she decided to speak again.

"Don't you have any questions? You're the least curious child I've seen here."

"You're already annoyed with me, sir," said Dabeet. "Perhaps because I wrote too many petitions and applications. I can't unwrite them, and whatever I say, including what I'm saying now, will only annoy you."

"You sound like a robot," said Kaluza. "They've sent me a robot to turn into a human."

Again, Dabeet remained silent. But he took her words and spun them into a series of thoughts. He knew he didn't really sound like a robot, partly because the software that produced speech for most robots nowadays was pretty natural-sounding, and partly because he spoke with normal intonation, as if he were giving directions to a lost traveler. His face might be expressionless, but his voice had the ordinary music of the English language, spoken calmly.

All that nonsense that Graff was so interested in, my story about a puppet who wanted to cut the strings. I *am* a puppet—but I control the strings myself. A self-operating puppet isn't a puppet at all, is it? Being a puppet means that someone else controls you. So the truth is that I'm the only non-puppet in a world of puppets—all of them responding to whatever emotional strings are pulled by people and events around them, while I alone am free to choose any or none of those responses.

"And stubborn," she said.

"Yes, sir," said Dabeet.

"Defiant," she added.

"I am not, sir," said Dabeet. "I'm waiting for directions or orders, which I intend to obey to the degree that they're within my power. I believe, sir, that obeying your orders to *your* satisfaction may be out of my power, but I intend to do my best, and I hope you'll come to judge who I really am by what I do in the days and weeks to come, rather than by how much I annoy you at our first meeting."

"Graff said you'd be my best student."

This seemed to require no answer, so Dabeet gave none.

"If I send him a vid of this meeting," said Kaluza, "he'll laugh and tell me that since I left you no possibility of an appropriate response, I had no choice but to accept your complete nonresponse."

If you know that, thought Dabeet, then why did you behave that way, and why are you still pissed off at me?

"I suppose this means that in Graff's eyes, you've passed yet one more examination. Perhaps he'll suggest I put you on the diplomacy track."

Diplomacy? That *was* a field where total control over face and voice could be useful. But what would diplomacy have to do with exploration and colonization?

"But I doubt you'll be in Fleet School by the time we start sorting you into tracks. Step outside the door, Mr. Ochoa, and Lieutenant Oddson will take you to your assigned barracks and introduce you to your team."

Team, and not army. So the old terminology of Battle School had been replaced. But would there be any real difference?

The door opened. Dabeet stepped through it. The door closed behind him.

"Well?" asked Oddson.

"She said you'd take me to my barracks and introduce me to my team."

"So you didn't annoy her enough to incur immediate punishment?"

"Is that a failure or a success on my part?" asked Dabeet.

"It's an interesting fact. Her normal method is to goad each new student into doing something that puts them on report, so they have to do some kind of unpleasant duty. It unites new students against a common enemy."

"So the commandant poses herself as our enemy?" asked Dabeet.

"Apparently not you," said Oddson. "Kind of a shame, since there's a sort of competition in the armies about who got the worst punishment after their first interview."

"Thanks for tipping me off, so I could make sure to get a spectacular one."

"Nobody's ever gotten away without a punishment, as far as I know," said Oddson. "Your colors are Green Blue Green, so if you're ever lost, you touch the wall on either side. Your colors will appear, and you can find your barracks, at least."

Dabeet wanted to say, "I don't *get* lost," but he decided that it was important not to boast. He recognized that his impulse to be boastful was the result of fear—no one knew him here, and so he wanted to assert his abilities as a means of winning respect. But this only worked on faculty members at Conn, and it was pretty plain that the IF didn't work like the faculty and staff at an elementary school for gifted students in Indiana.

Rather than asserting his strength, it might work better to show—no, not weakness, but vulnerability.

"I wish," said Dabeet, "that I could observe for a while before I actually have to interact with anyone."

"It can be a bit intimidating. But I can promise you, holding yourself aloof won't work at all. Don't just watch. Engage."

Engage. Dabeet had seen plenty of that, even at a school of intellectuals and artists like Conn. To engage usually meant to challenge, to compete. A new male baboon, demonstrating and asserting himself until the rest of the troop pummeled him enough that he felt like he belonged. The pummeling wasn't literal at Conn—or at least not usually—but here it might be. Because Kaluza might have called it a team, but Oddson still called it an army, and the military culture might have survived the name change.

Maybe I should have taken martial arts and self-defense classes seriously instead of regarding them as a waste of time.

No. If somebody wants to pound on me a little, to make sure I know my place, my best tactic is to give a couple of punches at first and then curl up in a ball and call out my surrender. Accept whatever place I'm assigned by the other kids, and then work to improve it over time. To live among baboons, you have to accept the baboon rituals and pretend to believe in the baboon religion, whatever it is.

And then try not to think of your peers as baboons, because if this is going to work out at all, you have to be able to lead them, rely on the ones who have useful abilities, and keep everybody happy.

6

—Whatever you expect this arrogant little git to accomplish, what makes you think Fleet School can help him?

—My question is whether he can help Fleet School.

The barracks was surprisingly small. When Oddson touched a panel and the door slid open, Dabeet stepped through and found himself at one end of a long narrow bunk-lined room that ran parallel to the corridor. This meant that the floor of the barracks rose up at the far end, so the last bunks weren't visible unless you knelt down.

Dabeet did not kneel down. Instead he looked at the boys in the nearer bunks. Most of them were reading, typing, or manipulating three-dimensional objects in the space above their holodesks. Only two of them looked up enough to notice him.

No. They didn't notice Dabeet. They noticed Oddson. And they immediately scrambled out of their bunks and stood at attention in front of their bunks.

Without a single word being spoken, each boy noticed the movement of the other boys near him, looked to see what was going on, and then immediately stood at attention by his bunk. The last boy to notice what was happening set his holodesk down with a sigh and stood at attention with a posture and facial expression that were eloquent with despair.

"I'm glad you concentrate so deeply on the things you read, Mr. Cabeza," said Oddson. "Standing order, young man."

Cabeza clambered up to the top bunk and stood on it. Only you couldn't stand on it—the ceiling was too low. So he struck a pose with his back flat along the ceiling, pressing upward from his half-bent legs. It looked very uncomfortable and wearying.

"I'm here to bring you the twenty-third member of your exalted company," said Oddson.

"We only have nineteen, sir," said a babyish boy near the door.

"You only have nineteen that bunk with you right now," said Oddson. "Nor do you know enough about the new boy's ability to assess whether he alone is enough to bring the whole team up to snuff."

"Too bad he doesn't have a name," said the babyish one.

"My name is Dabeet Ochoa."

"A talker," said one of the boys.

"What's his punishment?" asked another.

"None assigned," said Oddson.

This spread in a buzz of reaction to the far end of the room.

"Didn't he *meet* Commandant Kaluza?" asked the babyish one.

"He did, Mr. Timeon," said Oddson.

"And *no* punishment?"

A few chuckled. A few made faces of disgust and stared coldly at Dabeet.

"Must be a suckup," said someone not too far away.

"Kahlua punishes suckups worst of all," said Timeon scornfully.

"She must *love* him," said a kid well back from the door.

"Commandant Kaluza loves all the children," said Oddson.

That was greeted with snickers and hoots.

"She is deeply concerned about the happiness and well-being of every one of you," said Oddson.

"Except this new one," said Timeon. "This Ochoa."

"Oh, she punished me," said Dabeet—loudly enough to reach to the back of the barracks.

"Lying isn't going to gain you an advantage," said Oddson.

"The punishment was to give me no punishment, when apparently it's the custom for every new member of a troop to somehow offend the commandant and arrive here with hours of punishment. My lack of a punishment makes you all suspicious of me." He meant to go on, explaining, That isolates me even beyond the natural isolation of a new boy, arriving after everybody already knows everyone else. But he stopped himself, aware that his explanation wasn't convincing anybody.

"So your punishment is to have no punishment," said Timeon skeptically.

"What makes you so special that she singled you out like that?"

"I can't guess at her motive," said Dabeet. "But it might be because I've never been away from Earth before."

That got everyone's attention. "You've *never* been in null-gee before?" asked Timeon.

Dabeet shook his head, as he heard the grumbling.

"Earthsider."

"Mudbooter."

"You're going to kill us in the standings," said Timeon.

"Quite possibly," said Dabeet. "But I'll learn as quickly as I can. Especially if I get help."

There was no rush to volunteer. Dabeet had thought there might be at least a few offers or reassurances. Maybe there was something in his tone of voice. Maybe he really did sound arrogant and aloof. He'd never asked other children for help before; he wasn't good at it. Or maybe they hated Earthsiders so much that it overcame their need to get him up to speed so he didn't "kill" them in the standings. Or maybe they were a bunch of dull bobs and he'd have to make his way through this school alone.

"New Soldier Rule," said Oddson.

Immediately the boy on the lower bunk nearest the door got up and carried his holodesk and a small stack of clothes toward the back of the barracks.

"This is your bunk now," said Oddson to Dabeet.

"I didn't mean to make anybody move," said Dabeet.

"New Soldier Rule," said Oddson. "Weren't you listening? Can't you extrapolate? You need to be where you can listen to the more experienced students. Notice that the operative word here is 'listen.'"

Dabeet was about to answer, but realized that anything he said would be speaking, and therefore would prove the aptness of Oddson's warning. So he sat down.

"Press your hand on the back wall and your locker opens," said Oddson. "Don't expect any privacy here—anybody's hand opens your locker."

Dabeet refrained from pointing out that the word "locker" was clearly misapplied in this situation. He pressed the back wall, the locker popped open, and there was a holodesk.

"Is this mine?" he asked.

"Was it in your locker?" asked a nearby boy, his voice sarcastic enough that Dabeet got the point.

"How do I log in?" asked Dabeet.

Oddson answered before any sarcastic boys could do it. "The holodesk already knows who you are. The desks are completely interchangeable. Whatever you create on one desk will be available on any other. Anything you create will be looked at by monitoring software and, whenever they feel like it, by teachers and administrators. But no other students can read your files. That's all the privacy you get."

Generous, thought Dabeet. But he had had no privacy at Conn either. Until his abduction and his deal with his kidnappers, the only privacy that mattered was keeping things from Mother.

After Oddson left the barracks, Dabeet familiarized himself with his desk, but that only took a small fraction of his attention, especially since it didn't matter yet whether he did things wrong and had to do them over. What mattered was the other boys. If he was going to make this work, he had to figure out how to work with other children. And even though Conn had been a school for the gifted, Dabeet could not be sure that Fleet School was not composed of students who were far more intelligent; perhaps a few who were Dabeet's equals. Perhaps one, or several, or many, were cleverer than he.

After the first half hour, Dabeet reached the conclusion that if he had peers at this school, they were not in this particular barracks, though one or two showed promise. What surprised him, after having pored over the testimony and documents in the courts-martial of Graff and others who had supervised Battle School, was that these children did *not* seem to be obsessed with victory in the battleroom. They did not seem to form a single cohesive unit at all. They were not a team, much less an army.

Piecing together bits and pieces of information, he realized that the squad was divided into several groups. First, there were the "True Children"—the offspring of IF officers and soldiers. This group was further subdivided among the "Veterans," who had at least one parent who was active duty in space during the war, and the "Onlookers," whose parents were commissioned or enlisted, but stationed on Earth or Luna.

This seemed absurd to Dabeet, because anyone stationed in the solar system was an Onlooker, except the children in Ender Wiggin's jeesh, who directed the operations of the real fleets many lightyears away. Yet the three children here who had an ancestor in one of the actual combat fleets were called "grandchildren," because their IF relative had left after the Second Formic War several generations before. Apparently it wasn't just about where your parent served, but also about how many generations you were removed from the pertinent forebear.

The True Children all carried themselves as if they bore special authority or status, despite the pecking order among them. But the other kids were not at all deferent to them. One group was called "Inks," which, Dabeet learned from a quick inquiry on his desk, was derived from the American abbreviation for a corporation: "inc." These children had parents who worked for the big multinational corporations that owned all the best real estate in the Asteroid Belt and on Mars and the various moons that had stations.

Then there were the "Miners"—or, as they called themselves, the "Freeborn," whose families worked mostly in the Kuiper Belt as independent asteroid hunters. They were generally poor, compared to corporate families, but they had been crucial in the first two Formic Wars and had been granted full equality with the corporate and Fleet families by treaty after the Second Formic War.

Even within this lowest-status group, there were the children of the "Great" families—the rich, multi-ship free mining clans—and of the "Brave" families—the free mining families who had been most prominent in the first two Formic Wars, either by suffering terrible casualties or by astonishing feats of navigation and derring-do. There were only two of the Brave among the Freeborn, and they barely spoke to each other, since one of them, Delgado, did not believe that the other's ancestors had done anything noteworthy in the earlier combat.

How could *any* of these children be classified as smart, or even educable? These meaningless distinctions only kept them from forming anything like a real army. Even Ender himself could not have made anything out of them, because it was clear they cared more about maintaining status derived from their parents' positions than about anything they might accomplish here.

But Dabeet quickly learned that there was one other group, with only one member: "Dirt." Because he was directly from Earth, and had never even been in zero-gee until yesterday, he was the most worthless person there.

Which made him amazingly valuable to them all, because as long as he was on the bottom, everybody else could look down on him. They didn't persecute him, they mostly shunned him, except for those who, with exaggerated patience, answered his questions. Even when he managed to keep one of them engaged in conversation for more than a single answer, it was clear that they were being polite to him and nothing more. They got away as quickly as they could.

Dabeet had hoped to find a mentor in the group, someone who'd take pity on his plight and help speed up his learning process. Or if compassion failed, someone who would realize that this army's place in the standings would depend on bringing Dabeet up to snuff as quickly as possible.

Here's how that went.

"I'll need some help learning how to navigate and maneuver in zero-gee."

"No you won't."

"You've been doing it all your lives. I'm going to be terrible at it."

"No doubt."

"Don't you care that I'll damage your place in the standings?"

"Standings?" The boy—a Miner—laughed out loud and repeated what Dabeet had said.

"The war's over," said another boy. "This isn't Battle School. We don't care about the standings."

"Then why do they still have battles?" asked Dabeet.

"Because teachers be crazy," said a Veteran.

"Physical exercise," said an Ink.

"Because it's fun," said Cabeza.

"Listen," said Delgado, asserting a superiority over everyone that only he recognized, "nobody can teach you to navigate in zero-gee. You just do it. That's what the battleroom is for. You can make stupid baby mistakes and you don't drift off into space and get lost. So go in, fly around, make a kintama of yourself, and learn what you learn. It's what we all did."

"As little children," said Dabeet.

"We didn't make you do something as dumb as getting born on Earth," said Timeon.

End of discussion. He was on his own.

So much for trying *not* to be the loner that Graff had accused him of being. As far as Dabeet could see, he was the most cooperative of the whole group.

Or were they testing him?

No. The *teachers* might test him, but these kids really were as short-sighted and narrow-minded as they seemed.

And if he hadn't gotten the idea already that the battleroom combats weren't all that important, Oddson told him not to go to practices in the battleroom until he was fully up to speed on his coursework. "We have to know where you are in the curriculum."

So when the other kids went to the battleroom, Dabeet sat or lay on his bunk and read, taking little self-tests on the computer. He had no control over the testing, and had no idea what level he was revealing himself to be at. The tests were ludicrously simple at first, but finally got hard enough that he was actually having to think and work things out in his mind before writing.

And then Oddson came to him and told him the testing was over. "Here's your flash suit. Practice putting it on and taking it off until you can do it with your eyes closed."

"What did all these tests reveal?"

"That you're almost as smart as you think you are," said Oddson.

Dabeet did *not* say anything like "I could have told you that," because he recognized the thinly veiled insult and the challenge in Oddson's words.

"Look at you, trying not to gloat," said Oddson. "I've heard of people who could strut sitting down, but you can do a victory dance without even twitching."

"Victory dances," said Dabeet, "are apparently in the eye of the beholder."

"You'll attend classes, but everybody does work at their own level on their own desk. Just don't expect the teacher to waste the whole class's time by lecturing to you."

That far ahead of everybody. Dabeet was justifiably proud of his self-education. Though some of his ability had been honed by the handful of good teachers at Conn.

"When I've mastered putting on clothes and taking them off," said Dabeet, "could you explain why I'm going to waste my time trying to play games with this group?"

"Ah, there it is, the superiority complex I was warned about."

"I'm not superior to anybody," said Dabeet. "When it comes to the battleroom, I'm going to be like a snail clinging to the wall and leaving a slime trail. And even if I *could* fly like the others, so what? They aren't an army. They're barely a committee."

Then Dabeet proceeded to explain his observations about the groups that the children were divided into and how it made cohesive action impossible.

"Very good observations," said Oddson.

"They weren't observations, they were criticisms."

"You can hardly blame the children for divisions that affect the whole IF and everybody else who isn't on Earth or Luna."

"I don't *blame* anybody. Well, no, I *do* blame the administration and teachers at this school for tolerating this social situation. It must be completely counterproductive and yet you let it go on this way."

"We do," said Oddson. "So now that you've pointed out our culpability, I eagerly await your plan of action."

"Why should I have a plan? I'm a child."

"If you don't have a plan, then your criticisms are just blather."

"Oh, I'm supposed to reform the way teaching is done at this school?"

"You don't know anything about teaching, though you're a bit of a whiz at learning. So . . . *learn* what's wrong with this school, learn it so deeply and well that you can fix it. *Then* we'll all know how to do it, and Fleet School will be better from then on, all because a dirtboy named Dabeet Ochoa was allowed to come from Earth into space to save us."

Then Dabeet realized that Oddson was simply restating Graff's original challenges. "What qualities would make a good leader of an expedition?" Obviously this group was *not* ready to accomplish anything as a team, and so Dabeet's challenge was to somehow make a team out of them. Without even a shred of authority, without getting respect from any of the other children, Dabeet's challenge was to make a team out of these kids.

Had they deliberately let a team succumb to all these prejudices and divisions solely to pose a challenge for him? Was this all put together as a test for Dabeet?

No, that was solipsism, the idea that the whole world was set up solely for his benefit. This army was real, its problems were real, and Dabeet had been given his assignment—to reshape the children until they became a team.

He couldn't possibly tell anybody else what to do. He couldn't even make suggestions—he was already being treated with disdain, but if he uttered the criticisms that every suggestion was bound to imply, he would be even more isolated, treated with hostility rather than mere contempt.

He would have to do it without seeming to do anything at all.

Maybe Ender Wiggin could have done it. But Dabeet was not a natural leader of anything.

They're setting me up to fail.

Maybe I will and maybe I won't. But I'm going to work hard at learning to fly in zero-gee without puking or humiliating myself, and by then maybe I'll have an idea of how to influence people who despise me already for things completely beyond my control.

Somehow, I've got to become the kind of person that every kid in this army will want to follow.

He laughed aloud in his bunk that night, thinking about his impossible dilemma. Other boys, hearing him, were sure that he was crying himself to sleep. "Misses his mommy," one boy muttered—loudly and clearly enough to be sure Dabeet heard him.

"I do miss her," Dabeet said, loud enough to be heard by just as many people.

"Don't miss your father, though," said another.

"I've missed *him* my whole life," said Dabeet. "But I've never shed a tear for either of them."

This was not actually true, but it didn't matter, because there was no more response from anybody. He hadn't *silenced* them with his comment. They just didn't care enough to say anything more.

7

3. What are the most important problems the IF has been required to solve since the end of the Formic Wars?

There is no honest way to answer this question in the terms given, because it begs the question. We have no evidence, at least insofar as the public has been informed, that the Formic Wars are over.

We have seen the vids of the destruction of the presumptive Formic home world, and we have seen the vids of Formic warriors and workers collapsing and dying of their own accord, purportedly at the same moment that all the hive queens died on that home world.

However, since that planet is unable to provide us with an archaeological or fossil record demonstrating that it was the world on which the Formics evolved, this cannot be more than a supposition. Nor have we evidence that the inhabited worlds we invaded and seized were all the settled Formic worlds.

More to the point, it would be at least irresponsible and quite possibly insane to assume that the Formics did not have other colonizing expeditions underway at the time of Ender Wiggin's glorious victory. The expedition that came to our solar system and was defeated finally by Mazer Rackham's daring victory at the end of the Second Formic War had its own hive queen. Presumably other such expeditions would also have hive queens, and those hive queens would not have been destroyed when the "home world" smithereened.

Nor can we discount the possibility—or probability—that the Formics had launched a war fleet at least as terrible as our own, which cannot be detected yet because they are still traveling at a pace very close to lightspeed. We will only detect them when they decelerate.

So the biggest problem the IF had and has to deal with is the fact that most of the human race believes that the Formic threat has been completely extinguished, whereas we do not and cannot know that any such thing is true. We may be facing the most dire threat of all, potentially beginning at this instant or any other instant in the future. Since the Formics communicate mind to mind, they write nothing down. They make no maps. We cannot possibly have discovered their plans. It is insane for any student of military history to assume that because we have not detected an enemy fleet, it does not exist.

Yet even though we might face a savagely vengeful Formic armada at any moment, the government structures on Earth and Luna that provided funding and personnel for the International Fleet for half a century have now been allowed to lapse.

From this I believe we may conclude several things:

1. The IF has conclusive evidence of the non-existence of any Formic war fleets or colonial expeditions, so the claimed certainty that no Formics remain alive anywhere is actually a certainty, *or*

2. The IF has prepared such a massive and technologically advanced fleet, which now patrols the outskirts of the solar system, that no matter where a Formic armada assailed us, we could respond and give reliable protection to Earth, Luna, and all the important outposts of humanity in the solar system. This huge fleet is so capable that the Ministry of Colonization can make a great show of converting former warships into colonizing and exploratory ships in order to colonize the former Formic planets *and* discover new habitable planets where no Formic has ever been, *or*

3. The IF has reason to believe that the Formics were not capable of any of these things. I can imagine the scenario like

this: The hive queens were involved in a continuous civil war, competitive colonization like the European occupation and colonization of Africa in the 19th and 20th centuries. This savage warfare only ended just before the Formics sent out the colony that came to Earth to start the Formic Wars. Therefore this was the *only* expedition the Formics had launched.

Then, abashed at realizing, after Mazer Rackham's victory in the Second Formic War, that humanity was indeed sentient and capable of besting them in war, they humbly decided to leave us alone and hoped that we would do the same. All their resources were devoted to creating defensive fleets around each of their inhabited worlds and, most especially, around their home world, and they gathered all the hive queens together on the home world in the belief that they could protect it against anything we might throw against it. Thus the Second and Third Formic Wars resulted in the destruction of every living hive queen, and there are no fleets or expeditions with their own hive queens wandering through our region of the galaxy.

I believe that if number one were true, conclusive evidence would have been broadcast by the government to every sentient being in the solar system. I feel confident in ruling it out.

If number two is believed by the IF high command, then our own successful invasion of the Formic planets and the destruction of their massively defended home world clearly demonstrates that anyone who thinks a Maginot Line cannot be penetrated or circumvented by the enemy is a fool doomed to destruction.

The only story that leads to our certain survival as a species is number three, and that depends on so much wishful thinking about Formic psychology, of which we know nothing, that I would rather believe in Santa Claus, since there is so much more evidence of his existence.

If I, as a child in school, can see these obvious points, then the finest minds of the International Fleet cannot have missed them. I affirm that the effort to colonize hitherto unknown worlds is the only plan with any chance of bringing about the survival of the human species. Therefore our Ministry of Colonization is the most important portion of the International Fleet, and the faster they can find habitable worlds and get colonies established, the better our chance of riding out the attempted obliteration of humanity by an enemy that has every reason to hate us forever.

This is the *only* important problem faced by the IF after the "end" of the Formic Wars, precisely because we have no reason to imagine that those wars have ended.

Dabeet, your third essay on the diagnostic test was nonresponsive and shows a combative and rebellious attitude. It is inappropriate and imprudent to speak with such authority on matters you know so little about. If you bandy about such ideas and attitudes with other students, your continuation here at Fleet School will be in doubt.

Dabeet learned the theory and rules of the battleroom almost instantly. Hadn't everyone seen the movies about Ender and his jeesh, movies in which kids in flash suits skittered across the interior of the hundred-meter cube, carrying out intricate maneuvers and zapping each other, freezing parts of each other's suits or immobilizing them completely in death? Dabeet had found them interesting as he evaluated the physics of the computer simulations to see if they were accurate in depicting real null-gravity movement. Usually there were flaws; usually nobody at school or at home cared about Dabeet's explanations of why they would be impossible.

So Dabeet needed no introduction to the real flash suit, except to be shown how the pieces linked together as he put it on. Nor was he surprised at the way the handles on the wall popped out as his hand drew near to catch one, while remaining recessed if he approached in a different orientation, so that a protruding handle wouldn't injure him as he struck it, or interfere with the billiard-ball perfection of his rebound.

Dabeet thought: Bacana, smart walls. Nothing that happens in real war is analogous to *this*. The battlefield doesn't reach out to enfold soldiers in a cozy embrace. Not unless they're dead.

Only after a few practice sessions did Dabeet turn his analysis inward: I'm bad at this, and I'm not getting better fast enough to contribute to my team in actual games. Everybody's patient with me, but that's because the emphasis in Fleet School now is on cooperation as well as competition. Niceness counts. What do they really think of me? Not hard to guess. I'm a burden when I'm in play, and at my rate of improvement I always will be. I'll never catch up with any of the other kids.

And I don't care. I'm not even *interested* in becoming that good at this putative game. I don't want to spend the time it would take to overcome my natural clumsiness.

So maybe it's a good thing the game isn't as important in the life of Fleet School as it was in Battle School. Our worth as individuals isn't completely defined by our win-loss record on the leaderboards.

Yet I still have to spend hours a day in the battleroom for practice sessions, where I take up someone else's time trying to change this donkey into a steed. I need to find something else to do that doesn't waste other people's time.

It was in pursuit of that goal that Dabeet did something to annoy somebody, and now that he was standing in front of Urska Kaluza's desk, he assumed he was going to find out what.

"So if you can't immediately win at something, you won't continue?" she asked.

"I'll continue if you tell me that I must, sir," said Dabeet. "I didn't quit going, I simply asked if I could employ my time elsewhere, freeing up the time of whoever would have had to babysit me during practices. I really have tried to improve, Commandant Kaluza, and I *am* improving, but not fast enough."

"So you'll spend your time surpassing everyone in academic subjects," said Kaluza.

"If you don't think that's a better use of my time, sir, I'm happy to be guided by you in another direction."

"In Fleet School, we do teamwork. We do cooperation. We don't do solo grandstanding. So no, you may not be excused from practice time in the battleroom. You'll wear your flash suit and you'll be there ready to take part in whatever way your leaders require, or sit and do nothing if that's what they require. But *if* you do nothing, we'll be asking sharp questions of the other students."

"Thank you for the clarification, sir," said Dabeet.

"That wasn't a clarification," said Kaluza. "That was a denial of your request and a set of strictures and warnings. Don't use weasely words with me. We both know what's going on. You're a competitor in a cooperative place. You aren't willing to occupy the lowest rung on a ladder; if you can't climb as fast as the others, then you want to change ladders. Ain't happening . . . lad."

He was quite sure that what she wanted to call him was *not* "lad," but in the IF even the watchers were watched, and she couldn't be caught calling a boy "mudfoot" or one of the other charming words for someone who had never been off Earth before.

He saluted and left. She had judged him wrongly—he was actually trying to be cooperative and help accomplish the larger purposes of

Fleet School, but it was not surprising that she couldn't grasp the distinction. If a low motive could be attributed to him, then she would hear no argument. That's fine, *ma'am,* he thought. I'll work within whatever fence you build around me. *And* I'll find a way to build up my army in the process, until even you have to admit that I am *not* flying solo. I'm helping support and even form a community.

If, that is, I can't think of something to do in the battleroom that isn't just more of the same clumsy thumping around like the clodhopper I am.

Besides the battleroom practices, Dabeet threw himself into strength and dexterity training in the gym. Though there was definitely gravity in the gym and the martial arts training room, Dabeet was pretty sure it wasn't Earth-normal, or he wouldn't have been so strong. Here's the place where his recent departure from Earth would have given him an advantage—so of course the gravity was fudged to help out the breakable spaceborn children.

Not that those breakable children could help it. Long months and years away from gravity weakened the body, whether you came from Earth or were born in a ship or station with centrifuges or gravity manipulation. Most families tried to maintain a level of familiarity with gravity that would allow them to live on Luna with little or no transition—and to visit Earth without immediately dying. Dabeet could not begrudge them a little compensation for their fragility.

Everything evens out in the end—who said that? Mother? Some neighbor of hers? A teacher? Yes, it was a teacher, but he was being ironic, joking with a rather ugly girl that someday the very pretty girl who was the object of her envy at the moment would someday be in front of an audience or promotions board, and a huge bubble of snot would form, pushing out and sucking in with her breathing. "Everything evens out in the end."

"She'll still be a pretty girl with a snot-bubble," said the plain girl. "And she'll have the kind of cleavage that makes people not notice snot-bubbles."

"There's no cleavage *that* magical," said the teacher, and his laugh ended the conversation.

His point had obviously been that things do *not* even out in the end. Lucky people might bemoan this or that small thing that went wrong in their lives. But to others less lucky, they would seem to have sailed through life without trouble.

Like me, thought Dabeet. Nothing has gone wrong for me. Sure, my father's missing, but look at my genetic heritage. My devoted mother.

Good teachers, good books. My brains. Important enough to be kidnapped. Clever or useful enough to be let go. Taken up into Fleet School, where I'm mastering the coursework faster than anybody. My few setbacks are trivial, in areas that don't matter to me anyway.

So it was that Dabeet found himself clinging forlornly to one of the three-dimensionally floating objects in the battleroom that all the kids called "stars." They seemed to be made of the same material as the walls—their handholds extruded or receded as children approached each square.

Dabeet was holding tightly to one of the handholds, because his unconscious mind had noticed that the nearest wall or floor was as far away as if he were on a four-story building. He knew the vertigo would pass soon, and then he could let go and fly back to the wall.

As he thought these thoughts, a change in position caused him to give the handhold a hard twist, and something extraordinary happened. The whole face of that square extruded in the form of a pyramid, with the handhold perched on its top. The base of the pyramid was still aligned with the adjacent wall plates.

No one had mentioned that the surface plates could do such things. Dabeet twisted the handhold sharply back in the opposite direction. The pyramid was sucked back into the panel until it was completely flat.

Another twist, and this time the whole square panel moved forward, forming a cube. More torque, and the cube became a square pillar.

"Stop playing with the shapes," said Ragnar Olafson. "Are you three?" Ragnar had come out of nowhere and was instantly gone again.

So this was called "playing with the shapes." No doubt they all knew about it and had gotten tired of it years ago.

Dabeet gave the handhold another twist and the whole pillar snapped back into place, flush with the wall.

Dabeet had no idea why these panels had such capabilities, but perhaps by figuring out *what* they could do, he could think of a reason why they had been designed to do it. Dabeet launched himself toward a wall near one of the gates that armies used when they launched themselves into battle.

He began torquing the handles of the panels surrounding the door. Within a couple of minutes, he had shaped a low parapet all the way around the gate. It would be useless for the possessors of that gate— what defense could it offer when enemies could attack from above at any time?—but if an enemy team built such a low wall before the enemy emerged from their gate . . .

"That never does any good," said Ragnar again. "We tried all kinds of things back in the day. None of the teams waste time with the shapes anymore."

"I have to figure out what they can do," said Dabeet. "Especially if everybody else already knows."

"Nobody else cares," said Ragnar. "But play in the sandbox all you want."

Dabeet perked up at that reference. "Do they have sandboxes where you grew up?"

Ragnar looked confused. "A sandbox is a *thing*?" he asked.

"A box filled with sand where you can play. Digging and piling things up."

"I guess that would work, in gravity," said Ragnar. "Legal. I just thought it was an expression. Something you can play with that doesn't matter and does no harm. Makes sense that the thing came before the expression."

Dabeet might have allowed himself to get sidetracked into a discussion of idioms in various languages—one of his favorites was "raining cats and dogs," which was the equivalent of the Danish "It's raining shoemakers' apprentices" and the Greek "It's raining chair legs" and the French "It's raining frogs" and "It's raining like a pissing cow." The Serbian "The rain falls and kills the mice," the Welsh "It's raining old ladies and sticks"—Dabeet had memorized a long list of them and entertained a classroom during a rainstorm at Conn reciting the oddest ones until half the class was laughing hysterically, especially when they started making up new ones after "pissing cow," on related themes.

But this was not the moment to repeat that event, especially because he wasn't sure whether Ragnar had ever experienced rain at all.

Besides, at that moment Dabeet inadvertently pushed downward on one handle, and the beveled extrusion he had formed broke away from the wall behind it. It was as if the panel had come out of its socket, except that where it had been, there was a regular flat panel with a handhold, and on the bottom side of the block Dabeet was now holding there was another flat panel with a handhold.

"Did you know it would do *that*?" Dabeet asked Ragnar.

"I heard that they could come loose," said Ragnar. "What did you do?"

"Pushed down on the left side, pulled up on the right."

"Can you put it back?"

Dabeet set it back in place. It stayed, but it wasn't stuck. He could pull it off easily, rotate it, put it back. Then he tried repeating the motion that had made it come free. And he felt a clunk from inside the block as it reattached itself.

Well, no. Because when he pulled up the block came free, only now it was attached to another cube of panel material that came up easily, as a part of the structure.

"That's greeyaz," said Ragnar. "You can't do anything with it in combat."

"Throw it at somebody?"

"Accomplishing what? Doesn't freeze their suits, and they throw it back anyway. Just gets in the way."

"So you've seen people do this?"

"Never," said Ragnar. "But if it was useful, somebody would be doing it."

"Maybe nobody knows," said Dabeet.

"Same point."

"Nobody knew how to do archery till somebody invented arrows and bows," said Dabeet.

"You think that's like longbows at Agincourt?" asked Ragnar, laughing. "Good luck with that." And, once again, Ragnar launched himself away.

Still, it was the longest conversation he'd had with anybody in his team that didn't consist of them telling him what to do and how wrongly he was doing it.

Dabeet thought so much about the panels that turned into cubes and blocks that he began to dream about them, because after pulling them cube by cube out of the walls and joining them to each other, the shapes he made from them, the process of extrusion and connection, these became the forms and processes that went on in his dreams, endless pipes and bridges, arches and spirals, things he couldn't imagine the cubes might actually be able to become. He even hallucinated some of these shapes, watching them pass before his eyes while looking at a teacher, a diagram, his desk, blank walls. At any time he'd find his mind rotely putting blocks together, shaping them. Closing his eyes didn't get rid of the images. Nothing did. But he forced himself to continue concentrating on the lesson, making sure that his schoolwork didn't suffer because of this growing obsession with drawing shapes out of the battleroom walls.

How did Ender Wiggin and his jeesh ever get anything done, when they had these building blocks to play with?

If they had them. For all Dabeet knew, this feature of the walls had been added during the transition from Battle School into Fleet School. Maybe somebody realized that building things would be one of the most important tasks of the explorers and colonists. They would need shelter and defenses on these other worlds, for predators would not know that human flesh was indigestible, and resentful natives might be tempted to steal artifacts or take a biological trophy or two while the colonists slept.

But if it was worth creating these deep walls, with so many cubes hidden inside them, why hadn't anyone emphasized to the students the importance of building with them? Why wasn't the use of the cubes built into the game?

Or was it a test? Which students would keep doing the same old thing, and which would make a discovery and run with it?

It could be testing in the other direction, too, of course. To see how long Dabeet would keep working at this pointless, unappreciated, hypnotic, mind-numbing task until he realized that it was of no practical use. If that was the test, he was failing and had no intention of changing what he was doing.

The other kids on his team ignored him completely now, except when he built a structure that extended far into the battlespace. Some of them would mutter some kind of invective as they came closer to his building than they meant to. Others, saying nothing, simply grabbed on to one of the handholds on his pillar and used it to change direction. There *is* a use for these pillars, thought Dabeet.

But that was half an hour into a practice; in an actual competitive situation, the battle would be over before Dabeet's structure was half done.

Unless somebody was helping him build.

As he thought about this, Dabeet let his gaze wander around the battleroom. "Knowledge you have no use for is rarely worth having," Graff had said. "The secret is not to avoid learning useless knowledge. It's to make use of whatever knowledge you have."

Maybe there's a use for this knowledge about the blocks in the battleroom. . . . Maybe if I could put up a structure quickly enough, the instant we were allowed to pass through the gate, then the rest of the army could use my structure to change trajectories and be able to move through the battleroom using paths that weren't so ballistic, and with a decent amount of cover from enemy fire along the way.

When there are stars in the room, are they placed so that the blocks can be built out to link to them?

No sooner thought of than he had to try it, so Dabeet spent half the practice extruding boxes and building them up in a single rigid pillar that came to a stop exactly half a box-width away from the star, and not quite aligned with it.

Dabeet took the handhold of the square nearest his pillar's end, drawing it up from the surface of the star. He had only brought it half the distance to the end of his pillar when something shifted.

The star shifted. The whole star moved away from the pillar and sideways exactly the right amount to allow the box he was now extruding to line up perfectly with the end of the pillar.

Dabeet snaked his hand out from between the new cube and the pillar. They could hardly connect as long as he still had a body part involved.

As soon as his hand was clear, the new cube from the star finished extruding itself and snapped into place on the pillar. The star was now anchored to the wall by a long, inflexible tether.

The star had moved to make this happen. The cube had self-extruded in order to bridge the last gap. The blocks had locked together without his having to flip any lever or adjust anything at all. Clearly, the star had sensed his design and cooperated. Or, rather, the computer program controlling the behavior of the wall units had helped him achieve his goal.

The only possible conclusion was that the blocks had been designed with this exact process in mind. Bring wall blocks close enough to star blocks, and everything will self-adjust in order to fit.

"OK, that's amazing," said a boy.

It was Zhang He, who was rumored to be from the powerful Wu-Hu trading clan, a family both Great and Brave. This had been interesting enough that Dabeet had looked up his background, which revealed that Zhang He wasn't from a Miner clan. He was a True Child of the Fleet, and his family were Onlookers, stationed on Luna during the war. This information was part of his public bio, so Dabeet couldn't conceive of how the rumor of the Wu-Hu connection could have started.

"Glad you're amazed," said Dabeet. Then, hearing his own voice, he realized that this could probably be taken as sarcasm, so he added, "It amazed me, too."

"Did I see the star move?"

"I felt it and saw it," said Dabeet. "It moved."

"Eppur si muove," said Zhang He. The words that Galileo reputedly said after the Inquisition forced him to confess that the Earth does not move around the Sun; that it does not move at all. "And yet it moves," the great astronomer supposedly muttered.

Dabeet chuckled. "Not sure the discovery reaches Galileo's level."

"Good enough for the battleroom," said Zhang.

"I wish I'd timed how long it took me to build this pillar and connect it up," said Dabeet.

"You did time it," said Zhang. "You're wearing a flash suit. It times everything you do while you're wearing it."

Dabeet made an elaborate shrug, twisting his hands to show that *if* he was timed, he didn't know where to find the data.

Unfortunately, in making this gesture he drifted away from the star. He realized his plight almost immediately, and flashed out a hand to try to take hold. He was already just a hair too far away from a handhold—and the movement caused him to spin so that in a moment his feet were coming up and his hands were even farther from the nearest grip.

Zhang He caught him by the ankle and pulled him back to the pillar. "Happens to all of us," he said.

Dabeet smiled slightly at the attempt to salve his pride. "Thanks for saving me from a long slow trip to the far wall."

"Pull the back of your glove—either glove—up to your mouth, whisper your question, and then look at the glove."

Holding tightly to the handhold, Dabeet asked his other hand, "How long did it take me to build this pillar and connect it to the star?"

The back of his glove lit up with easily readable characters: "14:32."

"I hope that's minutes and seconds," said Dabeet.

"Still a long time," said Zhang He. "Longer than most battles."

So . . . still useless.

Unless somebody would help him. Learn how to create and manipulate the blocks as quickly as Dabeet did. Learn how to be his partner in this insane project.

Dabeet did not dare to ask. Zhang He was showing himself to have good will toward Dabeet, to be interested in what he was doing. But to ask one of the top soldiers in the team to apprentice himself to the lowest of the low, that might easily be an insult.

"What if we did it together?" asked Zhang He. "Would I be a help or would I just get in the way."

"You'd probably get in the way at first," said Dabeet, "and then be a great help as soon as you got skilled at extruding these cubic bubbles from the wall and sticking them together."

"I know," said Zhang He. "I'm a top soldier and you're kind of nothing, so people will say stupid things and some of them will get mad if I spend time doing this with you. I assume you've already taken enough shit to know how to ignore it?"

"I have," said Dabeet. "But have *you*?"

"I have to listen to them calling me Wu-Hu all the time, just to point up the shameful fact that my parents were both stationed on Luna during the war."

"How is it shameful to be a True Child of the Fleet?"

"Anything is shameful if people use it to ridicule you," said Zhang He. "But I know that they mostly do it because it's fun to say 'Wu-Hu.'"

Sure enough, Zhang He's toon leader and then the commander, Bartolomeo Ja, came to remonstrate with him. Zhang He answered cheerfully enough, but he neither obeyed them nor explained his reasons for working with Dabeet.

"This is taking pity way too far," said Bartolomeo. "*He's* useless, but you're the heart of your toon."

Zhang He's answer was a gratified smile. "Why, it's nice of you to say so."

The commander went on and on, to no avail, and then began yelling at Dabeet that he was *forbidden* to take up the time of such a valuable soldier.

Dabeet's answer was also mild. "Would you like to learn how to do this, too, sir, so we can get our time even faster?"

"I think we should try a timed run now," said Zhang He to Dabeet.

Bartolomeo gave one last warning. "There's no way that Kaluza will let you tear up my army like this," he said.

Dabeet thought he was probably right. But in the meantime, he and Zhang He had time enough for one real try. Zhang He was a quick learner, and even though his skill at extruding and binding the blocks wasn't up to Dabeet's level, he was nearly as quick.

They divided their activities. First they both extruded and linked pillars of eight blocks each until they had enough to make the whole bridge. Then Zhang He, staying at the wall, launched them up to Dabeet, who caught each one and joined it to the growing pillar. Finally, Zhang He tossed the penultimate piece and then carried the last one as he scrambled up the bridge. They set the last piece in place together.

"4:10," said both their hands.

"That's less than a third of my pace working alone," said Dabeet.

"That was your first time, and you had to keep making the trip back and forth to the wall," said Zhang He.

"If I could figure out how this would have any effect on the battle," said Dabeet, "then I'd be really excited that this can be built by two guys in about the time it takes for a battle to really get under way."

Zhang He grinned. "I wonder what we could do building four pillars at once. With a whole toon."

"Forget pillars," said Dabeet. "I wonder what would happen if we built a fort that completely enclosed the gate."

"Or built a bridge from one gate to the other," said Zhang He.

"Or a tube that you could crawl through, where nobody could shoot you from one side of the battleroom to the other."

"Nothing stops them from tearing the tube apart as fast as we build it, of course. Like Nehemiah's enemies tore down the walls of Jerusalem at night, after Nehemiah's people had worked on it all day."

"Nehemiah?" asked Dabeet.

"The book of Nehemiah in the Old Testament," said Zhang He. "Come on, Dabeet, you've read everything and you remember everything."

"But you're Chinese," said Dabeet.

"Chinese Christian," said Zhang He. "Not very well accepted in China, I'm afraid. Our family was already part of a Chinese Christian community on Luna before either of my parents enlisted in the IF. They didn't really enlist. The Fleet just took over the company they worked for, and they either took the oath or they were out of work."

"And you're a Christian?" asked Dabeet.

"We don't talk religion here in Fleet School," said Zhang He. "It's one of the rules."

The end-of-practice light was already flashing.

"Come on, let's head for chow," said Zhang He.

This implied that Zhang He was actually going to eat with him. Dabeet was baffled. "Don't we have to clean up all these blocks?" he asked.

"If we have to, they'll make us come back and do it. But I think the blocks know where they belong," said Zhang He.

Then it dawned on Dabeet. "Helping me was an act of Christian charity, wasn't it?"

Zhang He looked at him like he was crazy. "You're the only person here doing anything interesting," he said. "You letting me help you— *that* was charity."

Dabeet, trying to shape his responses to fit the expectations of others as normal people do, tried to detect any hint of humor or irony in Zhang He's words. Dabeet? Charity? He knew enough about the word to associate it with generosity, as well as Christian teachings and practice. How had it been generous of Dabeet to . . .

Well, he could have ordered Zhang He to go away and not interfere with Dabeet's work. This would have been a preemptive strike on Dabeet's part, to protect himself from ridicule. But Dabeet had not ordered Zhang He to leave him alone. He had felt no fear of him. Why was that?

Partly it was Zhang He himself. Dabeet had never seen him as one of the smug ones, who tried to elevate themselves by putting vulnerable kids down. And when he approached, Zhang He's soberness of manner never wavered. He seemed genuinely interested, and, as his hard work and quick mastery of the techniques soon demonstrated, he *was* interested.

Partly, though, Dabeet had to recognize a change in himself. At Conn, Dabeet never embarked on a project that would benefit from the help of others. His teachers always tried to intrude on his work in order to— as they imagined—give him guidance. Their guidance was always based on false assumptions about his purpose, their own ignorance making them worse than useless.

But Graff had set Dabeet to several tests, and now Dabeet was beginning to understand. Graff's tests were really teaching assignments. "What qualities would make a good leader of an expedition, or a colony, or a scouting or reconnaissance mission?"

More telling had been the second part of that assignment: "Which of those qualities do you lack, making it meaningless to bring you into Fleet School?"

Long before arriving at Fleet School, Dabeet had understood that leading other people under dangerous conditions—facing unknown dangers, or building a colony in a hostile environment—required that the team members trust their leaders, that they trust each other to do the jobs they were assigned to do. This meant helping each other, doing good work for each other—Dabeet could figure these things out as a thought experiment, and his readings only made the answer clearer: I can't work exclusively by myself and be of any use to the Ministry of Colonization or the IF's program of exploration.

But knowing that he must be cooperative and actually finding ways to do it were two very different projects. He had years of habitual introversion and surliness to overcome. He had to become patient with abuse and not flare up at provocations.

And he quickly learned that even when he offered to help, his offers were often rebuffed. He had tried to figure it out: Everybody by now understands that in academic subjects, I'm better than anybody in my age group. (Age groups are absurd anyway, but no complaining.) Why, when I offer to help students who are hopelessly struggling, or who look puzzled, or who shake their heads in frustration after a teacher's inept explanation, do they shrug me off, walk away, or stare me down until I stop offering?

Was it some conspiracy among them? Had they all agreed never to accept help from me?

Or is it something about *me*? Some manner I have that makes them take my offer wrong?

Now that Zhang He was letting Dabeet sit with him at lunch—no, to be exact, now that Zhang He was going to Dabeet's formerly solitary lunch-table seat—Dabeet could actually ask the question that mattered most.

"I know they bring fresh ingredients up here," said Zhang He. "But I think they freeze them all by storing them in bags in cold space, like the rubbish stashes."

Dabeet chuckled—he could tell that Zhang He was joking and, just to make things easier, the image struck Dabeet as genuinely amusing. "I hope they never get confused about which bags are which."

"I think what's on our trays is proof that they already have," said Zhang He.

Chuckle. Take a bite—no. Don't take a bite. Ask the question instead. "Zhang, can I ask you something kind of personal?"

"Can't promise to answer."

"Not about you. About me."

"I don't know anything personal about you. Just your school bio," said Zhang He.

"When I offer to help people. In their schoolwork, after class or in the library or even right there in the classroom. Nobody wants my help."

"Oh, they want it, all right," said Zhang He.

"They make it clear that they don't," said Dabeet, and then he did a pantomime of the normal response—the turning of the body, the raising of the shoulder nearest to Zhang.

"It's not always easy to accept help," said Zhang He.

"I know that better than anyone," said Dabeet. "But I repel anyone who might offer to help me because I'm an arrogant oomay. These guys are all normal and they have, you know, friends."

"But you aren't one of their friends," said Zhang He.

Dabeet could see that Zhang He was being evasive. "I can't get better if you don't tell me what I'm doing wrong."

"I'm here to help you on your wall extrusions," said Zhang He. "I'm not here to fix you."

"I intend to fix myself. But I can't even start till I know what parts are broken."

"Nothing's broken," said Zhang He. "You really *are* smarter than everybody. We've all seen you in class. You don't just read ahead, it's like you see the whole picture and understand the subject better than the teacher. You're doing great."

"Wrong answer," said Dabeet. "What is it you're *not* saying?"

Zhang He closed his eyes. "Look, it's the *way* you say things."

"Yes, please, what's wrong with it?"

"Like when you said 'wrong answer' just now," said Zhang. "We're friends, right? You don't hate me. Yet you said 'wrong answer' as if you had just found me like pus coming out of a sore."

Dabeet made another try. "Wrong answer," he said, much more mildly. And then, almost affectionately, "Wrong answer."

"Dabeet," said Zhang, trying not to laugh, it seemed. "The problem is that there's *no* way to use the words 'wrong answer' and not make them sound like 'you dull bob.'"

"I was asking you to help me communicate better, to find out why nobody accepts my offers of help. And you went off on how smart I was, like I was some moose who needed to be placated."

"Oh, I know that's what happened," said Zhang He. "And then you said, 'wrong answer' and proved exactly why I was right to try to placate you."

"I wasn't angry. I wasn't even rude."

"'Wrong answer' is rude, prima facie," said Zhang. "Teacher to student, it's even rude. But student to student, it's kind of awful. And friend to friend—well, you better smile when you say something that condescending."

"Smile?"

"To show me that the rude thing you're saying is between friends. That your rudeness is a joke, proving that we can trust each other."

"I'm such a zhopa," said Dabeet. "I know what you're talking about, I've seen other guys do it. I just don't know how to apply it to myself."

"Hey, at least you get it," said Zhang. "That's like being halfway there."

"Who's being condescending now?" asked Dabeet.

"Me," said Zhang. "But let's face it, if you really want to start taking human lessons, you have to recognize that you're starting at a pretty elementary level."

"I think the euphemism is that I 'show promise but have a long way to go.'"

"Except for showing promise, é, that's right."

"You were smiling. That's what you mean. You insult me that I don't show any promise, but your smile means that you think I *do* show promise, or at least that you think I have a chance here."

"When you're working on something," said Zhang, "you're perfectly easy to work with. You never get mad at me for making mistakes—"

"What would be the point of that?"

"Exactly," said Zhang. "You're sensible, you're respectful. *While* we're working on the blocks. The job is what matters, sure, but you also take care not to alienate anybody."

"You've got to remember, the only person I'm working with is you. Smart, hard-working, creative . . ."

Zhang He gave him a big grin. "So kind of you to say so."

"Sarcastic," said Dabeet.

"Completely sincere, but hiding behind a veneer of sarcasm so if you take it wrong, I have an out."

Dabeet sat there digesting these ideas.

"The food gets worse with age and falling temperature," Zhang He pointed out.

"Obviously false," said Dabeet. "This food could *not* get worse."

"Good smile. Got the signal," said Zhang. "And you're right, the food can't get worse, because long before that, it'll cease to be food." He grinned.

Dabeet grinned back. "Thanks for eating lunch with me."

"Friends don't thank each other for being friends."

"I just didn't know, for sure, that we were friends. Till now."

8

—You may not be able to confirm this, but I assume that this complaint originated with the Minister of Colonization.

—Complaints are all bastards. Father unknown. But it wouldn't surprise me.

—Since I'm not supposed to know about this, I can hardly offer any counter-arguments, but really, how absurd this is, to claim that it's inappropriate for IF personnel to provide services for inbound and outgoing ships. From the moment that the IF commandeered all fueling and supply and maintenance stations throughout the solar system at the end of the First War, IF personnel have been—

—The problem isn't IF personnel, it's Fleet School personnel—

—Do they imagine we're sending the *teachers* out to service the ships? It's our own maintenance staff that does that work, during their *copious* downtime.

—To which they would answer that if you have a surplus of maintenance personnel with nothing to do, your budget can be reduced accordingly and the redundant workers reassigned.

—Our budget? Are they innumerate? The fees we charge—which, I will add, are no higher than the fees charged at other near-Earth servicing and resupply stations—completely pay for the mechanical operating budget of Fleet School. Life support, orbit maintenance, communications, energy—we may be the only self-supporting agency in the IF.

—Most of the stations are self-supporting.

—There! That's my point! What Graff is demanding—

—If it's the Minister of Colonization—

—is that Fleet School's maintenance be returned to the general fund, so its expenses become a dead loss to the IF.

—Here's where the minister leaves his fingerprints: The proposal is that the funds come out of the Ministry of Colonization, since the school exists to supply the ministry's needs.

—This is a flimsy excuse for a bureaucratic budget grab. If Graff is paying, then he's in charge, and—

—Your arguments are cogent. Your books are in order—that was the first thing we checked. But these points are already known. I'll tell you what would make the biggest difference with the Defense Council.

—To arm Fleet School and call it a stationary battle cruiser?

—Glad you haven't lost your sense of humor.

—On the contrary, I have completely lost it.

—If you can show that bringing all these ships in to Fleet School for repair, resupply, and so on, has an *educational* purpose.

—I've been keeping the students strictly away from any depot operations.

—That was a wise policy, until now. If you could show that in the process of working with these ships, the students were learning teamwork skills, inventory and maintenance skills . . . you know, the kinds of things that they'll have to know how to manage if they ever actually run a remote colony—

—As if these exploratory missions to nowhere will ever happen.

—Oh, it *will* happen, and it *will* be very valuable for you, or your successor, if Fleet School grads play an important role in the exploratory and colonizing missions.

—Or my successor.

—What, were you hoping to stay in Fleet School forever?

—Bog no. I only thought I might be hearing a vague threat.

—There's nothing vague about it, Urska! How long do you think you'll remain in your present position if ColMin gets Fleet School on its books?

"You on this side of the room, you're on the inside team," said Lieutenant Oddson.

Groans from everybody except Dabeet. "It's because the mudfoot's on this side," said somebody.

"I wasn't going to send Dabeet outside no matter which team he was on," said Odd. "The outside team is going to do observation only, because look at yourselves. You're kids! You think somebody's going to trust you to attach a fuel hose? To replace vital outside parts? You're *watching*."

Groans from the other side of the barracks.

"Get a clue, bunducks," said Odd. "Get taller, show you're good for something, and the brass will trust you. What matters is, we're starting a new program here, and what you're going to be doing, inside team, and watching, outside team, is *real*. When you're exploring and colonizing, who do you think is going to tend to your ship?"

"Crew," said Dabeet.

"And which jobs that the crew do should the commander be completely ignorant of?"

"None of them!" shouted everybody, probably more for the pleasure of mocking Dabeet than for any eagerness to give an obvious answer.

"*You're* crew, or you can't command," said Odd. "You don't have to be as good at the job as somebody who specializes in it, but you have to know if it's being done right. And what if the crew member who knows how to do it best is killed? Eaten by an alien, smacked by a meteorite, killed by falling off a cliff? You think kuso like that is never going to happen on our expeditions? You have to know what he does—"

"Used to do," muttered Timeon.

"Used to do," said Odd. "You've got to know how to do it, how to train his replacement to do it, or understand what the machinery does well enough to jury-rig a workaround. Whatever it takes."

"What are we going to learn from watching?" asked Ragnar. "A lot of us grew up installing things on ships, in deep space and far away from any kind of supply station."

"Then you'll have an advantage in learning," said Odd. "Unless you get complacent and lazy, and then the other kids who work hard and think harder will pass you up like you lived your whole life in a high-rise in Taipei."

"But the inside crew?" asked Dabeet. "We're doing something real?"

"Kind of," said Odd. "You're shadowing the people who normally do the jobs. Inside installation, that'll just be watching, too. But inventory management, checking everything off to make sure nothing is left behind and everything goes where it's supposed to, you'll be working with the real software, the real numbers, the real lists. There'll just be somebody backing you up when you make mistakes."

"What if we find mistakes that *they* made?" asked Dabeet. "Will any-body listen to children when we report the error?"

"Won't it be interesting to find out," said Odd. "We've never done this before, so nobody knows yet what'll happen. But the people doing these jobs, they know their work and nobody's been reprimanded or fired since we started letting ships resupply and refit at Fleet School."

"They never did this stuff when it was Battle School, did they?" asked Dabeet.

Other kids groaned at Dabeet's asking yet another question.

"No," said Odd. "But that's because during the war there was no non-military traffic. Now it's peacetime, and Fleet School is perfectly situated at L-5, and if we *weren't* here some big corporation would build a station on this spot and make money hand over fist."

"So Fleet School makes a profit from this," said Dabeet.

No groans. The other kids were getting interested.

"This is not a class in interplanetary economics," said Odd. "But yes, I think so. I've heard that these refitting operations pay all the operating expenses of Fleet School."

Zhang He chimed in: "And tuition pays for the rest."

Several people laughed, since there *was* no tuition.

"You all have two hours of training—useless training, because it's all lecture, except for those of you working with the inventory software. And then the outside team will suit up and the inside team will wear your pussycat costumes."

That earned him a chuckle—Odd was always saying that this or that task was so easy that a pussycat could do it—but before Dabeet could get to Odd to ask for more information, he saw that Odd was putting the boy who had called Dabeet a mudfoot on report. Best for Dabeet to pretend he didn't know what was happening. He slid past them and headed out the door with the rest of the inside team.

Only as he saw the suited-up outside team pass the doorway to the office where Dabeet, Zhang, and a couple of others were getting an explanation of how bills of lading worked did it occur to Dabeet that if he was actually going to do what his South American masters demanded in order to keep them from harming Mother, he would have to know how to do real work while wearing a spacesuit. That was a skill that had never come up in a class at Conn. There was a space club, but they worked with telescopes and had no field trips even to the Moon. Dabeet's job, though, was to open a door and leave it open. Since that would lead to instant evacuation of atmosphere from whatever room he was in, there was no way to do that without a spacesuit. And he had no idea where the spacesuits were kept, what it took to get one, and how to put it on and use it even if he had one.

More to the point, every aperture in the Fleet School space station was electronically monitored. *Every* door—into barracks, into closets, into classrooms, into restrooms—reported its status to a central security system, which kept a record of it. How could he open a door without its being detected, closed, and then rigged with better security so it wouldn't happen again?

For that matter, every door already knew the identity of the person who approached it. They had palmpads beside them, but nobody ever had to use them because the door knew you were coming and, if you were authorized, slid open so you could pass through it. So even if Dabeet found an outside door he could mechanically open himself, the system would surely know that he was the one who was there opening it.

Dabeet wondered: How do they track us? We didn't get any implants—unless one of those injections before we launched actually put some kind of nano-ID into my body. Not likely. It's probably our clothing. Simple test: Try to get out of the barracks naked. But that's the other problem. Anything I do to defeat the door security system will keep me from leaving the barracks.

Anything I do will raise questions. Questions will get back to the commandant. And Urska Kaluza is not my friend.

If I can't do it, I can't do it. Didn't any of these security problems occur to the general or at least one of his brighter minions? Why did they think a *child* would have the ability to do anything, especially breach the exterior of a space station without its being noticed?

Dabeet could imagine the general's response. "You took the tests. They show you are very smart and resourceful. Find a way."

Whether or not Dabeet really believed Graff's story about Mother not having any genetic connection to him did not change the fact that she had spent *his* whole lifetime taking care of him, sacrificing whatever else she might have done with her life. With due candor, Dabeet recognized that he had not been an affectionate child—what reward had she received? She certainly did not deserve whatever the general would do to her if Dabeet failed to deliver on his promise.

Yet fail he would, fail he must. Children here were prisoners, not in status but in fact. Safety considerations alone would dictate that the one group that could *not* be given access to any passage into hard space was the students. Since bright kids—no, *sane* kids—would never *try* to open a door into space, there hadn't been any warnings. There weren't warnings issued about not drinking cleaning fluids or eating random medicines or sticking sharp objects into your eyes or ears, unless you counted what was printed on the containers. It was assumed that any kid who made it into Fleet School would have a healthy respect for the vacuum of space.

Dabeet imagined himself opening an outside door and then getting swept out into space with the rush of evacuating air. Nobody would be able to find him before he was long dead. Eventually, if he didn't plummet to Earth and burn up on reentry, somebody would run across his body. "Ah, a Fleet School student who was too dumb to graduate."

Rafa Ochoa deserved his loyalty. But he could not do what could not be done.

"I don't think you're paying attention, young man," said the accountant who was lecturing them.

Dabeet gave him a dead-eyed look and proceeded to continue the man's explanation from the point where he had left off to annoy Dabeet. The accountant's eyes widened. "I haven't gotten to that part yet," he said.

"While you were talking, what did we have to do but read ahead? Why give us these papers if you're just going to recite them aloud? Why not give us hands-on practice so you can *see* how well we understand?"

"We have a tried-and-true method of—"

"Of boring your trainees while preventing them from learning. Anyone who doesn't get it needs specific answers to the problems they have in working with the records. For instance, who makes sure that the items listed on the bill of lading are actually what the bill says they are?"

"People who aren't you," said the accountant.

Dabeet's guess was that the accountant had never thought of that question and had no idea of the answer. "So you look at the list, someone tells you—orally? on another list?—that all the items are here and have been sent to the right place, and—"

"I hope it's you doing the tally," said the accountant. "That would explain why they're using children for a serious job. *You* can crawl around among the shipping containers and check the numbers against the bill."

"So it's all shipping containers. The bill of lading says, 'Paper diapers for space babies,' but nobody ever opens the airtight container to make sure it isn't explosives or dehydrated dogs or military robots?"

"*Somebody* checks all of that, of course—at the time it's put into the container," said the accountant. "Then, as long as the seal is unbroken, we know it's the same stuff that was put into it in the first place."

"Unless somebody knows how to unseal and reseal those seals," said Dabeet.

"Only the proper authorities can do that."

"And there *are* no improper authorities, is that what you believe?"

The accountant was angry, and ready to utter a retort that would put Dabeet in his place, when Zhang He spoke up. "It's good to assume that everyone is faithful and law-abiding in carrying out their assignments."

The accountant seized on this seeming olive branch. "We *have* to believe that other people are reliable, or we could never board a spaceship or eat a meal or go under a surgeon's scalpel."

"And yet there are some incompetent surgeons, and some surgeons who are bribed to commit undetectable assassinations, and some surgeries that simply turn out badly despite everybody's best efforts," said Zhang He.

"We aren't doing surgery here!"

"I was merely agreeing with Dabeet that this system allows *anything* to be put aboard our space station, awaiting transfer to another vehicle, and we'd never know whether our own safety was being compromised," said Zhang He.

His tone was so mild, his expression so open and honest, that the accountant didn't show any anger at all. He took Zhang's I'm-so-helpful act at face value.

I have to learn how to do that, thought Dabeet. Instead of my you're-so-stupid attitude. Zhang really *is* helpful. And this man really *is* dim-witted. But Zhang is only helping *me,* yet convinces this git to react as if Zhang were helping *him.*

"I'm going to teach the whole lesson," said the accountant. "And you're going to listen."

"Why not let me continue the recitation, and you correct me if I get anything wrong? That way I'll have a task to keep me awake."

"They should have sent you outside," said the accountant. "Wise-asses die out there."

"And in here, too," said Dabeet. "Of boredom. Drowned in mindless rote. Do you even *remember* how to do this job? Are you capable of evaluating our hands-on work? Or do they bring in somebody else to actually teach?"

"You think you've mastered it, just because you have a photographic memory?" asked the accountant. "Show me."

"Show you what?"

"On that example bill of lading. Any errors?"

"I don't have any tallies to compare it to," said Dabeet. "But here are seven errors of spelling and punctuation." He tweaked them in the holo-display. "And here are three arithmetic mistakes that will cause the bill to be rejected by the computer. However, since the bill presumably came *out* of a computer, the real discovery here is that the computer must be seriously malfunctioning to produce an error-filled bill of lading like this."

"I think these errors were deliberately introduced," said Zhang He, "to test our ability to spot them."

"I think you're right," said Dabeet. "But what are they actually testing? Since *this* class of error *can't* come up on a computer-generated bill of lading, they're testing our ability to spot errors that will never exist. While the *real* errors remain impossible to see."

"And what real errors do you suppose those are?" asked the accountant.

"I imagine that most of the time, there aren't any errors at all. The tallyboys will spot any discrepancies. And the people who seal and unseal the containers are the only ones who can vouch for the contents, right? So examining the books and bills of lading at this level serves no purpose except proofreading the spelling of odd names, and serial numbers that spell-checkers can't catch."

Dabeet heard a very faint beep.

The accountant sighed. He left the room.

"I think his earpiece gave him an alert," said Zhang He.

"Didn't realize he had an earpiece," said Dabeet.

"I think it might only be on the side of his head that I can see."

One of the other kids said, "If you oomays have won us an early lunch, bacana. But if you've gotten us some kind of punishment, then eat kuso and die."

"I'm not from your culture," said Dabeet. "The flavor of kuso remains a mystery to me."

"'Kuso' means 'shit,'" said the boy.

"I knew what it meant," said Dabeet. You couldn't be in Fleet School for three days without getting a full vocabulary dump of all the offensive slang. "I just lacked your firsthand knowledge of how it tasted."

He gave the boy his best grin. The kind of grin, Dabeet realized, that several books he'd read described as "shit-eating." What a happy confluence of fecal references.

It was someone else who came back in. A woman. "My name is Enya Polonia. I'm the supervisor of loading and cargo here at Fleet School."

Dabeet, unintimidated, asked, "Is there really enough traffic that somebody has that as a fulltime job?"

"I'm also inventory manager for Fleet School. And one of the two purchasing agents. You're a very perceptive young man."

"I'm a child," said Dabeet. "One of several children who learn things very, very quickly. We're ready to learn the actual job that we're being trained to do, not just listen to memorized lessons and find typographical errors in bills of lading."

She studied Dabeet for a moment, then looked at the other children one by one. "It seems to me," said Enya Polonia, "that only one of these boys shares your criticisms of and amusement at our teaching methods." She indicated Zhang He. "The others wish you'd shut up."

"They wish I'd eat kuso and die," said Dabeet. "It was explicitly stated. But I'd rather spend my time learning something real, than eating the kuso that the other guy was laying down for us."

"We have two ships docked here," said Enya. "They both have to have a complete tally before they can be off-loaded. So we'll divide you into two teams. You, Dabeet, the self-assessed genius. And Zhang He, is it? A little quieter, not so confrontational, but the disciple of an arrogant git has voted for the gitty arrogance."

Zhang He smiled and nodded.

"I will give the two of you the slightly larger cargo, while the other four children will take the other ship. Your job is to tally—to make sure that every container on the bill of lading is present in the hold, and to identify any cargo that is *not* listed. In case you're tempted to check everything off and declare the job done, I should inform you that we have five items that are either listed but not present, or present but not listed. They may be all in one ship, or divided between them, or I might have lied about the total. If you try to goldbrick on this job, you *will* be caught. That's a matter of personal integrity and reliability, so it's not like failing an exam. It's failing as a human being. Am I clear?"

As Dabeet and Zhang He followed their wall bands to their ship's dock, Dabeet said, "I should be insulted that they would expect us to cheat, but for consistency's sake, how can I pretend to be surprised? My whole argument with Git Number One was about how easily corrupted their system was, so why shouldn't *they* assume that *we're* corrupt?"

"Only one correction," said Zhang He. "It was *our* argument about the corruptible system. Not just yours."

"Apologies," said Dabeet. "I'm really not used to doing anything *with* anybody, ever. I haven't had much need for the first-person plural."

"I'm not your disciple," said Zhang He. "She said that to hurt my feelings."

"Did it work?"

"No," said Zhang He. "But you're just vain enough to believe that she was right about that, so I thought it was wise to clarify the matter."

Dabeet laughed. "So you call me vain."

"Aren't you?" asked Zhang.

"Of course I am. But if you *were* my disciple, you'd find a nice way of saying it. 'Self-assured,' 'self-confident,' greeyaz like that."

"If you ever hear me using weaselly words like that instead of speaking plainly, then you can be sure they've done something to my brain."

"They're doing things to all our brains," said Dabeet. "Wasting them."

There was nothing about the passageways into the ship that in any way resembled a terrestrial dock or wharf or even an airport. They went through corridors, passed through an airlock security system into a large cargo bay, and then through another corridor and airlock into a somewhat smaller room that was filled with strapped-down shipping containers of every conceivable size.

"Here we are," said Zhang He.

"We're on another ship?" asked Dabeet.

"See the practical tie-downs to keep the cargo from shifting during ship movement?"

"When did Fleet School end and the ship begin?"

"The second airlock. That other big cargo space is where they offload this cargo once we've tallied it."

"It occurs to me that spaceships also store things they're going to consume in flight. Food. Water. Shouldn't some of these containers be open?"

"Only the tiniest ships use the same space for cargo and supplies," said Zhang He. "The crew would never let us near the ship's stores unsupervised. Their lives depend on that stuff."

"You lived your whole life on Luna," said Dabeet. "How do you know that?"

"We must have read different novels."

"We're in a race now," said Dabeet. "But I don't actually care about winning. Do you?"

"Not a whit," said Zhang He. "I care about doing a good job so they don't catch us in any mistakes."

"I also care about catching mistakes they *didn't* make deliberately in order to trap us," said Dabeet.

"If there are any."

"How should we do this?" asked Dabeet. "It makes no sense for each of us to carry a list and do separate tallies. That way we might *both* overlook something. I think we need to have one pair of eyes do all the inspections, calling out the ID of each container, while the other one checks it on the bill."

"I agree," said Zhang He. "And because you're the one with the least skill at moving through reduced-gravity environments—"

"Why aren't we floating, if—"

"Reduced-gee, not null-gee. You're sticking to the floor because our uniform boots are designed to do that. In case the anti-grav equipment piffs."

It took Dabeet a moment to realize that it was stupid of him to pretend to understand what he didn't. "I think I got the meaning from context, but . . . 'piffs'?"

"We lived in a Portuguese dome on Luna—they had room and took us in when my people fled China. So . . . separate slang. 'Piff' comes from 'pifar' which means to fall apart, fail, go blooey. English doesn't have a good enough word."

"So it does now," said Dabeet. "If I'm the worst at bouncing around in low-gee, then—"

"This hold is set to lunar gravity, so that containers stay in one orientation, but they're easier to move. They still have the same mass, so you can get crushed to death if you try to stop them by putting yourself between them and a wall. But there's *way* less friction so it's much easier to get them moving."

"We're not moving anything, though, right?"

"Just tallying."

"You grew up in lunar gravity."

"So won't it be good for you to work out how to move in that environment?"

"If I'm busy trying to control my movements, won't I be more likely to miss something?"

"I'll be keeping my eye on you when you're not actually reading labels. And I'll be right behind you. We'll *both* be making sure we don't miss anything."

It wasn't a bad system, and Dabeet learned that lunar gravity was a lot easier to work with than zero-gee in the battleroom. Though there were still tricks to it.

"Don't race up the stack so fast!" Zhang called out, and in a moment Dabeet found out why. When he reached the top container, he didn't stop. Couldn't stop. He just flew upward, hit the ceiling, and bounced back down.

"Sorry," said Zhang He. "I should have warned you sooner. Your momentum is based on your mass. Every kid on Luna learns that if you race up a ladder, you run out of ladder long before you run out of momentum."

"But there's still gravity," said Dabeet. "Even if I hadn't hit a ceiling I would have come back down, right?"

"Eventually. Somewhere," said Zhang. "Nice and easy wins the race."

It turned out that apparently all five trick items were in their ship— unless both ships had five. But Dabeet was skeptical. "Two of these 'mistakes' were those shallow containers stacked against the wall behind that massive one. We wouldn't have known they were there if we hadn't been so thorough about investigating every side of every stack."

"True," said Zhang He. "So they were messing with us."

"They were hiding it from *somebody*," said Dabeet. "The other three were obvious. Right out in the open. And we haven't finished the whole inventory, so we don't know whether we'll still find some on the list that weren't in the hold."

"So you're thinking that maybe those two hidden ones were *concealed* from lazy tallyboys, not a trap set to catch them."

"Let's finish, and then go back and look at them again."

Zhang He agreed. But before they got to the end of the cargo bay, some men came in with drags and drones and started off-loading the cargo nearest the door.

Zhang immediately bounded along the floor—a true lunar run, Dabeet realized, having seen vids of lunar movement before—and confronted them. He could hear Zhang in his earpiece: You can't take anything yet, we haven't signed off on the tally, and some adult is supposed to check our work before—

"There's always a schedule," said one of the men, "and this happens all the time. You're trainees, right? So you're being stupid-careful. We don't have time to wait for your training. You already checked everything at this end. Just keep going and we promise not to catch up with you."

Dabeet would probably have argued. Might even have followed Zhang, much more clumsily of course, to join in the discussion. But his body position marked the spot where their tally had stopped, so he waited till Zhang came back.

"You couldn't see his face from here," Zhang explained. "He sounded nice enough, but his face said for me to back off or we'd be the first cargo they off-loaded."

"So we keep at it," said Dabeet. "Because this is how the world works."

"Nothing is done by the book, ever. You just pretend not to see it."

It didn't take long to finish, but as they made their way to the door they realized that the stevedores had been moving cargo faster than the tallyboys could count it. If Dabeet and Zhang hadn't had such a head start, they would have had to count the last containers as they were being removed.

"What do you want to bet," said Zhang, "that a lot of tallies are made standing at the door, watching it all get loaded off."

"What I bet," said Dabeet, "is that a lot of tallies are made in the office without the tallyboy ever looking at the shipping containers or checking the labels."

"But not in the IF," said Zhang with a grin. "And certainly not at Fleet School."

"Where honor and integrity reign supreme."

They checked the bill of lading and found two missing items that hadn't been in the tally.

"So that's five," said Dabeet. "The three obvious extras, and the two that were missing."

"Then that's seven," said Zhang.

They were still in the loading dock, as the last items, hanging from drones, were being pulled by drags out of the ship.

"Unless the two hidden ones *were* the two on the bill that we didn't find."

"Different numbers," said Zhang He. "Different numbering *system*. Not the IF's standard codes, so . . . maybe not from a legitimate Fleet inspector?"

"Let's step out of here," said Dabeet. He didn't like the way the stevedores kept looking over at them.

"Shouldn't we look for those two shallow containers?" asked Zhang He.

"So let's say it's contraband. Either it won't be here and they'll deny ever seeing it, or it *will* be here and they'll have to put us out into space through a door in the ship," said Dabeet.

"So we leave this room and never know?" asked Zhang He.

"We know what we know," said Dabeet. "We're not doing anything that might risk our lives."

Zhang He suddenly grinned and whooped, then lifted up Dabeet's hand and slapped it.

"What are you . . ."

Dabeet saw that the stevedores had stopped their work. Zhang He turned to them and shouted. "We caught all five errors the teachers set for us! Done!"

In a moment they were in the corridors, heading back to the conference room they had started from. But as they were turning to go, Dabeet saw that the stevedores had turned back to their work without pausing for even a moment's thought. Having trainees do the tally at Fleet School might be new, but as long as the stevedores thought of them as exuberant children, they'd be in no danger.

"Good job," said Dabeet. "They've written us off as kids."

"Still wish we could have double-checked those two extras," said Zhang.

"We checked them thoroughly. We saw every side of them. There was no second label."

"We didn't see the front and back at a good angle," said Zhang. "If those two containers have disappeared, they'll never believe we found anything at all."

"If they've disappeared," said Dabeet, "then we know something corrupt is happening here. So we don't want to make a big deal of it."

"If they only left us five errors, and we found seven . . ."

"Then *they'll* make a big deal about it. See? If they don't already know about those two hidden ones, and they can't find them now, they'll want to claim we were lying, they'll say we failed the test, that we made stuff up. Do you care?"

Zhang He smiled a little. "É, I do. I don't like failing when I didn't fail."

"Neither do I. But look, Zhang, either they'll make a big deal about it or they won't. I think they won't. If nothing corrupt is going on, then either they left us seven mistakes, and we found them all, or they left us five deliberate mistakes, and a couple were genuine mistakes and they go looking for the extras and they find them and hey, we did good work."

"But if they don't find them . . ."

"If they *don't* find them, then something hinky is going on. If the brass here don't know about it, they call us in, make sure we stand by our story and that both of us agree on what we saw. Then they launch an investigation that we children of the Fleet never hear about. *Or* the brass is in on the scam, in which case they *know* we saw what we say we saw, but they never ask us about it at all, because they know that for all *we* know, they set all seven traps for us. So unless they bring it up, *we* won't think any more of it. It just disappears because, you know, we're children."

"So we don't even point out the difference in labeling."

"We act as if we think it's just one of their traps *unless* they ask about it. Then they're really investigating, and we tell everything we know, including that they were off-loaded while we were finishing our tally."

"Otherwise, we found seven mistakes when they said there'd be five, so aren't they tricky."

"And come on, Zhang. If there *is* something corrupt, how likely is it that they'd assign us to a ship carrying contraband?"

Zhang smiled. "Nobody planned this," he said. "This has all the markers of improvisation. Badly planned, ill-prepared teachers, letting us hijack their process—and the people carrying out this new program might not know anything about the smuggling operation, if there is one, and if those two containers were part of it."

"I still remember those lading numbers," said Dabeet. "But you're the only person I'm going to admit that to."

"Good idea."

"And I'm not going to do a search for those numbers to see what the system thinks they are or where they're from."

"You're not?"

"Not for a few weeks," said Dabeet.

"If you write them down, they'll find them in your desk."

"I won't type them into the desk."

"You're not going to use paper, are you?"

"I *have* those numbers, Zhang. When I have them, they don't go anywhere I don't want them to."

"You're so full of brag," said Zhang.

"If it's true, it ain't bragging."

"Yes it is. In fact, it's *especially* bragging when it's true."

"I don't forget numbers," said Dabeet. "And so I rely on that, because my brain has never let me down."

"Don't look them up, not even in a couple of weeks," said Zhang He.

"You're even more paranoid than I am."

"They monitor everything we do," said Zhang. "Even if they don't instantly recognize the numbers, they'll pass around a memo about what you looked for and what you found. You think that won't come under the gaze of the people who might feel a need to silence us?"

Dabeet had no answer for that.

"If somebody's smuggling, then that's a career-stopper if they're caught. That's Earthside jail and never going back out into space. Of course they'd kill us, especially you, once they realize that you'll never forget those numbers."

"You *won't* remember them?"

"Whether I have a good memory for numbers or not," said Zhang, "I don't know how it does me any good to say."

Dabeet smiled. "I think you're right. No search on those numbers. Not as long as I'm at Fleet School."

"Unless," said Zhang.

"Unless what?"

"Unless we both agree that there's somebody we can trust who might have the authority to investigate."

"And has protection enough that he *won't* get killed himself, along with us," added Dabeet.

"As if somebody at that level would ever talk to us!" scoffed Zhang.

"Hey, if they're *really* monitoring everywhere we go in Fleet School," said Dabeet, "what's to say they haven't recorded our whole conversation in the corridors?"

Zhang He smiled wanly. "Or simply read our lips from the security cameras."

They walked the last few strides to the conference room in silence. But Dabeet was thinking: I *do* know somebody who has the authority to investigate things, and probably wouldn't get killed if he launched an investigation.

But how can I get a message to Graff? thought Dabeet. And more to the point, how will I know that there's anything illegal to look into? If nobody is crooked and this is part of the test, then they'll all behave exactly as they would if everybody's in on a smuggling operation.

A dead end. Just like trying to get to a door so I can open it and save Mother's life. And I thought I was powerless on Earth.

9

—You told me to bring you anything concerning Dabeet Ochoa.

—What has he done this time?

—He's obsessing over the construction system inside the battleroom, but I wouldn't interrupt you for that. Look at this.

—He wrote to me. How sweet. A thank-you letter?

—What would you conclude if it were a thank-you letter?

—That he wanted something and thought that stroking me would help.

—Does it?

—If you had ever tried, you'd know.

—I suspect that if I had tried, I wouldn't be here today handing you this printout.

—True, but mostly because you'd probably be terrible at it. You've never been much of a sycophant.

—How about you?

—I was a champion at it. How do you think I got things done back when I was a junior officer? The vanity of high officers is a career-eating tiger, always needing to be fed on the blood of lesser ranks, but prone to purring when properly petted.

—You're a poet of bureaucratic maneuver, sir. How was that?

—Obvious, but also true, and therefore completely believable. The note?

—Should I leave while you read it?

—He wants a private conversation.

—Remarkable. That brings the number of people seeking a few minutes of your time to, let me see . . . everybody with ambition or a crackpot plan.

—Which of those is Dabeet, I wonder?

—He's already famous for his relentless ambition.

—Not sure yet how much of that was his upbringing and how much his innate character.

—I forgot, sir, that you're the one educated person in the world who believes in innate character.

—Most people believe in it. They just don't know what it would look like if they ever ran across its trail. So they pretend to believe that it doesn't exist.

—Just as you pretend to believe that all those tests for Fleet School you put out there actually measure something.

—They do measure something. They are excellent tests of the mental skills that we have agreed to call "intelligence."

—But you have long pretended that they also measure a child's future potential for leadership and command.

—And as long as we continue to censor any negative comments about the testing of children, we will continue to get excellent results from gathering the data from people who think their children are as clever as Andrew Wiggin.

—It brought you Dabeet.

—We've had Dabeet all along.

—What for? What do you see him for?

—Well, as Dabeet himself pointed out, we're not *quite* sure the Formic Wars are over. Now or three thousand years from now, the hive queens may suddenly burst upon the scene again, but this time much better armed and better prepared to take us on.

—I've watched Ender Wiggin and Bean and the whole jeesh, and I've seen no sign that Dabeet could ever have been fit to take part in *that*.

—I don't think Dabeet is a candidate to replace Ender Wiggin, should we ever need such a commander again, which I doubt.

—Then why do you indulge this arrogant child?

—Because someday we'll need a replacement for . . . well . . . me.

—I've read your file, sir. Your own test scores are not in the league of any of these children.

—We've known for a couple of centuries, at least, that great achievement— and yes, I know perfectly well that my achievements have changed the world—great achievement is not the result of inborn *talent*. It's about persistence. Courage. Measured self-regard.

—Dabeet has no shortage of self-regard.

—But the measurement has only just begun.

—And we have to give the boy credit for persistence.

—Relentlessness.

—But courage, now.

—All things in their time. He doesn't realize it, but he's in a dangerous place. So we'll see.

—So should I arrange your schedule to give him this meeting?

—It can't be by ansible. That would show Kaluza way too much about the importance I attach to the boy. I have to drop in for a sudden inspection, and then happen to bump into Dabeet. Kaluza will be certain that my visit is about *her*, so she'll think nothing of my incidental contacts with others.

—How urgent is this?

—Keep me within a shuttle trip of Fleet School. Earth or Luna or nearby space stations. Give no sign that I have my eye on Fleet School. Then, when I give the word, I want my arrival at Fleet School to be limited only by the physics of space travel.

—Are you going to answer the letter?

—Heavens no! And make the boy think that I care?

To Dabeet's surprise, other children began gathering with him and Zhang He in the battleroom. At first each newcomer would observe what they did. Some of them would then go off and start pulling cubes out of the walls. Some drew out only a few; others began a few small constructions and then drifted a meter or two away and looked at what they had built with apparent satisfaction.

Only a very few remained to listen as Dabeet and Zhang He talked through what they were doing. *Their* vision was to use pillar construction during an actual battle, and that demanded planning, speed, and a clear division of labor. Using the stopwatch function on their suits, each one timed the other on the basic tasks, then critiqued what they had seen.

"You're trying to move too quickly to start putting the pillars in place," Zhang He told Dabeet. "It isn't solid yet when you start moving it around, and so what you bring to the structure is still a kind of noodle, far too flexible. So you end up doing the solidifying twists again, on site, where it's much harder and more time-consuming to do it."

"So slower is faster," said Dabeet.

"That's just stupid. Slower is slower," said Zhang He. "It's *finishing* the job before you move on that will make a difference."

So Dabeet made sure each four-cube pillar was solid before he unlocked it from the wall and took it to the place where he needed to lock it in place to advance the structure.

The few kids who listened to them critiquing each other, or laying out the order of construction and assignment of jobs, didn't go off by themselves to try out this weird activity. Instead, each one in turn would come up to Dabeet or Zhang and ask if they could try.

"Of course," said Zhang He. "There's a lot of wall."

But Dabeet knew what they were really asking. "Yes," he said. "I'll watch you and tell you what you're doing wrong, till you get it right."

Soon Zhang picked up the same habit. Four kids went through this process and began to show some skill in pillar construction. In fact, it became a game, to start them all at the same moment, time them, and see who could finish first.

But one of the boys, Ignazio Cabeza, shrugged off the race. "I don't care if I'm faster or slower than *them*. I want to know if I'm improving over how fast I was before." And soon Dabeet stopped the competitive heats and turned to stopwatching each trainee in turn.

After a week of working with this new team, Zhang He teased Dabeet at lunch. "I thought you were the anti-social one, and here you brought these new guys in so deep that now *we're* hardly getting any practice time for ourselves."

"Aren't you learning from what they do?" asked Dabeet.

"We're all learning this useless set of skills, Dabeet," said Zhang He. "If this ever becomes a zero-gee Olympic event, we'll win. My point is that I don't get why you give up so much of your own time to help them."

"Because the six of us might conceivably build a structure quickly enough to be of use in an actual battle. The chance of just you and me doing it is pretty remote."

Zhang He thought about this. "So you need other people."

"I was working on structures that you and I alone could make in under two minutes. They weren't bad, depending on the configuration of stars in the room. But when these guys started actually paying attention and trying to improve, instead of just playing, I started designing more substantial structures, and pairs or trios of war machines."

"War machines," said Zhang He. "Sounds like catapults and trebuchets."

"More like turtles and pontoon bridges," said Dabeet, "but yes. War machines that can be made on the spot."

"So it's not that you suddenly became nice," said Zhang.

"I'm nice," said Dabeet, feeling a little hurt.

"You are," said Zhang. "You just kept it secret."

"It's easy to be nice when we have a purpose in common, when we're *working* together."

"If you treated classes that way, working together instead of trying to crush everybody else on every test, you'd have more friends."

"That kind of friend just distracts you from meaningful progress. If anybody really wanted help with classwork, I'd help them. But what would they do? Learn good habits of self-criticism so their work improved? So they could understand things *without* my help? Somehow I think not. Most of them just try to get the work over with so they can go off and 'have friends.'"

Zhang laughed. "So if people don't study as methodically as you do . . ."

"Then they're not interesting to me. And I'm quite sure that *I'm* not interesting to *them,* either."

That was their last private conversation at lunch, because starting the next day, the other kids on their team joined them, and they spent lunch hours planning structures and making assignments. "You have to memorize the dance you're going to do," said Dabeet. "This step, and the next step—it has to be out of your head and into your fingers and arms and feet and legs so that you move smoothly from one to the next without hesitation."

"So it's art," said Ragnar.

"Yes," said Dabeet. "Art that you do over and over again, perfectly each time. I want us to learn how to build six or seven really useful structures, and know the task so well that the moment the gate opens and reveals the configuration, I can say, 'Two flying turtles and a picket fence,' and all six of us know exactly the steps we'll do. We'll dance through it like a ballet company doing the same show for the fifteenth or fiftieth performance."

"No," said Timeon.

Everyone looked at him in startlement.

"I'm not *disagreeing,*" said Timeon, seeing the looks they gave him. "I'm just saying, it's not really like ballet. Somebody else sets up the stage for dancers. But we're making the stage."

"We're stagehands?" asked Monkey, the only girl who had joined Dabeet and Zhang.

"No," said Timeon. "I just think we're not dancing, we're *cooking*. We're like a team of chefs working in the same kitchen. We make the same dishes every single day, and they have to be exactly on time and exactly the same quality as every other time. Nothing different. And yet we have to do it from scratch, from the ingredients at hand."

"É," said Dabeet. "You're right, that's a better comparison. So next time we're in the kitchen, we'll know what's on our very small menu and we'll all be able to cook every dish."

They laughed and used forks and chopsticks to toss their food a little ways upward from their trays. "May we be better chefs than these!" Zhang chanted, as if it were an ancient Chinese prayer.

"Careful," said Ignazio. "If the cooks hear us abusing their food—"

"Then they'll know we're actually eating it," said Dabeet.

When everybody laughed, he felt himself blushing and his eyes watering. He had never said anything spontaneous that made a group of people laugh with delight.

No, he told himself honestly. I've never had real friends before. This is what it feels like. This is why people will sacrifice so many accomplishments in order to stay with their friends instead of their tasks.

But I have these friends *because* I stayed with my task. So instead of dragging each other down, we're building each other up. We're not just good friends, we're friends who do each other good.

And, for the first time, Dabeet thought of Ender Wiggin and wondered: Is this what it felt like for him to work with his famous jeesh? They weren't famous when they did their work. They were just kids who were working together, not to save the world, but to solve whatever problems the adults set before them. Did they all master their individual skills, and then Ender would deploy them, the way I intend to deploy these kids? But they could only be relied on when Ender himself had helped them train, had guided them into becoming as close to perfect as they were willing to become.

And they took correction and criticism from Ender, even before he had any official authority over them. Why?

At that moment, for the first time, Dabeet realized that he needed to learn what Ender Wiggin knew.

I'm never going to be an official leader, because Urska Kaluza hates me. But I created a task that didn't even exist, and worked hard to become good at it and to turn it into something useful for the whole army, the whole team. And by doing that, I accidentally drew these five people together.

Are they the best or worst of the players in the game? So far the leaders haven't come over and told us to stop playing around. They haven't demanded that any of my kids stop working with me. They might, of course, anytime they choose. But it's also possible that these are the worst players, so their absence isn't missed.

Some of them might be the worst players of *that* game, but they are the best players in the entire universe of the game *I'm* playing, and they're getting better with every practice. *I'm* getting better when I practice, too, no matter which of them is coaching me, because they've all learned to look for the right things. I taught them everything—Zhang and I taught them—but now they coach *us* and we all get better together.

Is this the great secret of Ender Wiggin's leadership? Do I have any chance of equaling him in a skill that I never thought I'd be able to learn—leading other kids?

Are there any records of his games and his practices when this was Battle School? Is there any chance I could watch them?

Not if I have to get Urska Kaluza's permission.

▬

"They don't allow me to go outside the ship," said Dabeet, almost as soon as he entered the office of the head of Fleet School Station security.

"Why am I hearing this sad tale?" asked Robota Smirnova. "It's not *my* policy. Pick a door, I'll let you go right out. Unless you want a spacesuit."

"I realize that you're the head of station security, not school security, so you don't normally deal with students," said Dabeet.

"You misunderstood completely. I don't deal with students. Period. Not 'normally' and not ever."

"I was never in space before I came here. I'm way behind the other students. And I'll never catch up, because Urska Kaluza hates me, for some reason."

"An excellent reason, I'm sure. What do you really imagine is going to come from meeting with me, Dabeet Ochoa?"

"It depends on how private this conversation is," said Dabeet.

"Is anyone else in the room? This is as private as it gets."

"I don't know who reports to whom," said Dabeet. "Do you report to Kaluza? Or to someone else, outside the station?"

Robota Smirnova looked at him, her half-lidded eyes showing no more interest than before. But that look went on for a long time. Five seconds. Fifteen seconds. An eternity.

Then Robota Smirnova arose from her desk and walked to the door. It opened as she approached. "Coming?" she said impatiently.

Dabeet followed her. Out into the corridor. Up one of the tubes toward the center of the station. Then into a corridor, then into a door a few steps up into the tubular wall, and this time their path was parallel to the axis of the station.

Dabeet was well-enough-oriented now to understand that they were moving from the main wheels of the station, where all the activities of Fleet School were conducted, to the next wheel up. Or over. When Dabeet helped with the cargo tally, he wasn't sure yet of the geography of the station, so he didn't know if they were now heading toward the wheel that held all the cargo, storage, mechanical, and port functions of the station, or the other direction, toward one of the unoccupied and, rumor had it, unfinished wheels on the other side.

Curious as he was, Dabeet said nothing, because this little expedition had come directly after, and therefore probably as a direct result of, his question about whom Robota Smirnova reported to.

He had meant this question *really* to mean, Is this conversation being recorded? If so, who will be able to hear the recording? I have things to say for you alone.

If she had taken it that way, then maybe she was leading him into an unwatched portion of the station. If anybody should know a place that was unrecorded, it was the head of station security.

It was the unfinished portion of the station. Not that it was stacked up with construction materials or anything—it looked every bit as clean and tidy as the occupied section. But there was a different smell, a lack of all the living smells of human occupation. And it was cold. This section was not maintained at the steady twenty-two degrees of the school. Closer to ten degrees, so as not to waste energy. They couldn't let it get lower than that, or condensation of water vapor would become a problem, and if it went to zero, the water would freeze. So . . . Dabeet had an answer to one question: At least part of the unused portion of the station was airtight, had atmosphere, and was connected to an air-heating system.

Robota Smirnova stopped at the door leading into an airlock. It took a moment for Dabeet to realize this, because there were no signs at all. But otherwise, it was identical to the personnel-sized emergency air-locks that came every fifty meters in the populated part of the station. This one also lacked the spacesuits, adult- and child-sized, that always hung in frames just outside the airlock.

"No suits," said Dabeet.

Robota's hand flashed out and covered Dabeet's mouth. Then her other hand reached around behind his neck and a little way down his uniform. She touched something. Pressed hard on something so it dug into his back. He felt a slight tingle, like the tiniest electric current. And then he didn't feel it.

"No," she said. "No suits, because nobody is authorized to be here anyway."

"So is this how you'll fulfil my request to let me go outside? Here? Without a suit?"

"This is where I can answer your question: Nobody is listening, nobody is recording, especially now that I've turned off all the tracking in your suit. And in case you think it would be fun to turn the track-ing off at any other time, I can assure you: The tracking system will not respond to your touch. Only to mine."

"*Only* yours?"

"And your barracks officer. Urska Kaluza can't even turn it off. Clear?"

"So I may speak freely?"

"If you mean, do I promise not to tell on you, absolutely not. If you're an egotistical idiot—which all accounts say that you are—I'll report whatever I want, to whoever I want. But if you have something of sub-stance to ask or to tell, then I'll do whatever a prudent and intelligent security officer would do. That's the best I *can* do, and if it isn't good enough, then back we go."

"She's Slovene and you're Russian," said Dabeet.

"She's Slovene and I have a made-up Russian name. Sort of. Robot is Czech for 'worker' and Smirnov is a Russian name meaning 'meek.' My name means 'docile worker.' It's ironic. I'm a Finn. There, now you know my dark secret. Finns have a long history of hating Russians and getting along with them anyway. But we have never cared a rat's ass about Slovenes, and vice versa. She's neither friend nor foe. Now say something worthwhile, Ochoa."

Dabeet wanted to go on with an explanation about how he wanted to know how to open doors and go outside so he could get some practice in the cold dark vacuum, but since that was all bullshit and a security officer probably had training in reading the microexpressions that betrayed even the best of liars, he closed his eyes, then reopened them and said, "I think Fleet School is being used as a base for smuggling, and I have no way of knowing how much of the current Fleet School administration is in on it."

"What if it's station security that's running the operation?" asked Robota. "What if you're telling your suspicions to the person who would be most likely to put you out this door without a suit in order to keep you silent?"

"If that were the case," said Dabeet, "I'd already be on the other side of that door with the air getting pumped out."

"So you took a flying leap and decided to trust me."

"I took a flying leap and decided that if anyone could be trusted, it was you, and if you couldn't be trusted, then we're all dead anyway."

"What an interesting theory. How would we all be dead?"

"Don't you want to hear my evidence about smuggling?"

"You were one of the tallyboys on a shipment several weeks ago. I'm betting you found several small and hidden crates that weren't on the manifest, and they were off-loaded before you could get the numbers."

"I know the numbers," said Dabeet. He repeated them, clearly articulating each number and letter.

"Interesting," said Robota. "Was this what you wanted to meet with MinCol about?"

"The Minister of Colonization is aware of some of the circumstances I now have no choice but to tell you about. I thought that if I could speak to him first, there'd be less to explain, and less chance of getting myself in deeper jeopardy. But he hasn't responded, and I thought I should report this to *somebody* before an unfortunate accident left me tetherless, slipping into the dark of space."

Robota nodded her understanding.

"Before I was accepted to Fleet School, but after I was first visited by MinCol and challenged to prepare myself for leadership rather than mere intelligence tests, I was kidnapped and taken from my school, on an airplane manned by various latinoamericanos."

"From?"

"They pretended to be from one country or another. Does it matter? Nothing they said was true, except this. They believed that some very dangerous weapons-grade bioagents were being smuggled to

Earth—presumably to some nation or faction that they opposed—and these bioagents were passing through Fleet School Station."

"So they already know. What is the point of this?"

"They didn't know. They suspected. They also suspected that the IF officers running Fleet School were all complicit."

"So why didn't they take their suspicions to MinCol?"

"For all they knew, it was this smuggling operation that funded Col-Min's ambitious program of colony ship construction."

"They couldn't trust anybody, but they trusted you."

"My mother is still on Earth. In effect, she's a hostage to guarantee my obedience."

"I know she's not your mother," said Robota.

"I know it, too," said Dabeet, "in the genetic sense. But Rafa Ochoa is the woman who raised me and educated me and was proud of my achievements and ambitious for my future. That makes her my mother, as you must already have surmised. They're waiting for my signal."

"Signal. You have some kind of enciphered message, then, to send in an email to Rafaella Ochoa?"

"Codes and ciphers reveal themselves to those who know how to detect them," said Dabeet. "It's something much simpler. If I don't respond at all, then my mother dies. If I do respond, I must send one of the following messages. 'There is no smuggling here.'"

"That's absurd," said Robota. "You could never find evidence that there was *no* trafficking."

"It's not absurd," said Dabeet. "I am who I am, and I detected the evidence of smuggling the first time I was involved in the loading and unloading process. If I had detected nothing—"

"It would mean they were cleverer than they actually are."

"There's no reason for them to be more than marginally clever, because it's an inside system. They've already bribed the man. Or in this case, the woman."

"Me?" asked Robota.

"Well, you'll tell me if *that's* true by what you do. But I didn't mean you."

"You don't like Urska."

"Nobody likes Urska," said Dabeet. "But Urska likes money. Or whatever coin she's being paid in."

"So one message is, no smuggling here."

"Which I think they wouldn't believe," said Dabeet. "The second signal is, smuggling is going on but there's no authority I can appeal to."

"You're appealing to me."

"The third signal is, I have found and reported the smuggling to the proper authorities, and it is being taken care of."

"Any more signals?"

"Three seemed enough. Especially since, as you pointed out, the first one is absurd."

"Are you going to tell me the signals? I'm guessing they involve the disposition of doors on the outside of Fleet School Station, on the side where telescopes in Latin America can detect it."

"Two doors open, with no vehicles nearby, means that there's no smuggling. Three doors open means that authority is dealing with it. One door open means that there *is* smuggling and nobody's going to take action."

Robota nodded. "How long will they remain open?"

"They assumed that I'd need to close the doors almost immediately, so to make sure they were observed, I'd wait for the next pass over Latin America and then the one after that. *Then* I open the same door or doors again."

"Very elaborate," said Robota. "And extremely stupid. Every door here is part of a system of alarms. If someone as much as touches the palmpad of any outside portal, I know it and so does my entire team."

"I told them that was likely."

"And they said?"

"They knew that I'd get caught, but they didn't care. I was supposed to invent some bullshit reason and what would they do to me, send me back to Earth? I'm a kid."

"So *they* could kidnap you and threaten to kill your mother, but they're counting on *us* to be nice?"

"I'm a child of the Fleet," said Dabeet. "They figured you weren't in the business of killing military children."

"A ruthless smuggling ring probably *is* in that business, or wouldn't think twice about entering into it."

"I didn't say that they cared about my life. Did I say that? No, they believe I care about my mother's life."

"To the point that, as an eleven-year-old, you'd sacrifice your own life to save hers."

"What son wouldn't do the same?" asked Dabeet.

"How do I know these signals mean what you say they mean?"

"Because I told you what they mean."

"And what signal do you mean to send?"

"*If* I am able to open doors without setting off alarms and getting arrested, then that means I have the cooperation of the authorities. So it's three doors."

"Three doors is ridiculous," said Robota. "You see how far apart they are. You open one, you have to run to the next, and then *another*. Then you have to close them all for the next revolution around Earth, and then open them again, then close them again."

"I'm a child of Earth. I have more stamina than spaceborn children."

"Here's what I think," said Robota. "I think three doors is a signal for *something*. Perhaps for a prearranged attack ship to seize all the ships using Fleet School Station as a port of call. Perhaps for the smugglers, who really work for your kidnappers, to know that the jig is up and to get away quick."

"You might be right, for all I know," said Dabeet. "They didn't tell me what they'd *do* about any of the signals, except that if there wasn't a signal within six months, my mother would die."

"So your little signals might be a far worse betrayal of the Fleet or of Fleet School than any petty smuggling operation."

"If they're bringing in weapons-grade space-made bioagents, then I don't see how my signals could be worse than *that*."

Robota had now positioned herself in such a way that Dabeet could not evade her close scrutiny of his face. He didn't try.

"Something that you've said is a lie," she said.

"Not as far as I know," said Dabeet. "Not *my* lie—I can't vouch for *them*."

"*Their* lie wouldn't show up in your face," said Robota.

"It defies logic," said Dabeet.

"You came to me to open these doors *for* you," said Robota, "because you knew that our security would be too good for you to accomplish it yourself."

"Yes," said Dabeet. "If *you* open them, then I don't get in trouble."

"Which means that you already planned to give the signal *before* you knew whether I'd believe you about the smuggling or betray you to the smugglers."

"I knew I had to give *some* signal to save my mother's life. Talking to you, I figured I'd either get your cooperation or not. Cooperation means three doors."

"And if I hadn't been cooperative?"

"Then we wouldn't still be having this conversation."

"And you believe that I've proven myself?" asked Robota.

"Either you have or you haven't. Either you're a traitor and a smuggler yourself, or you're a loyal officer who's prepared to cooperate with a kid who's being forced to accomplish an impossible task. If you want me to be able to concentrate on my studies up here, then you'll help me assure that my mother doesn't get killed."

"They'll probably kill her anyway."

"They might," said Dabeet. "I can't control that. If they kill her regardless of what I do, then it's on them alone. If it's because I failed her, then it's partly on me."

"What do the signals really mean?"

"That's what they told me they mean," said Dabeet. He almost added: As far as I remember. But Robota had obviously read his file, and his file would include data about the near perfection of his memory. She would never believe him if he tried to cast any doubt on the accuracy of what he claimed to remember.

"When do you have to open these doors?" asked Robota.

"O Meek Worker," said Dabeet, "I still have two months left."

"Exactly two months?"

"I have to calculate the time zones," said Dabeet.

"Oh, don't be a fool," said Robota. "You have those tables memorized."

"I have another fifty-five days, plus nine hours. But I wanted to be early."

"And if I say no?"

"Then I'll find another way to get the doors open," said Dabeet. "But this time, it will be only one door."

"I can keep opening doors randomly, in such numbers that your signal will be lost in the noise."

"What has my mother ever done to *you*?" asked Dabeet.

"I'm going to think about this," said Robota.

"You're going to consult with MinCol about this," said Dabeet. "I urge you not to."

"*You* were trying to talk to him."

"Face to face," said Dabeet. "Unrecorded. Whereas *you* will talk to him by ansible. And I doubt that Urska will miss out on anything you say by that means."

"You really are paranoid," said Robota.

"I have enemies," said Dabeet. "And now, because of what I just told you, so do you."

Robota shook her head. "You think you've got everything figured out."

"I know that I don't have *anything* figured out," said Dabeet. "I also know I'm a powerless child who needs the help of adults to get anything done. I hope that when you're through considering and consulting, you'll come down on my side. On the side of the Fleet. On the side of stopping the flow of plague agents to Earth."

"I hope to God you never run for public office," said Robota.

"I'm too intellectual. I don't have the common touch. I'd never win."

"You've given it some thought."

"Please don't think I'm boasting, Robota Smirnova, but I've given *everything* some thought."

10

—Are you who I think you are?

—If you think I'm Andrew Wiggin, governor of a yet-to-be-named colony planet, then yes.

—Ender Wiggin. What is—

—If you think I'm Ender Wiggin, heroic savior of the human species, then I can't believe we're wasting valuable ansible time.

—No, I'm just surprised, I'm—I didn't ask to talk to you. I didn't even know it was *possible* to talk to you.

—I was told you needed my advice.

—Maybe I do, I don't know. I mean, I'm in a storm of trouble but the person I asked to talk to was MinCol, and I thought *he* was the one going to pop up in the holospace.

—He's the one who told me you needed my—

—I can't believe this. *You're* the one he uses to blow me off?

—I don't know if you can call it—

—It's like I'm praying to Santiago and the saint says, not right now, Fleet boy, I'm going to send Jesus to talk to you instead. Here, make do with the Holy Mother.

—Every comparison gets worse and worse.

—Look, how secure is this?

—On my end? Officially, completely dead to outside electronics and no recording devices.

—Officially. That's the worry. When the officials who tell you it's totally private and secure are the very people you think are corrupt to the core *and* they hate you—

—So we're both taking this on trust. Trusting the untrustworthy.

—People who have no reason to keep their word.

—But MinCol thinks we should have this conversation, and since I don't know anything about you except you beat my test scores, but not *Bean's* test scores because that's not, you know, possible, then you're going to have to tell me things. Dangerous things, apparently. And live with the consequences if it isn't as secure as MinCol thinks.

—He wasn't Minister of Colonization when you knew him.

—He's MinCol *now*, and I still know him. You don't keep calling a man "colonel" when he now outranks every officer in the Fleet.

—Now, see, that answers one of my questions.

—A trivial one, I hope, since anyone with a brain could figure that out for themselves.

—Andrew. Ender. Governor Wiggin. What do I call you?

—I'm the only one you could possibly be talking to, so I'll assume that whenever you talk, you're talking to me.

—It's polite to tell the other person what to call you, when you're in the superior social position.

—Andrew. And what do I call you?

—I don't have a bunch of names and titles.

—And do you mind telling me what your unadorned name is?

—MinCol didn't tell you?

—Is it a secret? If your name gets out, do puppies somewhere die?

—Dabeet Ochoa.

—And you're at Fleet School. My alma mater with a name change. I can't really ask you what's different, because you weren't there before the change. But . . . do they still have the battleroom?

—Yes, but the win-loss record thing isn't as competitive. They tell me.

—But you know what your own record is, right?

—Zero. I haven't been in a battle yet. My team has, but I'm kind of doing my own thing. Me and a few others. Mostly Zhang He, he's this kid from Luna, he saw what I was doing and kind of made me let him help.

—What *were* you doing?

—I don't know if they had this before, but each panel of the battleroom walls can be pulled out to make up to four rigid boxes, joined or separate. You can throw them around but they get sticky and if they hit a wall or a star, they stay. You can build them into things. Pillars, pyramids. Walls. My team—if they're really mine, it's more like the team leader just ignores us— we've been learning how to build structures cooperatively, really fast, so that even though we're not fighting when the battle starts, our structures might make a difference before it's over.

—Toguro. I don't think the walls did that when I was there. If they did, nobody tried to use it, so nobody found out. I'm glad they have something to build with. So it isn't all lasers and flash suits and metaphorical death. You don't need my advice about that.

—I think MinCol wanted me to tell you about the thing that really has me scared.

—É. Speak.

—That's the thing. I'm really scared.

—Been there. I was right to be scared. People wanted me dead, it was scary, and nobody came to the rescue. *I* certainly can't come to *your* rescue from a ship that's already accelerated to a significant percentage of *c*.

—They have my mother hostage back on Earth.

—They?

—The people who threatened her. The people who kidnapped me and told me what to do or else she would die.

—MinCol knows about this?

—Do *you* ever know what MinCol knows? I wanted to tell him but he sent me to you.

—What do you have to do?

—Maybe I've already done it, so she's safe. But who thinks hostage takers will keep their word? She's still there, they're still there, so if they tell me to do something else what am I going to do?

—What did you already do that might be *it* so maybe she's safe?

—I lied to the head of security, because she was the only person with door access who didn't report to the Fleet School commandant.

—You don't trust the commandant.

—I don't trust Robota Smirnova, either—head of security—but the South Americans were going to kill my mother, so I had to trust somebody. And anyway I lied to her, said it was about the smuggling that goes on here—this place is so corrupt—but I got her to open some doors for me. It's a signal to them back on Earth. They see it when Fleet School is directly over them.

—A signal saying what.

—Saying that I can get to the doors and open them to let in a small raiding force.

—They want to raid Fleet School?

—They want to raid it *safely*. So nobody gets killed. The way I understand it, the free-for-all that's happening on Earth right now, with the Hegemon powerless, all the weak nations are afraid of getting crushed or absorbed by the strong nations. So some of them want to force the IF to get involved on Earth.

—Never happen.

—But if somebody from Earth takes the children of the Fleet hostage—

—Oh, they may come and pound the kuso out of whoever sent a raid against Fleet School. But they *can't* get involved on Earth in favor of any nation because it tears the whole fleet apart. Maybe in twenty or fifty or a hundred years, all the old loyalties will be gone, but Dabeet, get sane here. The Fleet will *never* intervene. Retaliate, but not intervene.

—I only know what they told me. Maybe that's what they actually believe. And maybe you're right, and it won't work the way they think. But they don't know that yet, so they're going to act as if they're right, né? And maybe it's all a lie, anyway, and they're really coming here to take over the smuggling operation, or shut it down, or assassinate somebody, or outrage the whole fleet by killing every kid up here. I don't know.

—So you're afraid you've jeopardized the lives of the other kids.

—Even if they don't intend to hurt anybody, as soon as you start shooting things up, people can die. Anybody might die. They might compromise life support, they might blow out a wall, entirely by accident but if it kills you, you don't care if it was on purpose.

—An excellent analysis. You did this to save your mother. One life, important to you. Unthinkable *not* to try to protect her.

—Except she's not my biological mother.

—Biological mothers lay their eggs and swim away and die. She's your primate mother, you don't let her get killed by the hyenas.

—But I'm still responsible for whatever happens when these raiders arrive.

—First, whoever set you this task may already be out of power in whatever country they thought they served. So absolutely nothing might happen. Right?

—É, but I'm not going to bet on that.

—Second, when they come, station security may drive them off right from the start. There's no way to *secretly* approach a space station at one of the Lagrange points. There's a lot of empty space but it's totally watched, so you'll get pinged even if you come in quiet and dark.

—Unless they think you're something else that's safe and expected.

—Deception might work. But if deception was a tool they were prepared to use, what would they need *you* for? They'd get in through the cargo ports, the entry bay, the docking tubes.

—So what they need me for is to take the blame. Look, this kid signaled us, he opened the door for us, he's the traitor.

—As if spaceships obeyed the commands of nine-year-olds.

—Eleven almost twelve, but that's right. They blamed *you*, though.

—They didn't court-martial me.

—You weren't allowed to go home to Earth.

—We children of the Fleet have all the universe before us, and only one place that we can't go.

—You're not a "child of the Fleet," technically speaking.

—I'm a child, and the Fleet owns me. Dabeet, what is your main concern here? To absolve yourself of any blame, no matter what happens?

—I want to keep anybody from being hurt. Not my mother, not any of the kids here, not the teachers, not even the corrupt administration.

—And not you, either.

—If possible.

—Minimize risk.

—As much as I can.

—Go to the commandant and tell her everything you've told me.

—As if she'd believe me. As if she'd even let me talk to her.

—You're talking by ansible to an unidentified person, Dabeet. That's making her insane even as we converse. You want to meet with her? Tell a teacher— tell whatever adult *is* talking to you—that the person you talked to by ansible told you to fully inform the commandant of everything you told me.

—And never tell her whom I talked to?

—She'll assume it's MinCol, and that serves your purpose better than invoking my famous but powerless name.

—What do you think will happen? She'll treble security and fight off the bad guys, then give me a medal?

—Oh, I think the likeliest thing is that she's the most corrupt person at the station, and the bad guys you met with have already bought their way past security in exchange for allowing her smuggling to continue. They'll promise not to hurt anybody, and then they'll kill her first thing. If you were those would-be raiders, wouldn't you do it that way?

—So what will I have accomplished?

—Moved responsibility to the adults, where it belongs. It's not supposed to be your job.

—But you're right, she probably won't do anything useful. Whether she believes me or not, she's probably committed to—

—You don't know what she's committed to. Maybe she *will* fight off the bad guys, and give you a medal when it's done. Or a court-martial. Does it matter, as long as the station is safe?

—Even if she fights them, there's still a good chance of kids dying or being injured as collateral damage. Or the whole station getting blown to smithereens. Same thing if she's in cahoots with them.

—I've always wondered what a cahoot is, and how many people can fit in one.

—You're playing language games?

—Why not? Our whole conversation is about games.

—No it's not. It's about a real threat to Fleet School.

—Oh, you remembered that.

—That's all I care about!

—I thought you were playing a game, Dabeet. The game of shifting the blame away from yourself, then hiding your head and hoping it all goes away.

—I told you it isn't about the blame!

—Isn't it? Because you don't seem interested in taking responsibility for what you've done, signaling people on Earth who want to attack Fleet School Station.

—I'll take responsibility! That's why I'm talking to you!

—No, no. You're still talking about blame. You'll take the *blame* when everything turns to kuso, very brave of you, but you're not taking *responsibility* for the invitation you just sent to the would-be invaders.

—I don't see what the difference is between—

—Don't you read history, Dabeet? MinCol said you were exceptionally bright and broadly educated.

—What does history have to do with—

—Weaseling politicians love to say, "I take full responsibility." "The buck stops here." But they only say that when they've been caught. When they're being blamed. What they always *mean* is, "Some underling of mine ran amok and I'll find him and lop off his head." Or his career, or whatever. They're taking charge of the *punishment,* if they can. But think about it: What does it look like when a disaster looms and somebody actually takes responsibility for it?

—You're not my teacher. Don't play Socratic games with me. Just tell me.

—If I just told you then I *would* be your teacher. *I'd* be taking responsibility for the problem you've known about and so far done nothing to prevent.

—So I'll tell Urska Kaluza what I did and—

—Put the responsibility on her. That's pretty much Plan A for dodging ultimate blame. "I told the commandant everything I knew, even though I know she's corrupt and unreliable and just as likely to flee the station on some pretext rather than try to prevent the attack."

—What do you want me to do?

—I don't *want* you to do anything. What do *you* want you to do? What kind of human being do *you* want to be?

—A living one. With a living mother. And all the kids on the station alive and safe.

—Who's responsible for making sure that happens?

—Greeyaz.

—No, not greeyaz.

—Me. I need to make that happen.

—You need to do all that you can do to make that happen. Is there *anything* you can do about your mother, that you haven't already done?

—If I work against them, then I put her in danger all over again.

—Go back into the brain-place where you keep the storage shed of historical information that you never thought you'd need. Why do you believe there's any scenario in which your mother doesn't die?

—Because I did what they said!

—Not what I was asking. Are they good and decent guys who keep their word? Or are they monsters who'll kill her just for the pleasure of showing you that they can do whatever they want and you're completely helpless to stop them?

—I don't know. I only met a couple of guys. I took them seriously but I don't know what they'll do.

—Probably neither do they, Dabeet. The bunducks you met are *not* the goons who'd be sent to kill your mother. *Those* guys might just kill her because they got sick of having to watch every move she made, so when they get the order to call off the surveillance, they may kill her just to get it out of their system. Can you do anything to control that?

—No.

—What *can* you control.

—Damn all. Nothing.

—Don't be stupid, Dabeet.

—I control what I do.

—And what you can plan and organize for others to help you with.

—Making structures in the battleroom.

—Making a team that works together to accomplish a difficult task.

—I'd have to . . .

—You'd have to tell them about betraying everybody. You'd have to trust your team *not* to spread it around what a traitor you are.

—I'm not a traitor! When I agreed to do it, I didn't know anybody at Fleet School, I only knew my mother, so I wasn't betraying the school, I was not-betraying my mother.

—But you can't possibly explain that to the others and then submit to their judgment.

—What if they hate me?

—You're an obnoxious little self-obsessed twit. What makes you think they don't already hate you?

—We talk for fifteen minutes and you think you know me?

—MinCol didn't tell me *nothing* about you, and I see that he's right. "What if they don't like me?" Come on, Dabeet. What's your real priority here. Keeping up the illusion of you as smartest kid? You did something dumb and potentially disastrous for everybody. Take responsibility. Warn them what's coming, tell them that it'll be up to the kids to organize themselves for defense of Fleet School because Urska Kaluza is corrupt and cowardly, if she turns out to be, and then watch as they appoint somebody *else*, somebody they like and trust, to be the leader of the kids' resistance. What does Dabeet Ochoa do then?

—I don't know.

—I do. Dabeet Ochoa runs off to his bunk, curls up and cries. Or he goes off to the library to do smart-guy stuff, or to plan his revenge, or—

—I'm not a baby.

—Good to hear.

—I'll . . . help them as much as they let me. I'll try to earn their trust again.

—They'll never give it to you.

—Why tell me *that*? You can't know that. Some of these guys really are my friends, you know!

—Why are they your friends? Because you were doing something, and they joined in. Why do you think they trust you? What have you done to earn it?

—I let them help. I trained them. I let them train me. We're getting really good at it.

—And you've never used it in battle. No tests. No trials. Still just a game. Building with blocks. All you did was let them help you and allow them to obey your orders.

—Why do you hate me? What have I ever done to you?

—I'm showing you a road out of the particular hell you got yourself into.

Is that what hate looks like? I've told you how to take responsibility. You do whatever you want, Mr. Test Scores.

Urska Kaluza looked bored when Dabeet came into her office. She had one elbow on her desk and leaned her head on that hand, regarding him as if she were barely able to stay awake. "You had your mysterious ansible chat," she said to him. "What do you want *now*."

"It was suggested to me that I inform you fully about a threat to this station."

She closed her eyes. "What threat could you possibly know about, that I don't? Did your ansible pal make threats?"

Dabeet really did not like her. But he was trying to train himself to pay better attention to what people actually did, as well as what they said. Urska Kaluza sounded contemptuous and looked lazy. But Dabeet thought he could detect a rigidity in her, tension that arose from what, fear? Dread? General anxiety? She believed that he had talked to Min-Col, and now he had something he'd been told to tell her. So she thinks this is some kind of danger to her career, *not* to the school. If she responds wrong, it might anger MinCol, who would either cashier her, transfer her, or . . . what, notice how resourceful she was and promote her?

Yes, thought Dabeet. She has the kind of ego that would believe somebody might want to promote her.

"Before I came up here from Earth," said Dabeet, "I was taken onto an airplane by some men with South American accents, who told me that many small nations were terrified of the chaos on Earth and wanted the International Fleet to intervene and stabilize things."

A smile flickered at the corners of her mouth.

"Yes," said Dabeet, "it *was* foolish of them to imagine that the IF would ever do any such thing, no matter the provocation."

He saw a bit of eye movement that he realized might have been the beginning of an eye roll, nipped in the bud. Her smile was not at his captors' foolishness. Her smile was at the lie she assumed Dabeet was telling. Didn't she realize that if he *were* lying, he'd at least try to come up with something halfway plausible?

"If you don't want to listen," Dabeet said, "it was only a suggestion that I should tell you."

"I'm listening," said Urska Kaluza.

"They intended to force the IF to intervene by means of a provocation involving Fleet School."

That got her attention. He could see her body grow more tense, her gaze sharper.

"They knew I was coming here. They instructed me to signal them when I got the capability to open exterior doors in the unfinished portion of this station."

"You don't have that capability," she said.

Dabeet ignored her. "If I didn't signal them that I had that capability within six months of my arrival here, they would kill my mother."

Now she did roll her eyes. "Haven't you been getting enough attention? After all your efforts to get here, are you trying to get me to send you home to Mommy?"

"The deadline was approaching, so I sent the signal."

"You did not," she said scornfully.

"I did," said Dabeet. "After all your time here with the brightest children of the Fleet, do you still think you're capable of predicting what is and is not within our ability?"

"You're a child," said Urska Kaluza. "You don't know anything."

"If that were true, that would be a pretty severe indictment of your incompetence as head of an educational institution."

"You don't know anything that the adults here do not know."

"Here's what I don't know: I don't know if the men who gave me my orders and threatened my mother are still in power in their home countries. I don't know if they actually have the ability to bring a raiding party here to Fleet School. I don't know how they expect to let me know *when* to open a door again."

She sniffed in disdain.

"I don't know if they're smart enough *not* to arm themselves with heavy projectile weapons. The shell of the station is self-sealing to a point, but too many bullets punching their way through and the nanooze on the surface won't be able to cope. They might also damage life-support equipment."

"You have no idea what you're talking about."

"So I said," Dabeet agreed. "All speculation about possibilities— which is what I was instructed to tell you. I don't know if the raiding party will be led by competent military leaders or by clowns. But most importantly, I don't know what their objective really is. The men who gave me my orders seemed to believe what they were telling me, but who knows if getting the Fleet to engage with Earth really is their goal? Nor can I even guess whether their purpose is extortion or terrorism."

A brief look of puzzlement passed across her face.

"If they take Fleet School and hold the children as hostages, then maybe they hope the IF will take steps to mollify them. But if the goal is to *make* the IF get involved on Earth, their most effective plan might be to kill everybody in the station and then shuttle on back to Earth. Or the Moon. Or wherever they've arranged to escape."

"You do understand," said Urska Kaluza coldly, "that by saying what you just said about terrorism, I am obligated to report this conversation, sending a full transcript to the authorities, because of the very strong likelihood that there *is* a terrorist threat, not from some mysterious cabal on Earth, but from you and your block-building friends."

"By all means pass this recording on up the chain. Make sure to include a complete report on the smuggling operations going on here, probably with your collusion. If you alter the recording by removing that reference, they'll detect it and it will still trigger an investigation. I could not be happier than to have you pass along this conversation."

"If only you *were* as smart as you think you are."

"If I were smart," said Dabeet, "I would have figured out a way to deal with this, keeping my mother alive and removing any threat to the school. But I'm not smart enough to do that, so I'm asking for your help."

"You're asking me to run around and do stupid, dangerous, time-wasting things, while you and your friends laugh about how you got me to jump through hoops."

"So you don't intend to take any extra precautions," said Dabeet.

"We already have a couple of boats doing defensive patrols. If there's any threat, I'll know of it in plenty of time."

"Just what the Formic Queen probably announced to all her soldiers, just before Mazer Rackham blew her to smithereens."

"What are you talking about?"

"The Second Formic War," said Dabeet. "It's called history. You should try it."

"Your insolence has no boundary, does it," she observed. "I'll tell you what steps I'm going to take. I'm going to put you under arrest and keep you in close, supervised confinement. That way you can't open any doors for them, and we'll be safe."

"I'm a child," said Dabeet. "You can't—"

"Psychotherapeutic confinement," said Urska Kaluza. "So I can."

"If my mother dies because of this arbitrary, ego-motivated action—"

"Dabeet, you don't seem to understand quite how stupid you are," she said. "Even if you actually believe the kuso you've been telling me, you gave me plenty of reason to make sure you never see anyone again."

"Empty threats," said Dabeet.

"I'm not going to let you risk everything I—"

"You know that I have the close interest and attention of people who are in a position to force you to produce me, alive and well, at any time."

She opened her mouth to answer. Thought better of it.

"So I'll be returning to my barracks and to my regular schoolwork and training," said Dabeet. "Nothing will change, unless you take action to resist any attempt to raid the school. If you do nothing, then that's your call. I've given you fair warning, a chance to do your duty—just in case some part of you still cares about that."

"For a powerless child, you have an obnoxious mouth."

"I'm offering you a chance to do the right thing."

"You're offering me a chance to humiliate myself."

"What if I'm telling the truth?"

"Oh, I think you believe everything you said. I just don't think you understand anything about what adults intend to do or even *can* do. Children's brains are simply incapable of grasping the adult world. If you tell other children or teachers the absurd story you just told me, I *will* put you in therapeutic confinement, because that will discredit your story completely. As long as you remain silent about these supposed threats, I'll leave you alone. Oh, and if you try to open any airlock doors, then all bets are off. Do you understand?"

"Probably not," said Dabeet, "since I have an incapable mind. But I'll do my best."

Dabeet walked to the door of her office.

"I haven't dismissed you," she said.

He would have ignored her, but the door didn't open at his approach. She had to trigger it, so he would have to wait. He turned and faced her.

"You will never have access to the ansible again, Dabeet. I've learned my lesson."

Somehow Dabeet did not laugh, or even let his face show a smile.

"Dismissed," said Urska Kaluza.

He heard the door open behind him. He turned and left.

—

He had told her everything—including the fact that he suspected her of being involved in the smuggling. At first he thought that he had failed completely, but no, he realized, I said those things and I'm *not* in custody. I'm not outside the station without a suit in a tragic accident. I was able to talk her to a standstill. That isn't failure.

I gave her a chance to do the right thing.

She didn't believe me, but I wouldn't believe me, either. Surprising facts rarely pass the plausibility test. If it hasn't happened before, it's hard to believe it can happen at all. Urska Kaluza didn't reject my story because she's stupid or evil. She rejected it because she's a liar herself, and therefore she assumes other people are lying.

In class, Dabeet was attentive—more so than for the past few weeks. He actually enjoyed class, and not just because he could show off what he learned by reading ahead. He realized that this was what Ender Wiggin had offered him—by telling an adult, it was no longer his responsibility.

Only she hadn't believed him, so she would do nothing, and that meant it was *still* his responsibility. Thanks, Andrew Wiggin.

In the battleroom, Dabeet's team built a few quick structures—familiar ones, nothing new, just to warm up. The one Zhang called "bridges," a series of arches rising from the four corners of the gate. The one Timeon called "walls," a series of three-by-three platforms that provided cover and hiding places.

"What's this for?" asked Bartolomeo Ja, the team leader; the commander of the army.

Dabeet looked at his team, who were still securing the links that held the whole structure together.

"Does it *have* a purpose?" Monkey asked Dabeet.

"If the enemy assaults us in an open room, this gives us cover. Behind this, you can move unobserved, but whenever you want you can come to dozens of different protected places from which to shoot."

"So, purely defensive," said Ja.

Dabeet didn't like the dismissive way he said that. Of course, it *was* purely defensive, rooted to the wall. But Dabeet didn't like being disdained.

"It's perfect for an open-room offense," he said.

Ja turned to face him. After Urska Kaluza's scornful responses, Dabeet appreciated the fact that Ja seemed ready to listen.

Dabeet turned to his squad and said, "Can we detach it from the wall and have it hold its integrity?"

"Who knows?" said Ignazio. "Let's find out."

Dabeet's first impulse was to stick with Ja and show him all the clever things they were doing. But no. Ja needed to hear it from people he knew and liked. "Zhang?" said Dabeet. "While we detach it, why don't you show Barto how it works."

"I know how the boxes work," said Ja.

"Not the boxes," said Zhang He. "The whole structure."

In about a minute, they were slowly propelling the jumbled structure across the battleroom. "How much mass?" asked Ja. "Can I propel myself backward?"

"It'll speed up the wall," said Zhang He. "You know, equal and opposite reaction."

"It'll flex the wall, too," said Ragnar. "Let's see how much flexion the connections can take."

Ja pushed off from the mobile wall, straight back toward the gate. He bounced off at an angle, getting past the edge of the structure. Then he coasted a side wall to get a view of the whole thing from the other side.

"Can't see a single person," he called out.

"If we let it hit the enemy's wall," said Dabeet, "it might stick and completely block their gate."

"The teachers wouldn't allow that," called Ja. "But come on, people, get to the enemy wall and prepare to catch this thing and push it back."

It was a ragged attempt, and there was a lot more testing of flexion. One corner of the wall detached. But Dabeet's people quickly put it back together and now they went back across the battleroom in the other direction, with the back of the wall now leading. It didn't matter. It was just as effective as a barrier to sight and weaponry.

"How long did it take you to put this together?" asked Ja, after he assigned his toons to spread out and find good protected vantage points for shooting at an imaginary enemy.

"With just the six of us," said Dabeet, "almost four minutes."

"Too long," said Ja. "In an empty room they'd slide the walls and be on you before you had it half built."

"But when there are only a couple of three-by-threes, those provide cover. They can protect us while we build."

"Or you can build it faster," suggested Ja.

"We're already pretty damn fast," said Monkey.

"What if you had a dozen builders?" asked Ja.

"They'd just get in our way," said Ignazio. "They haven't practiced."

"What if they practiced?" asked Ja.

"Then they'd get better," said Dabeet. "I don't know if it would cut the time in half. But we can get it under three, I bet."

"Maybe enough," said Ja. "What about a smaller wall?"

"It'll hide fewer people," said Dabeet.

"Look how many places aren't getting used with the whole army on this wall," said Ja. "Break it in half, let's see how many can use it."

They reached the home wall before Dabeet's squad had it broken into two parts. Now the structure made no sense, visually—but the whole army was able to swarm through it and find protected vantage points.

"So now," Ja asked Dabeet, "with half the wall, half the time?"

"Less than half," said Dabeet, "because we'll never anchor this to the floor when we start it."

"Midair assembly?" asked Ignazio skeptically.

"Let's try it in battle," said Ja. "Next time we have a clear battleroom."

"You want us to train more soldiers, then?" asked Zhang He.

"No," said Ja. "Build half a wall and float it, just the six of you."

"While some soldiers lay down protective fire?" asked Dabeet.

"We'll see how it goes," said Ja. "We have to respond to what the enemy does, and that may force us to use a different tactic. But if possible, yes, protective fire, we won't let them stop you."

For the first time, Dabeet began to attend battles. He still hovered near the home gate, observing, because his skills, though vastly better, were still not good enough for him to take part in a battle that counted on the stats. But he knew he had to be able to function in the midst of fighting and flying, not letting anything distract him.

After the first battle, Dabeet told his squad, "Since we're floating it anyway, we start with the outermost units, all right? Work our way back. That way we don't spend the whole time exposed to enemy fire, we can hide behind the first units while we build backward."

It caused them a lot of confusion for about fifteen minutes, but they were smart and, without Dabeet having to take over and tell everybody what to do, they worked it out. Now they built from the outside in, and they were down to two minutes by the third day.

11

From the landing parties that are establishing colonies on Formic worlds, we have learned that microbiota from two completely isolated genetic traditions are so incompatible that we are likely to have little to fear from microparasitic life-forms on planets we discover and explore. This does not mean we can shirk the precautionary measures etc. etc.

It stands to reason that the native flora and fauna of worlds we discover and explore also have little to fear from the microparasites we bring with us. The *War of the Worlds* scenario cannot take place. We, as invaders (although our hearts are pure), will not be overwhelmed by the local version of the common cold. Nor will we wipe out any species with smallpox.

Invasive species of macrofauna and macroflora are far more likely. Barnacles will not cling to our spaceships to overwhelm one world with another world's fauna, but because of the incompatibility of evolutionary traditions, we will have no recourse, when establishing colonies, but to introduce Earthborn species in new worlds.

As responsible explorers, we aspire to non-interference, but our very presence is potentially overwhelming on any life-bearing world, which we assume will be all rocky planets in the goldilocks zone. A casual visit, suited up, should do no harm, but even a brief colonial experiment of, say, five years, may provide opportunistic Terran species a chance to become invasive and outcompete the local life.

However, the problem may be self-curing. If herbivores get loose that can only eat gaiagenic vegetation, then they can only live where that vegetation continues to thrive. Therefore the local flora will be safe on any isolated continents. If carnivores get loose, they can only live on gaiagenic herbivores and each other. It can be assumed that any problems we cause will be localized or self-curing.

The only exception I foresee is the statistically most-invasive mammal species, the hyperpredator and hypercarnivore we call "housecat." *Felis catus* quickly returns to a wild foraging habit when cut off from human subsidies—if indeed it ever left that state.

Housecats have invaded every ecosystem that humans have entered, brought with us because of our fantasy that they love us and the reality that we love them. Having no loyalty except to food, housecats will inevitably stray into the wild.

They will always pose a danger to every small animal, bird, or fish that we try to establish, and it is also not far-fetched to imagine that if any creature can acquire the ability to make some use of the proteins found in alien life-forms, it will be the housecat, which kills without hunger, so that it would keep experimenting with every available ambulatory life-form until it found those whose proteins it could digest.

In addition, it seems highly unlikely that we could find a population of humans completely devoid of the toxoplasmosis parasite. Since this dangerous parasite can only complete its lifecycle in cats, banning the transportation of cats to any new world would also, within a generation, eliminate the oocytes of toxoplasmosis.

The ban on cats should be extended to every interstellar craft, because unplanned or accidental landings could inadvertently provide onboard pet cats an opportunity to get free and begin their astonishingly prolific breeding pattern.

This ban should not be extended to dogs, which, since we co-evolved with them for millennia, are useful companions and servants. Dogs are better at controlling seed-eating rodents and take their responsibilities far more seriously than cats, and humans would do the work of exploration and colonization far better and more safely with dogs. After all, we and our dogs shaped each other's bodies and minds for at least fifteen thousand years and quite possibly a hundred thousand. Dogs are irreplaceable as human companions. Their presence on spaceships should be encouraged. There is zero chance of dogs thriving on their own well enough and long enough to acclimatize themselves to become invasive outside the bounds of human settlement, or to acquire the ability to digest alien amino acids.

Cats do no useful work, unless we account it useful to provide a blank face for their owners to project emotions onto. They explore willingly, but take very inconsistent and unreliable notes. Leave them and their toxoplasmotic oocytes in the star system they've already infested.

From "Keep Cats Out Of Space," an in-class opinion essay by Dabeet Ochoa, for exogeography class.

It turned out to be surprisingly easy for the South Americans to get a message to Dabeet. It came in the form of a letter from his mother. The letter was genuine enough; it could not have been faked, since it was in her handwriting and it sparkled with her wit, slipped back and forth between Spanish and English in exactly her idiosyncratic way, and contained just enough pleading for him to write more and better letters that it was as if she sat in the room with him.

She had sat in some room with someone, for sure, because she included a word-search puzzle that "our old friend" had included for him. "It's especially challenging, he says, because it contains both Spanish and English. I told him, Why not Latin? Why not Russian? You didn't speak them here, but I imagine you could pick them up in no time, if there was a need."

Word searches were boring to Dabeet; he had outgrown them by age four. All they were was a series of treasure hunts with singularly unrewarding treasures. You search among seemingly random letters till you find the words that were laid in backward and forward, up and down, and diagonally. He had long since learned that all you do is move your eye back and forth, up and down on every line, finding words. Like plowing a field or mowing a lawn—not that Dabeet had ever done either task.

Only there weren't any words on any of the lines in any language Dabeet knew. Just a bunch of letters.

"Our old friend" meant nothing to Dabeet—they had no "old friend" unless she meant MinCol himself, which was highly unlikely, since she wouldn't have concealed his name, she would have used it openly, as a brag. So she might—*must*—be referring to the South Americans. As far as Dabeet knew, she hadn't met them when he left for Fleet School, but if they made themselves known to her, it would be in the guise of friends of Dabeet's. Unless they openly told her that she was their hostage for Dabeet's good behavior. It's not as if they were subtle men.

Dabeet received the letter at bedtime, when he was putting away his desk; it was a physical, paper letter in his mother's own hand, which meant that it had waited on Earth until a shuttle could take it on its regular rounds, probably first to the Moon and then from the Moon to Fleet School. The most important and least important messages traveled that way. But in this case, Dabeet assumed that the South Americans wanted it that way—probably so he would see Mother's handwriting on the letter. The puzzle, though, was a computer printout.

Dabeet tried reading something into every line in every direction but before long he had to conclude that this was a cipher. It couldn't be a code, because he had been given no key; they must expect him to realize there was a letter-for-letter cipher and figure it out on his own.

They knew he was smart, so they wouldn't need to make it so obvious that some teacher or military censor could see that it was anything but a puzzle. If they looked closely, they'd see that there were no recognizable words and so they might get suspicious. But of course any adult at Fleet School who saw a puzzle that had been sent by a mother to her child wouldn't bother trying to solve it.

It really was a puzzle. A different kind of word search. It's just that all the letters had been switched out with other letters.

If it was language, then he should be able to pick up patterns that looked like words and sentences. There were no spaces, of course, but there should be letters that were particularly common in each language, and he could make guesses.

How intelligent was the creator of this cipher? The goal wasn't to make it uncrackable, because any cipher could be broken by brute-force computing. The goal was to hide the fact that it was a ciphered message, but then make it easy to crack so there was no chance that Dabeet would miss any part of the message.

Whatever Dabeet did, he would need to rely on the power of his desk to help him. He scanned the puzzle into his desk and told the desk to treat the puzzle as individual letters, but keep the shape of the puzzle and not "correct" anything that looked like it was trying to be a word.

How would Dabeet himself create a bilingual cipher to a kid without a key?

He would choose a non-obvious direction and run the entire message consistently in that direction, maybe from bottom to top, right to left. Or perhaps one of the diagonals. They might use boustrophedon inscription, putting one line right to left, the next line left to right, as you would plow a field, back and forth in alternating directions.

Then there was the problem of part of the message being in Spanish, part in English—if that's what Mother's letter meant. Dabeet looked up character frequency in both languages and found that they were quite different. *E* led the way in both languages, but in Spanish the frequency went down from there as *E, A, O, S, N, R, I, L, D, T, U.* In English, it was *E, T, A, I, N, O, S, H, R, D, L, U.*

In a message this short, though, there was no guarantee that the frequency of letters would conform to the norms for the whole of literature.

And Dabeet's source on Spanish separated regular vowels and consonants from those with accent and tilde marks. The cipher couldn't use separate characters to stand for *N* and *Ñ*, along with two characters for every vowel, because they'd run out of letters in the English alphabet. So "señor" would be enciphered as "senor" and "aquí" as "aqui." Easy enough. Most Hispanics in America had long since stopped bothering with accent marks online, because it was such a bother on keyboards designed for American English.

The rule with simple ciphers was, of course, to first find the *E*s. A simple count of each character indicated two candidates for *E*. Letters *D* and *U* were fairly evenly matched in the cipher, with a slight edge for *U*. Dabeet then scanned the lines and columns and diagonals to see which direction looked more plausible.

None of them looked right. Whether he used *D* or *U*, there were formations that were impossible in both languages. Spanish and English both allow two *E*s in a row, but neither language ever allowed three. Neither language allowed *any* letter to be tripled. Yet in every direction, one letter or another was tripled. There was no direction in which he could scan the lines and detect a wordlike pattern.

Why would they make it so needlessly hard? He even tried spiraling in toward the center and still found impossible combinations.

Bleary-eyed and frustrated, Dabeet set down his desk and pressed the heels of his palms into his eyes. What if the message was urgent? What if they were already on the way and the message was "open the doors now"?

Their own fault if they were too dumb to make the cipher breakable.

"How long have you been awake?"

Dabeet opened his eyes. Bartolomeo Ja was standing there by his bunk. The other kids were still asleep, but commanders were always wakened fifteen minutes before regular soldiers.

"A while," said Dabeet. "Running a problem that was keeping me awake."

"You look bleary-eyed and ragged," said Ja. "How stupid are you?"

At first Dabeet took that to be a mean-spirited criticism, but his momentary anger was quickly defused.

"That came out wrong," said Ja. "What I mean is, how sleep-deprived are you? We have a battle, and if the conditions are right I want to battle-test your wall. But not if you're sleepy and slow."

"Doesn't matter if I am," said Dabeet. "The others will be sharp enough, and if I'm a little slow it won't matter because we can continue assembling it in flight."

"I'll take your word for it. *My* experience is that a tired soldier is a dead soldier."

"If I die, I die," said Dabeet.

"I know, it's only a game," said Ja as he walked away.

The battleroom had stars in the eight corners but nothing right up the middle. Dabeet's original wall would have had trouble forming up between those stars, but the scaled-down version was easy to maneuver. Dabeet was a little clumsier than usual, but they had practiced the assembly so much that he could almost do his part in his sleep—which is pretty much what he did.

Ja formed the rest of the army behind the wall before it was finished. They had practiced doing that, making sure not to get in the way of the builders, who had to mine the fixed wall in order to get the building blocks of the mobile wall. The structure was in motion half-built, but it moved slowly enough that Dabeet's newly expanded team could still pick up the last blocks, build them into three-by-three panels, and put them in place.

"Fire through the breaks," Ja reminded them. "Use your cover. But whatever you do, don't let them get edge-on to the wall, or we've got no place to hide."

They knew it, of course they knew it, but this was the first real test in a game, and if this whole structure-building thing was to get a fair test, they couldn't make mistakes.

They made mistakes, because *Homo sapiens* is not always sapient. But they adapted and recovered from their mistakes, and the battle ended with an overwhelming victory before the mobile wall was halfway across the battleroom. It was Odd Oddson who emerged from the teacher door and congratulated them, talking over the objections from the opponents, whose recriminations included words like "cheat" and "unfair" and "not what we trained for."

Oddson was amused by that last one. "The enemy that beats you is *always* the one who does something you didn't train for."

"*We* didn't get any building blocks!" one of them said.

Which led Oddson to invite Ja to demonstrate how the blocks were pulled out of the wall. Ja admitted he had never done it himself, so he called for the block squad to come demonstrate. Both armies gathered around to watch—including Dabeet, who was so exhausted by now that he was afraid he'd make hash of the demonstration.

Without saying anything, without delegating, he by default turned it over to Zhang He, who did an excellent job of showing how the wall panels could be pulled out to four blocks high, or separated into four individual blocks. Clear explanations, in very few words, as if he had written out the instructions and rehearsed them. Maybe he had.

They took another fifteen minutes in the battleroom for everybody to try pulling out blocks. Dabeet understood why Oddson allowed it—now that building something with blocks had won a decisive victory, every army would have to develop what amounted to a construction brigade.

While the others were playing, Zhang He came over to Dabeet. "What was *that* about?" he asked, looking annoyed.

Dabeet didn't know what he was talking about.

"Making me do the demonstration. People will think I'm the expert."

"You're as expert as I am. And today, much more expert."

"What do you mean, today?"

"I didn't sleep last night."

Zhang regarded him for a few moments. "Ja said you woke up early. Do you mean you never slept?"

"Working on a problem, time got away from me."

"Then things went pretty well today. I thought you were just testing us by not giving us any instructions or supervising us in any way."

"I don't usually, now that everybody knows what they're doing."

"But you're usually *watching,* so you can call out if one person's lagging or somebody else is doing careless work."

"Today it was all I could do to watch my own work and get it done."

Zhang He squinted at him. "What are you lying about?"

"Not lying."

That wasn't good enough for Zhang.

"Don't give me that San Tomás the Skeptic look," said Dabeet. "What's there to lie about?"

Zhang He shook his head. "I shouldn't have said 'lie.' What I meant was, you're hiding something, and I think it has to do with the problem you were working on all night. You never have to work even fifteen minutes on any problem from class."

"It wasn't from class."

"What, then? It's not like you have a day job with a mean boss."

I kind of do, thought Dabeet. "It's a puzzle my mother sent me."

Zhang He looked at him even more skeptically. Dabeet started moving toward the practice door as gravity faded back in, drawing them down to the floor.

"What, a mother can't send her son puzzles?" asked Dabeet.

"I didn't know you had a mother," said Zhang.

"Everybody does. Or did."

"You never talk about her."

"Nobody talks about their families."

"Everybody talks about their families," said Zhang. "With their friends."

And there it was, the real difference between them. Zhang He had friends. He had been here longer than Dabeet—everybody had—but Dabeet was nearly six months into his time at Fleet School and Zhang He was, as far as he could tell, his only friend.

Zhang He didn't say anything, because what could he say? He started to open his mouth, possibly preparing to apologize for saying such an insensitive thing, but Dabeet waved off his remark. "Can't be offensive if it's true," he said. "I'm not a friendable guy."

Zhang He gave the cruelest response: He didn't disagree. Mercifully, he changed the subject. "That puzzle. You said it was a puzzle?"

"Yes."

"Can I try it?"

Dabeet was nonplussed. On the one hand, whatever the South Americans were doing, it would become obvious soon enough, if they really came up here. Why keep it such an amazing dark secret? On the other hand, what if Zhang He *did* figure it out? Then the puzzle would be solved and Dabeet could read the message. Zhang He could read it, too. So was Dabeet ready for that?

Why was Dabeet worrying about this? If Dabeet couldn't read it, how could Zhang He? Either they were friends or they weren't. Trust or don't trust, there's no half-trust.

"Sure," said Dabeet.

Zhang He's mouth twisted into a wry little smile. "Took a few moments to decide. Good cop bad cop? Good angel bad devil?"

"I'm not used to discussing my business with anybody."

"Except whoever you get ansible calls from."

Of course the rumors had spread through the school. Kids didn't get use of the ansible unless somebody in their close family died, and usually not even then. There was an ethos of self-sufficiency; it was embarrassing to admit you needed your family. But Dabeet had an ansible call from somebody in the Fleet. Somebody so important that Urska Kaluza herself had been excluded from the conversation.

"Get yourself an ansible, I'll talk to you, too," said Dabeet.

Zhang He didn't laugh, he just sighed and walked through the barracks door ahead of Dabeet.

"Come on, that was funny," said Dabeet.

"To somebody, maybe," said Zhang He. "Maybe to everybody who knows who you were talking to."

"I was talking to Ender Wiggin," said Dabeet, impulsively.

"Still not funny," said Zhang He. "But I also don't care. So let me see the puzzle."

They went to Dabeet's bunk and Dabeet extracted the word-search puzzle from his locker. Zhang He looked it over. "There aren't any words here."

"That's why the puzzle took me all night."

Zhang He handed it back. "Is it in some weird language?"

"It's in English and Spanish, maybe half and half. And it's also in cipher."

Zhang He raised his eyebrows. "All right, that makes it a challenge."

Dabeet told him about letter frequency in both languages, and scanning for repetitions of *E*. "I also don't know if it's consistently in rows or columns or diagonals. Maybe the decoded puzzle really *is* a word search, so I have to find individual words and only then arrange them in order."

"Doesn't seem likely," said Zhang He. "That is, if anybody cares whether you ever read the message correctly. English is so positional that it's hard to come up with a statement of any length that doesn't lose all meaning if the words are jumbled, or mean the opposite of what's intended if you place one word out of order."

"That's why I looked for letter patterns only in straight lines. I kept running into triples."

"Oh. That's not entirely impossible, of course, since there aren't any spaces, so you could have a double letter followed by the same letter. 'Climb a tree, either the oak or the elm.' 'Tree' followed by 'either.'"

"That works in English. But the triples are all over, and I don't think that can happen in Spanish. The only doubled letter is *LL*. The *N* used to have a double, but when they palatalized it, the second *N* became the tilde."

"Adventures in etymology," said Zhang He.

Dabeet didn't like the sarcastic tone, but when it came to friends, beggars couldn't be choosers. "I just thought they might have replaced *Ñ* with double *NN*, for purposes of the puzzle."

"They've replaced everything with everything else," said Zhang He. "I haven't done a cipher since I was little. They get tedious too fast."

"Meaning you were pretty good at it, but when you deciphered them the messages weren't worth the work."

"'A stitch in time saves nine.'"

"'All's well that ends well,'" said Dabeet. "I only wish that were true."

"Who's the message from, really?" asked Zhang He.

"I told you, my—"

"Mother, right, only you wouldn't stay up all night deciphering a puzzle that probably says 'big loves and hugs' in two languages."

Dabeet closed his eyes. *Now* he was so tired he could drop off to sleep in a moment if he didn't work at staying awake. He was not going to make a good decision here. Decisions made on the edge of sleep were usually a mistake. Did that mean that he should think of what he really thought he should do, and then do the opposite?

"It might be a life and death message," Dabeet said, not knowing whether he was doing what he thought he ought to, or the opposite, or just being impulsive.

"Is that American exaggeration, or real?"

"I'm not all that American," said Dabeet. "I'm from the barrio."

Zhang He shrugged. "I'm a Chinese Christian, which means I'm not Chinese, I'm not Lunar, most other Christians wouldn't think me Christian, so I'm not anything."

"I'm saying it's life and death."

"Whose?" asked Zhang He.

"My mother's. When it was announced that I was accepted to Fleet School, it was in the papers and Mother's friends spread it through our church group. So then I'm at school, and out of the blue—literally— come these guys in uniform, pretend they're from my father in the Fleet, and in a minute I'm aboard a private airplane heading south by south-southeast over the Caribbean. Kidnapped."

Zhang He looked at Dabeet intently. Dabeet knew that he was deciding whether to believe this story or not.

"I'm not important, we don't have any money. What we had was me going to Fleet School, and that's what they wanted. I'm supposed to do something up here, or they'll hurt my mother."

"And by 'hurt' you mean 'kill.'"

"I don't mean anything. *They* mean it. And yes, probably that's what they mean. The idea is that if I don't follow their orders . . ."

"Orders to do what?" Zhang He asked.

"It's a puzzlement," said Dabeet.

It took Zhang a moment to realize that Dabeet was referring back to the enciphered message. "É, I can see how that might give you a sense of urgency about deciphering it. Only I wonder if they'd be happy to know that you told *me* about them. The point of a cipher is to keep the wrong people from reading it."   ·

"They'll never know," said Dabeet.

"Come on, if they're planning to do something inside Fleet School, they probably have spies up here," said Zhang.

Dabeet couldn't tell if Zhang was joking. "They do," he finally said, "and it's me."

"Oh," said Zhang. "But nothing is *happening* here. It's a school."

"Hence the need for a message."

Zhang looked at it again. "It doesn't look like it's divided into two languages."

"It wouldn't, it's enciphered."

"No, they'd look different. Languages look like themselves, even if they're in cipher."

"They do when you can see where the words divide," said Dabeet. "Or even which direction the lines run. Up and down? Diagonal? Boustrophedon? Maybe I can do it with a brute-strength attack, taking each possible orientation in turn, and trying to make sense of it letter by letter, guessing Spanish or English. The puzzle isn't all that long. If I work on nothing else, by my rough guess I could solve it in about three weeks. I just don't know if I have three weeks. If my mother has three weeks."

"It came on paper," said Zhang, "so it can't be *too* urgent."

"The shuttle schedules are known. They could have sent it to arrive just in time for whatever it is they want me to do."

"Have you told the commandant about this?" asked Zhang He.

Dabeet noticed that when Zhang was thinking of her as someone who might help solve Dabeet's problem, he called her by her title rather than "Urska Kaluza," as the students mostly did when she wasn't present.

"Not about the message, but about my mother's jeopardy, yes," said Dabeet. "She didn't believe me. Or pretended not to. For all I know, she's in collusion with the smugglers *and* the terrorists, and they only need me so they'll have a fall guy."

"Fall guy?"

"Someone they can blame no matter how it turns out."

"You said 'terrorists.' Kidnapping, spying, but . . . how are they terrorists?"

He wasn't ready to tell Zhang that they wanted Dabeet to open the outside door of Fleet School Station to their raiding party. So Dabeet only shook his head. "They're terrorizing me."

"Your brute-force method only works if the message is arranged the way you're guessing—all in one orientation, with the Spanish and English parts separated like the Rosetta stone."

"Rosetta stone. Do you think it's possible the two languages both say the same thing?"

"You didn't listen to me," said Zhang He. "They're not trying to make this too hard, but you have the reputation of being the smartest kid in the world. They expect you to be able to solve it quickly by getting some great insight. But to do that, there has to be an insight to be found. A trick that opens it all up."

"That's exactly what I need," said Dabeet. "A trick that solves it all! You don't happen to *have* one, do you?"

"Getting snotty with me?" asked Zhang He. "You're such an emossen dollback."

"I'm not trying to be snotty with *you*. I just—my mother's life depends on my cracking this, and you're right, I have this stupid reputation to live up to, and what if I can't? Passing tests designed by professional educators doesn't show whether I can actually *think*."

"Too bad everybody thinks those tests measure intelligence," said Zhang.

"Now who's being snotty?" asked Dabeet.

"Whose fault is it that you *have* that reputation?"

"Excuse me for doing my best on the examinations so I could win the prize of being up here with *you*."

"It's not your test scores that cause you problems, Dabeet, it's the fact that you can't shut up about them."

"I'm not the one who spread it all over Fleet School that I . . ." But Dabeet couldn't finish that, because yes, he *had* made sure to drop modest references to his higher-than-Ender test scores, not daily, but now and then, in a self-deprecating way, saying things like, "If those tests mean anything," and, "All I can do is try to live up to those tests." What a stupid lump of charach he had been. And it was compounded by the fact that Mother wouldn't shut up about it back in the barrio, at Conn. And then he made it worse by it by sending emails in her name to everybody with a shred of authority in the IF. That's what had drawn the attention of the South Americans in the first place. Unless it was that pointless visit by MinCol.

"É," said Dabeet. "You're right. I've been acting like I think I'm toguro, and I'm just a nuzhnik."

"Pretty much."

So they agreed on something. But Dabeet still had a message to decipher. "Look, do you have any idea what you were talking about?"

Zhang interrupted him. "No, how could anyone but *you* have any—"

"I didn't mean it that way. What you were talking about—the insight that would make it easy? Do you have any idea of the *kind* of thing it would be?"

"You already said one thing, that Greek word, boustrophon—"

"Boustrophedon, the lines alternating directions."

"É, that's the kind of idea."

"But it didn't help."

"I didn't say it was *the* idea, I said it was that *kind* of idea," said Zhang. "You really aren't willing to let go of your mindset, are you. Like this: What if the Spanish and English aren't in two separate sections. What if they're in alternating words—no, better yet, alternating letters. Like, 'como' and 'how,' spelled C-H-O-O-M-W-O."

"That's good," said Dabeet. "That produced a double letter that didn't exist in either word. That could be it."

"I wasn't saying that *was* it."

"But I'm saying that I can't do anything else till I at least *try* that. Most obvious case, both languages read left to right across the lines, from the top to the bottom of the word-search layout. Look." Dabeet started moving the letters into two separate boxes, the odd-numbered letters in one spot, the even-numbered ones in another. The desk quickly caught on to what he was doing and proposed a pair of completed boxes. Dabeet saved it, then began to look at each one.

"Two different languages, two different looks," said Zhang. "If this is an *A* and this is an *O,* here they are at the ends of a lot of words, nouns with gender. This one could be Spanish."

"And the other one—look how this pattern repeats. That has to be 'the,' which makes the *R* stand for *E.*"

"My work here is done," said Zhang He.

"Thank you," said Dabeet. "Really. I was too tired to think, but this works."

"Will you tell me what the message says, when you get it figured out?"

Dabeet wanted to say no, straight out, because he saw the way Zhang reacted when Dabeet referred to the South Americans as terrorists. If the message made it clear that Dabeet was supposed to open a back door for a raid, there was no way to predict how Zhang would react. The last thing Dabeet needed was to have to fight or sneak his way past a bunch of angry students trying to prevent him.

Or I could decide not to do what the message says. What then? Why *not* share it with Zhang? It's only a problem if I plan to carry out whatever assignment they give me.

Zhang rolled his eyes and started to turn away.

"Zhang, I don't know what the message says. I don't know if I *can* tell you."

"You don't know if you can trust me."

"I don't know if it would put you in danger to know."

Zhang gave a short nasty laugh. "I see, we're playing at spies. Glad I could help." Zhang walked languidly away.

Why didn't I just say yes? I could have changed my mind later, with an explanation. Or told him that I never figured it out. Instead I've offended him, which loses me the only offer of help I'm likely to get.

And what did he mean, "playing at spies." The cipher was real. Dabeet really was working on it all night. Why would Zhang help him, then dismiss the whole project as worthless? Who *is* Zhang to me? My only friend? Or the person who despises me most?

Yet I'm going to need *somebody.* I could use a second pair of hands, of feet. Somebody to run the airlock while I . . . no, stupid, Zhang doesn't have any more access to the system than I do, it won't obey students. But something. I have to do something in order to save Mother and . . .

Why am I valuing her above all the students here? Because her death is a sure thing if I fail, while the raid isn't supposed to kill anybody, or at least not any of the kids. Sure death versus a hard couple of days, maybe only hours? That's when the life of the one is more important than the convenience of the many. Right?

You're not in control of this, Dabeet. You can't predict any outcomes. You have to take action, or not take it, based on other criteria.

Dabeet woke up from a doze and realized it would take him three times as long to decipher the puzzle if he tried to do it now, without sleeping. He saved the bifurcated puzzle and lay down on the bed. He'd miss lunch. So what. Nap first.

Two thoughts just as he was drifting off.

I wonder if I got credit for creating the floating wall in the conversations about it all over the ship.

And when I was remonstrating with myself—"You're not in control of this, Dabeet"—it wasn't my own voice I imagined speaking to me. It was MinCol's.

12

From Spanish: your message received door must be in new unfinished sector open eighteen october lunar eight pm no atmo needed

From English: if defensive force ambushes us your mother is dead within half hour if our all clear not sent every half hour be smart

Once Dabeet tried Zhang He's idea, everything fell into place. The messages read, with alternating letters, from bottom to top, from right to left. The upper left corner contained sixteen letters of Spanish only, since the Spanish message took more letters than the English one. The weirdest thing was "atmo" because that just wasn't a Spanish word. But their phrasing and spelling must have been shaped by the exact number of letters that would fit into a perfect puzzle square.

Not a hard cipher at all, once Zhang He had come up with the key. But Dabeet had needed that key, so without Zhang's help he might have been pounding his head into the problem till the deadline passed.

More than a month away, though. And since all the near-Earth stations and depots used Lunar Time, which was tied to Eastern Standard

Time in the United States, there would be no problem getting the time right. They had used the English expression "pm" in the Spanish section, because any Latin American *or* soldier would have written the time using the twenty-four-hour system: two thousand or twenty hundred hours. "Ocho pm" took up the same number of characters as "dos mil," but they probably expected Dabeet to think like an American, even in the Spanish section.

So his job was to be door-opening again. Only this time, the head of station security would *not* be giving him a free pass into the unfinished part of the station, and would not be opening an airlock for him. Dabeet now faced a much harder puzzle than the cipher had been—how to get past the tracking system, so he could get where he needed to go without setting off an alarm, and then how to get an airlock to obey his unauthorized hand on the command plate.

Dabeet had already tried to hack his way into the computer system. He did it so easily that he knew at once the system was designed to be hacked—which meant that it wasn't the real system. Instead, everything the students accessed was part of a virtual machine completely firewalled from the *real* station operating system. There would be no way to get from inside the student system to the real station system, because nobody with any authority would ever need to access anything from a student desk.

To sign on to the real system would supposedly require having a teacher's fingerprint *and* knowing a password. But that was only true, Dabeet knew, if all the teachers followed security protocol all the time. It took careful and constant observation, but within three days Dabeet had a chance to use a teacher's computer for a few minutes when the teacher stepped away without logging off. What Dabeet quickly discovered was that the teachers operated inside yet another virtual system; they could do way more things than the students could, but the teachers, too, were shut out of real station operations.

This made sense. The last thing the station needed was to let any idiot reset a thermostat or open some outside airlock door. But since Dabeet was exactly the idiot they were trying to keep out, this became a serious matter. The countdown was running, and he still had no idea how to fulfil his assignment.

So maybe I don't fulfil it. What do these clowns expect? I'm a kid in a place designed specifically to contain really bright kids. He couldn't find any forgotten back doors because there had never *been* any paths from the virtual operating systems to the real one. If there *was* no solution to the problem, then the South Americans would be jaunting into space for nothing.

And Mother would die.

Was there some way to tell them he couldn't get the door open?

Yes. He could have failed to get the door open the first time. But he didn't fail. He got it open. They had no way of knowing he couldn't use the same method twice.

Meanwhile, classes went on, and Dabeet found himself struggling to pay attention, which meant he made a few mistakes here and there. Nothing out of the ordinary for an ordinary student, but two different teachers took Dabeet aside to ask him what was wrong. Nothing was wrong, of course. But to silence them, he smiled wanly and said, "I miss my mother." Did he want to talk about it? "Talking about it makes it worse. But thanks."

Apparently, if you tell the exact lie that they want to hear, they'll believe you without your having to make even the slightest effort at acting. Dabeet suspected that the flatter his voice while saying these emotional things, the more believable he seemed. And also the more seriously they took his rejection of them as counselors. No doubt they talked among themselves about how Dabeet was suddenly going through a crisis of homesickness, but nobody tried to talk to him. He knew it was only a matter of time before the resident shrink brought him in for sessions, but till that started, his slippage on coursework was explained to everyone's satisfaction.

Meanwhile, Dabeet kept looking for some way to get inside the bones of the station so he might be able to find a door that could be opened mechanically, or a back way into some station administrator's office where a real computer might allow him to create his own pathway into the system.

Since Dabeet had no access to current station blueprints, all he had to guide him was the regular map, which showed doors and rooms and corridors. He looked for gaps, for places where life-support machinery might be housed or weapons stored. But the maps were vague enough that such places could be anywhere or everywhere.

One thing he noticed was that each level of the station was proportionate to the one above and below. The top and bottom floors became quite narrow, because of the tubular shape of the station's wheels, but on the regular-width levels, the plan was basically the same. Visit one level, you've seen them all.

But was that really true? Access to life support would not need to be on *every* level. What Dabeet needed to find was a level that had a door or ceiling access that the other levels lacked. Anything important would certainly be locked. But once he found an anomalous door in the inhabited section of the station, he could then look for the *same* door in the unfinished part, where perhaps the same electronic safeguards weren't yet in place.

Wishful thinking, but it wasn't impossible. The station had been designed for security and isolation, but nobody expected sabotage or invasion, so it was easy to say, It can wait, there's no urgency about installing the locking system into the doors of the unfinished section.

How, though, could Dabeet explore the entire station, the finished and unfinished parts, without being tracked? He could bluff his way through questions about slippage in classroom performance, but he didn't know how he could plausibly answer the question, "What are you doing in this area?" Especially if it came up a second or third time in the same week.

Had Robota Smirnova reactivated the tracking device in his clothing? Dabeet couldn't be sure. She had put her hand on him several times—on his shoulder and even on his back, to propel him and steer him. But had she pressed in the exact center of his back, as she did when she turned off his tracker? Or did the tracker come back on automatically after a pause?

If his tracker was still off, then that meant nobody had noticed that he wasn't leaving any kind of trace in the student-monitoring system. No alarm had gone off. How could he find out whether his suit was broadcasting a signal?

He went places. This meant skipping meals, or arriving just before the mess-hall doors closed, or wolfing down his food and disappearing. He cut out of a couple of physical exercise sessions, but realized that was a bad idea—he needed to be in top shape when the raiding party came, because he could not predict what strenuous actions might be required of him. So he began skipping battleroom practices.

At first he asked Bartolomeo Ja's permission, but Ja's response was so indifferent—or even annoyed at the interruption—that Dabeet got the clear impression that Ja didn't care what Dabeet did. Ever since Dabeet stepped aside to let Zhang He demonstrate the techniques involved in building with wall blocks, Zhang had become the de facto leader of the block squad. When Dabeet did show up, he was reduced to asking, "What are we building?" or "What should I do?" because it was Zhang who was planning new structures.

Dabeet was human—he felt a stab of resentment more than once, that nobody thought he was essential or even valuable in an art that he had discovered and developed. But he was smart enough to realize that being inconsequential was an asset, when the most important thing he could do with his time was wander the station looking for hidden rooms and unexplained doors.

That is, it was important *if* there was anything to find.

It was only a couple of days before the halfway point to the deadline that Dabeet took a break to reassess his plans. The results weren't *nothing;* he may not have found anything, but he had toured every corridor available to students in the inhabited section and ascertained that there were no unexplained doors or gaps between rooms that might be filled with a service corridor or storage room.

This in itself was strange, he knew, because he had absorbed enough of spacer culture and lore from overhearing the other kids to know that even corporate and Fleet ships and stations always carried spare parts. Spare *everything,* because if something went wrong there was no time to order something from a warehouse and wait for it to be delivered. The goal in every Belter and Kuiper mining ship was to have on board everything needed to replace or rebuild everything on the ship, twice— and yet still have room for consumable supplies and cargo stowage.

Surely some of that mindset would have been involved in planning the Lagrange-point stations. Where was all that material? Air moved through the ductwork into every room; what was pushing that air? Where was it located? Solar power was wired into every room's lights and wall heating panels. Where were the power cables and the fiber optics? Of course they were in the walls and floors . . . but nobody would build such a system in space without creating complete access to every centimeter, so that nobody would have to tear out walls to get to the wiring, the piping, the air ducts.

I'm missing something, thought Dabeet, just like when I was trying to decipher the message. Only now I can't explain it to Zhang He, because he and I aren't talking all that much and I don't know how he'll react if he knows my mission.

The one positive outcome, so far, was this: Nobody had interfered with his wandering or asked him what business he had on teacher-only levels, or in corridors far from his own army's barracks. That might mean that he was not being tracked, or it might mean that they knew he was wandering around and didn't care.

Or it might mean that Urska Kaluza was secretly allied with the raiders and wanted him to obey their instructions. Therefore, she wouldn't allow anyone to interfere with him. Or it might mean that the security people were monitoring him very carefully, waiting to catch him in an overt act that would allow them to expel him from Fleet School.

Expel him from Fleet School? That would be the most elegant solution, wouldn't it! If they sent him back to Earth, he *couldn't* obey his orders. He'd be valueless to them through no fault of his own.

Unless they assumed, correctly, that he *planned* to get expelled and punished him—directly, or by hurting his mother.

I don't know enough to decide anything, he realized.

He found himself that day in the game room, which was full of kids competing in multi-player games or locking horns with the solo machines. There were stories about how Ender Wiggin had first made a splash at Battle School by beating older boys on these machines, but Dabeet found it hard to believe that somebody as smart as Ender would waste time on children's games.

Yet he needed to empty his head in the hope that his unconscious mind would bring out some useful idea.

The human brain was *such* a design nightmare, cobbled together from repurposed parts. What use was it to have his most productive thinking take place at a level where his conscious mind was unaware of it and incapable of retrieving it? Why couldn't it all happen where he could *see* it?

His reflexes quickly adapted to each game he tried; once he caught the movement patterns required to get past the obstacle, the game became boring. Maybe being bored with what his hands were doing was part of "emptying" his mind, but it didn't matter. He had to quit and move on to another game.

He went from game to game till he was in a back corner, where the less popular games were set up. He didn't want to play those games, either—they must have had these things installed for the days when they had younger kids in the school. He almost turned away to head back to the other games, or maybe he'd just head on out of the game room and go back to exploring and finding nothing. Except that he noticed there was an air intake down near the floor, in a spot where the view was blocked by the unused games.

There were air ducts everywhere in the station, but most of them were up high. There were a couple of them in the barracks, but there would be no way to examine them without attracting unwanted attention from the other students. This one, though, was down low, completely accessible, mostly out of sight.

Dabeet walked over and squatted to examine it. The grillwork framing and covering the duct looked as if it had been designed to come away from the wall rather easily, but it had been retrofitted with some clamps that attached to something on the other side of the wall. There would be no pulling it away.

There was no reason for that level of security unless someone had once used exactly this access point, and the station administrators were determined that no one would be able to do so again. Whatever the purpose for going into the ducts—sabotage? spying? hiding his collection of marbles?—it must have annoyed *somebody.*

It must have been a very small person who went into this duct. Even if the grill had not been permanently fixed in place, Dabeet was already too old, too big to get in there, or accomplish anything if he did.

"They say it was Bean."

Dabeet whirled so fast he lost his balance and had to catch himself with one hand to keep from toppling over from his squatting position.

It was Monkey—Cynthia Munk—the smallest and youngest of his squad of block-builders.

Before he could reply with the obvious question, Monkey answered it. "Legendary, I know. All the weird stories in this place seem to be ascribed to Bean."

"Bean is a name? A person?" It was something Dabeet had never quite believed.

"The smallest student ever admitted to Battle School, they say. Youngest. With test scores better than Ender Wiggin's."

Now Dabeet remembered having heard of Bean—in the context of test scores. His were the only benchmarks Dabeet had not surpassed. But when he saw "Bean" at the top of all the listings, he assumed it was a statistical term representing some kind of optimum.

"They emptied all the kids out of Battle School before they set up Fleet School," said Dabeet. "So how could Battle School kids pass on a legend to Fleet School?"

Monkey shrugged. "Some teachers were retained. Stories have a way of not dying. I'm not saying the stories are all true. Maybe not any. But if it was teachers who passed on the Bean stories, doesn't that mean they're more likely to be true? When I got here, because I'm kind of small, another kid told me I should start crawling around in the ductwork like Bean. And this exact intake was pointed out to me as Bean's first entry point into the air system."

To Dabeet it sounded like pure folklore. What kind of name was "Bean"? Frijole. Was the kid from Lima or something? There was no such kid.

Except that the name was there in the test-score tables, with numbers so high that Dabeet couldn't even aspire to equal them.

"He used to crawl through the ductwork all over the station," said Monkey. "Listening to the teachers talking, figuring out things that kids weren't supposed to know."

"He must have been tiny," said Dabeet. Now he realized there was no point in doubting her story openly. She enjoyed telling it, and Dabeet was in need of a friend. Well, an assistant, but the only way to get one was to turn an appropriate person into a friend.

She was still talking. "They locked down all the air-intake covers so tightly that no kid could possibly duplicate Bean's spying. Only who could do it anyway? Even *I* would get claustrophobic trying to go in there, and I'm not exactly a giant."

"Big enough in the battleroom," said Dabeet, trying to say nice things.

She looked at him quizzically. "What do you need me to do?" she asked.

Dabeet tried to hide his consternation.

"Oh, come on, Dabeet, you spend half a year hardly talking to anybody, not even when we were building pillars and towers and walls in the battleroom, and suddenly you're complimenting me and not sneering at the legends of Bean? He *is* real, you know. His name is Julian Delphiki and he was in Ender's jeesh in the war. It came up in the trial. Bean figured things out when Ender couldn't. Really brilliant people figure things out because they don't believe everything the adults tell them. When are *you* going to start doing that?"

"What's to figure out?" asked Dabeet.

She laughed softly. "You've been wandering around every level, every corridor, looking for *something*. Trying to figure out *something*. Zhang He says you got a coded message after that time you got a private meeting with somebody by ansible."

"I didn't know I was so obvious."

"It was obvious because I was looking. This whole school is full of the smartest kids in space, it's not like we're dumb as houseflies. But nobody cares what you do, so it doesn't matter," said Monkey.

Nobody cares. Well, he had tried to be invisible. Nobody caring what he did was pretty much the only way to disappear. "If nobody cares . . ."

"*I* care," said Monkey. "All this school stuff—you're good with the book learning, bad with the body-training, really bad with the friend-making. Zhang He *tried* to be your friend but it's like every word you said to him was a slap in the face."

Now Dabeet really was surprised. And hurt. He had tried to be *nice* to Zhang He right from the start.

"No, no," she said. "It was obvious you were trying to be nice, you're just bad at it, so you always sounded condescending. Yes you may help me if you like, and I'll be really patient when you screw things up. Like that."

"That's not even how I felt or thought," said Dabeet. "Zhang He never screwed anything up. I thought I was treating him like an equal."

Monkey rolled her eyes. "Dabeet. You've never *met* an equal. How would you know how to treat one?"

Dabeet felt a flash of despair. He knew nobody at Conn really liked him, but he chalked it up to envy. No, *Mother* told him it was envy. And maybe it was. But human beings need acceptance by a community, and Dabeet didn't have that—not at school, not in the barrio. Not even from the adults. He was never aware that this hurt him until this moment, when Monkey said it all outright. He had the normal human need to belong to a community, and he had actually believed that here in Fleet School, at least in the box-building squad that he had created, he finally had it for the first time in his life. He hadn't thought of it this way before, but yes, it had made him happy. And that was all stripped away.

"Come on, Dab," said Monkey. "I didn't realize it would hurt your feelings."

Dabeet heard her call him by an unthinkable nickname, and his first reaction was to lash out at her and forbid her *ever* to take such liberties. But he stopped himself instantly, because he realized that he was going to use the nickname as an excuse for hurting her back, rejecting her the way everyone rejected *him*. Only that was stupid and pointless because he needed her. And because she was being nice. She had shown him the respect and the kindness of telling him what was really going on.

"Don't go away," said Monkey. "Not right now. People will see your eyes are kind of red and they'll wonder what's going on."

"I thought they didn't notice me," said Dabeet.

"If you actually showed human emotion, Dab, they'd notice, believe me."

Dabeet brushed at his eyes with his sleeve. They came away wet. Which was really stupid. Counterproductive.

"I know you're really sad right now," said Monkey, "but I'm not. I'm kind of glad, because I figured that you were actually a human boy inside. Really, really deep inside. And here you are—first time I went looking for him, and he came right out. So I'm feeling really proud of myself. That's probably annoying but I'm not going to pretend I wasn't trying to get through to you because I've got nothing to hide. If you want me to go away, I'll go."

"I don't want you to go away," said Dabeet. He took a couple of deep breaths to clear his head and get rid of the unwelcome emotion.

"Because you need my help," said Monkey, "and I'm fine with that. Bacana, né? I'm eager to be part of it."

"Not if you can't keep it a secret," said Dabeet.

"There's nothing to be embarrassed about," said Monkey. "People won't think I'm your girlfriend or something. They really do think of me as a kind of pet and neither of us is anywhere near puberty."

"The secret isn't the fact that we're friends," said Dabeet.

"I'm glad that it's a fact," said Monkey.

"The secret belongs to somebody else. Some ugly things are about to happen and I have to get ready without letting anybody else know."

"Except me," said Monkey.

"You'll know what I ask you to do," said Dabeet, "but I'm not sure I can tell you why I'm doing it."

"Dab, I'm really smart. In the test scores, yes, but I'm ship-smart, too, I figure out how things work, I feel it in my bones. You really think I won't guess?"

"You're smart, but you're not insane," said Dabeet. "And my secret really is insane. So I don't know if you'll figure it out. But you have to promise me that you'll keep secret the things I ask you to do to help me, and also keep secret anything you figure out or *think* you've figured out or even *speculate* about."

"I get it," said Monkey. "I promise."

"Are you *good* at keeping secrets?"

"I'm brilliant at not blabbing," said Monkey, "because if you don't learn how to not-blab on a mining ship, especially a corporate ship like the one I mostly grew up on, then pretty soon you've got an eight-percent kuso atmosphere and you can't breathe *that*."

Dabeet grinned. "You sound pretty sure of that. Experience?"

"Toilet repairs. You know, sometimes the gravity generator goes down or misdirects when you're in the middle of your business. Not *me,* but a couple of little kids, both of them sick, and I was on the clean-up crew. *In* a hazmat suit. Because I told them I didn't mind getting the mess out from behind the appliances, and by the end, it was true. So yes, Dab, I've had my face mask covered in other people's vomit and poo and I only threw up twice inside my helmet, and both times I got it all into the spit bell so the suit could dispose of it. Well, almost all."

Just picturing this made Dabeet feel faintly nauseated, but because she was telling it humorously and a little bit proudly, he laughed instead of gagging. Or in addition to it. Gag-laughing.

"Don't choke to death," she said.

"I do need your help. Or I *will,* if I can find a way into the bones of the station."

Now the laughter ended. She regarded him steadily, then sat down on the floor. She patted the floor in front of her. "Sit," she said.

Dabeet sat.

"My shortness is mostly in my legs, so when we sit down we're more the same height so I don't spend the whole conversation craning my neck to look up at you. Also, if nobody can see us then nobody's going to come over to find out what we're talking about."

It made sense.

"I accept that you can't tell me everything, but you've got to tell me something or how can I figure out how to help you?" she asked.

Dabeet shook his head. "I've got to find some stuff out before you can possibly help me. There are jobs where I need another pair of hands, but before I get to those jobs—"

"Wrong answer," said Monkey. "Come on, Dab, don't be such an oomay. I'm *not* just an extra pair of hands, I've got a brain. Tell me what it is you're trying to find out. You said the bones of the station, what do you mean? What do you need to do?"

"I've already tried to break out of the student and teacher computer systems but they're both in a virtual box and the real system is inaccessible."

"And it's all fingerprint- and body-heat-sensitive," she said, "so you're never getting in unless they appoint you to the faculty."

"The faculty doesn't have access either," said Dabeet. "I'm talking about station stuff, not Fleet School stuff—mechanical things, life-support things."

Her eyes got a little wider. "You don't mess with life support, Dab," she said. "You're a dirtbaby, you can't help that but it means you don't get what it means to Inks and Miners. If anybody finds out you're planning to mess with *that,* somebody's going to try to kill you. I'm not exaggerating."

"Is one of them going to be you?" asked Dabeet.

"I don't know yet," said Monkey. "I told you I wouldn't tell anybody else, but that means that if you're endangering the survival of the station, I'll have to kill you myself. I really don't want to do that."

Dabeet almost said something boastful, like, "You're welcome to try," but then he realized that with his lack of agility in zero-gee—no, his lack of combat skills of any kind—she probably *could* kill him.

"I see that you get it," she said. "So now, you better tell me, really specifically, what it is you need to figure out how to do."

Dabeet nodded, but then held his silence for a long moment, trying to figure out how much he could tell her.

She started to speak but he held up a finger for silence.

And then he was ready. All his plans of telling her only bits and pieces had to be abandoned. Now that he realized how seriously Inks and Miners took the mechanicals, there was *nothing* he could safely tell her unless he told her everything. Except, maybe, that he sort of suggested the whole plan to the South Americans in the first place. And even then, she might not consent to helping him.

"Nothing I tell you will sound sane," he said, "unless I tell you pretty much everything. And it's not going to make me sound any better, except you'll see why I have to do it. Maybe you'll see."

"Don't *describe* what my reaction will be, because you don't know," said Monkey. "Just tell me what you can tell me, knowing I won't tell anybody else."

So Dabeet told her about the kidnapping by the South Americans, the threat against his mother, the signal using the outside doors of the station.

She listened, shaking her head, nodding gravely, all the appropriate responses as if she actually believed him—nothing like Urska Kaluza's reaction. Of course, he hadn't told Urska Kaluza *everything*. But he was pretty sure Monkey was not part of the smuggling ring, so he talked about that, too—the things that Zhang and he had found out.

Monkey grinned. "That emossen git. I mean Zhang. I can't believe he never breathed a word about this smuggling ring to *anybody*."

"If they knew that we knew, we'd be dead."

"That *is* an incentive to silence," said Monkey. "But you told Robota."

"And I'm not dead," said Dabeet, "so apparently I could trust her."

"But she's off station now."

"Everything I've told you so far, she knows, mostly because she helped me give the signal. I lied to her about the reasons. About what the signal meant."

Monkey cocked her head. "Buffering. Buffering."

"I'm telling you." He took a deep breath. Nothing came out of his mouth. He covered his face with his hands.

"Tell you what," said Monkey. "I promise *not* to kill you for just telling me. How about that?"

"What I'm afraid of is getting *you* killed," said Dabeet. "I'm afraid of getting everybody killed." Then he shook off his dread and told her, straight out, what the South Americans told him they were going to do.

"They really think this would work?" asked Monkey. "They think they can remain anonymous so that the Fleet would have to stop *all* the wars on Earth in order to respond to an act of terrorism?"

"I don't know what they really think," said Dabeet. "There's an old movie called *The Mouse that Roared*. Mother and I watched it and it was funny but not-funny. They had kind of the same plan. After World War II and the Marshall Plan—you know what that was?"

Monkey rolled her eyes. "I go to a world-class *school* and I'm a very good student, Dab. I get it already—some little country got the idea of invading America, losing the war, and then America would come in and occupy them and solve all their problems."

"You *guessed* that?"

She shook her head. "You Americans always think the rest of the world—"

"Stop," said Dabeet. "No sentence that begins, 'You Americans always,' is going to end productively."

She grinned. "Such a patriot."

"Not born there, but yes. We don't want to waste time on the argument about how the Americans in the twentieth century were the most beneficent empire in history, or not. Right?"

She opened her mouth and made a sound that could have been the beginning of a "just one more thing" kind of argument, and then she closed her mouth. "So the South Americans are going to come in through a door *you* open and peacefully take all the children and teachers and station workers hostage. Then the Fleet will go down to *Earth* to straighten things out. But you're forgetting one tiny thing."

"The Fleet will come get their children back, and they won't be nice about it."

"So you didn't forget it. Did *they*?"

"I don't know what they're thinking. They didn't ask me for my advice and there wasn't a question time for me to learn all about their plans."

"There's no way this doesn't end ugly," said Monkey.

"Even if they manage to take over the station without firing a shot," said Dabeet, "what are they going to do when the Fleet sends an attack squad?"

"Maybe they plan to leave the station right away," said Monkey. "Before the IF can respond. Take maybe ten or twenty kids down to Earth or Luna or some weird little space station they've already rented or something."

"Nothing will work as they planned," said Dabeet. "Because these guys are idiots. At least the ones I was kidnapped by. They could have taken me in a completely undetectable way, but instead they do it so that the cops and the principal *know* that I was kidnapped. The only reason it didn't make the news is that MinCol hushed it up."

"*He* knows about this?"

"I fed him a cock-and-bull story but I think he's better at pretending to believe me than I am at lying to him."

"You really stink at lying," said Monkey. "It takes a *lot* of human interaction to work up decent lying skills."

"I hope you teach classes in that someday soon, because *that's* a survival skill I really need."

"Oh, you're already doing the most important thing, which is, Don't talk. Don't tell anybody you have a secret. Don't *tell* lies, don't tell anything at all."

"Oh, é. I've got that down pretty well."

"So you have to save your mother. If they can't get into the station, she's dead."

"They *say* she'll die and I don't have any reason to doubt them."

"So let's say that they really mean for the station takeover to be bloodless."

"It can't be," said Dabeet. "There are enough security guys in the station, not to mention teachers who are experienced soldiers, that somebody's going to get killed."

"And they're dirts," said Monkey. Then, seeing the look on his face, she explained: "Dirtbabies. People from Earth."

"Like me," said Dabeet.

"Oh. You weren't puzzled, you were annoyed."

"They're dirts, yes. You were making some point?"

"They're going to bring guns."

Dabeet shrugged. "Possibly."

"Guns, on a station with an airtight hull."

She apparently took Dabeet's silence as incomprehension, so she elaborated. "You fire heavy bullets inside a ship, they're going to make holes in the walls. In the *outside* walls."

Dabeet already understood, but she was enjoying the explanation so much that he played dumb a little. It was annoying how completely she bought it. "But I thought all the outside surfaces of Fleet ships were coated in nanooze, so they seal up wherever they're breached."

"Let's test how efficient that is, and find out how much atmo can escape through six hundred machine-gun bullet holes before they heal over. Nanooze is like sticking your finger in the dike, it doesn't rebuild the original surface the way Formic ships did."

"So it's dangerous."

"Incredibly dangerous," said Monkey. "Now, if they're commanded by somebody who fought in space with the Fleet and then went back down to Earth—"

"There's no such person in the solar system," said Dabeet. "The only battles that were fought close enough in for the survivors to return to Earth were in the First and Second Formic Wars. Anybody who fought in *that* is seriously dead by now. And the people who fought in the Third War are dozens of lightyears away and they're *never* coming back."

Monkey nodded. "But it's part of their training. So let's say they've got a commander, maybe the whole raiding party, who used to be in the Fleet. I mean, come on, they can't be so stupid they'd send complete novices on a space raid."

"We don't know how stupid they are."

"You don't take automatic projectile weapons to a space battle," said Monkey. "They have to know that."

"They don't have to know anything," said Dabeet. "That's one more thing we have to be alert to. They might breach the hull all over the place."

"You can't let them in," said Monkey.

"I'm aware of the dangers. And now I'm *more* aware of *more* dangers. I don't know what my plan is yet because I can't think of a plan until I know what actions are possible. I'm just telling you the situation. If I don't let them in, my mother dies. If I do let them in, *maybe* nobody dies. Maybe no weapons are fired."

"Maybe we all die."

"That's what I think is most likely," said Dabeet.

"Oh," said Monkey. "That's right, I *heard* you were smart."

"I think they were lying when they talked about hostages. I think they're planning good old-fashioned terrorism. They're going to come into Fleet School Station and kill every one of us here, in some bloody and horrible way, and then flee. So the force that comes to save us is shocked and grieved and so angry that they *have* to retaliate, only they have no idea who did it because they're all gone."

"Or," said Monkey, "if they can't get away in time, they have enough explosives with them to smithereen the whole station so no bodies are ever recovered. That works, too."

"They didn't strike me as suicide-bomber types," said Dabeet.

"What type is that?"

"True believers in a cause they're willing to die for."

"The guys you met are the kind who are true believers in a cause they expect *other* people to die for."

Dabeet had to agree. "Anyway, you get my point. I think these clowns are planning to kill us all. Or if they aren't planning it, that's what's going to happen anyway because they'll fight to resist the IF's take-back of Fleet School. They can't afford to get caught, because then the IF would know whom to retaliate against. They either have to get away clean, or die in a way that leaves no bodies behind."

"Killing us all and then getting away is their Plan A," said Monkey. "And if they can't get away, blowing up the whole station including themselves is Plan B."

"I bet they come here on a hijacked ship," said Dabeet. "I bet they steal an outbound shuttle from the Moon and redirect it here. They'll only have the weapons and explosives they can carry in luggage."

"We're probably making up a far more effective plan than they actually thought of," said Monkey.

"But we'll be better off if we don't assume they're stupid."

They sat there looking at each other in silence.

"It doesn't matter if you open the door," said Monkey. "Because if you don't, they'll just lay down the explosives and blow the station from the outside."

Dabeet nodded. "That's probably their Plan C," he said. "But if I can, I *am* going to open the door, because, you know. Mother."

"You've got to realize your mother is going to die anyway," said Monkey. "Speaking realistically. She's a loose end."

Dabeet shook his head. "We don't know that."

"They're *killers*."

"We *think* they're killers because here we are in Fleet School, which used to be Battle School, so we're predisposed to think of brutal war against unfeeling enemies."

"You think we can *negotiate* with these guys? Let them in and have a nice chat?"

Dabeet shook his head. "Opening the door *or* not opening the door will lead to everybody dying, or a lot of people dying, or at least a few people dying, depending on how it goes. You think I haven't been living with this for the past months? I don't want anybody to die. I may not have any friends here, Cynthia, but I don't have any enemies, either. I don't want *anybody* to die, and I especially don't want them to die because some Earthside yiffa picked my mother as their hostage."

"So you have a plan?" asked Monkey.

"I do not," said Dabeet. "But if I *did* have a plan, it would depend on our having control of the mechanical stuff in the station, so we might be able to isolate them and cut off their air, or *something* that lets them inside but then we kill them all."

"Oh, I see," said Monkey. "That's a good plan, except that you don't actually have a plan."

"I know I don't," said Dabeet. "But if I could get inside the mechanical area of the station, I might be able to learn enough about the way the station works that I could come up with a plan."

"So why are you wandering around the whole inhabited portion of Fleet School instead of getting into the machinery?"

Dabeet buried his face in his hands. "Cynthia," he said.

"Please call me Monkey," she said. "I hate the name Cynthia."

"Monkey," said Dabeet, "what do you think I've been looking for? I can't find a single door leading into the mechanicals. Why do you think I was looking at that stupid locked vent that I couldn't possibly get my shoulders through?"

Monkey looked at him in something like awe. "You don't know?" she said.

"Know what?" asked Dabeet.

"There are doors all over the place. They don't all lead everywhere, but they all lead *somewhere,* and if you go into the right ones, you can get all over the station without having to go through some air duct."

"There are no doors," said Dabeet. "Not even trap doors in the ceilings."

"This from the koncho who discovered that you could make boxes out of the wall panels in the battleroom," said Monkey.

Dabeet thought about that for a moment. "Oh," he said. "The doors don't look like doors. They look like walls."

"You got it."

"I don't like you calling me a koncho," said Dabeet.

"It's just a word," said Monkey.

"A word that means 'traitor,'" said Dabeet. "I'm trying my best *not* to betray the school or anybody. Except for the kay-quops who kidnapped me and threatened my mother. I'm trying really hard to think of a way to betray *them*."

"So you're a koncho coming and going," said Monkey. "A double agent. Very thrilling. If either of us lives through this, they'll make movies about you."

"So how do I know which walls are really doors?"

"They'll always be panels of interior walls, with rectangular shapes."

Dabeet nodded. "But they don't just open for children, do they?"

Monkey grinned. "They're not supposed to, but I'm called Monkey, right? They have invisible palm panels, and our palms aren't keyed in to open them. So they *shouldn't* open for us."

"But they do?"

Monkey nodded. "They put the palm panels up high, so only full-size humans can reach them. But some of the teachers aren't all that tall. And if there were ever a hull breach and we had to get to spacesuits really quickly, those locking systems might kill us all. So I think that sometime along the way—maybe after it became Fleet School, maybe for most of the school's history—they keyed the palm panels to open to *any* warm hand."

"You've *done* this?"

"I got a friend to brace herself against the wall and I scrambled up her body and slapped my hand in the upper right-hand corner of the panel, and it popped open. Only a few centimeters, but it was enough to get my hand in and open it the rest of the way."

"You did this once?"

"We did it to every panel that looked like it might be a door. We were *bored* and it was fun to explore. We closed them all up tight again, or the adults might have gotten wise to us and rekeyed the palm panels to keep us out."

"Does everybody know about this except me?"

Monkey looked at him ruefully. "I don't know. *We* didn't tell people, but I'm sure people saw me do that scramble-up-and-palm-the-corner thing. And I can't swear we *always* reclosed the doors. It's a useful thing to have people know—for safety. Most of the doors have a dozen child-size atmo suits just inside. And a couple of adult ones."

"So when these intruders arrive we could just get everybody to suit up and shut down the atmo," said Dabeet.

"Not so easy," said Monkey. "If the system is designed right, it *can't* be shut down because it's designed with redundancy to make sure nobody can sabotage the station."

"Fine," said Dabeet. "I never thought it would be easy."

"You also never thought a door would look like a wall," said Monkey.

"If I can get inside, maybe I'll think of something that might actually work."

"Maybe if *we* get inside the mechanical spaces, *we'll* think of something that might work," said Monkey.

"Yes," said Dabeet. "We. Sorry."

"I know how ships in space function," said Monkey. "I know all the machinery and what it's for. Not *this* machinery, but the kinds of machines."

"And I don't know any of it, except theoretically."

"So you promise *me*," said Monkey. "You will not change anything, you will not break anything, you will not *touch* anything unless I have explained the machine to you *and* I agree with whatever your plan is."

It felt deeply wrong to Dabeet to have somebody else assert authority like that.

But she knew spaceships and Dabeet couldn't even function well in null-gee. There was no arguing with that. "Agreed," said Dabeet.

"No," said Monkey. "Words from your mouth. Whole sentences."

"I vow on my mother's life—because all of this is on my mother's life—that I will not make any alterations, I will not do any sabotage, I will not break anything, I will not *touch* anything—except to keep my balance—without your giving me the go-ahead."

"And you'll explain your plan to me every single time, very specifically."

"I will. What you said. I'll tell you my *whole* plan, and then you'll tell me why it won't work the way I think, and then we'll improve it together until it does work, or we'll give up and think of something else."

"And until *I* agree," said Monkey, "*you* don't do anything."

Dabeet said, "Yes. I swear to that."

"Then let me show you how to open the secret doors that everybody probably knows about except you."

13

—Cynthia Munk's response to the essay question "Please list and comment upon the five primary duties of an expedition leader."

The leader of a planetary exploration team must be aware of the nature of every specialist's work. The leader is not part of the redundancy system, because nobody can be a fully skilled practitioner of every specialty. But the leader has to know everyone's work well enough to:

1. Understand all reports from every specialist.

2. Make sure specialists are attending to all their duties and not just the most interesting ones.

3. Know how and when to assign tasks and portions of tasks to others in the redundancy system when a particular specialist's workload becomes too heavy to be competently performed.

4. Refrain from intervening in other people's decisions and workload as long as they are performing competently.

5. Recognize when issues and problems are beyond the leader's competence and then either consult with the entire team to work out solutions or determine whether the only viable solution is to shut down the station and return to space.

My only question about the leader's responsibilities is this: What training will prepare the expedition leader to make the determination in situation 5? What are the consequences to a leader who pulls the plug, as per 5, when examination of the data by superior officers reveals that the leader made a wrong or unnecessarily costly decision? Are there careerist incentives to avoid taking any of the steps in 5? Likewise, are there careerist and/or ego incentives to cause a leader to incorrectly violate 3 and 4?

In other words, how do we keep expeditions from functioning like every real-world bureaucracy ever known? Why should we imagine that this utopian culture can ever possibly exist? Is there something about being on another planet that will automatically transform human nature? Or will the Expeditionary Fleet only choose as its expedition leaders those persons who are already eligible for sainthood? By what system will such leaders be identified, and how will we get anybody else in the expeditions to follow them?

—Teacher comment: Coming from a corporate environment, it is not surprising that this student would assume that the well-known corporate tendency toward bureaucracy and careerism would also dominate in the Expeditionary Fleet. Will counsel student on the responsibility of leaders not to succumb to bureaucratic tendencies.

—Additional teacher comment: Student immediately agreed with all my comments and criticisms. Assume student was entirely ironic in doing so, and privately mocked our entire conversation after it was over.

—Conclusion: This student continues to show remarkable leadership promise.

Monkey was eager to demonstrate on a panel in the game room, but Dabeet said no. "How many kids come in here every hour? A vent near the floor is hidden, but a whole wall coming open?"

So they made their way to an upper level that had no active barracks. The rumor was that the IF had no intention of bringing Fleet School back to the number of students it sustained when it was Battle School. There was talk about quartering soldiers in the unused barracks, or housing faculty families there, or opening some kind of advanced school, but nothing real had happened and as far as Dabeet knew, the IF had no plans for these spaces at all. What mattered now was that nobody was likely to walk past the door while they had it open.

Dabeet braced himself on the panel just to the right of the one Monkey was going to try to open. "All the ones I tried opened from the right," she said, "but who knows?" This one fit the pattern: Monkey clambered up Dabeet's body, stood on his shoulders, and palmed the upper-right corner of the panel next to the one he was braced on. It sprang away from the wall about ten centimeters.

Monkey pulled it open farther and then held to the top of the door, swung off of Dabeet's shoulders, and then dropped down inside whatever space had just been revealed.

"What is it, a closet?" asked Dabeet.

"Come inside so we can close it again," said Monkey.

"How will we see?" asked Dabeet.

"Sonar," said Monkey. "Very quiet sonar. You don't know how to do that? Emit high squeaks and then listen for the echo."

It took Dabeet a moment to realize she was joking, and a moment longer to be sure that she wasn't ridiculing him, because it never occurred to her that anybody might not know, instantly, that it was a joke. Only after he had settled his emotional response did he step inside.

Monkey reached around him and pulled the door closed, using a mechanical handle. It was pitch black inside.

Monkey squeaked. Immediately a light came on. She was grinning. No, she was laughing silently, her shoulders shaking.

Dabeet almost asked her how she knew the pitch to squeak in order to turn on the light. Before he could humiliate himself, however, he saw that her left hand was leaning on a wall near a rocker switch. She flipped it down and the place was dark again.

"On please," said Dabeet.

"You have to squeak," said Monkey.

"I beg you, no," said Dabeet.

The light came on. "You have no sense of *play*," she said.

"I have no love of silliness," said Dabeet.

"Same thing," said Monkey. She started to head around a corner.

"Wait," said Dabeet. "You've seen this kind of thing before, but I haven't."

She waited while he looked at the six child-sized emergency suits and the two adult ones, each with a small air tank. "How long are these good for?"

"Half an hour if you hold still, fifteen minutes if you're active," said Monkey. "Come on, they trained you on these when you first got here."

Only then did Dabeet realize that yes, these were just like the training suits, except grey instead of white. "Right," he said. "What's this other stuff?"

"I don't know," said Monkey. "It looks like cleaning supplies." She indicated a shelf with plastic bottles.

Dabeet looked more closely. "If we were inclined to make explosives, these would do."

"You are insane," said Monkey. "These would make a poisonous smoke and one explosion could wipe out the entire school."

"Then let's not make one," said Dabeet, "unless the school is already doomed. But we should also look into the chemistry and see whether we can make some kind of flash-bang explosion that *doesn't* raise a poisonous smoke."

"Dirtbabies want things to go boom."

"Those who come against us will be dirtbabies too, most of them," said Dabeet. "I'm not making any decisions here, I'm taking inventory. But let's go on and see how deep this corridor runs."

There were many alcoves and doors identical to the one through which they had entered. The corridor itself was wide enough for a supply cart, and now and then there was a door on the other side, and an occasional trap door in the floor. Dabeet tried to open one; it was too heavy to lift it far, and while he held it up, Monkey looked and told him that it only gave access to a junction of various cables and pipes. "I could crawl along under the floor, though, I think," said Monkey. "This is a kind of invisible road, this crawlspace. Suppose we led the enemy along the corridor here, then ducked down under and made our way behind them."

"They might guess where we'd gone."

"They'll send men, not children," said Monkey. "And I'm not the only Ink or Belter who can move quickly through claustrophobic spaces, even if the gravity is switched off."

"If we could do *that*," said Dabeet, "then the children of Fleet School would have a huge advantage over dirtsiders."

"Except you, of course," said Monkey cheerfully.

"I don't think I'll be much use in any kind of battle," said Dabeet. Admitting it out loud was painful but it could not be denied. "Unless it comes down to making new walls and structures in a battleroom, and Zhang He is now the master of that."

"Not really," said Monkey. "Everyone knows that you were best at it, the one who could envision new structures and their uses in battle. But Zhang He won their hearts as well as their respect. If only you were likable."

If only. But Dabeet answered, "We don't know how the battle will work out, if there's a battle at all. But your plan is a good one, if opportunity presents itself, so everyone should know about it, in case you aren't where it's needed."

For about the fifteenth time, Monkey stopped moving farther along the corridor and turned around to face Dabeet, looking around him and over him as if she were wishing for someone more interesting to talk to.

"Why do you keep doing that?" asked Dabeet. "Can't you concentrate on exploring this place?"

"That's what I'm doing," said Monkey.

"I mean that dancing around and facing every which way," said Dabeet.

She shook her head. "Turn around and look back," she said.

She moved past him and pointed back the way they had come. Because of the curve of the station, the floor rose up like a hill, so that only the first two alcoves were visible. "Do you know how far we've come?"

"Well, a lot farther than I can see," he said.

"This is the fourteenth doorway, just behind us."

"You've been counting?"

"Counting is unreliable," she said. "Too easy to lose concentration. All numbers sound right and familiar, by the time you're our age. We've counted them all so many times. Look at the bottom shelf."

Dabeet looked. "What am I supposed to see?"

"Who cares what you're *supposed* to see," said Monkey. "This isn't a test made up by some teacher. What *do* you see?"

"Plastic bottles on all the shelves."

Monkey looked at his face. Waiting.

"I still see plastic bottles. And again, plastic bottles. Nothing's changing, Cynthia Munk. What am I missing?"

She just smiled benignly.

"You say you're not a teacher, but you're acting like one."

"I didn't say that I wasn't teaching you, only that I hadn't made up a test for you. I marked our path and kept the count. It's plainly visible. I've given you the answer now, so look and *see*."

Dabeet saw that on the bottom shelf in the nearest alcove, the second bottle on the outside edge of the shelf was a little bit pushed in, away from the edge. No more than a centimeter's difference. Then he looked at the farther alcove, and it was the front bottle that had been pushed in. "Your dancing involved pushing in the bottles. Did you just alternate the front and back ones?"

"And the second shelf up, the third shelf up. That gives me six places to mark. Every sixth place, when I push in the second bottle on the third shelf, I also push in a lower bottle. You can't see those because the sixth and twelfth alcoves aren't visible from here, but no matter which one I come to, I can see which group of six I'm at, and which member of that group of six, counting from our starting point."

Dabeet knew then that her dancing around had never been pointless or exuberant. Except it *had* been exuberant, which made him wonder if she had been mocking him, marking their trail like this without telling him, while making herself look silly and flighty in order to conceal what she was doing.

"So all the dancing was to keep me from noticing?"

"*You* kept you from noticing," she said. "My movements were all visible. But you thought you knew that they were meaningless, so you got annoyed instead of catching on."

"So you weren't testing me. You were making sure I failed the test."

"Was I?" she asked. "What an ugly world you live in, filled with enemies." She waved back at the marked alcoves. "Why do you think I pushed them in so slightly. I was trying for about a centimeter."

"So that if some custodian comes along here, he won't feel obliged to straighten the shelves."

"Custodians might straighten them anyway—you can't expect these to last forever—but yes, that's right. See? I'm not trying to make you fail, I'm trying to help you see how you keep track of a long series of identical locations. So we're coming up on the next one. *You* code it."

Dabeet started moving farther along the corridor. "The next one will be second shelf, front bottle, in a centimeter."

"Maybe," said Monkey.

"Come on," said Dabeet, growing impatient and embarrassed. "Why can't you just answer me?"

She stopped. He realized that the next alcove didn't have two ranks of bottles on the second shelf. Only the back one. So there was no way to continue the marking.

"Oh," said Dabeet.

"What *will* we do?"

Dabeet stopped, reached for the next bottle in from the edge, and slid it over to fill the position of the missing bottle. Then he pushed it a centimeter back. He looked at her for approval.

She looked back at him.

"You know more than me," said Dabeet. "Tell me if that's the right move."

"You have a brain of your own. Tell *me* if that's the right move."

"It's the same chemical, so any custodian coming along won't think it's out of place. Or at least not completely out of place."

She nodded. And waited.

"But the custodian might always take bottles from the outside edge and work inward. So having a gap between the edge bottle that we're using as a marker and the next one in will register as a mistake. The custodian will move it back."

"Erasing our marking," said Monkey. She waited.

Dabeet thought a moment more. "The custodian will also wonder who came in here and messed up the stacks. She'll comment on it to somebody. Or look up some duty roster and find out that officially nobody was in here. And she'll wonder."

Monkey grinned. "What will other people expect to see?" she said. "If you're doing an official job, it won't matter. But if you're a couple of sneaks like us, then it puts our ability to get into the service corridors at risk."

Dabeet pushed the bottle he had moved back into its original position.

"Now our marker is gone, but the custodian won't be surprised."

"Our marker isn't gone," said Dabeet. "We'll remember that in position fifteen, there *was* no bottle, but that still means that in exactly the right position, the bottle isn't flush on the outside edge."

"Except that we won't think 'fifteen,'" said Monkey. "We'll think position three, three. Third group of six, third alcove."

"Six plus six plus three," said Dabeet. "Fifteen."

"You think inside your own system, and the memories sustain each other."

"Now you sound like a Jesuit," he said.

"Mansions of memory," she said. "Exactly. The system works, so stay inside it."

"How many of these are there going to be?" he asked.

"You've walked all the corridors on every level of this wheel. You tell me."

"I wasn't counting," said Dabeet.

"Of course you were," said Monkey, "or you wouldn't have known whether you had checked the whole length of the corridor, all the way around the wheel."

Dabeet thought for a moment. "I just remembered the colors of the barracks I started at, and kept going till I reached those colors again. Green green brown, and keep on till I get to green green brown."

Monkey shook her head. "That's what you thought you were doing," she said. "But you have a number."

Dabeet thought a little more. The colors had a pattern. Green green brown was followed by green brown brown, then brown brown yellow, then brown yellow yellow, then . . . "Each color appears on three adjacent doors. There were sixteen colors. So three times—"

"*Two* times," she corrected him.

Embarrassed, he saw his mistake at once. "Each one overlaps with the two adjacent colors, so it's two times sixteen to get a total of thirty-two barracks, and therefore thirty-two of these alcove entrances."

Monkey still waited.

"Come on, that's *right*."

"Mess hall," she said.

Dabeet turned his face to the wall and leaned his forehead on it. "How stupid do I have to show myself to be?"

"One mess hall, with its kitchen," said Monkey. "And an upshaft and a downshaft."

"We should have hit a shaft already," said Dabeet.

"What would that look like?" she asked.

Dabeet thought about it. "Nothing. It would just be a longer space between alcoves."

Monkey grinned. "Except that maybe that was where we had doors going out the other side."

"Did I see *anything*?"

"I don't know. You were looking so carefully and methodically that I assumed you were seeing what you looked at."

"But not understanding it."

Monkey rested a hand on his shoulder. "Don't punish yourself by standing with your head against the wall. You were thinking like a dirt-baby, that's all. You were expecting that you'd see unusual things that would call attention to themselves. But inside a spaceship—which is all a space station is—things get repeated and *nothing* looks unusual because spaceships are artificial. They don't *have* scenery. Well they do, but nothing is designed to be scenery, so nothing will just happen to stick out."

"I did wonder where those right-hand doors led," said Dabeet.

"What was your conclusion?"

"I wondered if there were structures on that side of the wheel. Maybe ladderways going up and down from one level to another, so you didn't have to go all the way to a shaft to change levels."

"That sounds about right," said Monkey.

"Did you know that? Did you think of that?"

"Is this a competition?" asked Monkey. "Does it matter whether I thought of it? You thought of it, and you told me, so now we're both thinking of it."

"I have to know if I—"

"You have to know if you thought of *anything* I didn't think of? I, who grew up in spaceships, crawling around in service corridors because I was small and agile and smart and *observant* enough to report on any structural damage or other anomalies that might be symptoms of something dangerous to the ship? Compared to you, whose parents called the building superintendent when the plumbing didn't work?"

"We did our own repairs whenever we could. I learned how plumbing works and electricity and I fixed things."

"That's good," said Monkey. "Not useful here, but good. If we're ever on Earth and have a leaky toilet, I'll defer to your expertise."

"I can't help where I was born."

"I know that, and I don't criticize you for it," said Monkey. "Though if you were a friend, I could tease you about it."

"If you were a friend, you wouldn't want to."

"If you had ever had a friend, you'd know how idiotic that statement is. The way you know you have a friend is, they spill a little wind from your sails, when you're running before the wind. And then tighten your lashings when you've been a little storm-whipped. And yes, we study ocean sailing lore like crazy in space because it makes us feel as if we're still doing something human."

"I came from a place where I always did well," said Dabeet. "You have to understand that."

"No I don't," said Monkey. "Because it isn't true."

Dabeet now felt anger rise hot into his neck and face. "You don't know anything about my life before Fleet School."

"I know everything about it that matters here. You never tried anything back on Earth that you didn't *know* you could be best at. If you weren't best, right from the start, then you ran away from it. True or false?"

Dabeet wanted to lash out with some cruel retort, but everything that came to mind was foolish. Childish. Because there *was* no rational answer. "That's true," he said, grudgingly.

"When you got here, we all called you 'Test Boy,' because it was the only thing you were willing to do, because it was the only thing you were really good at. Anything you actually had to *work* at to learn, you hid from. The battleroom, martial arts, even the calisthenics that keep our bones strong and straight—anything that everyone else was good at, and you weren't, you didn't even try to learn. So . . . Test Boy."

"Why do you say it like it was . . . contemptible?"

"Because it is," said Monkey. "You and I are in this corridor, counting alcoves and looking for passages, because the whole station is in danger, partly because of decisions you made. And you're angry at me because *you* don't know as much as I do about things I've done all my life. That's not the contemptible part. What's contemptible is that you could have been *better* than you are by now, and you chose not to, because you couldn't *win* at it."

"But schoolwork isn't nothing. My being good at that isn't—"

"We're training to go out into space, discovering goldilocks planets and exploring them and reporting on life-forms and habitability, and getting perfect scores on schoolroom tests won't prepare you for that in any way."

"They're teaching us subjects that we need to know in order—"

"No, Dabeet. No and no and no. Think what it means to take a test in a class. They *say* they're giving us problems that we're supposed to solve. But that's never true, is it? Because they give us problems to which the solutions are already known. That's why they're able to give us grades. So all you do in classroom tests is solve problems that have already been solved."

Dabeet had never thought of it that way.

"Even that coded message you got, the one that Zhang He helped you with—it wasn't a *real* problem, it was a test, because there was already a known solution. *You* didn't know it, but you knew how to get it, and you would have solved it eventually, even without Zhang's help, because you *knew* there was a solution or it wouldn't have been sent to you. Right? All you know how to do is solve solvable problems."

"Outguess the teachers."

"You aren't *guessing*," said Monkey. "You really do figure things out. But there's no *pressure*, because you know that somebody, somewhere, already knows the answer, which means there *is* an answer."

"Well, what's the point of solving problems when there *isn't* an answer?"

"That's how we're going to spend our lives, Dabeet. When we go down to a planet, we'll have procedures we're supposed to follow—but only as long as those procedures yield desirable results. We have to know when to stop following them because they're not working, or they're counterproductive."

"They've never been solved," said Dabeet. "So we don't even know if there *is* a solution."

"If we fail spectacularly, everybody dies except the orbital team. If we find out that there's no way humans can establish any kind of permanent base on a planet, then we leave, right? And we don't even count that as a failure, because we now *know* that it's a goldilocks planet that, for whatever reasons we report, is off-limits for settlement. We go there with a test question—'Is this planet a potential human habitat?'—and if we do our work properly, then either 'yes' or 'no' will be the right answer."

"They sent me a coded message because they knew I'd solve it," said Dabeet. "They think of me as Test Boy, too."

"No, you *had* to solve it, I mean, there was nothing *wrong* with that. But *why* did they send it? Why do they want you to do the things they've told you to do? What will really happen to your mother? Why haven't you enlisted your secret pal on the ansible to protect her? Why are you letting them manipulate you and put all of us in danger?"

Dabeet covered his face with his hands. "Because she's the only person in the whole human race who cares whether I live or die."

"Well, I care," said Monkey. "Though I doubt I care as much as she does."

"I've been trying to figure out what's going on, but how can I know whether I'm right?"

"Exactly the problem," said Monkey. "You can't know whether you've found the right answer because there *is* no right answer. This isn't a problem to which a solution is already known. But you have to be ready to adapt to whatever happens. And here's what doesn't work: trying to solve it by yourself. On classroom tests, if you don't solve it alone, it's called cheating and they kick you out of school. But in space, if you try to solve things alone, you endanger everybody because we're all in it together, and no one person can think of everything."

"I get it, I get it," whispered Dabeet. "I'm the most stupid useless person here because I don't have *any* useful skill."

"It's not about you," said Monkey. "It's not about whether you're the most of this or the least of that. It's about the whole community that lives in this fragile habitat. I'm sounding like my own father now, but it's the lesson we all learned by the time we were four. We never, never, never do anything without telling somebody else what we're doing, and where, and why, and for how long, because our lives all depend on knowing everything about everybody else."

"I shouldn't have kept my problem a secret."

"Obviously," said Monkey. "And when Zhang He realized that whatever was going on, it was a potential threat to all of us, he told everybody in our building club. The people who actually know you and work with you. We know you're not stupid, but we also know you do everything solo, and we decided we couldn't let you keep acting like that because it was going to get us all killed."

"You couldn't have known that, because you didn't know about the threat from—"

"We know all about the threat from people thinking they can fix big problems without the embarrassment of telling other people how they screwed up. When it affects everybody, there's *no shame* in telling about your mistakes and the potential bad results. Until you learn that, you can't be trusted on any exploratory team."

"The South Americans have me jumping through hoops."

"Which means they almost certainly aren't South Americans at all. Oh, the people who kidnapped you probably are, but they're obeying somebody else's orders."

"You can't possibly know that."

"Somebody who was tracking you. *You.* Why would your name even come up in any South American country?"

"Because of my test scores."

"If it's because of your test scores, then they really are stupid and our danger is probably a great deal less, though they could still screw up and kill us all. Dabeet, haven't you followed any news reports from Earth? Battle School students and graduates back on Earth are getting kidnapped, only they don't get returned, like you did. But you were kidnapped *before* all the other kidnappings, weren't you?"

"I don't know. I heard of a couple, so . . ." Dabeet thought carefully about what that could mean. What if his kidnapping wasn't an isolated event? What if it was merely an early kidnapping? "Those kids were taken because they were trained military leaders."

"And you were a trained test-taker. Test-taking is an *obedience* test. Will you do what the test tells you to do?"

"So I wasn't picked because of my ability," said Dabeet. "I was picked because I follow instructions. Because if they told me the right story, I'd betray everybody in Fleet School."

"There's no shame in that," said Monkey. "They didn't choose you because you *wanted* to be a traitor, they chose you because you were extremely skilled at figuring out very hard problems with known solutions, and because you had one person in the whole world that you loved."

"I don't even know if I love her," said Dabeet. "She isn't even my biological mother. No genetic connection. All I know is that she loves *me*."

"Do you think the people who kidnapped you were smart enough to figure all that out?"

Dabeet shook his head. "I wondered how they knew so much about me," said Dabeet.

"Come on, Dabeet, you were so proud of being smart that it didn't surprise you at *all* that they found you."

Dabeet was almost dizzy with Monkey's heartless, relentless cataloguing of his mistakes and ignorance. "*You* figured it out."

"I figured things out mostly because I walked these corridors with you and you also told me about your mom and the South Americans. Nobody else knew all that, and neither did anybody on Earth. So who is really behind this? Not some South American country trying to get the IF to intervene. Maybe those clowns who took you believe that, but whoever *told* them about you, whoever came up with whatever asinine plan they're following, *that's* who figured out that you were the one they needed."

"And who was that?" asked Dabeet.

"Nobody knows who's taking all those Battle School alumni," said

Monkey. "But whoever it is has found a way to track every one of them, wherever they went all over the world."

"Maybe it's a whole bunch of countries taking the kids."

"No, Dabeet. Read the news. All the countries used legal process before Battle School even closed down. Very openly. All the kids were repatriated to their legal country of origin. The kidnappers are taking them somewhere else. Or killing them."

"But why take me? The most ignorant kid in Fleet School, the least experienced in space—"

"They knew you'd be feeling disconnected. No loyalty to Fleet School, no friends," said Monkey. "Easy to intimidate."

"Scaring me doesn't confer on me the competence to do anything. And who is it who's manipulating me?"

"I don't know," said Monkey. "But *that's* a *real* question. We don't know if there *is* a solution. Maybe all my assumptions are wrong. There's no answer key that will be compared to our decisions and checked off whenever we get an answer wrong."

"I'm so out of my league."

"By ourselves, we all are. Together, maybe just as badly off. But with more brains working on it, bringing different experiences and perspectives to the problem, maybe we can come up with better hypotheses."

"I get it now, Monkey, I really do. It would be insane for me to keep this secret any longer."

"Well, don't go crazy on me here," said Monkey. "You don't know that there isn't a co-conspirator here on the station."

"You mean, besides me."

"You're not a conspirator, you're a tool. Like somebody who holds up a bank because the real robbers are holding their family hostage."

"If there's another conspirator, then what's with all the door-opening?"

"If investigators afterward are steered to evidence showing that *you* opened the doors and *you* let them in—because they held your mother hostage—then they're not going to look to see who the real inside guys were here in Fleet School, are they?"

"So I'm not just a tool, I'm the patsy."

"See? Isn't it a *lot* more fun to count alcoves in the corridor?"

"When did you figure all this out?" asked Dabeet.

She looked at him in consternation. "I haven't figured anything out. We don't know if we're right about anything. I've been brainstorming this with you *right now,* I only know what I think of when I hear myself say it. Like you. That's how working things out as a team *works.*"

Dabeet could only agree with her. "Of course I'm only really useful because I'm the sole witness of the original kidnapping. I mean, this is bound to work out like doing the wall structures in the battleroom. You or Zhang He or somebody will take over and make all the plans and—"

"Maybe that's how it'll go," said Monkey. "So what?"

"I'm just saying, it's not like I'm useful for anything except telling everybody how stupid I am."

"Self-pity—that'll make them all respect you."

"I'm a traitor. Nobody's going to respect me."

"Well, if you tell us your history, and then you shut us all out the way you did with the wall-building team, then é, that's right, everybody else will solve the problem without you because you'll do your normal thing and refuse to take part. Otherwise, you'll be part of the team, and you'll think of whatever you think of, and so will everybody else. And nobody will care who thought of what, as long as it works."

"In utopia, maybe. People care who thinks of stuff."

She nodded. "Yes, that's right, you're right. We had a major system failure on my ship when we were three months out of the nearest port. The problem was enormously technical so let me just summarize it by saying that there wasn't enough breathable air to get us all to a port alive. People set up all kinds of possible solutions, including having about half of us voluntarily step out into space so there'd be enough air for the remaining half."

"Would they have done that?" asked Dabeet.

"Maybe. We'll never know. Because somebody thought of a much better idea that involved an alteration in the way the hydroponics functioned. We'd stop growing food crops and convert everything to oxygen production—a different set of plants—but it could be done in time. And we did it, and it worked, and nobody had to leave the ship."

Dabeet nodded. "You thought of the solution," he said.

"I hung around in the hydroponics fields a lot because it was fresh air. I used to pretend I was on Earth and I was in a meadow. Only it was a meadow stacked up in ten layers under artificial sunlight."

"So it was you."

"In recognition of my valuable contribution, my parents' corporation paid for my place here in Fleet School. This is my prize—meeting you and maybe getting blown to smithereens by the criminals who are manipulating you."

"So it *does* matter who thinks up solutions."

"I was also the person who screwed up the oxygen-delivery system in the first place," said Monkey.

Dabeet digested that for a while.

"It was a clumsy accident but I *immediately* told my parents what I had done and they told the ship staff and that's when everybody started brainstorming solutions."

"So you were the idiot who caused it *and* the genius who solved it."

"Happens that way a lot," said Monkey. "But we were on a ship, and even though it was corporate we long since became like family to each other. Nobody condemned me for my mistake, because they all knew that everybody makes mistakes, and I hadn't tried to hide it, so there was still maybe time enough to do something before we all died."

"Did *I* tell anybody when there was still time?" asked Dabeet.

"Well, I'm the first student you told, so . . . we'll find out if this leaves us enough time."

"So maybe we should go tell everybody else on the wall squad," said Dabeet.

"Are we through mapping this interior corridor?"

"No, but—"

"Let's go to them with data. Actual knowledge. Maybe even some potential ideas for a plan."

"Though we still don't have any idea what the raiders will do, when and if they actually raid Fleet School."

"Here's what I think, based on what you've told me so far. I think that whoever is behind all the kidnappings, yours and everybody else's, I think it's somebody who hates Battle School and every kid who was ever in it."

"But this isn't—"

"It's the same Lagrange-point station that used to be Battle School. Let's say it was somebody who was up here and washed out. Somebody familiar with the layout of the station. And they hate this place. They— he or she—they want to punish everybody. What happens if *that's* the motive behind all the kidnappings?"

"They aren't coming here to hold us all hostage so the IF will intervene on Earth," said Dabeet.

"They're coming here to kill everybody," said Monkey.

"So they don't even have to come inside," said Dabeet. "Just breach the hull and—"

"Too many hulls, so it isn't feasible, and besides, they don't just want to destroy Battle School or Fleet School or whatever we are. They want to *punish* the school and everybody who was ever in it."

"They want the Fleet to find the bodies," said Dabeet. "And not just dead from oxygen deprivation. Dead with blood and guts everywhere."

"Dead so that when the bodies of children are shown on the nets back on Earth and out in space, it makes everybody so sick and angry, so insanely furious, that . . ."

When her voice trailed off, Dabeet prompted her. "So insanely furious that *what*?"

"I have no idea. And I hope I'm completely wrong. But I think we need to act as if *that* is their plan."

"You mean, we should treat them as killers even before they've killed anybody," said Dabeet.

"*That's* what we need to discuss, don't you think?"

14

**Submission from Dabeet Ochoa in Basic
Decision-Making 01.**

The assignment is to explain the difference between the decision-making
process in exploratory expeditions as opposed to military ones.

The only important differences are (1) the tools used and (2) the overall
imperative not to harm the enemy.

In all other ways, the geology, atmospherics, and biota of a thitherto unknown planet *are* the enemy, in that they conceal the means they would use
to destroy us, they cannot be trusted to act as they seem arrayed to act, and
they adapt their tactics to our actions, including direct assault and passive
reconnaissance. Also, it remains true that no plan we make will survive first
contact with the enemy.

Instead of shuddering and pretending that our presence is not an assault
on a planet whose systems are determined to resist us, let us simply admit
that our entire program of exploration and colonization is designed to promote the dispersal and therefore survival of the human race regardless of
the fact that this cannot possibly be accomplished in any case without ex-

tensive collateral damage to the enemy—the planets and ecosystems into which we obtrude ourselves.

We differ from the Formics' assault on Earth only in that we are alert to the possibility of encountering intelligent life, and we are determined to abandon any world which contains it.

I do not believe that this noble self-restraint will survive the first encounter with such a sentient species. First, we will have every motive to find that they are not sentient, including redefining sentience upward until we ourselves do not meet the criteria.

Second, if their land is desirable and they seem not to be using extensive tracts of it, we will delude ourselves that the land is "empty" and will allow "limited" colonization. We will do this because the planet will already be promised to a group of colonists, who will already be on the way to it and cannot be turned back until they arrive.

Co-occupation of a planet with an indigenous sentient species will inevitably lead to genocide or sequestration of the natives, unless their technology is equal or superior to our own, in which case our outnumbered colonizing force will be destroyed.

Therefore, any approach to an alien goldilocks planet must be conducted exactly as one would approach an enemy whose intentions are not yet known.

This does not mean that the normal military decision-making process will be appropriate, primarily because the normal military decision-making process is not appropriate for the military, so it would be insane to transfer it to exploratory expeditions.

Good commanders, military and otherwise, recognize these laws:

1. Nobody thinks of everything.

2. Not everybody thinks of anything.

3. In a genuine emergency, the course of action will be unanimously and immediately recognized and carried out; good leadership in such a case consists of maintaining order and keeping records.

4. If it is not a genuine emergency, then inaction is the best policy until there is enough information to allow the decision-making group to pool information and offer multiple suggestions.

5. Retreat is a course of action. In most emergencies it is the obvious best course. Otherwise, desirable inaction includes not retreating.

6. The leader who consults only himself is so stupid and dangerous as to constitute an emergency requiring his immediate removal. The process of removal must not be treated as mutiny.

7. Consultation requires asking, listening, and considering. It does not require compliance. The leader must explain the reasons for the ultimate decision.

8. The duty of team members who are not the leader is to provide the leader and other team members with as much information and as many possible courses of action as possible, including irrelevant information, since the determination of relevancy is preemptive decision-making.

From MinCol: Dabeet is finally getting some idea of why he is alive.

To MinCol: A purpose imposed on a child by another, however well-intentioned, will invariably cause the child to regard it as the most detestable of all possible goals and he will devote his life to obliterating or obliviating it.

From MinCol: Unless the purpose-imposer is actually helping the child realize the child's own unconscious desires.

To MinCol: Thus do parents and teachers deceive themselves into believing they are omniscient. The belief in one's own omniscience is the least reparable form of ignorance.

From MinCol: The fact that I continue to consult with you is proof that I have mastered Dabeet's eight principles. And also the dozens of principles he has not yet detected.

To MinCol: The fact that you continue to meddle in Dabeet's life in every circumstance *except* actual emergencies is proof that the time I spend consulting with you is completely wasted.

From MinCol: Keep up the good work.

Dabeet knew perfectly well that nobody would see anything suspicious about a meeting of the team of builders. Toons and special squads met together whenever they needed to decide something or plan something or get some kind of training.

But Dabeet was so tense and alert as the team assembled that he felt a little nauseated and a little faint. He had never felt this way before, and he even wondered if he might be coming down with something.

Then, when everyone was there, Dabeet realized that he wasn't tense out of fear that the teachers or staff would suspect something strange or dangerous was going on. He was tense because he didn't know whose meeting this was. While he and Monkey had decided to assemble everybody, she was the one who actually notified the others. Did that mean she was in charge of this meeting? Or would it be Zhang He?

And now that they were all here, he knew. It was Monkey's meeting. That came as a great relief. Dabeet briefly tried to figure out why. Had he been *afraid* that it would be Zhang's meeting? Despite Zhang's recent hostility, Dabeet still regarded him with great respect. And, if he was really to be honest with himself, he still felt trust in and affection toward Zhang He.

Why not? Zhang was the first to join him in the battleroom, the first to accept Dabeet's leadership. Who cared what his motive was? *Nobody* was ever going to be Dabeet's friend because they thought he was so bacana. And he wouldn't want to have friends who chose their friends on the basis of general coolness. Merit was what mattered, and no matter what Zhang He said, Dabeet knew that Zhang had joined with him because Dabeet was doing something interesting and useful that nobody else was doing.

That was then. This meeting wasn't about innovative battleroom tactics. And another reason Dabeet felt relieved, he realized, was that because Monkey took charge of the meeting, it meant Dabeet didn't have to. That would have been very hard, since the meeting was about dealing with danger that Dabeet had brought to Fleet School with him.

Not by *my* choice, thought Dabeet. But whom was he arguing with? Keep silent, he told himself. Let others say what they will. All that matters is that this group of innovative, cooperative, intelligent people participate in trying to solve the problem.

And then Dabeet thought: Am I one of that group?

Maybe that's what this meeting is really supposed to decide.

"This isn't about the battleroom," said Monkey. "Or anything inside the school. The whole station may be in serious danger from outside. From Earth, or at least from a conspiracy that has its roots on Earth."

"And you learned about this from your last dirtside visit?" Ignazio asked her.

"I learned about it from the obvious source," said Monkey. Then she outlined very briefly the threat to Dabeet's mother, what the kidnappers had told Dabeet their plan was, and the action Dabeet had already taken to signal the potential raiders.

Then there was silence. A long silence, in which nobody looked at Dabeet.

Dabeet wanted to assure them, to *convince* them, that there had been no choice, that when he arrived at Fleet School, he hadn't known anybody yet, so why should he have felt any loyalty? In other words, he wanted to persuade them not to be angry with him.

But what was the point of that? They *should* be angry and afraid, because Fleet School was in serious danger. Or might be. They had to plan as if it were. So their anger, even if it was temporarily directed at him, was still a positive. At least they hadn't laughed at Monkey's assessment of the threat. They were taking the problem seriously.

"What do you already have?" asked Zhang He.

That was his leadership, thought Dabeet. Zhang was asserting that Monkey was reporting to *him,* and through him, to the whole group.

"Dabeet and I went into the back passages."

"The ducts?" asked Timeon. "Like Bean?"

Ragnar rolled his eyes. "The service corridor, right?"

"Easy to get into, on every level," said Monkey.

"Easy to get trapped in," said Ignazio.

"No more so than the public corridors," said Monkey. "Also, lots of chemicals and solvents, as well as emergency atmo suits."

"What, you think we should make bombs, blow up the station, and then float around in spacesuits until the grownups come to save us?" asked Timeon.

Monkey looked like she meant to respond angrily, but Zhang He intercepted her. "If need be," said Zhang He. "She was listing our resources, not making plans, and it's good to know that we have chemicals and what we *could* do with them."

"Explosives, definitely," said Monkey. "Some oxygen-dependent, some that could work without O-two. Not sure if anything would work as a rapid solvent, at least not on whatever suits the raiders might be wearing."

"We'll work out the chemistry later, when we have the full inventory," said Zhang He. He glanced around the group. "Does that make sense?"

Dabeet assumed for a moment that what Zhang was really saying was, Anybody want to argue with me? But no, thought Dabeet. There was no anger or assertiveness in Zhang's voice or face or body when he asked if it made sense to defer the discussion about explosives.

"What about just telling the teachers and letting the security forces take care of it?" asked Ignazio.

Monkey looked at Dabeet. So did Zhang. And then, finally, so did everybody.

"I told Robota Smirnova about the threat," said Dabeet. "Before she was moved out of the station itself. If she isn't part of the conspiracy, then I can only assume that she has alerted the appropriate people in the security force."

Ignazio shrugged. "Well then, if they've got it in hand, what's it to us?"

Dabeet wanted to retort that as anyone with half a brain would realize, assumptions about what Robota might or might not have done meant nothing. What guarantee did he have that she had believed his story? But he held his tongue.

"If we see signs that the security forces are ready, fine," said Monkey. "But have there been any changes in routine? Has our brilliant military contingent been increased? Are they responding to the potential threat?"

She was referring to the two IF marines detailed to maintain discipline and security inside the station.

"They don't seem any *less* lazy and stupid than usual," said Ragnar.

"The real security needs to take place outside of the station," said Zhang He. "So the raiders never get inside. We won't see their preparations for *that*."

"I have a pretty radical idea," said Timeon. "What if Dabeet didn't open the door?"

"His mother will be killed," said Monkey. She looked at Zhang. "That was in the message you helped him decode."

"Will *my* mother be killed?" asked Ragnar. He looked around the group.

Everybody except Dabeet avoided his gaze. Most of them looked down at the floor.

"Sorry," said Ragnar. "I just don't know how many people should die on this station to save one kid's mother from what might be an empty threat."

"This is all hypothetical," said Zhang He. "It might all be kuso. But we're navigating in unmapped space. So we can't afford to assume anything. And we can't just write off anybody. Or anybody's mom. Not now."

Dabeet knew he shouldn't be resentful of Ragnar's suggestion that Maria Rafaella Ochoa might be expendable—he had harbored the thought himself. But the crassness with which Ragnar asked, "Will *my* mother be killed?" rankled deeply.

Ragnar saw Dabeet's inadvertent response. He gestured toward Dabeet. "Why is he even here? He shouldn't have heard my comment, but I *did* need to say it, and it's not as if he's contributing anything."

Monkey leaned her head against Ragnar's shoulder. "You're so sweet, Ragnar. He's keeping his mouth shut precisely so that you *can* say such stupendously insensitive things, as if Dabeet were not a human being with feelings. I think he's doing it so splendidly that we should let him remain as long as he can stand it."

Ragnar shrugged her away. "If we have to be *nice,* we can't make an honest assessment."

"Nobody's worried that we'll suffer from an excess of niceness," said Zhang He. "It may be that Dabeet will be prompted to remember information that he doesn't know that he knows. He's also quite possibly the smartest person in Fleet School, so it's not inconceivable that he'll have an idea worth thinking about."

"*Test* smart," murmured Timeon.

"I'd rather have test-smart," said Ignazio, "than everything-stupid."

"If I had a plan," said Dabeet softly, "I would have either proposed it or carried it out. I only just got into the back corridors, thanks to Monkey. I'm going to explore a lot more, just to see what's there. I'll tell you what I find."

"We already have your list of cleaning supplies," said Ragnar.

"And if that's all that's back there, won't it be good to know that?" asked Dabeet. "I know that I brought some aspects of this problem with me, but do you really believe that if they're determined to do this, my noncooperation would have stopped them? It's quite possible that I'm in this only so that after it's all a disaster, I'll be available to blame it on."

"And all the families of the dead Fleet School kids," said Ragnar, "will feel much better if you can prove that you tried to stop it."

"I think the only question we need to answer today," said Dabeet, "is whether we're going to try to kill them the moment they appear, or keep our violence level low until they escalate."

"Your question contains the answer," said Timeon. "We have to wait till they prove they're terrorists."

Monkey shook her head firmly. "That could be with one big station-shattering explosion. If they come, they start dying right away."

"Make them attend meetings like this till they die of boredom," said Ragnar.

"You can leave when you want," said Zhang He.

"*I* think the real question, the first question, the one we need to decide right now," said Ignazio, "is why we think *we* can decide for everybody. Isn't the whole population of the station at risk? Why do we think *we're* fit to decide for all?"

"Because we make really cool structures in the battleroom," said Monkey, as if this should be obvious to all.

"Very funny," said Ignazio. "But if we keep this confined to the six of us, how are we different from Dirt Boy keeping this secret for all these months?"

"No name-calling," said Zhang He.

"Because we might hurt the kay-quop's feelings?" asked Ignazio. "*He's* free to leave, too."

Dabeet stood up. "I think you'll be able to speak more freely if I'm not here. I hope you'll let me know what you decide." He walked out of the barracks room they were using.

It was rumored to be the barracks that Ender Wiggin's Dragon Army had used during Battle School days. But if there was an aura of success and brilliance that would spread to anyone using it for a planning meeting, Dabeet had not detected it.

They would think he left because he was angry, but that was only partly right. He agreed with all the scorn they directed at him. He deserved it. But it also wouldn't help them think well, so it needed to stop. The best way to stop it was to remove the target.

Dabeet went to the first closet door in the corridor, jumped up to tap the palm lock, and was about to go inside when he heard someone coming. He pushed the door back into closed position and sat down against the door with his head resting on his knees.

Adult steps. They came to a stop next to him. "Where are you sup-posed to be?" asked a man's voice.

"In a barrio in Indiana," said Dabeet.

"Oh, it's you." Dabeet knew the voice now. It was Gusti, the account-ing teacher.

"I lost track of time," said Dabeet.

"You don't lose track of anything," said Gusti. "But I'm looking for Teburoro Timeon. Somebody said he went up to this level and maybe you've seen him."

Dabeet lifted his head from his knees, not having to pretend to feel despondent. "All I've been looking at is my knees," he said. "But you're the only person I heard walk by."

"Get back to . . . whatever . . ." said Gusti. "Or don't. You may be right about Indiana. I'd rather be there myself."

Dabeet shook his head. "Everybody had a choice at the end of the war."

"Some of us thought we'd have a brilliant military career," said Gusti, "instead of being stuck in a near-Earth station babysitting a bunch of innumerate children."

Since Dabeet had a better understanding of higher mathematics than Gusti, he was pretty sure that gibe didn't apply to him.

Gusti walked away, continuing to pass along the corridor. He didn't stop to open any of the barracks doors, as if it didn't occur to him that the child he sought might be in one of the rooms. Then again, the children were not supposed to be able to open barracks doors without having their palms authorized.

Maybe the system was supposed to work that way. But Monkey had read the transcripts of the trials of Hyrum Graff and others after the war, and among the details she thought she remembered reading was a document that included a code-number override to Dragon Army bar-racks. And since it had worked, everybody assumed that what they had been told about station security was true.

But what if it wasn't? Dabeet got up from the floor and walked along the corridor in the direction he had been going before, toward the up-shaft. He stopped at the first door he came to, which was definitely *not* Dragon Army's barracks door, and entered the same code into the virtual keypad.

The door opened.

Was the code a universal override?

Dabeet closed the door and went along to the next barracks door. Since the whole length of each barracks ran parallel to the corridor on the opposite side from the hidden service corridors, the distance from one door to the next was considerable. And, just as with the service corridors, the curvature of the wheel of the station made it so that two barracks entrances were the most that were ever visible at a time.

At the third door, Dabeet didn't enter any code. He just palmed the barracks door.

Nothing happened.

He palmed it again. It opened.

At the next door he learned that double-palming worked as well as the code. There was no security here at all.

Was it because these barracks were unused? Or would the same procedure open the occupied barracks on the next two levels down?

He thought of going back to tell the others, but then he thought of something else.

Why would an adult teacher, an officer, be wandering an unused corridor looking for a student? Why would he be *asking* other students where Timeon had gone? Wasn't the station system tracking all the children by chips in their uniforms?

Dabeet had been thinking that the reason he hadn't been caught exploring was because Roboto Smirnova hadn't turned his chip back on after their foray to the door, and it was dumb luck that nobody had tried, and failed, to locate Dabeet on the tracking system. But he had been worried that the more he went around with Monkey into places where they didn't belong, the likelier it would be that *her* chip would give the game away.

But no. Gusti had to *look* for Timeon because there were no tracking chips. There was no security system. Doors could be opened by anyone, kids could go wherever they wanted, because the adults in this place didn't care where the kids went or what they did. At least not enough to encumber themselves with an elaborate system of codes and IDs in order to open doors.

It sounded so careless to Dabeet that he was sure there must be another explanation. But what could that be? They shut down student-tracking because some rats had swallowed a lot of chips and they were now flooding the system with false locations? The system was being updated and rebooted so the lack of tracking was only temporary?

Stupidity and carelessness sounded more plausible to him.

Was it possible that airlock doors were just as easy to open? Had security become *that* lax in the station?

Then, a more chilling thought: Was the security system turned off so that the raiders could open any door by double-palming it? Could they possibly be on their way already? Could Dabeet's "assignment" be a smoke screen, to lull him into a false sense of security about how long he had before they arrived?

But if they wanted their arrival time to be a surprise, why tell Dabeet anything at all? If the security system was this disabled, why did they need Dabeet to open anything for them? What was the *point* of involving Dabeet if their inside people in the station were this effective?

No. Likeliest reason for the lax security was the normal one: laziness. Close runner-up: incompetence. Third place: stupidity. These were always the likeliest explanations for procedural lapses. Constant vigilance might be essential to keep a system safe, but constant vigilance was also unbearably tedious, and it was easy to talk yourself into reasons why it wasn't all *that* important.

Battle School had held the brightest minds of Earth and trained them to save the human race. Security made sense because important things were happening here.

But *Fleet* School was only training spacer kids to go off and explore distant planets. These kids weren't being trained to kill, they were trained to collect plant specimens and read scientific instruments. So . . . palm-palm, and anybody can open any door. Security consists of not telling the students.

And, amazingly enough, it had worked till now.

Or it hadn't, but Dabeet wasn't an insider so nobody had told him.

If I go back and tell them now, they'll look at me like I'm an idiot because they already know and it never occurred to them that I didn't know. Like Monkey with the closet doors.

But if you could open the doors to other teams' barracks, there was no chance that nobody would have used it to commit pranks. We're children here, thought Dabeet. Some temptations are irresistible.

Dabeet headed briskly back toward the barracks where the meeting was going on. If he ran into Gusti coming back the other way, he'd claim he was now trying to walk off his homesickness. Vigorous exercise, that's the ticket!

He didn't encounter Gusti.

He double-palmed the door to the supposed Dragon Army barracks. The others stopped talking and looked at him—clearly they had been expecting an adult when the door suddenly opened.

"Something I think you should know," said Dabeet. He told them about double-palming, and how Monkey's code worked on other doors. "Maybe it's only on this level," said Dabeet. "Maybe not. Maybe all the teachers know about this, maybe not. Did any of *you* know that double-palming would open any barracks door?"

"Maybe it's your magical palms," said Zhang He, already walking to the door. He went outside. The door closed. A moment later, it opened again. "Toguro," said Zhang He.

"If we have a bunch of people chasing us," said Monkey, "it might be useful to know we can open any door."

"Unless they also know it," said Zhang He.

Then Dabeet told them about Gusti looking for Teburoro Timeon. "They're not tracking us," he said. "Whatever Gusti wants with you, Tim, it must be urgent enough that he forgot that he's not supposed to drop clues that the teachers don't always know the location of every student."

"Maybe the system's down for a few hours," said Ignazio.

"Maybe," said Monkey. "But Dabeet and I were gone for more than an hour yesterday and nobody challenged us about it. Nobody came looking for us, nobody said, 'What were you two kids doing in the service corridors.'"

"That doesn't prove anything," said Ragnar.

"You're right," said Monkey. "So let's get some *real* evidence by *asking* about it. Then the adults will know that they have to reinstitute the security and tracking systems."

"I was afraid that if I went exploring," said Dabeet, "I mean really deep exploring, I'd have to do it without any of my clothes, because supposedly they're *all* equipped with a tracking device."

"Talk about getting caught with your pants down," said Ragnar.

"It's a good thing if we can go anywhere," said Zhang He, "and the bad guys don't know how to open doors we close behind us. But we can't know what *they* know until they get here."

"*If* they get here," said Ragnar.

"Obviously," said Monkey.

"Sorry I interrupted the meeting," said Dabeet. "I thought you might have already known this, but if you didn't, then you needed to." He turned and left. Nobody called for him to come back.

Dabeet opened the first closet again, and this time nobody came along to prevent him from using the door. Inside the service corridor he was careful to use Monkey's method of marking his trail, since this was a different level. And the first time he came to one of the outside doors that they had speculated might provide access between levels, he reached out to palm it open.

Access between levels—but inside or outside the closed atmosphere system?

He went back to the nearest closet door and put on a child-sized atmo suit. Then he went back to the outside door. If the suit sensed a drop in pressure, it would automatically attach him to the nearest exterior wall and activate the breathing system. It would also set off a distress call—unless some lazy moron had also disabled *that* safety feature.

But getting caught outside in an atmo suit wouldn't necessarily be a disaster, because Dabeet was already regarded as a pathetic loser. "I just wanted to get some experience in space because they didn't train me before," he could say. "All these other kids knew what they were doing when they got here. How am I supposed to catch up?" Yes, he could sell the idea that he was just a needy stupid kid doing loser stuff in the effort not to be such a loser.

The door did not lead into cold space. It opened on a narrow vertical passage which, unlike the upshaft and downshaft you could enter from the main corridor, relied on ladders with no gravity assist.

Ladders weren't easy in an atmo suit. Dabeet thought of taking the thing off as soon as he got to the next level up, but then he realized that his pathetic-loser story was also true. He really did need to get experience doing tasks while wearing an atmo suit. He would never be as adroit and agile as the kids who had grown up in spaceships and space stations—but *now* he understood that he didn't have to be the best at space stuff, or even good at it. He only had to be able to perform adequately enough to stay alive in dangerous situations.

He walked around the next level up—marking, again, how far he'd gone each time he passed a shelf unit. But this time he saw that there were different chemicals stored on each shelf unit, and some different tools, too. This made him curious enough to try going out into the main corridor, where he found that he was definitely *not* on a student barracks level.

Dabeet wanted to test to see if the doors here—which came about three or four times more frequently than barracks doors—responded to the same simple double-palm code. But what if these were teacher sleeping quarters? Those were supposedly on the level below the kitchens, mess halls, gyms, and classrooms, but common knowledge wasn't always right. He was beginning to wonder whether it was *ever* right.

And teachers' sleeping quarters weren't the only possible uses for these rooms. They could be offices or conference rooms, and if he palmed open a door he might find himself facing six adults having an earnest meeting about what they imagined Monkey and Dabeet had been doing yesterday in the service corridors.

Then again, they might be storage rooms, and one of them might be filled with useful laser weapons. Or maybe they were filled with uniforms from long-defunct student armies from Battle School days, and extra flash suits from the time when twice as many kids needed them constantly for practice and competition.

Or something really crazy, like the frozen corpses of Formics that died at the end of the war and were being saved up for later study.

That was stupid. After the first and second wars, no Formics ever got this close to Earth, and so there'd be no reason at all to transport the corpses here.

Except that Lagrange stations were convenient depots, near to Earth and the Moon but not in orbit. That's why smugglers were using it, right?

What if these rooms were being used by the smugglers?

Very inconvenient location for warehousing, thought Dabeet. But then, the parcels that he and Zhang had seen were small. The big stuff stayed in the warehouses in the docking area, and the small secret stuff was stowed up here.

He listened at a door and heard nothing. That meant either excellent sound isolation or the room had no conversation going on.

He double-palmed it. It slid open just like a barracks door. A light came on, just as in a barracks. Shelves lined the back wall—deep shelves, deeper than a single row of bunks. And some of them—but not all—were laden with metal crates and trunks.

Each one was tagged with the name of an officer.

This was where they stowed their possessions—whatever they didn't need in daily life in Fleet School. If somebody wanted to hide something dangerous, it might be here—but then, smugglers would hardly put their contraband in trunks labeled with their own names.

There weren't enough staff and faculty here to account for *all* the rooms on this level. So Dabeet stepped out and closed the door.

Keep exploring here, or go back into the service corridor?

He opted for the service corridor. Exploring all these rooms would be a job for the whole team, if they decided it was worth it. Maybe there *were* weapons on this level, maybe not. But they needed to get a map of what rooms contained what kind of stuff. It was too big a job for

Dabeet alone. What he wanted was not a specific inventory, but rather a general map of the station.

So he went back to the outside laddershaft he had come through and went up one more level.

This time the ladder tilted sharply inward, so it wasn't really a ladder anymore. More like a stairway with very narrow treads. And when he got to the top, it wasn't a full standing-height door. Dabeet opened it, and found himself in a completely different kind of corridor.

This must be the top level, where the wheel of the Fleet School station narrowed. There was no room for a public corridor at all. And nothing was stored up here. Instead, ductwork, cables, and pipes lined both sides of the narrow corridor.

The floor consisted of sections about a meter long, with smooth, solid outer edges and open-weave centers, so Dabeet could see through the floor to the additional cables and pipes that ran below it. The solid edges bore the unmistakable marks of wheels; this was a kind of track, on which some kind of vehicle ran.

When Dabeet tried to stand, he found that he could—but anybody taller than him would be completely unable to do so. Even Dabeet had to move his head to one side or stoop over whenever he came to a light fixture.

The place wasn't dim, though—if somebody needed to come up here to repair or replace something, they'd have plenty of light to see what they were doing.

Dabeet had to walk along the corridor for a while, just to see if there was any change. There was, of course. Since the level below this one had lots of rooms instead of a series of long barracks rooms parallel with the main corridor, there were ducts and wiring leading down into those spaces at appropriate intervals.

But at intervals that suggested the size of a barracks room, there were much thicker arrays of ductwork, cables, and pipes leading downward. These, Dabeet decided, must pass through a thicker-than-usual wall in the next level, in order to service the barracks rooms two, three, and four levels down.

A little mental calculation made it plain that these ducts couldn't possibly provide atmo and heating for more than three levels, so beginning four levels down, a different duct-and-pipe system must service the lower levels. Maybe a corridor just like this one, only upside down, ran along under the lowest level, with ducts rising upward to the levels above. Or maybe there was an "empty" floor like this one in the middle somewhere.

Good to know this existed, because most of the kids in Fleet School could run along this corridor, while it would be nothing but trouble for adults. A reasonable escape route, especially because the floor curved even more steeply upward, restricting visibility more than on the lower levels.

Then he came to a place where something was attached to the ceiling, forcing him to get down on all fours to get past it. When he was under the thing, it took little time for him to realize that he was looking at the cart designed to run along the track—four wheels and some kind of propulsion system. No steering, though—just guide wheels mounted sideways, so that the cart was running along the sides as well as the base of the segmented floor.

Dabeet examined the floor sections again, and realized now that there was a flange running along the raised edges—except right here, where the cart was attached to the ceiling. If the cart was lowered straight down, it would settle right in between the edges, and the wheels would go right into their place. Once the cart moved forward or backward a meter, the side-wheels would be under the flange, so that in case there was a loss of gravity—or centrifugal force—the cart would not rise away from the floor.

This cart-and-track system must have been used before the station was set to spinning, so it was able to carry a tied-down cargo even in zero-gee.

Judging from the tracks, the cart must have seen a lot of use for a long time. But there was also dust on the floor, so . . . how long had it been since anybody used it?

Since Dabeet had no basis for estimating the normal rate of deposition of dust in this corridor, he had no way to estimate. But it was possible, wasn't it, that this corridor had fallen out of use since Battle School made way for Fleet School?

Maybe these systems aren't even used now, thought Dabeet. New and better systems were installed on another level—a more convenient one—and all this was left here because it wasn't worth the effort to dismantle it. It's not as if you can do anything *else* with this space.

He placed a hand against an air duct.

Warm.

So it *was* in use. And that meant it might fail, and so this access track might still be used from time to time.

Was Bean up here? Or did he do all his exploring *inside* the ducts, as Monkey seemed to believe?

Well, more fool he, to cram himself into such tiny spaces when he could have walked upright along here.

Only Dabeet wasn't interested in walking. He had to see how the cart was supposed to be lowered, and whether it still worked.

Lowering it required nothing more than double-palming the control box beside the cart. Immediately four mechanical arms lowered the cart to the floor and then withdrew back into the ceiling.

The cart was in two identical parts. But a little pulling and pushing showed Dabeet that either end could be adapted into a passenger space. Unexpectedly, the rider or driver had to lie on his back and watch his forward progress in a couple of mirrors that popped up on either side. Dabeet crawled into the space, which was designed for a much larger body. For a moment he thought it might be like a car, using feet to control speed and braking—in which case his lack of adult height might make it impossible for him to use the thing.

But no, the controls were all in a single hard-wired appliance that he could hold while lying on his back. Actually, there were two remotes, one on either side, so that left-handed or right-, you could drive using your dominant hand.

Dabeet started pressing the buttons and yes, the cart moved easily and fairly rapidly along. He soon got used to the weird upside-down mirror image of the track ahead of him. And it wasn't as if there were any obstacles ahead of him. It took very little time for him to complete a circuit of this level. There were four more suspended carts, for a total of five.

When he had the cart back under its hanging-place, Dabeet turned himself over and crawled off the cart. This was designed to carry two adults, at need—one in each half. But kids Dabeet's size could double up and piggyback. Might be able to carry six or eight kids, depending on the power of the motor and, of course, the battery life.

Double-palming brought the arms back down to pick up the cart and draw it up to the ceiling.

These carts would probably never be useful, because the students would probably never have a reason to flee upward into this top corridor. Yet if they *were* needed, the carts existed and it might be possible for some of the students to become proficient drivers.

For a moment he thought of waiting to tell anybody until he had really mastered driving a cart while lying on his back looking into a mirror.

Then he stifled his ego. It's more important for as many people as possible to be proficient drivers than for me to have the pleasure of being the best at something really fun.

In fact, he knew that he needed to get the others up here, so that lots of people could be proficient with the carts. And he needed to do it at once, before he talked himself into doing something egotistical and counterproductive.

I really hate this atmo suit, he realized. He was soaked with sweat and it was rolling into his eyes, making them sting. Weren't there supposed to be temperature controls in the atmo suit?

Oh. That's right. Dabeet found the temperature controls easily, just where the instructor had shown him when he first came to the station. It helped a lot. Cooler air fanned across his face and he didn't feel so claustrophobic in the suit.

He couldn't take off the suit up here. He had to get back down to the level where he found it, and hang it back in its place.

He went down a different ladderway and soon had the atmo suit back in place. Then, still a little sweat-soaked, he stepped out into the corridor.

The others were still conversing in the barracks, and once again they fell stone silent when he entered. "I think you need to see the top level."

"Not right now," said Zhang He. "We're making progress, and we can go up on our own, one or two at a time, after we've decided the things we have to decide."

"Fine," said Dabeet. Then he briefly told them about the ladderways and the carts. "Imagine if somebody was injured. The cart could get them from one side of the station's wheel to the other in far less time than walking."

"Injured people are going to be hard to get up that ladder," said Monkey, smiling.

Dabeet smiled back. "I guess we'll have to wait to injure them until they're already up," he said.

His message had been delivered. Time for him to leave again, so they could decide how to deal with the problem Dabeet had brought to Fleet School.

15

—Mind-reading is essential to human life, but we're all so bad at it.

—I knew you would say that.

—Some people are so predictable that all their decisions seem to be by reflex. Provoked, they get mad. Stroked, they purr and snuggle. Fed, they fall asleep.

—I like it when you're all metaphorical.

—Even when people try to be unpredictable, they usually do it in completely predictable ways. Adolescents who show their originality exactly as all their friends do.

—You're saying all this because Achilles is truly unpredictable and it makes you afraid.

—I don't like being wrong, and I don't like acting blindly.

—So you figure him out, you take action, and when you turn out to have been wrong, not only do your actions fail to contain him, but also you feel resentful that he led you to make wrong decisions.

—He's not trying to deceive us. He isn't thinking about us. He's trying to accomplish something, but his goal is rooted so deeply in his psyche that he himself doesn't know what it is.

—Thus you project onto Achilles your own ignorance of his purposes.

—Can you do better?

—I can fail less often, by never trying to read his mind.

—You can afford that luxury because stopping him isn't your responsibility.

—It isn't yours, either.

—I make it mine.

—And by so doing, you doom yourself to failure.

—Satisfying some unconscious inner hunger of my own. Except that my *conscious* hunger is to stop that boy before he does some real damage.

—He has so many plots under way that it's easy to think that every terrifying path leads back to his door.

—You think all this business about a raid on Fleet School *isn't* Achilles after all?

—Achilles has been kidnapping Battle School graduates. That fits with his normal pattern of relentless revenge against anyone who saw him weak.

—Which is everyone he ever met.

—But he only notices that they see his weakness when *he* sees his weakness and sees them seeing it.

—And none of the kids in Fleet School had anything to do with Battle School. The only thing they have in common is venue. Battle School happened in the same Lagrange-point station. Is he taking vengeance on terrastationary habitats?

—Maybe he sees it as an act of altruism: If he destroys the school, then teachers and fellow students there can never humiliate somebody like Achilles again.

—Doing a favor to the kids he blows to bits.

—To be fair, we don't *know* that's his plan.

—Is it the most vile, violent, and incomprehensible act you could imagine?

—As applies to a space station, smithereens is about as total a triumph as you can aspire to.

—We have to assume he means to do the worst.

—But not everybody working for him will have that goal. Evil isn't best served by equally evil servants.

—A thing little understood by war-crimes tribunals dealing with civil servants in an evil regime. In what way did administrators of the water supply or transportation system absorb the evil of the regime? The more virtuous these civil servants are, the more the evil ruler can count on them to keep their word. Then all he has to do is conceal from them the most likely consequences of their actions.

—Like what you and I did to Andrew Wiggin.

—We were saving humanity. Ender knew that was the goal. He wanted us to succeed with him.

—I notice you're not openly embracing the title "evil ruler." Or rejecting it, either.

—If I die before you, you can have that inscribed on my tombstone.

Maybe somebody else went to that innermost—topmost—ring of the station in the next few days after Dabeet discovered it, but Monkey was the only one who asked him to take her there. They indulged in a little playing with the carts—it was impossible for venturous children not to see what happened if they collided two of them on the same track. Not at high speed, of course. But it didn't matter. The carts had collision-avoidance so all they did was stop abruptly, tossing Monkey and Dabeet a little and making them laugh.

"Now my original plan of making all the bad guys lie down on these tracks so we could run over them won't work," said Monkey.

"We can't make them do anything," said Dabeet.

Monkey narrowed her eyes at him. "Have you ever heard of 'humor'?"

"I knew you were joking, if that's what you're asking. I simply chose to remind myself of the ludicrousness of making *any* plans until we see what they actually want to do once they get here."

"That's why I'm here with you," said Monkey, "instead of sitting around with the bigger kids listening to them make elaborate plans about 'luring them' here or 'driving them' there."

"Just for amusement," said Dabeet, "where do they plan to lure them or drive them?"

"Mostly to a battleroom. All four of them or just one of them. And when they get there, they find that teams of builders have constructed elaborate forts or mazes out of wall cubes."

Dabeet nodded. "That was my first impulse, too."

"You think our little wall forts would slow them down?"

"They can't use projectile weapons, or they'll perforate the hull and drain the whole place until the nanooze on the outside walls can seal the holes. So inside a battleroom, our wall forts will behave to their weapons just like walls."

"But come on, Dabeet. Even if our wall forts are *brilliant,* they aren't weapons. We can't build traps into them. They'll figure out how to dismantle them as fast as we did."

"Well, maybe. Maybe not. Defensive structures don't win battles, they only delay them while you wait for relief or hope they give up and go away."

"Because if they get delayed for a couple of minutes, they're bound to get discouraged."

"So the only plan that matters is how to stop them from reaching their objective, and unless their objective is in the battlerooms, there's no reason they'd ever go there."

"Well . . ." said Monkey.

Dabeet tried to guess what she was thinking. "You're right. *We're* the objective."

"We have no idea what the objective is," said Monkey, "so I don't know what *you* think I was going to say."

Dabeet started to explain why he thought she had been about to contradict him, but she cut him off.

"So because you *imagined* you could guess that I was going to contradict you," said Monkey, "you immediately thought of a deep hole in your previous statement, and talked as if *I* had said it."

That was exactly what Dabeet had done. "Yes."

"I think you've just discovered a new mental discipline. Self-contradiction as a spur to creative thinking. You think up something, then you assume it's an idiotic idea and figure out *why* it's dumb, then you think of ways to make it less dumb, and then think of why *those* things are idiotic—"

"And meanwhile I also assume that the assumption of idioticness is also idiotic and poke holes in *that*—"

"And in the end, you never reach any useful conclusion or plan of action."

"Once they hear of this new mental discipline," said Dabeet, "geniuses everywhere are bound to adopt it as their primary means of analysis."

"Until it occurs to them that such a mental discipline is also idiotic."

"Leading to exactly the same result that most commanders get to in war with far less effort," said Dabeet, "which is why the *real* geniuses beat them."

"Why?" asked Monkey. "What result is that?"

"When you focus on trying to figure out the enemy's plan before he's shown it to you by taking action, you're basically playing mental chess against yourself and *doing* nothing. What if the enemy is so much smarter than you that all your guesses are ridiculously wrong? Or what if the enemy is so stupid that you give them way too much credit?"

"It's stupid to assume your enemy is stupid," said Monkey.

"True," said Dabeet, "but it's even stupider to try to wage war by outguessing the enemy."

"Well, you *have* to try."

"What you mean is, you can't *help* but try," said Dabeet, "but it's such a waste of time that you can't regard anything you think of as a 'plan.'"

"So we just sit here trying not to think," said Monkey.

"Not at all. We spend our time planning what *we* will do to *them*."

"How is that better? We don't know a bit more about them than before, so anything we plan is just a waste of time."

"Here are the huge differences," said Dabeet. "First, defensive plans are wasted if the enemy won't attack where you need him to. But offensive plans don't require the enemy to act in a certain way. *We* initiate the action, so we don't guess what they'll do, we simply *see* what they've *done* and where they actually are."

"They're not here," said Monkey, "so we can't see what they've done."

"And we *do* know a lot about them," said Dabeet.

Monkey immediately looked suspicious. "Have you held back information that we need to have?"

"I haven't held back anything," said Dabeet. He did not say how hurtful it was that she went straight to that assumption. Why shouldn't she? She didn't know Dabeet. She didn't know she could trust him.

Dabeet wasn't even sure she could trust him, because he didn't trust himself. He wouldn't know what *he* could do until he did it. He wouldn't know if he could be trusted until he actually accomplished something.

"Monkey," said Dabeet. "You *know* that we know a lot about these raiders. They have to arrive here in a spaceworthy vehicle."

"Well, duh."

"Not *duh*, Monkey. That's not guessing, it's something we know. We *know* it. And that means that *you*—and everybody like you, who grew up in a spacefaring culture—you already know way more than nothing about their arrival vehicle. *I* don't know that stuff, except, like, they have to be able to contain and replenish atmosphere, there'll be airlocks, some kind of propulsion system. Places for passengers and crew to sit during the voyage. Food. Water."

"That's like saying, we know the enemy has to poop sometime. Yeah, but so what?"

Dabeet couldn't help but laugh. "Monkey, knowing that the enemy has to poop is actually important. On Earth, there's the whole disposal problem. If their poo gets into their drinking water, they're going to start getting dysentery and that can destroy your enemy *for* you."

"On a spaceship, you'd have to work really hard to get poo into your drinking water," said Monkey.

"Right. But peeing and pooing are right up there with breathing and drinking and eating, when it comes to necessities. As long as you aren't facing a robot army—"

Monkey looked surprised. "Do you think they really *would?*"

"They tried robot soldiers against the Formics," said Dabeet. "Drones are better. Human soldiers are best. It's not just speed, strength, and accuracy, it's also adaptability and knowing where to strike in the first place. And making independent decisions."

"I thought the whole point of massed armies was to make them all submit to the single will of the commander."

"You see any massed armies around here? You think we're going to go toe to toe with whatever *men* they send against us? This will be asymmetric fighting, and our actions will be individual or small squad."

Monkey looked thoughtful. "They don't really teach us military stuff here, do they."

"When I was trying to get into Fleet School, I read everything. Watched everything."

"But you knew this wasn't a military school anymore."

"It's the school where the IF sends their own children."

"So we should all be listening to you because you read more books?"

"Nobody should listen to me. Everybody should prepare themselves to carry out their own plans. Cooperating where we can, but not falling apart if we find ourselves alone."

Monkey looked at him a little sideways. "You're preparing to go off and do crazy things on your own."

"You see anybody inviting me to be part of their army?"

Monkey gave him the eyebrow equivalent of a shrug.

"I'm making plans to do what I can. I'm practicing the skills I think I'm going to need."

"And what are those skills?"

"Moving in freefall," said Dabeet. "Working in a spacesuit. Or an atmo suit. Figuring out how the electronics work. Improving my skills with hand tools, in and out of gravity."

"That sounds very specific," said Monkey. "You already know what you're going to do."

"It isn't and I don't. But if everybody else is going to the battlerooms— which is no worse than any of the idiotic ideas I've come up with, by the way—somebody needs to see what's going on in the ship they came in."

"So you, the one with the fewest space skills, have appointed yourself to reconnaissance."

"I'm the only one who'll recognize my mother if they actually have her on their ship."

"Are you serious? Why in the world would they bring her *here*?"

"My first thought, too. But there are a few things to consider. If they're planning to use me as the fall guy, then bringing her here gets a prime witness to my innocence off Earth and makes her look like part of the expedition."

"Not a very good reason."

"The second reason they might bring her is also the answer to your objection: Who says these clowns are reasonable?"

"What happened to 'It's stupid to assume your enemy is stupid'?"

"It's right there with 'It's stupid to assume your enemy will only do reasonable things.'"

"You got any other reasons why they'd bring your mother?"

"So she can die along with the rest of us. So everyone I know and love will be extinguished."

"You really *do* think this is all about you."

"I can't rule it out," said Dabeet.

"*I* can. It's not about *you*."

"Monkey, I know this is far-fetched. But look, I don't know who my father is except that the woman who raised me believes that he's an officer in the IF. What if he's a very high official? What if he's kept me hidden because his enemies would use me against him if they knew about me? So, maybe they found out about me, and they want to kill me in some spectacular way so that whoever my father is, he'll know that his son was killed, along with the woman who raised me, and the act of terrorism was blamed on me."

"You're a loon," said Monkey. "I don't mean that in a teasing way. I mean a jackboot strapped-in lubricated paranoid."

"I don't *believe* that, Monkey. My father really is with the IF somehow, because they let me in here. But beyond that, he's probably just a guy. I *know* that. But I don't know that I'm not being used to target *him*. What if he's powerful, and this is a way to get to him?"

"Delusions of grandeur," said Monkey. "They usually go along with paranoia. Why would everybody be spying on you? Because I'm so important. How do you know you're so important? If I weren't, why would they all be spying on me?"

"And yet important people often have children, and they get their education somewhere," said Dabeet. "As I said, he's probably just a guy."

"So tell me, genius test boy," said Monkey, "were you planning to do your freefall practice outside the ship?"

"That's where they keep the zero-gee."

"There's the battleroom."

"Where there's always somebody watching."

"Well, you certainly have privacy in outer space. One miss and you're gone forever. Is this just a way of concealing from yourself your unconscious decision to commit suicide?"

"Quite possibly. But maybe you could coach me."

"I could. But maybe I should be making my *own* war plans."

"Are you?"

"I didn't realize I needed to till now."

"So maybe you train me so I can accomplish the stealth mission of spying on a ship that's docked with Fleet School, and maybe sabotaging it or rescuing somebody inside it."

"Literally everybody here is better qualified for that mission than you, Dabeet."

"And yet it's my mission," said Dabeet.

"*I'll* do it," said Monkey. "It needs doing, I think you're right, but you don't have the skills."

"Help me with that," said Dabeet.

"There's no possibility of your being competent by the time they get here."

"There's no chance I'll be as competent as *you*. But this isn't a competition. I only have to be competent enough to do the job. And you'll be needed elsewhere. You already *are,* they've already assigned you."

Monkey grimaced slightly. "Building walls in the battleroom."

"You have *that* skill, too."

"Thanks to you," said Monkey. "And also, no thanks."

"You have a team," said Dabeet. "I don't. I'm expendable. If no one can think of a use for me, I'm expendable, unless I think of a use for myself."

"Don't do this dangerous thing," said Monkey. "Annoying as you are, I'm kind of used to you. I'd miss you a little if you died."

"That is, truly, the nicest thing that anybody's said to me in Fleet School."

"É, well, I'm not going to spend the time to train you." To Dabeet she sounded a little defiant, as if she felt she were doing something wrong by refusing to help him.

Dabeet's first impulse was to play off of this, to try to persuade her.

But he thought better of it immediately. He was not going to treat other people as things to be manipulated until he got what he wanted. She had a right to make her own decision, and if Dabeet was her friend, he would respect that.

"I get it," said Dabeet. "You have to practice with your team of incompetent wall-builders."

Monkey smiled at his characterization of her team. "It's my assignment."

"It's the role you play in the community," said Dabeet. "Teacher, shepherd, guide." Only when he said it did he realize that this was true. As she had appointed herself *his* teacher, shepherd, guide.

He could see her relent . . . a little. Instead of Dabeet arguing her into it, she was responding to his respect. Maybe. It wasn't as if Dabeet could reliably decode what was going on in anybody's mind.

"I don't have time to teach you," she said, "but I'll tell you the rules they tell little children who are doing their first tasks outside the ship. The children who follow these rules live. The ones who don't, don't. Do you understand that?"

"Yes." Even though he would remember everything she said without making any special effort, he faced her directly and made steady eye contact, which would show her that he was listening, paying attention. Another gesture of respect.

"One," said Monkey. "Don't let go of one thing until you're holding something else that's attached to the ship."

"Doesn't sound like freefall to me."

"Freefall comes after about a year of these rules. Get it? Now *listen*."

Listening meant not questioning. Dabeet flashed on Monkey as a two-year-old, hearing her father or mother tell her these rules. With children of that age, the adults would have to work to make sure they were being heard and understood, and Monkey was treating him as she herself might have been treated. Must have been.

"Rule One, don't let go till you're holding something else attached to the ship, you got that. Rule Two. The ship is always *above* you. If you let go you fall *away* from the ship."

"In zero-gee . . ." Dabeet began, but at the narrowing of Monkey's eyes he fell silent.

"It's how you *think*. You use your gravity sense to pretend that you'll fall if you let go. Got it?"

"So it's really Rule One all over again," said Dabeet.

"It's Rule Two," said Monkey.

"Sí, Maestra," said Dabeet.

"Rule Three," said Monkey. "Before you move from your present position, name *out loud* the thing you're reaching for."

"But you won't be there to hear me," said Dabeet.

"Name it," said Monkey, "or die."

Dabeet thought: It isn't about naming it for the adult. It's about having a clear idea of what you're reaching for before you reach, so you don't get sloppy in your habits. "Name it out loud. I will."

"Rule Four. Find where your target is attached to the ship and say it out loud."

Made sense. So you don't reach for some piece of debris only because you assume it *must* be attached to the ship. "I assume by 'ship' we mean 'station' in this context."

"Is the station moving through space?" asked Monkey.

"Sí, Maestra," said Dabeet. "And I want to keep moving with it at exactly the same velocity."

"Rule Five."

"How many rules do you expect your two-year-olds to memorize?"

"All of them," said Monkey. "Rule Five. If you ever come loose from the ship, wrap your arms around any object that you come near. Do not use your hands to catch on to it. Wrap your arms around it."

"Such a waste of opposable thumbs," said Dabeet.

"The rule is actually simpler: Wrap your arms around it, not your fingers."

"Because the hands of babies are too small to grab anything."

"Because humans are deceived by their own weightlessness into forgetting how much mass they have, and therefore how much momentum."

"I'll think I can grasp something, but I won't have enough grip strength to hold it."

"And there's no guarantee that with the slight vision distortion of even the best-made spacesuits your eyes will guide your hand to the exact spot. It's been a long time since our lives depended on being able to grab branches."

"These are good rules," said Dabeet.

"Rule Six."

"Good thing I can count to six."

"Don't walk. Don't run."

Dabeet immediately thought of a little girl running along the outside surface of a ship and launching herself into space with the first step.

"You learn to walk and run inside ship's gravity, but none of that works on the outside surface."

"Most ships these days have hulls covered with nanooze. Besides self-sealing any punctures in the hull, the nanooze grips human feet. But you don't run—the nanooze won't let go fast enough and you'll fall over. You don't even walk, because that implies a steady rhythm of movement. You carefully pry up one foot and set it down in the new location. You give the nanooze a moment to grip, and then you pull up the other foot and put it in a new place. That isn't walking."

"Very wise."

"Tell me the rules," said Monkey.

"One. Don't let go of one thing till I'm holding something else that's attached to the ship. Two. The ship is always above me. Three. Before I move from my present position, I name *out loud* the thing I'm reaching for. Rule Four. Find where my target is attached to the ship and say it out loud. Five. If I ever come loose, wrap my arms around any object I come near. No hand-grasping. Six. Don't walk, don't run."

Monkey looked at him oddly. "You didn't even have to try."

"I don't forget things."

"Knowing the words won't help you unless you *do* everything the rules say."

"I'll do them, Monkey. And thank you for teaching me this much."

"Follow these rules, Dabeet, and you'll live. Don't and you won't."

"Got it."

"Good luck, Test Boy."

And that was it. She jogged off down that uppermost corridor and was almost immediately out of sight behind the curvature of the ceiling.

She had really meant it. Just tell him the rules and he was on his own.

But this would be better, wouldn't it? He had discovered in his first attempts in the battleroom that, unlike the way he could learn any words or numbers or sounds or images that he encountered, he had a hard time getting his body to do what he wanted.

No, his body did everything he wanted. What was hard was figuring out where his body actually was, and what movements followed each other in a sequence.

I'm not a dancer, that's what it is. I can't learn sequences of movements easily. And I'm about to trust my survival to my ability to acquire new habits of carefulness.

But that's what these rules are for, thought Dabeet. If I'm obeying them, then I'm not acquiring habits of anything. Each movement is methodical and new. Not part of a sequence—a single movement. Reaching for a named, attached location. Or wrapping my arms around an object.

If I ever have to wrap my arms around something, it'll be because I'm loose from the ship. A drowning man, flailing around, panicking. That's why I can't trust my twitchy fingers. Too frightened to be functional. When a drowning man attaches himself to his rescuer, there's no brain involved. Just clutching. But Rule Five gives me a plan to recite. Overcome my panic. No flailing. Just arm-wrapping. These are good rules.

Because I'm going to panic.

Not that he was ever afraid in the battleroom. Why would he be? He was wearing armor in an enclosed space with plenty of atmosphere.

Out there, though. He had read about it—the awareness of a huge universe of downward movement. A place without horizons.

Rule Two. The ship is upward. I'm holding on so I don't fall forever into that nothing.

I can do this. Forewarned is forearmed.

Dabeet got into a spacesuit and felt it compress in the limbs and neck to fit his small size. The gloves also tightened. But not enough. They were still almost as fisty as mittens. Another reason not to imagine he could grasp anything that was flying past in a blur. The gloves were supposed to augment his grip—but he had to aim his hand exactly right so the object he wanted to hold would be in the crease of his palm. Now, wearing gloves, would that mean the crease of the *glove's* palm, or of his hand inside the—

He knew what this internal monologue was about. There was no doubt in his mind—the crease of the glove was the thing that would come into contact with any object out there. No, he was chattering to himself in his own mind to postpone the inevitable moment when he went through the tiny workman's airlock and found himself outside.

Because he had caught himself procrastinating, he moved immediately. Suit sealed? Confirmed by the row of green lights along the bottom of the heads-up display inside the helmet. Breathing suit atmo? Yes. How many minutes? Only an emergency suit, not recently recharged—two hours of air, but only half an hour of full battery. Got to get a bunch of these fully charged before they . . .

Procrastinating again. Inside the airlock, he sealed the interior door, then carefully thought through the steps in airlock training. If you just pop the outer door, you'll be ejected along with the air. Don't even *imagine* you're strong enough to hold on to something and not get blown out the door. Even though this airlock was much tinier than the cargo airlocks they had trained them on, Dabeet wasn't taking chances. First activate the pump and get as much air out of the chamber as possible. Done. Wait wait wait. Didn't take long—air cleared.

Not all of it, of course, but there wouldn't be any rapid puff of air when the outer door opened.

Even so, Dabeet hooked an arm through the bar on the inner door— no doubt put there for just this purpose, since it stood out far enough to insert an entire spacesuit arm into the gap. Only when he was securely in place did he push the button to open the outer door.

He had thought there would be some kind of metal-on-metal prang, but no, he had to turn his body to see that the door was open. No sound at all.

Do I leave the door open for when I come back?

Airlock discipline. Always close the door. Always always always. Because your rescuers may need an airlock. And you can't be sure you'll return to the same spot.

But to close the door, Dabeet had to pass through it.

There were arm-grip bars on all four sides of the door. At first Dabeet tried to snake an arm around and push it through the gap, but no. These bars were meant to be held by hands, not by arms.

He tested the grip. Sure enough, it was clumsy and fumbly when he first tried to attach, but when he pressed the crease of the palm into the bar, the gloves activated and gripped like steel.

Bacana. He could go out the door now.

Right now. Any second now.

Because he became impatient with his own fear, Dabeet almost pushed himself right out, but he stopped himself. He had no idea how much force he should use. With his hand gripping the outside bar, his back was to the doorway. The last thing he wanted to do was push so hard he broke the glove's grip on the bar. Or broke his arm. Could that happen?

Dabeet pulled his other arm away from his handhold on an interior bar and used his fingers to push his body out into . . . space . . . no, just the area outside the . . .

He felt his breathing growing fast and ragged as he seemed to *whirl* out of the door.

But his grip on the outside bar held as a kind of pivot, and it did not let go when he whumped against the hull of the station.

He expected himself to bounce off, but no. The nanooze gripped him immediately. It was holding his back firmly to the hull.

By reflex, he almost pulled his hand away from the bar, almost let go. After all, this was like lying on a hill, wasn't it? The nanooze holding him like gravity.

The ship is always above me. I am not lying *on* the ship. I am hanging *from* the ship. I'm holding on to the ship for dear life. Obey these rules and live.

Dabeet opened his eyes and allowed himself to see and understand his situation.

He was on the upper curve of the inside of the wheel of the station. He could see the under-construction wheel "down" near his feet. It was actually parallel to the wheel he was on, but that would only be obvious down near the fattest part of the tube. Up here near the top, it could have been a separate vehicle.

Dabeet looked left, then, slowly, right. The wheel he was on curved like a huge halo above and around him. The unfinished parallel wheel went only partway in one direction, where it left off with construction materials and equipment fastened to it at the end. In the other direction, he could see that it went much farther, before it ended in a similar welter of supplies and tools. The wheel he was on was complete.

He thought of the inside of a bicycle wheel. There were no spokes here, though. Just tubes snaking out to the four cubes of the battlerooms. It took a bit of study to figure out that yes, all four cubes were in place, one of them mostly occluded by the other three.

Those tubes had to be the corridors. But they were so small. Forty at a time, kids would run along those corridors and . . .

No. Those tubes must be life support, because *there* was the corridor. A single corridor, because that's how the children experienced it. One corridor leading to each end of the one battleroom it was attached to. Rigid, rectangular. Like airplane jetways, only longer.

Now Dabeet could see how that single corridor always stayed attached to the same battleroom. But it also continued around the outside of the first battleroom and then forked to go on to the second, the third, the fourth. That's how it looked from the inside, too. They never saw where the other corridors led off. They only ran the path that was open to them, lit up with their team colors. Each one leading to one end or the other of the square. The enemy's gate, our gate. And then the corridors leading to the teacher door, the observation rooms. The mysteries of the battleroom now laid out clearly before him.

Completely irrelevant to the task at hand.

Or not. Because there was something quite pertinent that had never occurred to him before. There were no airlocks leading out of the battleroom cubes. If something happened to damage the station so severely that the battleroom corridors were compromised, there was no other escape route. Ultimately, just the one corridor providing an exit from *all* the battlerooms.

The most terrible place to be if somebody attacked the station, because there would be no escape.

That was important information. He would tell Monkey, she would tell the others. Maybe they'd change their plans. Maybe they wouldn't. He could imagine Zhang He saying, "Dabeet just doesn't like the plan because he didn't think of it."

So unfair of Dabeet to think that. Zhang He wasn't his friend, he understood that now. But it didn't mean he was Dabeet's enemy. That sense of betrayal, Dabeet couldn't give it any weight. In all likelihood, Zhang He would be the one who'd instantly recognize the danger, argue on the same side as Monkey. We can't stake our survival on the sturdiness of the corridor connections.

Dabeet shut his eyes. He hadn't come out here to play through imaginary scenarios of how the other students would react to any information that came from him. This wasn't the time or place to indulge his hurt feelings. His loneliness.

He opened his eyes and stared straight forward. With the hoops of the station in his peripheral vision, the battleroom boxes mostly above him, all he could see straight forward was . . . nothing. Stars.

And then, suddenly, not nothing. The luminous blue and white of Earth, larger from here than the Moon was from Earth.

His eyes immediately tried to find recognizable objects on the globe. Was that Africa? No, it was clouds. Were those mountains? Maybe, doesn't matter. Does *not* matter.

And then the stab of light as the Sun first edged into view. At once his screen darkened in a single patch, making a near-total eclipse of the Sun inside his suit. Good design, thought Dabeet. Good for people wearing these suits not to go blind whenever they happen to spin to face a star.

The station was rotating at a decent clip. He hadn't realized how fast they were moving.

But not moving in a straight line. Spinning. So if he fell away from the station, he would continue, not in the station's general line of movement through the universe, but rather in the exact line where he *happened* to be going when he let go of the station. It would basically shoot him in that direction like a ball flying out of a jai alai player's cesta. He'd have to work out the physics of that. . . .

Later.

Still gripping the bar outside the airlock door, Dabeet tried to push himself up—no, *down*—from the surface of the hull by pressing with his other hand. But all that happened was his other hand got caught in the nanooze.

Br'er Rabbit and the tar baby. Whatever you touch to get leverage, you're stuck to that, too.

Not possible. Nanooze wouldn't be useful if you couldn't unstick yourself, and easily.

He raised his hand from the nanooze. There was only a momentary tug and his hand was free.

Instead of trying to push himself off the hull, Dabeet simply rolled toward the side where he was gripping the bar. The nanooze let him go quite easily. Good thing he hadn't trusted it to hold him. It was there to seal breaches in the hull, not to fasten stupid boys to the surface.

So let's say that the enemy ship is docked at an airlock on the main level of the . . . which ring? This uppermost ring?

He needed a clearer map of the station in his head. He remembered what he had seen. Not this ring, the next ring down. The middle one.

He tried to imagine what the jointure between the rings would be like. Could he get from this ring to the other one without letting go and just flying there?

No flying. Rule One.

Because he was now hovering just over the open airlock door, he was tempted to go back inside. Hadn't he learned a lot already? That was a good first day, wasn't it?

Dabeet tried to imagine two-year-old Monkey doing just this much, and her father saying, Come inside now, Monkey, come inside. And Monkey would say, No, Papa, no, no, I want to do more, I haven't done nothin' yet.

Am I afraid of Monkey's contempt?

Yes sir, that I am.

What goal would be reasonable for this first expedition? Dabeet cast his gaze along the tube and saw that the next airlock was only about . . . about . . . he had no idea of the distance. He remembered inside the tube.

How far to the next airlock? Much farther than it seemed to be out here. But that was a reasonable goal.

He looked around the perimeter of the open airlock door and found the CLOSE button. He almost pressed it before realizing that perhaps he should make sure no part of his body would be between the closing door and the frame. Ouch, that would have been nasty. He pulled himself away from the open door, which involved holding on to the bar with both gloves.

Then he could hardly bring himself to let go of the bar with one hand so he could press the button.

I'm going to have to let go of things all the time. Not till I have hold of other things, right, but still. Most of the time, only one hand will hold me to this ship that's right overhead.

Overhead.

Dabeet gently pulled his legs free of the nanooze and let them drift up . . . no, *downward,* so that now he really was hanging from the bar by both hands. Gravity wasn't tugging him "downward," but at least now he could feel like both hands were his connection to the station. Yet he could let go with one hand and reach upward to the button. Push. Slow but steady closure of the door. Dabeet counted. Four seconds to close. Looked slow, was actually fairly quick.

Now I'm here. Outside the ship. Hanging here with the next airlock only about fifty meters away.

He could see the bars around that other airlock.

And absolutely nothing to hold on to between this airlock and that one.

Oh, this is such a very bad design. Maybe I'm not supposed to have any handholds at all. Maybe I'm supposed to walk along in the nanooze and—

Don't walk. Don't run.

Dabeet looked at the curved metal sheet that was riveted to the frame of the wheel. Smooth, unbroken . . .

Except that the corners were rounded. And since each corner was aligned with three other corners, each junction had about a ten-centimeter gap. A full-sized person could easily reach one of those corners, but . . .

So could a child. Dabeet slid himself along the bar to one end, then reached out his hand.

"Reaching for that gap between plates," he said aloud. "Definitely attached to the ship by a bunch of rivets."

He found that the rounded corners had a gap behind them, so there was room for gloves to reach in and get a grip. He could easily hang from this.

But could he reach the next one?

That was nowhere near as important as the question, Could he get back to the bar around the airlock door, if he once let go of it?

It took him a long time to let go of that bar, move his free hand up to the same gap, and hang there by both hands. Then, almost convulsively, he started to reach again for the bar. But he stopped himself. "Reaching for the airlock bar. Left hand stays here, right hand moves to the bar."

It turned out to be easy.

Slow at first, Dabeet began to get a rhythm once he realized that even a child could bridge from gap to gap. Each time, he'd say, "Next gap. Next gap." But about halfway across to the other airlock, he stopped himself. He had been getting too comfortable with it. The process was repetitive, and he had the illusion that he had mastered the physical routine of it.

But that's how I'll die, thought Dabeet. The first time I let go before realizing that the gap isn't at the same spot in this place.

And, sure enough, even though he hadn't consciously noticed it before stopping himself, the plates aligned differently in one band around the hull. He remembered now that inside the hull, there was another structure that intruded into the topmost corridor. And here on the outside, that structure was represented by longer, narrower plates. Their corners were not rounded. There was no gap.

But the whole band was raised about three centimeters above the level of the regular plates. He reached his glove into the space and found that it was deep enough for his hands to find purchase there. But the reaching hand was facing the wrong way, his hand didn't bend that way, he—

I'm hanging *below* the ship, he reminded himself. He pulled his hand back to the gap he was hanging from and now reached again, this time with his hand held the other way, palm out from the station surface. "Reaching for the lip of that plate," he said. Now his fingers went under the plate in the right direction. Once his grip there was secure, he let go of the old gap and rotated his body so that when he reached the other side . . .

There was no gap between the two narrow plates. Combined, they were wider than the spaces between corner gaps. He hadn't reached the far side, where presumably there was another lip. Immediately he laid his palm flat against the surface. The nanooze gripped his glove. But he didn't count on it. He was *hanging* from the station, he couldn't count on the nanooze holding him.

I didn't say, "The other side of these plates" out loud, thought Dabeet. And he realized that if he had *said* it, he would have looked to estimate the distance, would have been prepared for this.

He slid his extended hand through the nanooze toward the far side. Stretched farther and farther.

Could I reach it with my toe? Or is the toe of the boot too thick to fit into the gap?

By tilting his head backward so his chest was pressed against the plates, he was able to reach far enough that his fingers caught the lip. He gripped as tightly as he could. Finally his heads-up display showed him that both gloves were locked into their life grip on the ship's hull.

He let go with the first hand. At once his body relaxed into its new position, beyond the narrow patch, hanging in place. He inserted his other hand into the same gap. Gripped with both. Breathed slowly and carefully.

Now he was back to the land of the corner gaps. He could see that this path continued unbroken to the next airlock. Slowly, word by word and grip by grip, he made his way across. He forced himself to push the VACATE button before he pressed the OPEN button on the airlock. The last thing he needed was a tsunami-force puff of air to blow him off the face of the station.

Do not feel relieved, he warned himself. Relief makes you careless. I can lose my grip here in the airlock entrance as easily as anywhere else. "Reaching for the bar above the airlock door." Then, "Reaching for the bar inside the airlock."

With his arm hooked through the bar on the interior door, he pushed the CLOSE button and saw the band of dazzling sunlight disappear as the door blocked it.

RECHARGE. It took about ten seconds for atmo to level out, yet when the light turned green, Dabeet wasn't yet ready to open the interior door.

I'm alive. But that was harder than I ever thought it would be.

He tried to imagine making that same passage with Monkey supervising. She would have been helpful. He would have been more confident. Or would he? Monkey was kind, but she couldn't have kept the "of course" tone out of her voice each time he figured something out.

Better that I did this alone.

I don't want her to watch me do this till I'm a lot better.

I'll never be good enough for her not to demand that I name my next grip before reaching for it. I'll never be as good as her. As good as *anybody* else who grew up in space.

I never want her to watch me do this.

But then he realized: It won't matter. Maybe whatever needs doing will require more than one of us. Her or somebody else. Somebody who hates me, somebody with disdain. Somebody I have contempt for. It won't matter. I'll concentrate and say my next grip out loud, just like a two-year-old, and they can think what they want. I'll be alive. I'll get where I'm going.

16

—Dabeet isn't Ender, my friend, and he's not facing a fellow student. Get him out of there.

—I can't.

—You most certainly can. I know the disposition of the ships near the station, and you have three close enough to get there with hours to spare.

—Suppose only one person is saved from Fleet School, and he happens to be the very child that all the evidence is designed to point at. I think not.

—Alive is better than dead.

—I believe that's almost certainly his opinion, too.

—He matters to you. Apparently more than you understand. Unless you have fifty more scions scattered around the solar system. Do you have a spare?

—He's the only one.

—All your eggs in one basket. Doesn't sound like you.

—Sounds exactly like me. It's what I did with Ender.

—Get him off that station.

—Can I evacuate everybody?

—In a pinch, maybe.

—Count the ships, estimate the life support. And what would that teach

Dabeet? All of them? Adults will step in and save you. These kids are supposed to go on exploratory missions, colonization, with *no* recourse closer than ten, fifteen, twenty years away. They can't expect God to come out of the machine and save them. Ever.

—I wonder how useful that lesson will be to them when they're dead.

—I wonder how many times that lesson will save their lives.

—Who saves their lives this time?

—Dabeet.

—You hesitated. Because you don't believe he can do it.

—I know he can do it.

—Can, but it relies on luck, it relies on . . .

—He's doing his best to prepare himself, isn't he?

—How about giving them a serious security force to help.

—You know that won't do any good. *And* it's just another variant of adults stepping in to save them. They'll all let down, they'll all think, *Now* it's up to *them* to protect us.

—I know you're right. I do know that. But I also know what can go wrong.

—Everything can go wrong.

—Good. I wasn't sure you knew the whole list.

—Tell you what. I'll make you a bet. Let's send a ship, demanding that he be removed for reassignment. If he goes willingly, then we also blow the raiders out of the sky, everybody's safe, they don't even know *if* the raiders would even have come.

—That sounds good.

—But I'm betting that he won't go.

—You think you know him?

—Yes.

—You sure you're not assuming that he'll be like you?

—Oh, I would have taken the chance to leave. At that age? You have no idea how careful I already was.

—So you're counting on his mother's genes to—

—I'm counting on Dabeet. I'm counting on him. Is it a bet?

—If I win, *you* get Dabeet alive and safe and also all the kids in Fleet School. Safe. But what if *you* win? What kind of fool makes a bet where if he wins, he loses?

—We really shouldn't bet on this, I get your point.

—I'm still going to give the orders and make a try to save him. Can you live with that?

—He won't come.

—

Nobody treated Dabeet any differently in the mess hall or during classes, and from this Dabeet learned that Monkey hadn't told anybody about his plan to become competent outside the safety of the station's atmosphere. She kept her word. The way Zhang He also kept his word. You didn't have to be a friend to be loyal. You only needed to have honor.

Do I have honor?

I do if I want it. All I have to do is keep my word.

No, I have to mean my promises when I make them. When I say I'll do something, I *mean* to do it, and then I do it. That's honor. Not to give your word unless you *can* keep it, unless you intend to keep it. To be the kind of person who, when they say they'll do a thing, the other people can go about their business because that job is as good as done.

How did I get through this many years of life without understanding that?

Because I was always competing. Always working to win, to be best. Nobody to promise anything to.

Except Mother. Never promised her anything, but I knew my duty. I did whatever it took to keep her safe.

Only I don't have it in my power to keep her safe.

Trying my best to be honorable, but it isn't in my power. Finally told the truth to the others, so they could prepare, but . . . was that honor, or the need to tell them before they found out some other way? Leaving them ignorant would certainly have been a betrayal. So I could have been *less* honorable.

Such were Dabeet's thoughts as he ate alone in the mess hall. Everybody else was divided into their squads and teams for the coming crisis. And won't I feel stupid if nothing ever happens? Embarrassed, yes, but relieved.

He also had other scattered thoughts. For instance, he was glad that he hadn't thrown up in his spacesuit. Atmo suits were claustrophobic and clumsy, but outside the ship it was different. Then he had to deal with vertigo, genuine danger, the momentary terror of being surprised by the terrain. And he never threw up. Never even got nauseated. That was something, wasn't it? Not a virtue, but . . . a strength? Maybe a sign that he wasn't a complete . . .

It was a sign that he didn't have to deal with vomit inside his helmet.

That's all it was. No hidden talent suddenly revealed. No path from here to being impressive to anybody. His highest aspiration right now was adequacy, and not puking helped.

And he thought about his schoolwork. That was his refuge. The thing he knew he could do well.

From what he overheard, he had a general idea of the other kids' strategy. It was all about luring the raiders to the battlerooms, and then . . . something. At least they weren't talking about trying to find some weapons stash, probably because they sent everybody through all the hidden corridors one day and didn't find anything. As if they could possibly match trained soldiers after only a few days or weeks of practice.

Like I'm trying to match trained spacewalkers after . . .

Not trying to match anybody. Just trying to be adequate.

And thus his mind went round and round.

One conversation that mattered. Zhang He and a couple of other leaders came to his lone table in the mess hall and sat across from him. "What's the signal?"

"I already told you everything I knew," said Dabeet. "The complete decipherment of the sole message I've received. It told me October 18th but I think they'll come earlier."

They pondered that for a moment.

"When?" said one of the boys Dabeet didn't know.

"Because that's what I would do."

"What if they don't come till after?"

"For all I know, they've been caught by authorities on Earth and I'll never hear from them again. For all I know, the whole thing has been called off. Or maybe they never meant to do it. I don't know anything beyond what I've already told you. I'm not holding anything back."

"Including what a koncho you are."

Dabeet said nothing to that. He hadn't betrayed them. He had warned them. But they'd spin it however they wanted. Arguing wouldn't change that.

They left him then, and there were no more conversations. When he had cooled down a little, he realized: Zhang He must have already told them this, but the older boys didn't believe him. They needed to hear it for themselves. Zhang He didn't think he was holding back.

It came as an announcement on all their desks, during class.

NOTICE
THE FOLLOWING ARE ORDERED TO
EMBARCATION 2 FOR IMMEDIATE
NEW ASSIGNMENT

The list was headed by Urska Kaluza's name, followed by the names of all the training masters, including Odd Oddson. There was only one student's name on the list. Dabeet Ochoa.

Dabeet got up from his seat.

"Sit down, Cadet," said the teacher.

"His name is on the list," said Monkey, who happened to be in the same logistics class with him.

The teacher, nonplussed, looked down the list again, starting to say, "No he . . ." and then "This is ridiculous . . ."

Dabeet didn't wait for him. Halfway to the door he realized that with what he intended to do right now—hide from whatever they were summoning him for—he shouldn't carry his desk along with him. He handed it to Monkey as if he were returning something that belonged to her. "Thanks," he said. Then he was out the door, which closed to cut off the teacher's voice saying, "I really need to check on . . ."

They would know what class I'm in, so they'll already have somebody heading here. Whoever "they" is.

Dabeet ducked into the first janitorial closet he reached and pulled the door closed behind him. Then he got to the first ladderway and went to the uppermost passage on the middle level.

In a few moments, he was in a spacesuit, in an airlock, and then outside.

Good thing he had already practiced getting from the middle wheel to the upper wheel of the station. He could get back inside somewhere other than the classroom level. But for the moment, he held on to the outside bar, with the airlock closed and recharging beside him.

Why am I running? When did I decide to hide?

It wasn't implausible that he would be reassigned. With all the nasty reports Urska Kaluza had certainly made about him, getting him out of Fleet School might well be a priority.

But Urska Kaluza was also being reassigned. And why all the training officers?

That was what didn't ring true. There was no reason to take them all at once—nothing could be more disruptive to their education. Teachers could come and go, as their assignments expired or new expertise was needed. Nobody much cared. There were teachers they liked, even some they respected, but they weren't part of their lives. The training officers, though, they were a different story entirely.

If the station were attacked, the training officers might take command, and if they did, their students would rally around them and obey. That would be a potential disaster for their defense preparations, since they were not *part* of any of the team organizations, and it would completely disrupt whatever the kids had already planned. But if you knew the station was going to be raided, and you didn't know that the students were planning an organized resistance, then getting the training officers out of Fleet School would look like an essential move.

Likewise, getting rid of Urska Kaluza—if they thought she was really worth something as a leader, then of course they wanted her gone. And if she was in collusion with the raiders, having her off the station would have been part of their deal.

Whoever was moving them off the station knew about the raid, that was clear enough. Dabeet might have reasoned it out only now, clinging to the outside of the hull, but apparently at some limbic level he had known it instantly.

If he left the station now, and then the raid came, nobody would believe he hadn't been warned in advance. They would be sure he had lied to them, concealed information, betrayed them.

Here I am, clinging to the outside of the station. I'm as gone, as far as the other kids know, as if I had been spirited away on whatever ship was taking good old Urska Kaluza.

Poor me.

Dabeet forced himself to calm down and think. Was there something useful he could do right now? Yes. He could see Embarcation 2 from here. Or, rather, he could see any ship that was docked there.

But not very well. The tail end of something.

He wouldn't have to move *very* far along the wheel to get a better view. One airlock away. Maybe two.

He was about to move across the closed airlock door, but then he stopped himself. "The bar on the other side of the airlock. Attached to the hull." Then he reached for it. Naming each gap in the plates, the lips on the center band, he made it to the next airlock.

Clearly the back end of a ship. But that much he already knew.

Carefully, gap by gap, plate by plate, he made it to the airlock after that. And now he could see the IF insignia. An official ship, not a raider, not a yacht, a real ship. Small. Not even a cruiser, more like a messenger. But it would be armed, because all IF ships were armed. This little packet boat could probably blow the raiders out of the sky. But it wouldn't be here. It would be gone.

Well, it would be gone if they gave up on finding Dabeet and went without him.

If I don't go with them, I may well die.

He immediately answered his own thought with another: If I go with them, all the others may die.

He almost laughed at himself. You think you can save everybody? You think your absence will doom them to a miserable death? Even if we're facing Goliath, Dabeet, you're no David.

I will be if that's what I need to be, Dabeet told himself. I won't be a great hero-king whose name will live for three thousand years. But I'll do an adequate job of whatever needs doing.

He memorized the ship's number and then settled down to wait.

After only a few minutes, he remembered that even if they weren't tracking his suit, they certainly would have a record of his airlock door opening. If somebody poked their head out right now, he'd be in plain view.

Carefully, naming every gap, every reach, Dabeet made his way from the middle wheel to the inner one, the topmost of the three. It was tricky because the three wheels hadn't been designed to move together. Instead, the inner wheel ran on a track along the inside of the middle wheel, just as the outer wheel ran on a track along the outside of the middle wheel.

Originally, the three wheels had moved at their own rate, so that the false gravity from centrifugal force would be roughly even among the wheels, innermost to outermost. Ah, the things that engineers had to cope with, in the days before the Jukes corporation did its breakthrough work with gravitics.

But how did they get from wheel to wheel? Now, with the wheels in lockstep, they had the elevator shafts from level to level and wheel to wheel. In the original design, how would teachers and students get from their residential levels to the classroom level?

It wasn't a school, then, of course. The station was built before the arrival of the first Formic ship, before there was an International Fleet. It was meant to be a permanent way station between Earth and Moon, perhaps a depot or transshipment facility. Maybe a way station for Terran and Lunar shuttles. Maybe a resort, a hotel and restaurant and spa for people who were ridiculously rich.

Maybe one wheel for each purpose. Each one supplied and administered separately. All this expense for what, commerce? The tourist trade?

But all this was back in the days before Jukes's breakthroughs in the science of gravity led to the technology of gravitics. Before the Jukes Gravic Downmaster eliminated freefall inside space vehicles, except where you wanted it. Gravic fields could be fine-tuned to provide just the right downward pull in every location. Science was amazing in those days—before the Formics ever came. Maybe because space was still new, the solar system was still pioneer territory.

Why, the people who built this primitive wheel design probably still thought there were only four forces, and still imagined they could find the Grand Unified Theory—a notion that had gone the way of the Philosopher's Stone and Aether and the elements of Earth, Air, Fire, and Water. Yet the station was still in place, still turning—for stability now rather than for illusory gravity—and still protecting its inhabitants from radiation, dust collisions, and the near-vacuum of space. Rather like the Roman roads whose pavement, however overgrown, still ran across Britain, Gaul, Italy, Iberia, and northern Africa.

Old space stations like this could be retrofitted fairly safely because they weren't going anywhere. They didn't have to be built to withstand powerful acceleration and deceleration, or to cope with collisions with high-velocity dust as a spaceship neared lightspeed. There was no way to keep the really old spaceships in service except in near-Earth traffic, shuttling among stations, ships, and the Moon. A station like Fleet School, though, stayed in its position at L-5, used for whatever purpose the IF still had for it.

The differential in movement between the wheels had never been very fast. Because workmen were expected to have to work on the juncture between the wheels, there were handrails above and below the tracks, precisely so that workers could do exactly what Dabeet needed to do—move from wheel to wheel without danger.

Only Dabeet was thinking the way Monkey had taught him to think: What is the safest way? The rings were now locked in place by struts connecting the wheels, and by moving only a few panels to the nearest strut, Dabeet could grip the strut and walk it hand-over-hand "up" to the next wheel. It was a safer grip, a shorter path, and didn't require him to go into the wedgelike space between tubes.

Having climbed the strut, Dabeet was on the inner ring now, and he made his way easily but carefully up to a position near the top. He would be far more visible here than he was down near the juncture, but who would be looking? It wasn't as if anybody ever looked out the window— there were never any windows on a station like this. Any kind of see-through panel would last only a couple of years at most before microcollisions with dust and debris scored the surface so much that you couldn't see through it at all. And anything that mattered would have to be detected from *much* farther away than you could see with the naked eye through a window.

So nobody would see him unless they were using instruments to deliberately scan the wheels of the school in order to find him. If they wanted him *that* badly, there was nowhere he could hide.

From this position, Dabeet had a good view of near space. He knew that any ship that wanted to approach unseen could do it by switching off its blinkers—except when sunlight caught it. Nothing could hide from the stark searchlight of the Sun. Even nanooze didn't make a ship's surface completely nonreflective.

But of course the raiders wouldn't come *now,* while the IF packet boat was still docked.

How long before they gave up on Dabeet?

How long before he had to go inside to change suits, to replenish his atmo? He had made sure that the top-level spacesuits were fully charged, but he was wearing one from the middle wheel. Less than fifteen minutes left.

Dabeet made his way to the nearest airlock and clung to the bar there. He couldn't see whether any ships were approaching, but it was more important to get inside quickly when the time came, change into a fully loaded spacesuit, and then get back out.

Just as he was about to press the OPEN button on the airlock, he saw the packet boat drift backward out of Embarcation 2. They had stopped looking for him.

He was watching it clear the embarcation center when his suit alarm went off. Oh, that's right. The atmo in the spacesuit didn't care whether they were looking for him or not. He had exactly one minute to get inside before he started to suffer mental degradation from lack of oxygen.

He made it with thirty-five seconds to spare.

They had left without him. So he didn't need to go back outside. Did he?

What if the teachers had orders to arrest him and hold him for the next ship?

One thing was clear. If the raiders really had arranged for this IF ship to get him, Urska Kaluza, and the training officers out of the way, that meant he would *never* get an instruction to open an access door. Which meant that he didn't have to figure out how to open one of the main airlocks for them when they arrived.

They didn't need him. Maybe they had never needed him. Maybe all of this was for no other purpose than to create evidence that he was the Fleet School traitor who was taking orders from the raiders.

Did that mean Mother was dead? Or soon would be?

Or had she been dead all along?

Or had she never been in danger?

There was no way to know.

What he *could* do was keep watch, so when the raiders came, he'd know where their ship was, and which airlock on which wheel they entered through.

Probably one of the wheels under construction, Dabeet thought.

I have no basis for deciding what is and is not probable, he replied to himself. It could be anywhere on the station. It could be Embarcation 1 or 2, for all I know. It could be one of the cargo bays. It could be the one-man emergency airlock that I just used to come into the ship. It could be *any* of them, because they couldn't be locked. Any worker or soldier or other spacewalker would never be locked out of access to air, on any IF installation, anywhere. Miners and corporate ships and stations followed the same protocol. Hundreds of back doors on this space station. The only security measure was the alarms that went off when an airlock door was opened.

Mine didn't set off an alarm, thought Dabeet. I opened it in plenty of time for them to find me, but nobody came in search of me. I was *so* findable, yet I remained unfound.

With Robota Smirnova gone, was it possible that the adults didn't know how to check to see which open airlock had set off an alarm?

Or was shutting down the alarm system part of the raiders' plan?

Or had Urska Kaluza shut the system down as part of her deal with them?

How can I waste time speculating when I have *no* pertinent information?

All this time, Dabeet had been putting on the new, fully charged suit. He would be good for sixteen hours now, before he had to come back in.

No he wouldn't.

He peeled down the suit, opened his uniform, and peed into the first mop bucket he could reach with his suit around his ankles. Very awkward. He had to hold the bucket up above where the suit bunched around his shins, so he wouldn't spatter urine all over inside the suit. Ah, the glories of being in space.

The suit itself held plenty of water to keep him hydrated. Real workers would wear a honey suit under the spacesuit to deal with waste elimination, if they expected to be outside for the full sixteen-hour charge. But Dabeet knew that if it became necessary, he'd pee all over inside the suit rather than come inside if his job wasn't complete.

What was his job? Sentry. He was the lone sentry on the circular walls of the station. He imagined some solitary Chinese soldier on the Great Wall. Or perhaps the lone Quechua warrior on a pinnacle of the Andes, ready to run and give warning of the approaching Spaniards. He was pretty sure that heroic soldiers didn't wet themselves. Then again, they could pee off the wall or the pinnacle whenever they wanted, because they weren't wearing spacesuits.

He got the suit on, double-checked it even as the suit double-checked itself. All connections secure. All systems fully charged and ready.

Dabeet stepped back into the airlock, closed the inner door, discharged the air, and in a few moments he was back at the peak of the inner wheel, scanning nearby space, looking for the flash of light that would mean a stealthy ship was approaching through sunlight.

17

—Let's pretend that Dabeet will figure out a way to defeat the terrorists. Let's say that he and everybody else survive.

—You're pretending. I'm predicting.

—Are you going to tell him who he is? Who *you* are?

—What good would that do? It might raise expectations that he would inherit my—what is it I've built?

—Secret government.

—Web of influence. But it can't be inherited, it can't be used by anybody but me, because it's all personal. Not this office liaising with that office, but me talking to this friend.

—Or you talking to that mousy, intimidated official, or that ambitious-but-stupid officer—

—Not really many of those. They aren't of much use to someone like me. I need the help of competent women and men who share my vision of spreading the human species among as many colonies as possible. I often have to explain to each one how the thing I'm asking them to do relates to that overall purpose. They help me because they can see that I'm leading them to accomplish the only cause that matters now.

—No coercion at all? No extortion, no blackmailing, no log-rolling?

—You were one of the toughest birds I ever brought into the aviary. Did I do any of those things to you?

—Wouldn't have worked.

—It wouldn't work with *any* of the people I need. Fearless, independent, insightful, generous people. People who use their own wits to solve problems instead of wringing their hands and wondering what I would want them to do.

—Too bad people like that rarely run for public office.

—They do, all the time. Then they lose. There's always a secret government that nobody knows about except the people who are in it. And they don't think of it that way. They just know that if they need something done, *this* is the person to talk to in this department, and *that* is the person to talk to in another.

—And you hold all this inside your head.

—If Dabeet is going to be part of the secret government, he won't have any trouble holding everything in his head. Perfect memory has its uses.

—Until you get old and it fades.

—He's not old yet. And *yours* hasn't faded.

—Has so. I'd give you an example, but I can't remember any.

—Your memory hasn't faded. Neither will his. Look, I'm doing the job I'm doing, and, once we get enough colonies established, it'll be done. Over, accomplished. The whole colonization project will take on momentum of its own because people will found new colonies out of pure self-interest. Adam Smith's invisible hand. So Dabeet won't *need* to have my job, because my job won't exist.

—Doesn't mean he won't still try to do it, if he knows who you are and what you've done. He's competitive. He'll have to find a way to be better than dear old Dad.

—You're wrong about that. Dabeet was raised to be arrogant, his amour propre depended on being the best, the smartest. But I think that's already been taken out of him. He's at the level of amour de soi, to use Rousseau's terms precisely. He doesn't choose his actions based on what other people think *of him.* He hasn't made any effort to force the other kids to do things his way.

—He's smart enough to realize you can't lead if nobody will follow.

—But ambitious people *don't* learn that. They just break their hearts trying.

—You sure Dabeet isn't walking around with a broken heart?

—The heart of that fatherless boy was broken from birth, do you think I don't know that? But he never tried to assert ownership of this crisis. He never tried to take charge of things. He only looked for ways he could help. Isn't that right?

—Yes, you're right. I should have realized how remarkable that was.

—Could *you* have been that self-restrained?

—In all the charges brought against me in what we laughingly call my military career, I was never accused of self-restraint.

—My whole career consisted of deliberate self-restraint—but I was only biding my time until I could get my way, enact my plan. I don't think Dabeet *has* a plan.

—Wise boy.

—We'll just have to see how well and quickly he reacts to whatever comes.

—What if there's no time to react? What if they simply blast the station to bits upon arrival?

—The soldiers on this raid don't know it's a one-way ticket. They think they're coming home. They don't even think they're going to have to kill anybody.

—Somebody must know.

—Are you sure of that? Remember who put this all together. Achilles isn't happy when he has to trust other people to cooperate with his plans. He prefers to deceive everybody, betray everybody. He serves no higher cause that other people would willingly die for. So if he wants everybody to die, he has to fool them into thinking and acting as if they were all going to survive.

—I'm not sure what's more disturbing: that you think you know Dabeet, or that you think you understand Achilles.

—Achilles has had plenty of time to teach us who he is. Dabeet is still finding out. So I don't think I know Dabeet. And I think I know Achilles only well enough to predict how he'll treat anybody who trusts him.

It became a question of sleep. Specifically, this was the question:

If watching for the raiders' ship is so unimportant that it's all right for me to take a ten- or six- or four-hour break in order to sleep, then why is it important enough to warrant my spending every waking moment doing it?

And then there was the obvious corollary:

If I don't sleep, isn't it possible I'll doze off while outside the station? Would the suit's gloves still hold me in place? Or if I'm awake, after a fashion, and I see the ship, what then? If I'm so sleepy that my mental function is impaired, how can I possibly do anything useful?

Then there was the question of food. He was hungry. The suits—he was rotating among three, recharging two while he wore the third—kept him hydrated, but he was already weak with hunger. Yet how would he get food without revealing himself to someone?

Was there any danger from revealing himself? He imagined that most kids thought he had gone with Urska Kaluza, but he was equally certain that none of them cared whether he had or not. And if they saw him, what would be the negative consequence?

Here's what he imagined: He wasn't important at Fleet School, but he might be important to the raiders. They had singled him out by holding Mother hostage and getting him to open that door. What if they had some use for him, and looked for him as soon as they arrived? Would it be better to have the other kids say, He left with Urska Kaluza on a packet ship, or to have them say, He's here somewhere?

He couldn't function if he was weak from hunger. He *really* couldn't function without sleep. Compared to this, the problem of the stinking urine bucket was trivial.

Dabeet remembered back to his time at the Charles G. Conn School for the Gifted. If you missed a meal in the cafeteria, there was a snack buffet. If everything there was stale or dried out or simply gone or not to your liking, you could use vending machines in the study hall. There were choices.

In Fleet School, there was whatever mess you were assigned to, and nothing else. There were mealtimes, and no other times.

The suits had internal clocks, so he knew that it was almost breakfast time in his mess. He could eat, then maybe shower, then sleep up here in the top corridor for fifteen minutes, and *then* go back on duty.

He could not, could *not*, enlist some other kid to keep watch with him. Everybody else had assignments that were important to whatever defense command had been created among the students. Dabeet couldn't be seen as thinking his foolish self-assigned watch duty took priority over official jobs. The last thing he needed was more grounds for resentment or hostility to him. There might well come a time when he needed to be able to present a plan for immediate action and have it evaluated on its merits, rather than through a haze of hatred.

Eat, shower, sleep. That was his decision.

He woke up about an hour before lunch, having inadvertently skipped ahead to the sleep portion of his plan. He was still half in his suit, which he had not hung back up to recharge.

Go back outside and scan the sky again, before eating and showering?

If they come, they come. I'm really *not* doing anything important. I'm only keeping watch because it was what I could think of that I could do alone. Except I can't do it alone. My marvelous brilliant superior brain still needs sleep just like any other animal. Too bad I can't have the sides of my brain take turns sleeping, like a dolphin. Dolphins don't go into space. They can't get their flippers properly into spacesuit gloves. Stop trying to think and go eat. Be first in line.

Instead, he went to the shower because nobody else would be there. Either they were all in class—what else would the teachers do with them?—or they were doing some assignment for the Fleet School Defense Command, or whatever the name was, if it had a name. Nobody would be assigned to shower.

It felt good to be clean. Even when he put back on the same unwashed uniform it felt good.

He was still first in line at the mess. Nobody else was there early. Apparently they were busy. Or in class. That's right, the last morning class let out fifteen minutes after the official lunch mess began because, of course, this was the IF.

The lunchroom staff wasn't so much surprised to see Dabeet as it was surprised to see anybody. They were apparently so used to having nobody show up until fifteen minutes later that the door didn't slide open on time and he had to slap the door hard to get the attention of the people inside.

"Well, we're impatient, aren't we," said the noncom who opened it.

"Hungry. Sorry," said Dabeet. What he had wanted to say, what he *would* have said at Charles G. Conn, was, How about doing your job so people don't *have* to get impatient? But Dabeet was trying to extend his new, human, less-despicable personality to everyone, not just people he needed things from.

Though actually he needed something from the kitchen staff, didn't he.

"You don't show up on the roster."

"You know my face. You see me here all the time."

"But your name isn't on the list anymore."

"That's because somebody thought I was leaving the station a couple of days ago, and then I didn't, and the people who could have put me back on the list *went* with that ship, so what am I supposed to do, starve? Then you'll just have to drag my desiccating skeleton away from the door. Isn't it simpler to give me food?"

He tried to say it with wry humor. One of the cooks got a smile, but nobody else seemed to think he was amusing at all.

"What did you do for the last five meals, when you didn't show up?" asked the noncom.

"Starved," said Dabeet.

"That's your best bet," said the noncom.

"You have the food. You always throw some away after every meal. Please throw some away now by giving it to a beggar boy who's not on the list but is still, by evidence of your own eyes, alive and present at mealtime."

"What can you do?" said the head cook, who was probably the noncom's boss. "He said 'please.'"

Dabeet was relieved that instead of skimping, they had taken his skipping of five meals seriously, and he had extra-large portions of everything. None of the food was as tasty as what even the poorest families in the barrio got, but that was the military and he was used to it. What he needed now was calories. He tried to eat methodically, not taking a new bite until he had thoroughly chewed and swallowed the previous one. Still, he polished it off in less than ten minutes. None of the other students had arrived when he carefully took his tray to the cleaning stack, sorted the silverware and cup, and scraped the leftover biomass.

Dabeet stopped at the serving window. They looked at him like they were getting ready to say, Didn't we already give you enough? But before anyone else could speak, Dabeet said, from the heart, "Thank you so much. That was very kind of you." Then he pushed away from the counter and headed for the door.

"Wait," called the noncom.

Dabeet turned, saw her beckon, and walked back to the window. She handed him a bag. "Rolls," she said. "They'll stay fresh in this bag for a couple of days. In case you have to skip the next five meals."

It was a sign of how tired Dabeet was that tears sprang into his eyes. "Thank you," he said, and turned away to hide his emotions. Of course it didn't work, he knew they had seen, but except for Mother such unasked-for kindness had never happened to him. He didn't know how to deal with the combination of weariness, surprise, and gratitude.

"Go save the world," said the noncom. It had been the standard farewell from the kitchen staff during Battle School days. They were the only ones left from that era.

Won't save the world, thought Dabeet as he went through the messhall door. Just the station. Maybe.

There were students coming toward the mess hall now, all from the same direction, because that was the nearest elevator. Dabeet turned and walked the other way. These corridors were wheels, after all. He didn't want to talk to anybody, explain anything, or even have rumors flying: I saw him. Coming out of the mess hall. He's still on the ship.

Not that anybody would care enough to spread a rumor.

Not that the kids he saw wouldn't have recognized him, so it was already too late to stop the rumors.

Nobody was on the up elevator, and soon he was back at his station, where all three suits were in their charging stations. He took the one that was next in line.

There are suits at all the other airlock doors, he reminded himself. And the other airlock doors don't have stinking piss buckets standing by.

No time to go empty it.

No, you're not going to dump it into space. No reason anybody should have to cope with little pellets of piss-ice out there, colliding with all the surfaces of the station.

Besides which I'd probably get it all over the spacesuit. If it didn't freeze in the bottom of the bucket the moment I got it outside.

He made it through the airlock again, and closed the door while gripping the outside bar, as usual. Then he made his way to the top of the inner wheel and looked toward the loading dock of the bottom ring of the unfinished portion of the station.

There was a ship attaching to the loading dock.

It was bigger than the packet, and while it displayed a registry number, it was *not* an IF ship. In fact, if Dabeet had learned his corporate sigils, this wasn't just a corporate ship, it was a Juke vessel, and it was designed to carry passengers and a cargo, too.

Why would a Juke vessel come here? Jukes had nothing to do with Fleet School. So there was no innocent explanation. The raiders had commandeered, hijacked, or simply chartered a Juke vessel for this attack on the school.

So now what do I do, go back inside and race up and down the corridors shouting, "Run for your lives, the bogeymen are here!"?

Wouldn't it be nice if he had his desk.

Dabeet supposed that he could get from this set of station wheels to that one without going inside. The connecting passage was only a quarter of the way around the wheel. He could do that, naming every handhold, in a couple of hours.

Or he could go inside, take off the suit, maybe give a warning to somebody, and then run through the corridors and be in place in about ten minutes.

In place? What place? Had the airlocks in the new part of the station been equipped with spacesuits? Recharging stations? Did the emergency one-man airlocks even work?

The airlocks had to work because who would be insane enough not to have a way for workmen to get back inside safely. The suits, though, were iffy.

He got inside, took off the suit, then detached the next suit, fully charged, from its station. Carrying it, he went along to the highest corridor, closed the access door behind him, and began to jog along toward the pass-through to the new wheel.

As he expected, in the down elevator to the middle level of the middle wheel, he ran into a couple of older girls he sort of knew.

"Going home, Dirtman?" asked one of them.

"You know those suits can't do reentry, right?"

Dabeet showed neither annoyance nor amusement. "The raiders are here. They just docked on the bottom level of the new construction."

They looked at him blankly.

"Do you know who Monkey is? Zhang He?"

One rolled her eyes. The other seemed to realize that he was serious. "Yes," she said.

"Please tell them that Dabeet says they're here. I saw the ship, not the people, so I don't know how many. I'm going to do recon and I'll report to whoever makes it to the topmost corridor in the new wheel. Got it?"

"Got it," she said. The other one also nodded.

"Whatever plan they've cooked up, it starts now," said Dabeet.

"Yes sir," said the girl whose eyes hadn't rolled.

Then Dabeet got out and ran to the pass-through.

Depending on how quickly the raiders debarked and deployed, it might already be too late to get into the hidden corridors unseen.

But it wasn't. They were taking their time. Or maybe docking took longer than Dabeet had feared. He didn't see or hear anyone before he got up to the top corridor and then to the uppermost secret corridor. There were no suits at the first airlock. Well, that made sense. He attached his suit to a recharge station. Another bust. The stations didn't have water, they didn't have air, they didn't have power. He'd have whatever was in this suit and nothing else.

So he couldn't afford to waste time traversing a long section of the hull. He needed an airlock as close to the docked ship as he could get. Only how to translate outside distances to inside ones? Why hadn't he counted airlocks when he saw the ship dock?

Well, he *had* counted them, because he had *looked* along the whole distance from the Juke ship to the pass-through. He closed his eyes and calmly reviewed his memory. There were two easy ways to find the right airlock. First, he could count to eleven. Second, he could go until the corridor dead-ended where the workers had sealed it off, because on the inner ring, the Juke ship was docked almost directly below the last airlock before the inner ring's construction had left off.

His count was right. Eleven. And there was the end. Nice to know he could still trust his memory.

The recharge stations didn't work, there were no suits, but the airlocks *had* to work—which meant they must have several charges of atmo, too. And . . . yes. Once inside the airlock, he flushed the atmo back into the system and everything worked exactly right. He opened the door, held on to the outside bar, and . . .

And the corner gaps weren't there. He looked closely and realized that the surface of the hull-under-construction hadn't been plated yet. It had nanooze all over it, so it looked the same from across the gap between wheels. But the system of plates with gaps at the corners had not yet been installed.

Well, wouldn't it have been nice to find *that* out a few days ago? Or even during the time I was supposedly watching for these raiders to arrive.

Is Mother on that ship?

He pushed that thought aside and considered his options.

He could go to a lower airlock, on the level just above the docked ship, but that would mean using corridors that the raiders might be watching.

Or he could creep down the hull like a silverfish scurrying along a ceiling, letting the nanooze hold him to the ship.

Completely different technique, one he had never tried. If he gave a sudden lurch, he might push himself free of the nanooze. The stuff had been designed so people in spacesuits could *walk* on it.

Don't walk. Don't run.

É, Monkey, I'll do neither. I'll creep. Not slither, not crawl. I'll keep maximum body contact with the nanooze and let it hold me right down the outside of the hull, to the docking area, so I can . . .

Do what? Look through the ship's windows to see if Mother's tied to a chair inside with duct tape over her mouth? What kind of idiotic movie do I think I'm in?

A Juke ship would also have a nanooze surface. It would also have emergency airlocks on the outside. He might be able to get into the ship. That way, the raiders could conveniently kill him right on their own ship instead of having to hunt for him through the whole station.

They don't want to kill me.

I don't know what they want. If I come into their ship from the outside, dressed in a regular spacesuit, they'll kill me before they realize from my size that I'm a child.

Well, what else did I think I was going to do? I can't do recon from inside the station. What will I learn there, without exposing myself to detection and capture? The only thing we don't know about is the ship. How many soldiers does it have seats for? What kind of weapons are they carrying? Can we steal any of them for our own use? Do they have room to take hostages with them? If they don't, does that mean they plan to kill us all?

While these questions and speculations ran through Dabeet's mind, he was experimenting with the nanooze—without ever letting go of the airlock bar. He found that it did take some effort to pull away from the nanooze. Being composed of millions of tiny intelligent-networking robots, the nanooze knew the difference between full-body contact and boot or glove contact. When he attached to the nanooze with only one hand and both knees, the nanooze held tightly, so it took a deliberate effort to pull any of those body parts free. And he couldn't pull more than one part free at a time. So the nanooze had the rule about not letting go of one handhold till you've got a grip on the next. It was designed specifically for his purpose. It was meant to hold somebody to the hull without preventing them from moving.

Even after these tests, Dabeet could hardly bring himself to let go of the bar. He was trembling. But he did it, and without too much delay, either, because if the information he gathered was going to be worth something, he had to get it now.

Can I still think of the hull of the station as "up"?

No. That really was too much like a silverfish. He had to think of it as down, so that what he was doing was crawling along sloping ground, not clinging to a down-curving ceiling.

With his mind properly oriented, he began creeping. He wasn't quick—especially at the junctures between the wheels—but his steady movement got him there quickly enough. Only twenty-two minutes since he saw the docking vessel.

Was that even possible? It felt like it took forever to run through the pass-through and get up to the top corridor. And twice as much of forever to get down the side of the wheel. Twenty-two minutes of forever.

There was no nanooze on the dockbridge between station and ship. Nor were there handholds. He couldn't exploit the physical connection between Fleet School and the Juke vessel, not without a serious risk of coming loose and drifting along to an unshielded reentry.

I'd die of the heat long before I actually burst into flames. So, it could be worse.

Of course, if I didn't get sucked into Earth's gravity well, there'd be more than fifteen hours of using up all the oxygen in this suit, singing old Spanish lullabies to myself and weeping for Mother as I drifted off into the cold black of space.

Why didn't these suits have directional rockets to allow a person to maneuver and save himself if he came loose?

A quick scan of the heads-up display showed a little icon labeled DIR. He focused on it for one, two, three beats and the icon expanded into a menu.

DIRECTIONALS

GL   BL   D

GR   BR   V

He made it a point not to focus on any of these long enough to activate them. Decoding them wasn't hard, especially because now he could remember hearing an explanation of the directionals in a lecture when everybody else was going outside. Glove Left, Glove Right, Boot Left, Boot Right, Dorsal, Ventral.

No, no, no, no. His first attempt with directional rockets was *not* going to be all by himself out here. He didn't even know what part of the glove and boot the rocket blast would come from.

Yes he did. Sole of the boot just under the pad of the foot behind the toes. Middle finger of the glove but only when the finger was rigidly extended. And the rocket blast would be only the tiniest trickle so that any effects would be slight.

He could almost hear Monkey saying it—though he knew she had never mentioned the directionals to him: One second of that tiny trickle will put your frozen corpse a hundred kilometers off your original trajectory within a minute, so search parties will never, never find you. Stay on your original trajectory.

Monkey hadn't said it. An instructor had said it. Odd Oddson had said it. But it sounded much more important and believable in Monkey's voice.

It was disconcerting how easily he could recast his memories. How often did such distortions happen inadvertently? If he couldn't trust his memory . . .

The nanooze won't let me break free with two feet at a time. What do I have to do in order to simply jump this very, very short distance of maybe ten meters? That's a short distance, isn't it? Must I balance on one foot and then hope I can take off straight up and then catch myself on the Juke vessel's nanooze?

He migrated over to the nearest emergency airlock door on the hull of this wheel, and took hold of the bar there. Holding on with both hands, with both feet firmly planted in the nanooze, he pushed off very gently, both feet at the same time.

They didn't budge.

Bacana. A safety feature that made his mission impossible.

He tried again, harder. Was there a little give before his feet were sucked back down, hard against the hull?

Now, instead of standing flat-footed, he flexed the boots enough that he was held only by the toe portion of the soles. He pushed off, a little harder than before, and . . .

His legs shot out away from the hull.

His gloves' grip on the bar didn't even bend. He swung out as if his hands were a hinge, and then his heels and buttocks slammed against the hull on the other side. The nanooze caught and gripped him.

This is good. Stand on tiptoe and jump, and the nanooze on the Juke vessel will catch me.

Probably.

If I can aim well enough for any part of my body to touch any part of that ship.

No time to waste. Dabeet crawled along the surface of the hull until he was positioned directly under—across from? over?—the widest part of the Juke vessel. It was not an atmospheric craft so there was no non-sense with wings or fins. Just a fine smooth surface with two visible emergency airlocks on it. Very tall from top to bottom of the ship. He *could* reach it. Especially if he didn't have to use a lot of force to break free of the hull of the station.

He tucked up his feet, one at a time, until they were under the trunk of his body. Then he let go of one hand and balanced himself on boots flat against the hull.

It took ten seconds to persuade himself to push away with the other hand.

It took a lot of strength to organize his body to stand upright instead of swaying and wavering. Then his suit understood what he was doing and suddenly it was as if he were in a pillar attached to the ground at a ninety-degree angle. No wavering. His body was pointed directly at the Juke vessel.

Maybe I should have tried to jump so I'd land like a belly flop in a swimming pool.

Maybe I could never push off accurately in that position. So I'm doing this. Now.

No he wasn't. The nanooze wouldn't let go of his flat feet at the same time.

He rose to his toes. But the suit maintained his balance perfectly. All he had to do was try to stay in that position, and the suit, reading the tiny adjustments in his muscles, did the rest. Whoever designed this suit, thank you. And whoever died so that they would know these refinements were necessary, I honor your memory, because maybe I'll live through this because of you.

He pushed off gently. As if he only meant to jump a couple of centimeters from the ground.

The nanooze let go. He drifted upward. He tilted his helmet back to see where he was going. Just like swimming. Just like diving. He wasn't going up anymore, he was falling down toward the ship. *Straight* toward the ship.

He splayed out his gloves to make maximum contact with the nanooze. Then landed. They stuck.

I just freefell ten meters through space from one vessel to another. To the kids who were adept at maneuvers in the battleroom, this would have seemed like nothing. They made this jump from walls to stars in the battleroom all the time, and longer jumps, too, while shooting weapons. But for me this was, this *is,* unbelievably good luck.

Sorry for breaking your rules, Monkey. If I did break them. I mean, I didn't walk, I didn't run. But I kind of did let go of one handhold before . . .

I'm alive. That's a passing grade even if I broke some rules.

There were no friendly corner gaps on the Juke vessel, either, and the nanooze didn't feel as if it was holding him as tightly. But by moving carefully, he had no trouble making his way to the aft airlock, farthest from the dockbridge. He had no idea what alarms would go off inside the ship, but if he was arrested or killed the moment he opened the door, at least he tried to do something useful. It might turn out to be incredibly stupid, but he didn't leave it all up to the others to clean up his mess. And it was possible, wasn't it, that with him in custody the others might be safer, right?

The airlock worked more quickly than the clunky old design of the station airlocks. Zip, in. Zip, door closed. Whoosh, atmo recharged. Zip, inner door open. He didn't have to push a single button or any other kind of control once he had called for the outside door to open. An excellent design, since a person in serious trouble in space might not be able to push a sequence of buttons. Just push the one button, and the airlock itself would do the rest.

And here he was inside the enemy ship, wearing a spacesuit. The display told him he could breathe without the suit, so he took off the helmet and set it near the airlock. He took two steps and then climbed out of the suit. He was too clumsy while wearing it to handle this reconnaissance as rapidly and thoroughly as he needed to. Wearing it wouldn't save him a moment of time if he had to run away, because a butterfly could catch him while he suit-lurched his way back to the airlock.

To his surprise, the suit and helmet interfaced with the recharge connections beside the airlock. A standardized interface that they hadn't messed with in half a century or more. Very nice.

There seemed to be nobody in this area, which looked to be a cargo bay. Like the cargo bay he and Zhang had inspected together months ago, helping with the tally. When they first discovered evidence that somebody was smuggling contraband through Fleet School.

The trunks were large, about as big around and half the length of a coffin. Could they be loaded with weapons? Dabeet had no idea. They didn't look long enough for rifles or automatic weapons, but who would bring projectile weapons into space?

They were all firmly lashed to the shelves and frames. And because the boxes clung to the shelves, Dabeet realized: The ship was fully equipped with gravitics. There was no hint of freefall inside this space.

Dabeet climbed onto a shelf and slid between boxes to the back wall. What did he expect to find? Maybe he only did it because it was behind big cargo containers that he found the small packages that turned out to be contraband. This time he found no secret parcels. Instead he saw that every single box had wires coming out of the end nearest the wall, and all those wires were bundled together, running the length of the cargo bay, getting thicker and thicker as they neared the front.

What was this, a burglar alarm system?

Dabeet made his way toward the front. From the central corridor, if you looked between the boxes you couldn't see the wires. They were the same color as the walls, and the shadows were too dense behind and between the boxes.

At the front, though, because he knew what to look for, he could see that the bundles of wires ran to a single box that looked just like the other boxes except it was not attached, electrically, to the ship in any way.

Whatever those wires did, they were *not* part of the ship. It was quite possible that they were not under the ship's control at all. Possible that the captain or pilot or whoever had no idea that the cargo was wired together.

If I try to open one of these boxes, will it detonate a little explosive or poison dart or something to kill me?

Let's find out.

No detonation. No dart. And also no opening a box, because there was a digital pad that needed either a passcode or a fingerprint, or both.

His fingerprint would be useless, but he could try a few passwords, the kind that lazy stupid people used—and also the kind that lazy smart arrogant people used because they thought that stupider people wouldn't guess them. One of them worked. BIRTHPLACE. Too lazy and stupid to type in "London" or "Boise" or "Caracas." *Any* city would be better than just typing in the prompt.

The lid was heavy and it couldn't rise very far because of the shelf above it. If Dabeet were a grown man he might have tried to wrestle the box far enough out to open it completely, but that would probably pull the wires too far. So he'd just have to try to see. . . .

Where light came into the box, near the end facing the central corridor, he could see a bunch of regular rectangles, slightly rounded at the corners, completely filling the space. Each one had what looked like a tiny dart stuck into it with a wire coming out. The wires all headed toward the back end of the box—no doubt, these were the wires attached to the box in front.

Dabeet saw the letters V-A-C in a wedge of light and knew that these were all nice little packets of Vacoplaz, a very high explosive that worked with or without atmo. Dabeet had heard that space miners called it "wreck-roid," or "ass-pop" for "asteroid popper," because it could be used to blow the center of asteroids to dust. And each packet was equipped with a detonator connected to a central control, so they could all be made to explode at once.

With his view of the contents already memorized, Dabeet lowered the lid, whereupon it relocked automatically. He was thinking: These are not meant to be carried inside the station, to be used to blow up selected locations. You don't wire them together anywhere but the place where they're meant to be used.

If each box contains explosives all the way to the bottom, and all of them blow at once, not only will this ship be turned to small metal and plastic fragments, but also the resulting blast will breach the integrity of every structure in the station. All the wheels, all four battlerooms, the embarcation hub, everything.

Do the raiders understand what they're carrying here? Do they know that this ship will never take them home?

If the purpose is to destroy the station, the ship, and all their contents, human and otherwise, why hasn't it already taken place?

Because whoever set this up doesn't want to just blast it all to bits. They want an alarm to be sent out by the teachers, calling on the IF to send ships to rescue them. Maybe they're hoping to blow up the first wave of rescue ships along with the station. Of course they are.

And the explosives aren't under the control of the raiders who came aboard the ship. That control box at the front is expecting to get the detonation signal from somewhere else.

Is there anybody on this ship? If I leave the cargo bay and go to the front and . . .

No, that's the wrong thing to worry about. What if the person at the detonator controls is only waiting for the station to rotate enough to see that the docking is complete? I don't have time to put on the suit, go back out the airlock, fly back to the station, get inside an airlock there, and then find somebody to help me figure out what to do. I got here fast, but not fast enough.

So Dabeet simply palmed the door leading from the cargo bay to the passenger cabin. It opened easily—no reason for security there unless they were being attacked by pirates—and Dabeet was relieved to see that all the rows of seats were empty. There were twelve pairs of seats on either side of a central corridor, wide and comfortable seats as befitted a corporate vessel. Forty-eight passengers.

Dabeet strode up the corridor to the door leading to the control room, the bridge, whatever they called it in their attempt to maintain outmoded nautical terminology. Again, the door palmed open. Again, there was nobody inside.

That had to be a strict order from whoever held the detonation button. If somebody stayed on board, they might decide to check the cargo. They might find—would easily find—what Dabeet had seen, and reach the same conclusions. The central control box was bound to be booby-trapped, but there were no traps on the bricks of Vacoplaz. Half a dozen men could open every box and pull every detonator in what, half an hour? Maybe fifteen minutes. Better to tell them to clear the ship completely because . . . because . . .

Because we're sending another ship to pick you up from the main embarcation hub. You and all the children. Just gather the children in the hub and a much larger passenger ship will arrive within minutes of your signal.

That would be a good lie. Dabeet hoped it was the lie they had been told. Because *that* would mean that any delaying action from the students might delay the moment of detonation.

Might delay it long enough to . . .

Dabeet was pleased to see that the main airlock stood open to the ship's interior; only the outer door, the space door, was closed. And, like any good airlock, it responded to anybody pushing the button. The door whooshed open. The atmo of the ship and of the station had already equalized. There was no puff of air in either direction. And the door was unguarded. For the moment, at least.

They really don't think the students on this station pose any threat. And why should they? This wasn't Battle School anymore. It was more like Eton than Sandhurst. More Phillips Exeter than West Point. And with the training officers gone, there weren't any *real* military personnel. Just teachers, cooks, and children. *They* would be easy to round up, but there were so many it would take all their people to do it.

Dabeet reclosed the outer airlock door and ran through the open airlock at the station end of the dockbridge. Now there would really be a danger of running into some of the enemy as they patrolled the corridors in search of stray students.

Or not. Because, after all, this was the unfinished, never-occupied portion of the station. No students would be in class here, no teachers walking the halls. No doubt they had posted guards at the pass-through, to keep anybody from the finished station from trying to escape to the unfinished area. But they wouldn't have guards in the upper, maintenance corridor that Monkey and Dabeet knew ran along the top of the pass-through structure, or the lower one, either. His friends could get to the rendezvous point easily—at least, they could if Monkey was with them.

Them?

Who did he think they were going to be? He had sent word with two older girls who ordinarily would despise anything said by a younger student like Dabeet. The one who had seemed to take him seriously might have been mocked into noncompliance by her eye-rolling friend thirty seconds after Dabeet left them. Why did he imagine that his message had been delivered?

He laddered his way through the elevator shaft to the top level, then got into the maintenance corridors and climbed to the uppermost service corridor. There were carts here, just like in the finished portion, and as soon as Dabeet came to one he got on and ordered it to move forward toward the rendezvous point.

Even if they got the message, what guarantee did he have that Monkey and Zhang or anybody else would be allowed to come and meet with him, even if they wanted to? "You want to desert your post and go get more information from the koncho who brought all this down on us?" "Yes sir, because unbeknownst to everybody, he's actually not a bag of charach, he's a wise and reliable hareess, looking out for all of us from his watchtower."

There's nobody there. Nobody there.

And then the cart brought the rendezvous point into view, the floor coming into view first. There were feet. More than two pairs of feet. Six pairs. And soon they had faces. Zhang He and Monkey, yes, and the rest of that original team: Ignazio Cabeza, Teburoro Timeon, Ragnar Olafson. And, unbelievably, Bartolomeo Ja, the commander of their army.

Dabeet wanted to weep in relief. He wanted to kneel down and thank every one of them for coming at his call.

Instead, his first words were, "There's nobody guarding the raiders' ship. It's loaded with explosives, enough to destroy the whole station and kill everybody. I think detonation is under the control of somebody on Earth or Luna, and the raiders don't even know this is a suicide mission."

They stared at him. In disbelief, he assumed at first, but how could he convince them if they didn't simply take his word?

Then he realized that their long, long pause had been only a microsecond as they processed everything he said.

"So what's the plan?" asked Bartolomeo.

"I kind of hoped that you guys who grew up in space would have an idea."

"Can we pull all the detonators from the explosives?" asked Ignazio.

"I didn't try," said Dabeet, "in case pulling one might set off all the rest. And there are . . ." Dabeet performed the calculation. "I estimate there are 26,928 individual parcels of explosive, each with its own detonator."

Nobody questioned his arithmetic.

Zhang He said, "I wasn't raised in space. Luna."

Ignazio nodded. "Earth for me, till the war ended and Mom brought us up to join her with the Fleet."

Timeon grinned. "Playing videogames all through a wasted childhood on the Ilha do Fogo."

Dabeet was genuinely surprised. "You've got as much dirt under your nails as I do."

"It's Ragnar and me," said Monkey, "and I think we need to see the setup."

"Right," said Ragnar.

"Nobody guarding it?" asked Bartolomeo. "I grew up in Macau, by the way. Dirty feet, too."

"None of us is even close to grown up," Zhang He reminded them.

As they swiftly made their way along corridors and down the elevator shaft, Dabeet asked the questions that were on his mind. "I thought you'd be in the thick of things," he said to Zhang He.

Ja laughed.

Zhang answered, "After we designed all the defensive walls for all four battlerooms and trained everybody in how to build them, they suddenly noticed how young and short we were."

"It's all about the alpha males, binoon," said Timeon. "Once they get the stash of fruit we found, it's bye bye bunducks."

"What are the raiders doing?" asked Dabeet.

"Don't know," said Ja. "We came to meet you."

"Over the top of the pass-through?" asked Dabeet.

"Well, indoors, but yes," said Ignazio.

"And you just sauntered up to their ship and found it was open?" asked Zhang He.

"No," said Dabeet.

"You came in from outside," said Monkey.

"I left my suit on the ship," said Dabeet.

"Can we possibly talk any louder?" asked Ragnar.

More quietly, Monkey persisted. "So you walked the station hull onto the ship?"

"Never walked," said Dabeet. "Crawled like a silverfish. Had to let the nanooze hold me. And then I jumped the last ten meters."

Monkey's lips tightened and she walked ahead a little faster.

They were at the open airlock.

Monkey immediately began putting on one of the suits arrayed there. A major airlock like this, even on the construction side, was going to be equipped.

"What are you doing?" asked Ja. "I didn't know we had a plan."

"There's no plan that doesn't include me needing a suit," said Monkey. "Kintama Boy made one incredibly lucky first jump—"

Dabeet tried to correct the record. "A carefully planned and flawlessly executed—"

"But if anybody's doing anything that requires space-walking . . ."

Ragnar had opened a panel low in the wall of the station airlock. "Two kilometers of cable," he said. "Firmly attached, load limit five hundred kilos."

"We don't want to attach the ship to the school," said Ja.

"Blow it off the airlock?" Monkey asked Ragnar.

"Get some serious distance, fast," Ragnar answered.

"Gotta be the ship's airlock that blows," said Monkey. "Manual override, evacuating all the atmo in the ship. All propulsion, blowing the ship away from us."

Everybody seemed to agree that nothing else would work.

"All right then," said Monkey. "You all stay *inside* the airlock here, doors closed, suits on. After I blow the ship off the station, I'll jump back."

"Using your mighty legs of steel, O Wonder Woman," said Timeon. "What's the velocity of the ship at that point?"

"Maybe I just ride it out," said Monkey with a grin.

"No suicide missions," said Ja, with real heat.

"What, I can't fall on a grenade cause I'm a girl?" asked Monkey.

Ragnar put a hand on her shoulder. "We know you're the best at this kind of thing, Monkey. But here's the problem. Anybody can open the ship's airlock on a manual override, and anybody can jump toward the station. But there's only one person with a decent chance of going out and catching them."

"You're search-and-rescue, Monkey," said Ja.

"You're not actually the commander on this operation, Ja," said Monkey.

"No, I am," said Dabeet.

They all looked at him as if they had forgotten he existed. "I have a suit on board the ship. Fully charged by now. I go in, put it on, you seal your airlock. I do a manual override on the ship's airlock, which blasts all the atmo out of the ship and it rockets away. Then I go through that open airlock door and jump for home. When I do, Monkey comes out to catch me, is that the plan?"

"It's about a third of the plan," said Monkey. "The big movements. What's missing is all the little stuff that keeps you from dying."

"Tell it to me quick because we don't know how long we have." To Dabeet's terror and chagrin, nobody argued with him about his being the one on board the ship to blow out the airlock. It was his job now.

"First," said Monkey, "the manual override is designed for one weakened and dying person to be able to trigger it. So easy that they have to protect it inside a door track so that it doesn't get triggered by accident. You already have to be inside the airlock with only the outer door closed, and then, where the inner door runs up, there's a button embedded inside the door's track. Always on the aft side. Toward the back of the ship. When you push it, whoosh."

"Got it."

"You've got nothing yet," said Monkey. "Because the system is designed so that you push the button and *you* get blown out along with everything else that isn't riveted in place. Only that won't work this time because we'd never find you and if you haven't noticed, we don't have a search-and-rescue ship to go looking for you. So you have to stay inside. And here's how you do it. The inside bar of the airlock is right *here* around the corner. . . ." She demonstrated the position. "And there's another handhold about a meter farther along the wall."

Dabeet remembered seeing both of them on the way out.

"It's not enough to hold on to the first bar, because even though your suit has a strong lock-on grip, it's not strong enough, especially with one hand."

"Why only—" Dabeet began, and then realized, and shut up.

"You're pushing the button with your other hand," Ragnar said helpfully.

"You have to lock one leg *through* the second bar. An adult can do it, but they always break the leg. You're smaller, you twist your boot and get it through, and then you try to get the other boot through but don't try for long because maybe you can't, the bars are different lengths. Main thing here is to get your knee under the bar and your leg exactly straight, not twisted. Then you bend your knee so that your lower leg is a big hook holding you on."

It was starting to sound very hard and complicated to Dabeet.

"If it isn't straight before you bend it, you'll break that leg," said Monkey.

"Probably break it anyway," said Ragnar helpfully.

"But it'll keep you in the ship," said Monkey, glaring at Ragnar. "But the second, and I mean the very second, after the atmo is completely blown, pull that leg free no matter how much it hurts, and I mean even if you've got six knees and three elbows in that leg, forget the pain and pull it out. Now you'll be in freefall because the gravitics cut out when atmo goes. You still hang on to the first handrail with one hand, swing around and grab the handrail just inside the *outer* door." Then she paused, thinking.

"Losing count of the handrails," said Zhang He.

"Dabeet isn't," said Monkey. "He's been working with airlocks for weeks now, and besides, he never loses count." She turned back to Dabeet. "The airlock is too big for you to reach that outer handrail without a little jump, so you have to disobey Rule One."

Dabeet nodded.

"But don't let that little jump carry you out the door, because you have no idea which way the ship will be facing by then. The launch won't be stable, the ship will probably be in three kinds of spin, so you have to wait in the door until just the right moment to jump toward the station."

"Toward this airlock," said Dabeet.

"Don't waste time looking for this airlock," said Monkey. "Jump toward the station. Period. And as soon as you do, look on the heads-up display for the SIG command, call up the menu, and light yourself up like a Christmas tree. Then it's my job to come out and get you."

"Got it," said Dabeet.

"No you don't," said Monkey. "Don't wait to jump. The *first* time you can see the station, you jump. That's it. Even if you don't have your legs under you, even if you can't get much power into the jump, even if you only push off with your hands, you go the *first time*. Because every second on that ship, you're getting farther from us here and I only have a two-kilometer line."

"Jump immediately, wait for nothing," said Dabeet.

"Last thing. Listen closely. What did I teach you about grasping?"

"Hug, don't hold."

"I'm going to get way more specific than that, Dirt Boy," said Monkey.

"Do not reach for me. Do not touch me. Even if I come *this close* to you, *no* physical contact between you and me because the friction of any contact will send us both spinning out of control."

Dabeet was confused. She saw it in his face.

"Yes, I'm coming out to get you. I'll use my directionals to get as close to you as I can. But I will not grab you, and you will not grab me. You will hug the *line.* You'll wrap your arms around it and hold on. I'll send a signal that it's time to start reeling in, but not until you're holding that line. Then as it draws me in, you and I will collide, and when we do, you have to be holding so tightly I won't knock you loose. Then as the line draws me in, it draws you in. Got it?"

"Line will be invisible," said Ragnar.

"That's possible," said Monkey. "You may have to simply trust that the line is straight as an arrow between me and the station. But if you have all your lights on, then there'll be a very tight beam straight forward from your helmet. Look toward where you know the line is supposed to be, and you'll catch a sparkle. You won't see a *line,* just sparkles, and you won't be able to tell if they're in a row or not, but nothing out there will be sparkling *except* the line, so you'll know that's it, it's reflecting your light. Spread your arms wide and when you're near it, grab. Hug. *Nothing* breaks that hug. Né?"

"É," said Dabeet.

"That was a three-month course in line rescues," said Monkey. "Now go earn us both an A on the test."

Dabeet saluted, and even though it began as a playful gesture, he wasn't playing. He knew that some part of this ridiculously elaborate plan was going to fail, and even if he got the ship away, he would probably die. But Monkey was willing to risk her life to come get him, and so he meant that salute with all his heart.

She saluted him back. Dabeet turned and jogged up to the outer airlock of the ship, pressed the OPEN button, went inside, and closed the outer door behind him.

18

—We bent all our efforts to finding another Mazer Rackham, someone whose genius—

—Genius?

—Would bring a desperate war to a quick, successful conclusion.

—Luck.

—Luck that we had you in the Second Formic War, and that you were in a place, at a time, with a weapon, when your brilliant insight could be put into action. Dumb luck. I agree.

—And you knew that if you didn't have a commander of genius in the Third War . . .

—If we waited for them to come at us again, their many worlds against our single world would be our doom. A war of attrition that we couldn't win, no matter how spunky we were.

—Not sure "spunky" is the—

—It's true that we invented some powerful new technologies under pressure. They didn't have our nanobots, or our gravitics, which led to the molecular-disruption device, but that would no more have won the war, if the endgame had taken place here in our solar system, than the V-1 and V-2 saved the Nazis.

—If we're talking about World War II, don't forget the atomic bomb.

—It came at the end of a crushing war of attrition. If the Japanese hadn't already lost the war, by every measure, the A-bomb would have been no more effective than the fire-bombing of Dresden. You know what I'm saying. We should have lost all three Formic Wars. We *did* lose them, except for a single, miraculous, decisive battle, the rarest form of victory.

—Hannibal had Cannae but Carthage lost the Punic Wars, the English had Agincourt and Crécy and they still lost the Hundred Years' War. I know.

—With multiple planets and the ability to reconfigure their fleet on the fly, their endless supply of soldiers, their—

—You learned the right lesson from the wars, my friend. The human race was doomed if we remained on only one world.

—We can't count on our gene pool squeezing out military geniuses whenever we need them. Good commanders are hard to find, but even the best commanders can't win lopsided wars of attrition, and a species confined to one planet is a single roach waiting to be stepped on.

—Not a roach. Roaches can scurry.

—So we're a fly caught in a web of our own weaving.

—Better.

—The sheer luck of having you in the Second Formic War, the miracle of Ender Wiggin and, let's be fair, the unsung Julian Delphiki—

—And, even fairer, you.

—Ain't we grand.

—But we did have Ender Wiggin.

—Won't happen again. We'll revert to the normal pattern of war. For all we know, there are six Formic fleets heading toward us right now, seriously pissed off and ready to exact vengeance against us. Carthage. That's what we are. A single city on the edge of the desert of space, waiting to be obliterated and have salt sown in our fields.

—So, having won the last war, you're winning the next one by dispersing the human species.

—Like a dandelion, blown out by a little child to take root wherever the breeze carries the tiny seeds.

—And you're the little boy with the puff of air.

—Which is why I'm not preparing my son to be the genius who will save the human race in a grand, spectacular battle.

—You're preparing him to be one of those little windblown seeds.

—Not even a seed. A part of the wisp of filament that serves as the kite to carry the seed along till it finds broken, fertile ground.

—It's called the "pappus." The achene, the beak, the stalk. I paid attention when we did dandelions in botany class.

—You took botany.

—The best preparation for a soldier. So that when the war is over, I can return, like Cincinnatus, to the farm, and make war against dandelion, thistle, nettle, and vetch.

—Andrew Wiggin is going to try to live the life of Cincinnatus, without any kind of preparation to suit him for the task. Dabeet, by his inborn character, was doomed to a life of arrogant isolation, useless to any community, more damaged from the start than Ender was. I had no way of knowing how he would respond to a crisis that showed him the futility of isolation.

—I think he's done rather well.

—If he lives, it will have been worth it.

—And if he dies?

—Then I am a Darwinian dead end, the brazen fiery Molech, Saturn devouring his son.

—Having adopted the human race, my old friend, you have billions of children, your dandelions in the lawn of the galaxy.

—I love the little bastard. I want my boy to live.

—Which will require him and his team to score an unlikely tactical victory against the most talented monster in centuries.

—That's what our geniuses are born for. Not to fight off aliens, not to prevent astronomical or ecological catastrophes, but to stop our own home-grown monsters from eating us alive from the inside out.

Dabeet found his suit where he had left it, now fully charged. Oh good, he thought. When Monkey fails to catch me—or, more likely, I fail to catch *her*—I'll have *plenty* of time to regret my many flaws and failures as I drift into the fires of reentry or the bitter cold of space.

He moved carefully, making sure that every piece of the suit fit. The suit reported itself to be intact and functional. Dabeet walked up the passage between the cartons of Vacoplaz, touching nothing. Then along the aisle between the passenger seats, which had so recently held the raiders who came here, wittingly or not, to kill a school full of children, along with themselves.

He stood in the open inner doorway of the airlock and found the button. Then raised his right leg and twisted his boot to fit between the second handrail and the wall. He didn't bother trying to fit his other leg into the same space. Instead he pushed himself down until his knee was directly under the rail. He bent his leg so his calf rose up to make a hook.

He tried an overhand grip, then switched to underhand, locking his right glove on to the handrail nearest the door. Only then did he reach out, slide his left glove down the track of the inner airlock door until he found the gap that contained the emergency OPEN button.

Nothing to wait for. Either they had closed their own outer airlock door or they hadn't. Not his job. Dabeet pushed the button.

Two things happened at once. The gravitics stopped, so that Dabeet was no longer sagging downward from his perch between the two handrails. But this barely registered with him because there was an enormous force trying to pry him out and hurl him through the door.

He was struck by several items, but the suit did its job so that nothing injured him. He couldn't see anything that flew out the airlock door because the wind of the escaping atmo pushed his head against the wall so that his faceplate showed him nothing. His heads-up display was blinking with warnings—he was no longer in a breathable atmosphere, he was no longer in gravity, he was going onto suit atmospherics, the suit was beginning to provide warmth as the ambient temperature plummeted, and oh, yes, equilibrium was gone because Dabeet was inside a spaceship that was now spinning in every possible direction, roll, pitch, and yaw.

And then, after only a few seconds, it was over. The atmo was gone and so was the wind pushing his face against the wall and the force trying to pry his leg out from the handrail.

No bones broken. His grip still held. But now he needed to get his leg out, and to do that he had to pull himself forward.

It didn't take long. His leg, being uninjured, turned, straightened, then bent as he needed it to. His boot came free of the handrail. This immediately caused him to float outward but his hand grip held.

He pulled himself into the wide-open airlock and took the short jump to the rail beside the outer door—almost without thinking, except that he did murmur to himself, "Outer handrail," and saw how it attached to the ship, even though he knew he wasn't supposed to let go of the previous rail until—

His toe snagged on the frame of the inner door, causing him to spin ass-over-teakettle and now his reaching hand wasn't actually reaching for anything and he was going to go out the door, he knew it—

But then his head fetched up against the side wall of the airlock and he caught the handrail near the inner door and caught himself and controlled himself, with the help of the suit's power assist. He loved the design of this suit, because how else could a child have held on with one hand and managed to straighten himself and still his motion? He had no such strength in his wrist, in his arm, but the suit was strong enough, and now he held himself in place, his feet toward the outer door as he saw the station float past.

This was the first time he saw it through the door but he could not possibly have made any kind of jump that took him toward the station. By the time he saw it, it was already too late, any exit movement would have taken him through the door heading somewhere else, somewhere random.

The rotation was not as bad as he feared—the station had not passed so *very* quickly in front of the doorway.

There was no guarantee that it would ever be visible through the door again, though, because the ship was rotating in every direction.

Dabeet gathered himself, pulled his legs toward his chest, and again reached for the rail near the outer door. This time he caught it easily, despite a bit of coriolis effect from the multiple spinning.

Was the nanooze still on the outside surface?

Yes. Trying not to see the spinning, trying not to think about how far he already was from the Fleet School station, Dabeet clung to the doorframe while getting his body through the door and his feet planted squarely on the nanooze.

Then he looked for the station. The previous jump hadn't been possible, but the next one would be.

He couldn't see the station at all, though there were several points of light that might have been nearby ships catching sunlight. But "nearby" could mean five hundred kilometers and he would be invisible to them and anyway, Monkey might already have jumped, mightn't she?

No, it had only been thirty seconds or so—a minute?—since he pushed the button and ejected the Juke ship from the airlock. They must have retracted the dockbridge before he—

No distractions! Look in the direction you're spinning *toward,* he told himself. See it *before* it's directly overhead.

It was never going to be directly overhead. He saw the station, the completed wheel, the half-completed wheel, the battleroom cubes attached to the center, but he wasn't going to get a chance at a straight-up jump from this surface. Yet if he tried to walk—Don't Walk! Don't Run!—he wouldn't get into a better position because in a few moments the station would be invisible again so, leaning in the direction of the station as best he could, Dabeet rose onto his toes and pushed off.

Only after he had left the surface did it occur to him that the rotating ship might collide with him, hitting him with the nose or tail of the vehicle.

It didn't. He had pushed off with such vigor that the whole thing was already behind him.

He was not headed directly for the station. It could have been worse. He was moving on a course that would take him past the station by about a quarter of its diameter. Under the circumstances, that was pretty good aim. But also under the circumstances, that was certain death because he would *miss* the ship and—

Monkey has to catch me, and if she's going to catch me she has to see me. Dabeet looked away from the ship, concentrated on the SIG icon on his heads-up display and then chose ALL LIGHTS from the menu. He spread his arms and looked at them—like a Christmas tree. Like the neon sign over a bar.

If I use my suit's directionals, I could point myself closer to the station, and—

No directionals. No! He didn't know how to use them and Monkey had to be able to predict his course. She wasn't supposed to smack into him directly, so even at this angle, she could probably pull the tether right in front of him so he could hug it and she could drag him in.

Except for one problem. The station wasn't getting any closer. In fact, it was obvious that he was still moving *away* from the station.

Am I still attached to the ship somehow?

No, he realized. He had been moving away from the station at exactly the velocity of the ship. He took his strongest leap toward the station, but all his strength couldn't have overcome the ship's speed. The push that the escaping atmo gave the Juke ship was far stronger than anything his legs could have achieved. I didn't reverse my direction of movement, I merely slowed my outbound movement a little. I'm not going to pass near the station because I'm still moving away from it.

That's why he was supposed to leave the ship as quickly as possible. So that Monkey could outstrip his outbound movement using her directionals. He had no way of guessing if he was even within her two-kilometer range. The time it took him to catch himself in the airlock, reorient, stand on the surface, search for the station, and then, finally, leap—

I had to do all that. I had no choice. What good was leaving the ship if I wasn't somehow aimed toward the station so my movement away would be somewhat slower?

If she can reach me, Monkey will reach me. If she can't, then I knew this might be how I died, I knew it and I chose to do it because who else should take this risk? I'm the one that the kidnappers chose. Now they can pin the whole raid on me and I won't care because I'll be dead.

A light appeared in front of the station. It had to be Monkey turning on all the lights of her suit. It took a while, concentrating on that spot of light, before he could be sure that he was looking at a spacesuit moving toward him. Moving a lot faster than *he* was moving, so she would overtake him, she really would. If the tether was long enough.

The suit was tracking her, too, because she was in motion and he had focused on her for three seconds. It reported that she was on a good course. No, not a good course, she was going to pass *behind* him. She had aimed and missed!

No, fool, Dabeet told himself. Just because your head is pointed toward the station doesn't mean you're *moving* that direction. Since you're moving away from the station, she's not passing behind you, she's going to pass ahead of where you're going to be.

Only now you're upside down, fool. You can't grab the tether with your legs.

He scanned the heads-up display and saw an icon labeled ORI. He vaguely knew that the suit could use the directionals automatically to reorient him, and ORI seemed like the best candidate for the menu he needed. Could it reorient him without changing his direction of movement? Time to find out.

He first selected REV but all that did was rotate him on the vertical axis so now his back was toward the approaching spacesuit. REV again and he could see her. He tried INV and this time the suit spun him upside down. His feet were now vaguely toward the station and as Monkey approached, he could see that their heads were now pointing in roughly the same direction. At moments he thought she was going to miss him by a hundred meters; at other times it looked as if she was going to collide with him. How could his perspective change like that?

It wasn't his perspective. The heads-up display showed that her trajectory really was changing, because she was using her directionals to perfect her aim.

He saw the sparkles behind her and realized that he was catching glimpses of the tether. The sparkles ran straight back toward the ship, though they looked like a series of dragonflies darting straight toward Monkey.

Don't look at her face, don't try to communicate, all that matters is the tether. No distraction. The tether. Wrap your arms around it and—

Dabeet pulled his arms back to his sides. In the position he was in, it was quite possible that in order to bring the tether close to him, Monkey would pass so close that his wide-open arms would touch her, put them both into a spin, and make the rescue impossible. Only after she passed could he open his arms to hug the line.

She drifted past him, slowly enough that she wasn't a blur, he could see the elements of her suit. But not her face. He didn't even try to see through her faceplate. His eyes were down, toward the tether.

The heads-up display was showing him the tether.

"Not helping," he murmured to the suit. He looked past the display, through the faceplate. He couldn't see the sparkles at all now. But she was past him, he flung his arms wide, and then he felt his left forearm hit the tether. It started to spin him but he immediately pulled against the tension and drew his body toward the tether, wrapped his arms around it. This was working. He had the tether. Still couldn't see it, but the heads-up display confirmed that he was on the line, he was wrapped around it, and he glanced and gazed at the LOCK command. Now the suit would hold on even if he was unconscious. He could nap now, and Monkey would bring him in.

He could hear a whishing, humming sound inside the suit, and it took a moment for him to realize that the tether was now reversed. Instead of playing out to let Monkey catch him, it was reeling her in.

They would collide soon. He hoped that she had used her directionals to make her change of direction more gradual, that she would also make their collision gradual enough to pose no danger to them—

Then he realized that there were bright objects whizzing past him, and he felt a force suddenly hurtle him rapidly toward the station. Was this how fast Monkey was going when she hit him?

She hadn't hit him. Instead, he saw her spacesuit flash past him. And then her new movement made the tether jerk in his arms. Without the strength of the locked suit he could never have held on. Why was she moving so fast?

Not her choice, Dabeet realized. The ship had blown up. All the force that would have torn apart the station had blasted in every direction from the ship. They were far enough to cut that force in half, maybe to a quarter of what it would have been, but they were still way too close, and the debris had hit them, most of it pulverized to dust, so it hit them like wind; but some of it was still in chunks, mostly tiny, but some the size of a leaf, some the size of a basketball—

Dabeet was now going the same speed as Monkey, dragging along behind her, moving toward the station. The tether was still reeling them in—whoever was controlling it must have sped it up to match and surpass their new velocity and it was pulling him a little sideways, so his angle changed, and now he could see that . . .

Monkey's suit was torn. Not a big tear, but she was trying to cover it with her hand, and the glove wasn't big enough. Atmo was escaping and turning instantly into a cloud of ice. Dabeet remembered the lecture they all heard about leaking spacesuits and it didn't take any complicated math to realize that unless that leak could be slowed, Monkey would arrive at the station airlock door dead.

Dabeet didn't even have to think about it. He pushed against the force of the suit-lock and his right arm came free. He found the tether with his glove and locked on to it. Found the tether with his other glove. Hand over hand, he climbed up the tether until he reached Monkey.

Then he climbed Monkey's suit. Each grasp, he thought the name of the spot he was reaching for, he gripped and let the glove take hold, too much haste and he'd lose her completely, he had to stay close, stay *attached*.

Now he was almost even with her, his chest pressed against the abdominal tear in her suit. He wrapped his arms around her body and gripped. Tighter. Tighter. Tighter. Was this close enough that his suit was blocking the leak? Did his suit somehow know what he was trying to do? Was it helping him? Or had he missed, was he clinging to her dying body as atmo kept escaping because he wasn't blocking the hole?

I won't know, I can't know till the tether brings us in, and I don't dare let go to check because then atmo will *definitely* escape.

Do the suits self-seal at all? There's no nanooze, but surely there's some kind of self-sealing mechanism. Her suit couldn't cope with the size of the tear, but maybe the two suits together could do it, especially if he *was* blocking the hole so that no more atmo was escaping.

There was a harsh jolt as the two of them collided with the hull of the station. His suit's lock held, so they weren't pulled apart. They slid along the nanooze only a little way, with only a couple of bounces, till they were dragged around the corner of the airlock doorframe and toward the tether's root in the inside wall.

Hands grabbed at them, tried to pull them apart, but Dabeet held on to the locked position until he could see that the outer airlock door was closed. Then the inner door opened, atmo whooshed into the space, and now he unlocked his hold on Monkey and the other kids pulled the two of them apart.

He reached up and pulled off his helmet.

"Rip in her suit!"

"Get the helmet off!"

"Is she breathing? Is she conscious?"

So he wouldn't have to tell them about the torn suit. He stood on the floor, grateful to be back with working gravitics. He made the suit loosen and drop down from his body, and he stepped out of it.

"Is she alive?" he asked.

"Yes," said Zhang He. He had apparently been inside the station corridor, not in the open airlock, because he wasn't wearing a spacesuit. Dabeet saw and instantly registered that it was Bartolomeo Ja who had been in the open airlock, wearing a suit, monitoring and controlling the tether. And also Timeon. Those were the catchers, there to pull them in.

They had Monkey out of her spacesuit. Ragnar was checking her pulse, her breathing; he put his hand flat on her chest, nodded. "Heartbeat strong, breathing strong. But who knows how long she was oxygen deprived?"

Monkey's eyes opened. "The only thing depriving me of oxygen," she said, "was Dabeet crushing the life out of me."

"I was trying to block the hole in your suit, I didn't mean to—"

"Saved my life, oomay, that's what you did. Alarms going off in my suit, estimate of five seconds till total atmo loss when you plugged the hole, you saved my stupid life."

"I let go of the tether, though," said Dabeet.

"I forgive you," said Monkey.

"And I used the directionals to reorient myself," said Dabeet.

"If you hadn't, would you have seen that my suit was torn?"

Zhang He spoke up. "Back from death for two seconds and she's already arguing."

"Thank you for saving me, Monkey," said Dabeet.

"Felt like I was back with my family, on a real ship," said Monkey.

And then silence. They were all breathing heavily. Coming down from an adrenaline high.

Finally somebody moved. Bartolomeo Ja. He walked toward Dabeet, held out his hand. Dabeet took it, not sure what was happening. "Thank you, sir," said Ja. "For saving us all."

"We saw the raiders' ship blow up," said Timeon. "If it had still been attached to the station when it blew . . ."

"Maybe two minutes at the most after you blew the airlock," said Ja.

"Did you know how much time we had left?" asked Ignazio.

Dabeet shook his head. "I don't think it was on a timer. I think it was detonated from Earth the moment they saw that the ship was detached from the station. The only thing that gave us the time we had was that the ship was moving mostly away from Earth so it took a minute before anybody on Earth could see that it had detached. Plus time to realize and push the button, plus the time lag for the electronic signal to reach the ship—"

"Shut up," said Monkey. "We can all do the math."

"I'm not *telling* you," said Dabeet, "I'm just *realizing* it."

"What took you so long to get out of the ship?" asked Ragnar.

"I tripped," said Dabeet. "And then it took a few seconds to get through the door and stand on the surface and find where the station *was,* so I could jump toward it."

"You call that jumping 'toward' the station?" asked Ragnar.

"Best I could—"

They laughed. Ragnar slapped him lightly upside the head.

"Joking," said Ragnar.

"Take a joke, dollback," said Ignazio.

"Sorry," said Dabeet. "Give me a few minutes, I'll see how funny it is."

"No you won't," said Zhang He, "because it isn't. We're just relieved. And yes, zhopa-brain, you saved us all. We know you didn't choose for these marubos to come up here and you *sure* didn't choose for them to try to blow us out of the sky, but you lissed into their ship and you sussed it all and you got us with you and—"

"I'm really glad you came. I didn't know if you would."

"What if we hadn't?" asked Ja.

"I don't know," said Dabeet. "Maybe I would have thought of blowing the airlock to get the ship away. But I sure hadn't thought of it up till you guys started saying it was the obvious thing to do."

"You're going to be a lousy bureaucrat," said Zhang. "You don't even know how to modestly take all the credit."

"If you *had* thought of it," said Ragnar. "By yourself. Alone. What then?"

Dabeet shrugged. "I don't know," he said. "I wouldn't have known where to look for the airlock release button."

"You would have found it," said Ja. "Because of the sign all over the inside of the inner door that says, 'Airlock Release Button.'"

Ragnar scoffed. "But would you have—"

"He would have pressed it," said Zhang He. "You know he would. Because he's taking this whole thing onto himself. He thinks it's his fault. He would have done it."

Dabeet had no idea if Zhang He was right, but with everybody else nodding and murmuring, "é, certo, claro, right," he didn't see any reason to raise an argument.

But he had to say something. "I'm glad you guys showed up. I'm glad Monkey knew how to pull somebody out of space like that. I'm glad you knew how to run the tether. I'm glad it took them long enough to detonate that we could get away from the ship. Thank you." Then he burst into tears. He didn't know why. They just erupted from his eyes, his body convulsed in sobs.

Only for a couple of seconds. Maybe five. Or ten. Monkey was hugging him, a couple of others had their hands on him, gripping his shoulders, his upper arms. "Good job," said Ja. "Proud to know you," said Zhang He.

And then the crying stopped, as quickly and involuntarily as it had started.

"We've still got a bunch of bunducks on this station," said Dabeet.

"If the plans worked," said Ja, "they're all in the four battlerooms by now, along with all the older students. Teachers in the embarcation hub with the younger kids. You know, the ones our age."

"And a year older," added Ignazio, snickering.

"They can still do a lot of damage," said Monkey.

"Could you feel the explosion here? Inside the station?" asked Dabeet.

"Whole thing shuddered," said Ragnar.

"Earthquake," said Ja. "Felt like a major quake."

"So they know *something* happened," said Dabeet. "If we put the right spin on this, maybe we can talk them into surrendering."

"Surrendering to kids?"

"Surrendering to whatever IF forces come racing here after they detected the explosion," said Dabeet.

"Oh, *those* guys," said Ragnar.

"Got to talk to them before anybody gets hurt or killed in the battlerooms," said Monkey.

"Controls in Urska Kaluza's quarters, public-address system all over the station," said Ignazio.

"If we can get in there," said Timeon.

"Let's go find out," said Ja.

Two minutes to run the pass-through and get to the commandant's quarters. Didn't meet a single raider. The door was wide open. An old-fashioned microphone sat on the table. It took Ignazio a few seconds to bring up the commands from the control panel. "Should be wide now, they can hear it everywhere," said Ignazio.

"You sure?"

"I'm sure I selected 'All Speakers' and 'All Area' and 'Full Volume,'" said Ignazio.

Dabeet pushed the microphone toward Ja.

"Não, bicho," said Ja. "Not me."

"You're the commander," said Zhang He.

"I'm team leader of a bunch of children," said Ja. Then he pushed the microphone toward Dabeet.

"Me?" asked Dabeet. "Why?"

"No time to find a grownup," said Monkey.

"Nobody here knows how to talk with authority," said Zhang He. "So we'll have to make do with insufferable arrogance." Zhang He grinned. Almost sincerely.

Dabeet put his hand on the microphone and took a couple of breaths. Composing himself. He still had no idea what to say, but they were right. He had withered adults with his scorn back in the Charles G. Conn School for the Gifted. That was the closest they were going to come to a voice of command.

Monkey whispered, "No school slang."

Dabeet nodded. "Greetings, all you soldiers who made this unprovoked attack against the children of Fleet School. Everybody stop whatever you're doing and listen. Now!"

He made his voice like a whip. But he sure wished that he knew if anybody was listening.

"Whatever you thought your mission was, they lied to you. Your mission was really this: To bring a ship filled with Vacoplaz, attach it to Fleet School Station, and blow us all to hell. Including you. Every one of you. There was no escape plan, there was no evacuation plan, the only plan was to get you here and kill everybody on the station."

He tried to imagine what they might be saying in the four battlerooms. Doubts? Challenges? Officers ordering the others to pay no attention? Time to prove what he was saying, as best he could.

"We got on board your unguarded ship and found the Vacoplaz. There was no way we could pull thousands of blasting caps out of the 'plaz. So we popped the airlock and blew your ship away from the station. Whoever was controlling the Vacoplaz back on Earth took long enough to realize what had happened and trigger it that the ship was far enough that the station wasn't destroyed. But you felt the blast. Like an earthquake. You felt it. What do you think could cause a jolt like that? All the kids in Fleet School stomping their feet at the same moment? You know I'm telling you the truth."

Dabeet looked at the others. The ones who weren't grinning were nodding.

"Your ship is a bunch of dust and chunks heading toward Earth re-entry, the Moon, and mostly outer space. There's nobody coming to pick you up because they expected the whole station, including your bodies, to be dust and chunks by now. You've been betrayed. And any officers telling you not to listen to me, they're still part of that betrayal. Shut them up so you can hear what I'm going to tell you now."

Dabeet looked at Ja, who was smiling tightly and shaking his head. Dabeet shrugged, in effect asking him, If that was wrong, what should I say instead?

But Ja smiled more broadly and gestured to him to go on. Thumbs-up from Ragnar. Slap on the back from Timeon.

"A relieving force from the IF will be here soon. If they find you holding any child or teacher as a hostage, you can be sure that there'll be a lot of dying here today. Maybe some of us, but most definitely all of you. The IF doesn't take it kindly when somebody kidnaps their children. So forget any idea of hostage negotiation. We're not your hostages anyway. You are now our prisoners. Do you understand that? If the IF comes here and finds that you are all in custody, having surrendered to the students of Fleet School, then there will be no killing. Except for whatever officers you had to kill just now to get them to shut up."

Monkey rolled her eyes, but he got thumbs-up from Zhang He and Ragnar.

"Let go of your weapons and come out into open space. The students will gather up your weapons and take them out of the battlerooms. You invaders will remain in the battlerooms until the IF forces enter to formally accept your surrender and to interrogate you about whoever it was on Earth who sent you here. I suggest full cooperation. And don't bother waiting till you have legal representation. It's military law out here. Tell them everything. You don't owe a thing to those lying bastards back on Earth."

Dabeet stood there for a moment, trying to think if there was anything else he needed to say.

Just one thing. "If any of the invaders are *not* in a battleroom, then you will either get yourself *into* a battleroom, or you can head for the airlock where you left your ship, open the door, and jump on out."

That was it. That was all. Dabeet looked at Ignazio and made a throat-cutting gesture. Ignazio punched a spot in the holospace and then grinned. "Mike's off," he said. "Toguro, man."

"Should I repeat it?" asked Dabeet. "Was it clear?"

"You got a voice like a whip," said Ja. "You were the man for the job."

"So that's my career now," said Dabeet. "Public relations."

A couple of them laughed. The ones who had lived on Earth. The spaceborn had no reason to know what "public relations" even meant.

"I think we need to go and see whether they're actually doing what Dabeet said," Zhang He suggested.

Dabeet made as if to go with them, but Ja put a hand on his chest and stopped him. "You stay here. You, too, Cynthia."

Monkey's eyes flashed with resentment, but whether it was at the instruction to stay behind or at the use of her given name, Dabeet couldn't guess.

"You two have been through enough," said Ja. "Taken enough risk. If these bunducks are still shooting or taking hostages or whatever, you don't need to be in it. You've done your part."

"Leave Ignazio with us?" asked Dabeet. "In case we need to make another announcement?"

"Koncho," said Ignazio. But he also stayed.

After a few minutes with the three of them alone in Urska Kaluza's quarters, Dabeet began to go around the room, palming open everything that looked like a door. Lots of cupboards. Enough dishes to serve a six-course meal at the big table. Two different bathrooms, presumably one for guests and the other, with a luxurious bath and shower, for the commandant. A cupboard of snacks, which they immediately began sampling, and a refrigerator with food and drinks, with and without alcohol.

"Don't even think about it," Monkey told Ignazio, who was fingering a bottle of scotch. "You have no idea what your body's tolerance for alcohol is, and you don't want the official report on this to say that they found you drunk."

"Besides, if somebody's keeping scotch in the fridge," said Dabeet, "it means they're too stupid to choose decent scotch in the first place."

"Oh, you're the expert," said Monkey.

"Room temperature except for American beer and a few wines," said Dabeet. "I was raised by a civilized mother."

Ignazio set down the bottle and picked up a soft-drink can with a label printed in cyrillic characters. He poured it out into a glass and it looked like some kind of fizzy fruit juice. Pretty soon they were working their way through the fridge and the snack cupboard, reviewing it all as snidely as possible.

After a half hour or so, Ragnar came back with news. Two officers dead, killed by their own men when Dabeet told them, over the public-address system, to shut them up. Otherwise, no casualties.

The raid hadn't gotten that far, anyway. When the raiders pursued the students into the battlerooms, they had been confused by the network of walls and pillars and bridges they had built. They couldn't see any kids and they didn't know how to find their way through the maze. Then the shock hit the station and everybody stopped moving while the officers screamed about how they had a job to do, now do it . . . and nobody did anything.

"So what are they doing now?" asked Monkey.

"One of the older kids got some teachers out of Embarcation and they turned on the gravitics in the battlerooms. All the kids are out, all the raiders are in. The doors are locked."

Dabeet felt relieved.

"And here's the thing," said Ragnar. "Not one person asked, 'Who was that on the loudspeakers?' They all knew."

Dabeet knew exactly what that meant, but he tried to put a good face on it. "When the job requires an asshole," he said, "I'm your man."

"It wasn't a bad thing," said Ragnar. "I didn't mean that as a bad thing."

"I know," said Dabeet. And he *did* know. But despite Ragnar's intention, it *was* a bad thing. It meant that with not all that much time at Fleet School, Dabeet was famous for sounding arrogant and scornful. It might have been useful this time, but it wasn't something Dabeet would ever be proud of.

It took three hours for the first IF ship to dock at Embarcation. By the time any marines made it to the battlerooms, the teachers had already filled them in on what happened. It was another couple of hours before anybody came to the commandant's quarters.

The marine colonel who led a couple of noncoms into the room looked surprised to see Monkey, Ignazio, and Dabeet there.

"This is the best of the soft drinks," said Monkey. "There's still plenty in the fridge." Of course she had indicated the one that they all hated worst, because she was, after all, still Monkey.

"What are you kids doing in here?" asked the colonel.

"Being naughty," said Ignazio. "After ejecting the raiders' ship and getting the ones still on the station to surrender, we figured it was time for a snack and Urska Kaluza kept all the best stuff for herself."

"Are you drunk?" asked the colonel.

Ignazio looked at Monkey and Dabeet. "If they think I'm drunk anyway, you could have let me actually *have* some of the scotch."

"Not scotch from a fridge," said Dabeet. "You deserve better."

By then a couple of teachers had come into the room. "This is where they made the announcement from," said the astrogation teacher. "It was that one." She pointed at Dabeet. "Said all the right things and they complied."

The marine colonel looked at Dabeet, then at Monkey and Ignazio. His attitude changed visibly. "Good show, then," he said.

"I think," said the astrogation teacher, "that they were also on the team that detached the ship before it blew."

"You seriously did that?" asked the colonel.

"Is the station completely pulverized and everybody dead?" asked Monkey. "No? Then yes, we did it very seriously." She pointed at Dabeet. "He was the one who blew the airlock on the ship. Also found the Vacoplaz and figured out what was going on. Dabeet Ochoa."

"And she came out and brought me back to the station," said Dabeet. "She almost died doing it. Her name is Munk."

"Cynthia Munk," said Ignazio, ducking as she slapped at his head.

Dabeet named the rest of the team, starting with Ignazio.

"You planned this?" asked the colonel.

"Hell no," said Monkey. "How could we figure somebody would bring two thousand–plus packets of Vacoplaz to blow up a school full of children? We just made it up as we went along."

The colonel turned to the teachers. "I thought this wasn't a military school anymore."

"We're space kids," said Ignazio. Considering that he had grown up in Cádiz, that was stretching the truth a little. But not much. They were space kids *now*. Even Dabeet. All of them.

Monkey backed him up. "This wasn't a military situation, not with the ship and the Vacoplaz. It was an equipment malfunction and we did exactly what we would have done on any mining ship in the Belt."

The marine colonel grinned. "Got it," he said. He waved a hand toward the treat-strewn table. "Carry on."

As he was leaving, Dabeet asked, "Are all the kids OK? All the teachers? All the kitchen staff?"

The colonel turned. "No casualties among station personnel. Didn't know you had kitchen staff aboard."

"Maybe they stayed in the kitchen," said Ignazio. "In which case, maybe they'll serve dinner."

"I'll check on that," said the history teacher. "Everybody must be about starving by now."

"Two officers dead, two seriously injured. One from each battleroom. We've listened to the recording of your announcement." He looked at Dabeet. "You, right?"

Dabeet nodded.

"If you ever need a job as a drill sergeant," he said. Then he grinned. "You asked about the other kids," he said. "And the teachers, and the kitchen staff. That's how a commander thinks. That's what I heard in that recording. A commander."

Then the marines and the teachers left and it was just the three of them again.

"A commander," said Ignazio, in exaggerated awe.

"Still a yelda," said Monkey. "But you've got kintamas."

"Giant ones," said Ignazio. "Don't know how you get your pants on."

19

—So what's your plan now? Live forever? Not much point in that, I can tell you. Endless voyaging at lightspeed is indistinguishable from prison.

—Except you get a better quality of visitor.

—You visited me on that horrible voyage only because you wanted something from me.

—And I got it. Because you wanted to give it.

—When you consider, sir, how little you intervene, will it make any difference whether you live to see the fruits of your labors?

—Curiosity is a reasonable ambition.

—There are no reasonable ambitions. They all involve hope for a future in which your favorite things remain unchanged, and the things you detest are transformed into something wonderful.

—My curiosity is just as satisfied with bad results.

—There is no curiosity without hope, and there is no hope without disappointment. If all the colonies failed, or if the Formics return with a vast armada and do to Earth what we did to their home world, would you really want to be there to see it?

—Must you always see the worst?

—I'm never disappointed. Pleasantly surprised sometimes. But not often.

—I watched my son discover what kind of man he is, what kind he wants to be. I'm glad I have lived this long.

—Living forever requires fabulous wealth. But in your absence, don't expect your network of influence to endure. The people who cooperate with you will either die or will assume that you've died already. You'll come out of your lightspeed voyage and discover that you're powerless, but you can afford a good hotel.

—I think you've depressed me enough for one day. I'm going to go see my son.

—And tell him the gladsome tidings?

—If you mean, tell him that I'm his father—I don't think so. He wouldn't be impressed, he'd be angry that I hadn't told him before. And he'd be disappointed that I'm not smarter than I am.

—But pleased that he's smarter than you.

—There *is* that. But I don't think he cares as much about measured intelligence as he used to.

—Ender Wiggin is more your son than Dabeet is. You spent so much more time with him.

—He's like a son to me, yes. And so is Julian. But neither of them is *more* my son than Dabeet. You're forgetting the joy that comes from knowing that your genes have reproduced themselves in a person who is likely to survive.

—I *am* forgetting that. I have reason to.

—You love your grandchildren and great-grandchildren.

—I don't know them.

—You still care about them. Whether they live or die. Whether they're happy.

—But I don't love them as much as I love Ender Wiggin. Because I didn't raise them, I didn't teach them. But Ender—him I taught, and knew, and trained, and hurt, and tried to heal.

—You guided him to victory.

—For *that* I'm not sure he'll be grateful for very long. Because I lied to him every bit as much as you've lied to Dabeet.

—Keeping a secret is not telling a lie.

—You tell yourself that, Hyrum. Chant it every night and every morning. I wonder if you'll come to believe it.

The kitchen staff had not stopped working through the entire raid. The invaders paid no attention to them, and the cooks recognized that no matter who won, people would be hungry.

So after the IF relief ships had taken complete authority, and loaded the prisoners and the corpses into vessels and taken them wherever such people would be taken, the students and faculty of Fleet School were summoned to their various mess halls and fed an unusually flavorful supper. As if the cooks wanted to prove that they, too, had been worth saving.

Dabeet sat at a table with Monkey, Zhang He, Ragnar, Timeon, and Ignazio, the original wall-building team. Bartolomeo joined them for part of the meal, but there were enough people crowding around to say whatever they had to say that Bartolomeo moved to another table to make room for them.

It was hard to eat while making polite responses to all the kids with comments or questions. Dabeet still had half his food left when the others were done. Monkey leaned over and spoke into Dabeet's ear. "You're allowed to eat. You don't have to answer everybody."

"Yes I do," said Dabeet mildly. He had such a name for arrogance already that he couldn't leave anybody to walk away saying, "I just wanted to congratulate him but he was too important to listen to me."

It was Zhang who took action. "People, come on, let the boy eat. He's as hungry as anybody and he's hardly eaten anything yet."

A few people backed away then, and Bartolomeo and some of the other team leaders came over and dispersed the crowd. Finally, Dabeet was able to eat his mostly-cold food and pass those five minutes without having to say anything to anybody. He finally looked around at his team and said, "You got enough to eat?"

"Plenty," said Monkey. "I don't know how, but the harder the cooks try, the worse the food gets."

"She's not used to spicy," said Ignazio. "Poor child."

"This all began," said Dabeet, "because you came over to help me build pillars and walls in the battleroom."

"That was the flame," said Timeon. "We were the moths."

"You were willing to take me seriously when nobody else was. That's how you ended up saving my life, and Monkey's life."

"And everybody's life on the whole station," said Ignazio.

"I'm just saying," said Dabeet. "Thanks for giving me a chance."

"Biggest mistake of my life," said Monkey. "Almost killed me."

"É, I know," said Dabeet. "I'm a dangerous friend."

His words fell into a gathering silence in the mess hall. Had everyone left?

Quite the opposite. All the students and faculty seemed to be there, which meant that they had been summoned. Supper had just turned into a meeting, and standing on a table near the main door was Robota Smirnova.

"You all know," said Robota, "how the bold action of the students of Fleet School forestalled the raid and prevented the bloodbath that some-one intended. We don't yet know who instigated this act of terrorism, but we do know it began on Earth. We also know that there were col-laborators here on the Fleet School station, and we are happy to report that, upon receipt of our messages, the crew of the packet ship that car-ried off the commandant and training officers shortly before the attack arrested Urska Kaluza with charges of smuggling, conspiracy, and trea-son against the Fleet. We expect that all the training officers will be exonerated, and the packet ship is turning around and bringing them all back here."

There was applause and some cheering from the kids—they knew and liked their training officers more than anyone on the faculty. And the idea of Urska Kaluza being arrested pleased many.

"As head of station security, I am assigned as acting commandant until the Fleet makes a temporary or permanent appointment. For those who are wondering why I was not here when the raid occurred, I was ordered to withdraw to an observing position on a nearby vessel sev-eral months ago. We were preparing a boarding operation against the terrorist vessel when several students took matters into their own hands, blew the airlock, ejected the ship, and then escaped from it before it blew up. We have every reason to believe that our boarding operation would have been observed from Earth and would have triggered a dev-astating explosion, probably killing every soul on this station. So the actions of the students involved were the only plan that could possibly have succeeded, and even then it depended on flawless execution, which was achieved."

To this, the assembled students and faculty erupted in deafening cheers and applause and arm-waving and a bit of food-tray-tossing. Only those at Dabeet's table remained silent, grinning at the enthusiasm of their fellow students.

Except Dabeet, who slid aside his food tray and lowered his head onto his arms.

"Quiet, quiet," said Robota Smirnova. "Quiet, please. Because there's one more piece of information that I must deliver, and instead of wait-ing for a private meeting, let me say it now, so there's no delay. Dabeet Ochoa, I am happy to inform you that Maria Rafaella Ochoa was rescued from hostile custody in a police action by Cuban authorities, who located her in an embassy in Havana. I don't know which embassy or what the international repercussions will be, but she had been taken there when the terrorist ship was launched, and only the swift coopera-tion of several nations and the International Fleet allowed her to be lo-cated and rescued so quickly. Let me be clear, Dabeet Ochoa. Your mother is safe."

Again, some cheers, lots of applause. But Dabeet wept into his hands, great body-racking sobs that he could not control. He felt the hands of his friends touching him, patting him, gripping him. He felt Monkey's arms around his body. Yet in the midst of all this emotion, he was able to think: The threat against Mother was real, but I did not fail her. The threat against Fleet School was real, but I did not fail my friends. I did not fail.

Was this how Ender Wiggin felt, when he stopped a war, won the war? Not the triumph of victory, but the deep relief of knowing that with everything at stake, he did not fail?

Maybe Ender Wiggin didn't expect to fail.

No. The only person that arrogant was the Dabeet Ochoa who arrived at Fleet School about a year ago, planning to betray everyone here in order to save his mother. That boy expected to succeed at everything because nobody was as clever as he was.

What a fool, thought Dabeet. And how hard it was to break that ar-rogance and find something useful to put in its place.

It was these friends, with their hands on my shoulders, on my head, arms around my chest. It was this community of generous children who saw value in what I was doing, and eventually found—no, *made*—something valuable in me.

He wept all the harder, and was even more grateful for the touch of their hands.

—

A few days later, everything was back to normal in the station. It took half a day to unbuild all the walls and pillars in the battlerooms and return the frames to their proper locations in the walls. And then a gen-eral tournament of all the teams, just to exhaust the pent-up energy in the children.

But all of that came to an end, and there were the teachers in their classrooms, making assignments and reviewing material that the stu-dents had not learned well in the past weeks, as they waited and pre-pared for the coming of the raiders. A lot of ground to cover.

Not for Dabeet, though. His memory still functioned as always, so that he had not actually lost any classroom time. So the review made him impatient, in part because he had no recourse: If he tried to get out of class, or even to do extra assignments, it would look to everyone, including Dabeet himself, like the old Dabeet, the one who had to show he was smarter than everybody.

So it came as a relief when a message banner appeared on his desk, and the teacher's voice came at the same time: "Dabeet, please report to the commandant's office immediately."

Dabeet got up, blanked his desk, and carried it with him out of the room. Maybe he'd come back to this classroom, maybe not. But if he had to sit and wait somewhere, it was better to have the tools to accomplish something than to twiddle his thumbs. The one thing he didn't want to do was sit and think, because inevitably his thoughts would run back to his nearly-disastrous expedition into the enemy ship. What if he'd tried to keep his suit on once he breached the ship? What if he hadn't thought to open a box so he didn't know about the Vacoplaz? What if the other kids hadn't shown up to the rendezvous he called? What if those two older girls had failed to deliver the message?

What if he had tried to jump the first time he saw the station, and gotten completely off course? As it was, he now knew that when Monkey reached him, she only had about a hundred meters of tether left. If his trajectory had made it so she couldn't reach him with that length of cable, he would have died. And perhaps she as well, because the explosion would have caught her even closer to the ship, and there would have been no one to cover and plug any tears in her spacesuit.

What if, what if. He knew that this was idiotic, to imagine all that could have gone wrong. Especially because it *hadn't* gone wrong. But whenever he didn't keep his mind busy with *something,* that was where it went.

Robota Smirnova sat behind the commandant's desk, where not that long ago Dabeet had sat eating snacks and drinking carbonated beverages with his friends. But after only a glance at her, Dabeet's attention was drawn to the other person in the room.

Dabeet walked to the Minister of Colonization and extended his hand. "I know I have you to thank for rescuing my mother, sir," said Dabeet.

Graff took his hand, but shook his head with a wry smile. "I did help prepare the ground a little, but it was all the officials in the IF and the various governments, not to mention the Cuban police, who did everything that mattered. I'm glad she's safe, though. And you, too, Dabeet."

Dabeet glanced over at Robota.

"I asked Robota to remain here for a short time," said Graff. "She has been given a one-year appointment as interim commandant of Fleet School, and she wanted me to help train her in school administration, which is why I'm here."

Dabeet immediately thought: You came here to see me, and training Robota is only an excuse. But then he quashed that conclusion, because it was borderline narcissistic.

"Congratulations," said Dabeet to Robota.

"And I wanted you to know that I was the one who arranged for Robota Smirnova to be withdrawn from Fleet School during the weeks before the arrival of the terrorists," said Graff. "She wanted to be aboard the station with a beefed-up security force, but it was my belief that the only result of that would have been the needless death of many on both sides, including, in all likelihood, faculty and children."

"I think if there had been resistance of that kind, sir," said Dabeet, "the explosives would have been detonated much sooner."

"That's a reasonable conclusion," said Graff.

"Damn right," said Robota. "I hated the orders I got, but I obeyed them, and because of you, Dabeet, everything worked out well. I'll leave you two now, and go present my new credentials to the faculty and staff." She was already at the door by the time she finished speaking. It closed behind her.

"She's a good officer," said Graff. "When she helped you open a door, she was *not* acting under my orders. She made the right decision, don't you think?"

Dabeet could only shrug. She should have been court-martialed for it. But if it helped keep Mother alive, Dabeet was glad that Robota had done it.

"I need to ask you to make a decision, and you don't have much time to make it. Your position here in Fleet School has become complicated. There will be a court of inquiry and your name will be all over it. If you're needed for examination or testimony, that will take priority, of course, but it shouldn't interfere with your studies here."

Dabeet said nothing, as he tried to figure out where this was leading. He was trying not to jump to conclusions.

"Details of your actions will be known throughout the Fleet, but not on Earth. I can return you to Earth at any time, to resume normal schooling there—if any schooling that involves you can be called 'normal.'

In other words, you can escape from whatever public opinion gathers about you and your actions."

"But I can also stay here, if I choose?"

Graff obviously understood that this was Dabeet's immediate choice. "Why would you stay?" he asked.

"I'd like to say something noble, like, 'If Ender Wiggin couldn't return to Earth after saving all of humanity from the Formics, how can it be right for me to go back when all I did was push a dangerous ship away from the school?'"

"Very noble indeed," said Graff. "And complete goffno, if I'm using the word correctly."

"I don't want to leave here," said Dabeet, "because for the first time in my life, I have friends."

"Not everybody will be your friend, after the inquiry's results are published through the Fleet."

"I don't need *everybody* to be my friend," said Dabeet. "I'm pretty astonished that *anybody* is, and I like it, and I want to stay."

"They're a good group," said Graff.

"Is it possible I could go home just long enough to see Mother?" asked Dabeet. "And then come back here?"

"Let's be reasonable," said Graff. "Nobody else gets to go to Earth to—"

"With all due respect, sir, people whose families are in space have the chance for annual visits, at least. And if I can't go there, perhaps she could come here. Or somewhere nearby."

Graff studied Dabeet intently. "You do remember that she's not actually your mother."

"She's the only mother I have," said Dabeet.

"She's an officer of the Fleet. She was assigned to you, Dabeet. The assignment is over, and she'll be given new responsibilities somewhere else."

Dabeet felt this as a slap in the face. But then he took time to think. "That's bullshit, sir. She loved me. She cared about me. She didn't just switch that off because she got a new assignment."

Graff raised his eyebrows. "You're probably right. I'll check with her and see what she wants to do. If she's willing, then something can be arranged. But you must understand that there was never a legal adoption. You have no legal claim on her, nor she on you."

Dabeet sat down across from Graff. "Let me sort this out a little, sir. Am I to understand that I'm legally an orphan, a ward of the state? And my time being raised by Rafa Ochoa constituted kidnapping, under your authority?"

"It was under Fleet authority, not mine," said Graff.

"A distinction without a difference, I'm guessing."

"You're guessing incorrectly," said Graff. "You are not an orphan."

"I don't know of any living parents."

"You may *feel* like an orphan, and that's tragic," said Graff. "I weep for all the children who are in such a situation. The children of all the soldiers and pilots who traveled with the fleets that conquered the Formic empire grew up with no hope of ever seeing their missing parents."

"They knew who they were," said Dabeet, "and they knew *where* they were, and what they were doing. They knew what their sacrifice was about."

"Then let me assure you of this. Your parents are alive. They both know that you're alive. They are distressed at the necessity that keeps them from being a part of your life."

"You know who my parents are."

"Of course I do," said Graff. "And I know why you have been deprived of their presence in your life, and I, and they, agree that this is your best chance for a normal life."

"Why?" said Dabeet. "Are they too famous to raise me? Famous people have had children before. They don't all turn into horrible human beings."

"Fame doesn't enter into it," said Graff. "Beyond that, I will neither confirm nor disconfirm any guesses you make. Please don't waste time."

Dabeet wanted to strike out at that complacent face across the table. To scream at him for his smug decisions about what was good for Dabeet, without any attempt to let Dabeet be part of the decision.

"I can see that you are determined to deprive me of knowledge about my parentage, and to conspire in keeping me from having any kind of parent in my life."

"You had years with Rafa Ochoa," said Graff.

"And now those years have ended."

"You were not deprived of love. You still aren't."

Dabeet thought immediately of his friends, and his eyes watered. He calmed himself and answered with a steady voice. "So my only family, here on forward, is whatever brothers and sisters I can find for myself."

Graff nodded slightly. "A good way of looking at it."

"And my real father and mother consent to this," he said.

"They do," said Graff. "Though not happily."

"The fact that they gave consent at all means that part of my education must now include trying to overcome the soullessness they have bequeathed to me in my genes."

"Yes," said Graff.

Something flickered across his face and Dabeet wondered if it might be pain.

Why would Graff have felt pain at Dabeet's words?

An answer came immediately to Dabeet's mind. "Sir," he asked, "are you my father?"

Graff immediately shook his head. "I am not," he said. "But I would be proud to claim you as mine, if it were so."

Graff pushed himself up from the table. Dabeet knew dismissal when he saw it, so he also got up from his chair. "Thank you for meeting with me, sir," he said. "Thank you for being candid with me."

"I suspect that you're determined to go to great lengths to discover your parentage," said Graff. "Don't waste your time. If there's any human being alive who knows better than me how to erase every trace of certain information from the databases and archives, I will hire him and make him check my work. You'll never succeed, so I urge you not to try."

"I'll spend my life trying to figure out why you're so grimly determined never to let me know who I really am," said Dabeet.

"Speculate all you want," said Graff. "Guessing is free. It's also bound to fail."

"Then you, sir, are my enemy," said Dabeet. "I once counted you as my only friend."

"Wrong on both counts," said Graff. "You have until I leave Fleet School, probably near noon tomorrow, to change your mind and return to Earth."

"Do you have a new mommy waiting to be assigned to me there?" asked Dabeet.

"Do you need a new mommy?" asked Graff.

Dabeet had no answer. Because the only true answer was: I need my real mommy and daddy, sir. Not another substitute.

"I didn't think so," said Graff. "But of course you would be assigned to a foster family of very high quality. With foster siblings who would welcome you."

"If I were still the kind of boy who would accept that situation," said Dabeet, "then they would be fools to welcome me. But I'm not that kind of boy. I'll be staying here."

Graff extended his hand. "You did well here, Dabeet, under very difficult circumstances."

"Are you saying that I passed your test, sir?"

Dabeet watched as Graff seemed to puzzle over what he had been referring to.

So Dabeet quoted it back to him. "'Why not apply your adequate intelligence to figuring out what qualities would make a good leader of an expedition, or a colony, or a scouting or reconnaissance mission? Then see which of those qualities you lack.'"

Graff nodded. "Do you know which of those qualities you lack?"

Dabeet replied instantly. "All of them," he said. "But I'm getting better, and I'll never learn them anywhere but here."

"Was that the whole test?"

"You gave me advice," said Dabeet. "'Knowledge you have no use for is rarely worth having. The secret is not to avoid learning useless knowledge. It's to make use of whatever knowledge you have.'"

"Have you followed my advice?" asked Graff.

"It was bad advice," said Dabeet. "What I have lived by is this: Whatever I need to know, and don't, I must learn. And if learning it fights against my natural inclinations, then it's all the more important that I learn it anyway."

"My advice was good enough," said Graff. "You merely found a higher priority. Good for you. You learned to crawl around on the surface of space vehicles and how to jump from one to another without dying. Are you good at it now?"

"No sir, not compared to pretty much every other student in the school. But I was good enough for the job I had to do."

"Well said. I spend my life doing things I was very bad at, starting out. So far, I've usually made myself skilled enough for the jobs I had to do. As long as you continue thinking and acting by that principle, your life will be worth something to you and, quite possibly, other human beings as well."

"Am I dismissed, sir?"

"I assume that by 'sir' you mean, 'My enemy'?"

"Yes, sir," said Dabeet.

"Then yes, you are dismissed for now, my friend."

Dabeet left the commandant's quarters and managed to calm himself as he walked briskly back to the barracks that he shared with his friends. He was greeted warmly by the few who noticed him come in. They were all buzzing with the news that Robota Smirnova was the new commandant, and he gave them no hint that he already knew, or that he had spent fifteen minutes in a painful interview with the Minister of Colonization. It was better to let them tell *him*. It was comforting to know that they cared enough to tell him things.

Maybe making and keeping friends will always require me to think through the steps of it, the way I had to name what I was reaching for as I moved along the outside of the ship. Maybe it will never be natural for me, never reflexive, never *easy*. So be it. I can't live without it, can't accomplish anything without it, so I will become adequate at forcing myself, against my inclinations, to be a friend to my friends. If I'm good enough at it, they'll never guess the effort that it requires.

In a day or two, we'll stop talking about the raid, the explosion, the danger, the heroics, and the changes in the school. This will all become the new normal. But the new normal of Fleet School has a place for me in it. This is home now.

ACKNOWLEDGMENTS

This novel began when Cameron Dayton found a likely sponsor for a game set in Battle School; but the game needed to be less warlike and more constructive than one based on *Ender's Game*. That's when I came up with the idea of the wall panels that pop up to form boxes, out of which the children could build structures in the battleroom. As for the school itself, it would now serve as a training ground, not for military leaders, but for explorers and colonizers of the new worlds to which humanity was spreading. The game never happened, because the would-be sponsor flaked on us; but it would have been a good one, Cameron! Meanwhile, the novel series about the children of Fleet School lives on. It's odd that I keep writing novels based on games that never happen.

Cyndie Swindlehurst has proven over and over again that lawyers make superb proofreaders and editors. While I was writing this book, she dealt with a new edition of *Ender's Game*. In proofreading it, she discovered that somehow the wrong version of the novel was being used. Her thoroughness saved us endless toil in more than one edition. Yet I didn't have to give it a moment's thought: Cyndie freed me to concentrate on Dabeet, leaving Ender to others. She then gave this book a superb copyedit.

People whom I have counted on for years—Kathleen Bellamy as our line of last defense, Kathy Kidd as one of my circle of first readers—died before they could contribute to this book. Yet I still feel the need to thank them, because they were part of all my work for so many years, and because it was hard not to type their email addresses into my sendings of newly-completed chapters and my askings of questions about what had gone before in the *Ender's Game* universe. I am grateful they were part of my life and my work for so many years.

Scott Allen kept my computers working, despite the mischief caused by Microsoft, with its carelessly-designed hardware and software. Good ideas, badly executed, can become very nearly worthless; but Scott Allen kept saving me from drowning in digital despair. Meanwhile, Nicholas and Sarah Allen joined him in keeping the wheels of our little factory turning. My thanks to all three.

Erin and Phillip Absher provided me with good counsel and encouragement, chapter by chapter, as I wrote this book. Charley and Gracie Rankin spent several weeks providing glorious distraction and inspiration. For a book that I had imagined would be easy to write, my editor for thirty-five years, Beth Meacham, provided me with the time and the guidance to complete a story that turned out, in many ways, to be the most challenging of my career.

As always, my wisest counselor, my constant support, and my firstest reader has been Kristine Allen Card. Because of her, I have a life worth living.

Orson Scott Card, Greensboro, 2 May 2017